THE NEXT TO DIE

The cabin's sturdy new door is still closed and padlocked, just as it was left in the wee hours Saturday morning . . .

And then there were two.

"Yoo-hoo! Ladies!"

Oh, wait, it's not good manners to neglect to knock before dropping in, so . . .

The rubber-grip end of the heavy flashlight beats a satisfying rhythm on the new door of the small brick house.

The key turns easily; the padlock falls away with a clanking sound. The door doesn't even creak as it swings open . . .

A wall of stench rolls out through the open door.

The flashlight's beam arcs across the exposed brick walls, the doll furniture, the maggot-filled carcass that used to be Pammy Sue. Then it falls on what looks like a heap of rags on the dirt—or rather, mud—floor in the far corner.

After a swift, hard kick, the pile of rags in the opposite corner squirms to life.

Phyllida Remington gazes up from the filth, blinking into the light.

Miss Beverly Hills is beautiful no more.

The artfully sculpted nose was shattered by the antique andiron she never saw coming at her.

Those surgically enhanced cheekbones are swollen purple and smeared with blackened streaks of dried blood.

And her blue eyes are round with fear, bewilderment and, most satisfying of all: horrified, shocked recognition . . .

Books by Wendy Corsi Staub

DEARLY BELOVED

FADE TO BLACK

ALL THE WAY HOME

THE LAST TO KNOW

IN THE BLINK OF AN EYE

SHE LOVES ME NOT

KISS HER GOODBYE

LULLABY AND GOODNIGHT

THE FINAL VICTIM

Published by Kensington Publishing Corporation

There's no escape
when you're the
last to die...

χ

WENDY
CORSI
STAUB

THE FINAL
VICTIM

ZEBRA BOOKS
KENSINGTON PUBLISHING CORP.
www.kensingtonbooks.com

ZEBRA BOOKS are published by

Kensington Publishing Corp.
850 Third Avenue
New York, NY 10022

All Kensington titles, imprints, and distributed lines are available at special quantity discounts for bulk purchases for sales
promotion, premiums, fund-raising, educational or institutional
use.

Special book excerpts or customized printings can also be
created to fit specific needs. For details, write or phone the
office of the Kensington Special Sales Manager: Attn. Special
Sales Department. Kensington Publishing Corp., 850 Third
Avenue, New York, NY 10022. Phone: 1-800-221-2647.

Zebra and the Z logo Reg. U.S. Pat. & TM Off.

ISBN 0-8217-7971-0

First Printing: April 2006
10 9 8 7 6 5 4 3 2 1

Printed in the United States of America

For Mark, Morgan, and Brody.

For my beloved father, known to most as Reg Corsi,
and to a lucky few as simply "Poppo."

And in loving memory of my cherished mother,
Francella Corsi,
April 1942–May 2005.

ACKNOWLEDGMENTS

The author extends deepest gratitude to Laura Blake Peterson, Nathan Bransford, and the staff at Curtis Brown, Ltd.; John Scognamiglio and the staff at Kensington Books; and Nancy Berland and the staff at Nancy Berland Public Relations. In addition, the author wishes to thank the staff at Boone Hall Plantation; the staff at The Isaiah Davenport House; Barbara McQueeney, the concierge Marty Weiss, and the efficient staff at Marriott Savannah Riverfront; the knowledgeable guides at Savannah's Old Town Trolley Tours; and last alphabetically but never least, Wendy Zemanski.

The author also acknowledges having taken deliberate liberties with the timing of actual events depicted within this fictional plot, having opted for literary license over historic accuracy.

PROLOGUE

It took two years for her to come back to the beach.

Two years, the divorce, and the realization that life must go on.

Charlotte Remington, who took back her maiden name after her husband left, has no choice but to keep getting up in the morning, keep moving, keep breathing . . . if only for her remaining child's sake.

Breathe.

How many times during the initial shock did she have to remind herself to do just that?

Breathe, Charlotte. In and out. Just breathe. Keep breathing, even though your chest is constricted and your heart is breaking; even though you want to stop breathing . . .

Even though you want to die.

Charlotte Remington thought she had everything: loyal husband, loving son, happy-go-lucky daughter, loyal friends.

Now they're all gone.

Now there is only Charlotte, haunted and bereft; and

a sad-eyed little girl who watched her big brother drown on a beautiful July day, just yards from the shoreline.

This shoreline.

But it happened a long time ago; a lifetime ago.

The first time, afterward, that Charlotte returned to the southeastern shore of Achoco Island to inhale brackish air, feel sand beneath her feet, and gaze again over the sea, she wanted to flee.

But she forced herself to stay.

Breathe. Just keep breathing.

And she forced herself to keep coming back, all through that first summer without Adam. And again the following year. And the one after that . . .

It's been five years now.

Five years and seven weeks, to be exact.

Here she sits amidst the Labor Day weekend crowd, the day after a lavish family wedding. She has a pounding headache, though not from overindulging last night: the wedding was dry. Grandaddy, a fiercely dedicated teetotaler, won't allow liquor to cross his threshold. But there was a band, and a crowd, and Charlotte danced too much, and stayed up far too late chatting with people she hadn't seen in years.

It was fun. She has few regrets about last night as she lounges in her blue and white striped canvas sand chair with her woven sweetgrass hat on her aching head, a romance novel in her hands, and her daughter at her side.

Lianna never goes into the water. Not here. Not anywhere. Not even a pool.

The other parents in Charlotte's bereavement support group back in Savannah have experienced similar reactions in their surviving children. One, who lost a teenager in a traffic accident, said his younger son had panic attacks for months every time they got into the car. Another, whose toddler succumbed to a rare stomach disease, said the older sibling eventually developed anorexia, afraid to eat lest she somehow "catch" what her little sister had.

Perhaps Lianna will never venture into the water again. Then again, maybe she will. The child psychiatrist she's been seeing since the tragedy told Charlotte not to push her.

So she doesn't.

She just brings her to the island beach on beautiful summer days, where they sit companionably side by side with their books, and they breathe salt air.

Just breathe.

The beach is postcard-perfection on this, the last official weekend of summer.

Down beyond the dunes, where sea oats sway in the warm salt breeze, bright-colored blankets and umbrellas dot powdery sand. Crisp white sails skim the horizon. The ocean air is rife with the sounds of gleeful children splashing in the surf, the incessant roar of the waves, the squawking of circling gulls, the hum of banner-toting planes cruising the coast.

Largely unpopulated until the last decade or so, Achoco Island lies off the coast of Georgia, about midway between Tybee and the Golden Isles; nowhere near the tourist hub of either. The entire northern end, above the longer of the two mainland causeways, consists of a wetland wildlife refuge and what remains of the Remington family's private estate.

But the island's southeastern shore is teeming with activity on this cloudless September afternoon. A steady

stream of beach traffic snakes from the boardwalk beyond the dunes to both the north and south causeways,
and no doubt all the way back to the mainland highway
to Interstate 95.

That's why this day was chosen. Because of all the people.

The holiday crowd surpasses every expectation and
will serve its purpose. Nobody pays the least bit of attention to the lone occupant of a blanket carefully
spread a strategic distance from any of the three lifeguard towers.

Nobody suspects that this idyllic holiday weekend is
about to give way to chaos—and tragedy—the likes of
which this beach hasn't seen in five years.

Or, to be more precise, five years and seven weeks.

"Well, look at you! If it isn't Mimi Gaspar, all grown
up and gorgeous!"

Perched high above the sun-baked sand on the
wooden lifeguard tower, Mimi—nee Martha Maude—
Gaspar doesn't allow her gaze to leave the surf for even
a split second.

The waters off Georgia's crowded island beach are
choppy today, courtesy of a new tropical depression
churning six hundred miles southeast in the Caribbean.

Anyway, she can identify the speaker by his voice
alone, though it's been a few years since she heard Gib
Remington's trademark low-pitched, lazy drawl. A fake
drawl, as far as Mimi is concerned.

He didn't even grow up in the South—he was raised
in Rhode Island, where his mother's family lived. After
he was kicked out of his boarding school there, he was
sent to Telfair Academy, his father's and grandfather's
alma mater down here, presumably where his stern

Grandaddy could keep an eye on him. A lot of good that did.

"What's the matter, you're still not speaking to me?" he asks.

"I figured y'all were back for your sister's wedding yesterday," Mimi says at last.

The beautiful Phyllida Remington might be living among the movie stars in California's Beverly Hills—with hopes of becoming one herself—but she chose to marry at the family's nineteenth-century mansion right here in the Low Country. The wedding was the social event of the summer for the hundreds who were invited.

Mimi was not among them. She doubts she'd have been welcome even if she was still dating Gib. He never did bring her home to meet his family.

"I'm only here till tomorrow. I'm flying back up to Boston first thing in the morning," Gib informs her importantly. "The fall semester starts Wednesday."

Law school. Some fancy one in New England, maybe Ivy League. She doesn't know for certain, and she doesn't care.

"What about yours?" Gib asks.

"My what?" She skims the whitecaps for the pale head of a surfer who just took a harrowing tumble off his board. It's one of the Tinkston brothers, probably Kevin, the youngest of the four notorious local hell-raisers. Down at the water's edge, two fellow lifeguards stand at the ready with orange rescue tubes.

"Your fall semester."

Yeah, right.

Once upon a time, her future was promising. She had been a full-scholarship student at Telfair Academy—live out, of course—and followed up her high school career with another free ride at Georgia Southern. She was working on a degree in international studies, dreaming of one day moving abroad.

But that was before Daddy, a fisherman and heavy smoker, was diagnosed with lung disease.

Now, as beach season draws to a close and her pals prepare to head back to dormitories and lecture halls, she'll be peddling her meager resume around Savannah. She has to get a regular job and help her parents make ends meet—never an easy task for them, but nearly impossible now.

"Let's hook up tonight and catch up," Gib suggests, undaunted by her failure to respond to his last question. "What time are you off duty?"

Ignoring that as well, Mimi watches the Tinkston boy resurface among the breakers and promptly paddle back out with his board in tow, resilient, she thinks, as her ex-boyfriend here at the base of the lifeguard tower. Gib seems to have forgotten that the last time they saw each other she informed him she never wanted to see him again.

Technically, she still hasn't. Seen him, that is.

But curiosity gets the best of her now. She flicks her gaze downward to catch a glimpse of him.

Big mistake.

Law school obviously agrees with Gilbert Xavier Remington IV.

So does yet another summer spent in New England as a lifeguard on a coastal island presumably worlds away from this one.

Deeply tanned, clad only in red and white hibiscus-print board shorts and sunglasses, Gib is all abs and biceps. His hair is longer than it was when he lived under his father's roof. The sea breeze whips the sun-streaked locks back from his face to reveal a familiar jawline Mimi often traced with her fingertips, and the full lips that have been kissing other girls—countless other girls, she's sure.

She shouldn't have looked at him, damn it.

Now it's almost impossible to drag her eyes away and focus them back on the water, where they belong.

She's already got a boyfriend: Jed Johnston, whom she's known her whole life. His family lives a few doors down from hers in Tidewater Meadow, a low-income island housing development. The two of them were inseparable until Mimi went to prestigious Telfair Academy and Jed to tiny Achoco Public.

It isn't that she turned her back on her old friend— just that they moved in different circles. Especially in high school.

Especially when Mimi fell hard for Gilbert Xavier Remington IV.

Now, when Gib persists in asking what time she gets off, it's almost impossible to emit a casual laugh and say, "You're kidding, right?"

But she does manage to say it, and is rewarded by a moment's silence from below.

Then, his voice laced with incredulity, Gib responds, "You're still not over it."

"It" being the most traumatic event of her teenaged life, Mimi ignores the comment and watches a young mother in the water. Pale-skinned, obviously a tourist, the woman is wading knee-deep, stooped over and clutching both of her wriggling toddler's hands tightly as an incoming wave washes over them.

"You know, I said you were all grown up and gorgeous," Gib comments, "but I guess I was only half-right. You're just gorgeous."

Mimi thrusts her silver whistle between her lips to keep from responding, unsure, even as she does so, what she would say.

Part of her—the giddy, girly part—is flattered that Gib is still attracted to her. That part longs to take him up on his offer to get together later.

But another part of her—the mature adult part—is so dismayed she's still attracted to him that she wants to lash out, tell him to get lost.

Then a huge wave breaks. She cups her whistle and blasts it abruptly, standing to motion the clueless tourist mom to bring her toddler closer to shore. The tide is coming in and the water is too rough; the child could easily be swept from her hands.

The woman obliges and begins to move toward the beach.

Mimi removes the whistle from her mouth and sits again to resume her vigil while pondering whether she might accept Gib's invitation after all.

Maybe she should. Just to show him that she's over "It." Over *him.* Just to prove she's both grown up and gorgeous.

Yes. She should. She should see him. For closure, if nothing else.

Again, she shifts her gaze from the water to the sand . . .

And finds that the spot where Gib once stood has been taken over by a lone seagull.

Her heart sinking, Mimi spots him sauntering toward the grassy dunes.

Why are you surprised? He never was the type to stay by your side for very long.

She shakes her head, remembering the bad times.

And, reluctantly, the good.

Forget it. Forget him. You don't need that jerk in your life.

Then, above the crashing surf and distant buzz of a seaplane, she hears a frantic shout in the distance.

"Help! Please, help!"

A man is running down the beach, waving his arms at her.

"My son!" he screams, and gestures at the water. "Theo! I can't find him! Oh, God, please, help me!"

All thoughts of Gib are obliterated as Mimi hurtles herself from the lifeguard stand, frantically blowing her whistle to summon the other lifeguards for rescue.

Long after sunset, sheriff's boats bob in the increasingly rough water off the beach, the surf eerily lit by dozens of floating spotlights.

Divers plunge again and again into the murky, sandy, churned-up depths in their grisly search for the victim of today's tragic drowning accident.

Be careful. Don't smile, not even to yourself. Not even out here in the dark, when you think nobody is looking at you.

You just never know.

From this point on, it will be crucial to keep up the façade at all costs, treading carefully every step of the way.

A sudden splash and shout heralds the possible discovery of the child's waterlogged body.

No. Another false alarm.

The boy has yet to be found.

The tide is coming in. Soon, they'll call off the search for tonight, with the waves and undertows ripping dangerously due to that storm in the Caribbean.

But they'll resume tomorrow if they can. They'll probably search for days, just like the last time, with the Remington boy.

Will it make a difference that he was the scion of a powerful local family, while today's victim was an outsider?

Maybe.

Maybe not.

In the end, who cares?

In the end, all that matters is that after many months of planning, it has begun at last.

PART I

THE FIRST VICTIM

CHAPTER 1

Three summers later

"You look pale. Why don't I ask Nydia to bring you a fresh glass of sweet tea?"

Startled by her husband's voice, Charlotte Remington Maitland looks up from the novel she's been pretending to read.

Royce is standing in the broad archway that separates this large front parlor from its twin just beyond. She didn't even hear him open the French doors.

"No, thank you," she murmurs, setting the book on the doily-decked piecrust table that once belonged to her great-great-great-grandmother, the first mistress of Oakgate. There, on an embroidered coaster, sits the full glass of now-lukewarm tea the housekeeper had brought her a little while ago.

Or maybe it's been longer than that.

Sunlight, spilling through the filmy lace curtains that cover the narrow, twelve-foot floor-to-ceiling windows, falls at a different angle now: more blue than golden, casting long shadows across the patterned Aubusson rug.

Charlotte glances at the clock on the marble mantel, studiously avoiding her grandfather's vintage portable electric radio that still sits beside it.

"Is that the right time?" she asks, startled to see that the hands indicate nearly seven o'clock. Maybe Nydia forgot her clock-winding ritual this morning, with all that's gone on.

But Royce assures her, "That's the right time."

Unbelievable. Charlotte had sat down at half-past four, promising herself a few quiet moments with her own ritual: afternoon sweet tea and a book.

"You must be hungry," she tells her husband as he crosses the room and sits beside her on the antique yellow-silk sofa.

She notices that his black hair is damp from a recent shower and his handsome face, prone to five o'clock shadow, is clean-shaven. He's changed out of his black suit and into clothes that are, for Royce, casual. Pressed chinos, white linen, long sleeved, button down shirt, leather loafers. With socks.

She loves that about him; loves the way he always manages to look as though he just stepped out of the pages of a catalogue, even when he rolls out of bed in the morning. Not a day goes by that she isn't thankful for him in her life; the proverbial sunshine after the darkest of storms.

"I'm not that hungry." He rests a warm hand on her shoulder. "I could eat anyway, though. I had two sandwiches at the luncheon after the service, but you didn't touch a thing. You must be famished."

She shakes her head. She hasn't been hungry in a few days now, her usual voracious appetite having given way to the dull pain of grief.

She didn't expect her grandfather's death to hit her this hard. After all, Gilbert Xavier Remington II was an old man, closing in on ninety. He wasn't going to live forever.

But he always said he'd be around to escort Lianna down the aisle when the time came, even if he had to roll by her side in a wheelchair. Until a few days ago, the idea of the formidable Remington patriarch in a wheelchair was far more outlandish than the presumption that he'd be at his adolescent granddaughter's wedding one day.

And the way he died . . .

Maybe if he'd been sick, Charlotte would have been prepared for the inevitable. But he wasn't. She can't recall her grandfather ever being sick, even with a cold. He was indestructible.

In fact, the closest thing to vulnerability she had ever seen in the man was his reaction to the death last year of his stalwart lifelong friend old Doc Neville. Grandaddy, who in his lifetime had stoically buried his parents, wife, two sons, and young grandchild in the family plot, had seemed haggard and prone to uncharacteristic emotion for a long time after that loss.

"It was a beautiful service, wasn't it?" Royce is asking Charlotte, dragging her thoughts back to the present. "You did your Grandaddy proud."

She swallows hard. "I wonder if he was up there somewhere, watching."

"And counting heads."

Charlotte laughs despite the grief welling in her throat. If there was ever any doubt that Gilbert Xavier Remington II maintained a prominent place in Low Country society after all these years, today's turnout at the little Baptist church overlooking the sea put it to rest.

"I'll bet there were three hundred people at the service. And probably almost as many at the reception," she adds, remembering the crowd that gathered in the shade of the plantation's oversized portico for an elegant luncheon.

"And at least one who skipped the church but showed up for the free food after."

Yes. Vincent Champlain.

Royce is immediately contrite. "I'm sorry, I didn't mean to get in a dig at your ex today, of all days."

"Feel free to dig him any day, Royce. He sure doesn't hesitate to do it to you every chance he gets."

She finds it ironic that although her ex-husband chose to walk away from her and Lianna, he resents another man stepping in to fill his shoes. Especially a man like Royce, who has everything Vince has striven desperately to achieve—and, when all else fails, does his best to fake.

Like class, and good looks, and good taste, and a means of supporting himself.

"He 'accidentally' tripped me with those big feet of his when I was walking to the buffet table," Royce tells Charlotte, "then he fell all over himself apologizing. But believe me, he was about as transparent as that white blouse Phyllida put on after the funeral."

Again, Charlotte laughs. Leave it to her cousin, the would-be Hollywood actress, to go directly from mourning black to red-carpet sexiness.

Yes, and leave it to Charlotte's first husband to miss the lengthy church service and the burial beneath the blazing midday sun, arriving just in time for the catered reception. He claimed he got held up in traffic driving up from Jacksonville, but she doesn't believe him.

She learned years ago never to believe anything he said. If only their daughter would do the same.

"The irony," she tells Royce, "is that Vince couldn't stand my grandfather, and vice versa."

"Well, at least he was there today for Lianna."

"He wasn't there for her." *He never has been.* "He was there to rub shoulders with the Reynolds, the Chathams . . . people who might be able to do something for him someday."

She shakes her head, remembering how Vince finally sauntered over to extend his sympathy to her, devouring several jumbo shrimp as he spoke.

"So sorry about your grandfather, Charlotte. What a shame."

He said all the right words, but his tone was utterly indifferent.

And that, right there, was the story of their lives together.

The marriage was dying long before their firstborn drowned off Achoco Island eight years ago. Vincent blamed her for Adam's death, of course—she was there; he wasn't.

She never knew where he was that day, but she has her suspicions.

Not that any of it matters now.

Adam is gone; so is Vince, for the most part, as well as the friends she once had as a young wife and mother. They turned away from her after she lost Adam—or maybe it was the other way around. Maybe it was she who severed the ties, unable to see them with their intact families when her own was shattered.

And now Grandaddy is gone, too.

Now all she has left are Royce and Lianna.

Nothing else, nobody else, matters.

Deep in the thicket beyond Oakgate, broad stretches of marsh are broken by dense wooded clumps of maritime forest: oaks, pines, cabbage palms, and a tangle of native vines. Abundant Spanish moss threads its scaly tendrils over every living bough. Years ago, a good portion of this marshy acreage behind Oakgate must have been dry land.

Dry enough, anyway, to house the row of slave cabins that are surprisingly well preserved after decades of neglect and encroaching tidal surges.

Of course, the cabins aren't *in* the water—yet. Just surrounded by it, and well sheltered from human destruction by acres upon acres of wetlands and dense undergrowth.

If there remains anyone on this earth who even remembers that the cabins exist, they certainly don't care enough to go to the trouble of paying a visit.

The structures poke their sturdy crowns through the tangle of foliage, looking for all the world like something out of a nursery rhyme . . . except that all three are made of brick.

Pity there's no door on the nearest, and most easily accessible of the three.

Yes, otherwise I could knock and say, "Little pig, little pig . . . Let me come in!"

Only there's no one inside to hear . . . Yet.

Along with the roof, the wooden door has long since rotted away in the unforgiving, damp climate, leaving only a few scattered, spongy remains of hand-hewn timbers. But a door can easily be replaced.

A cursory examination of the interior, courtesy of a handy flashlight, shows that there are no windows here, and no other doors. Where the ceiling used to be, a jungle of moss and leaves block out the light. The only thing that breaks the expanse of brick wall within is a shallow fireplace. There doesn't seem to be even a toehold, should a future prisoner want to escape the sturdy cell by scaling a wall.

This will do. This will do quite nicely.

It's obvious that no living soul has been out here recently, though a proliferation of webbing and a rustling in the overhead foliation indicates countless living creatures have made the old slave cabin their home.

Bats, snakes, rodents, reptiles, bugs, spiders . . . It will be a daunting job to rid just one of the three cabins of its furry and creepy-crawly twenty-first-century residents.

But one cabin is all that's needed.

One cabin that has been outfitted with everything that's needed for this . . . *project*.

Yes, *project* is a good way to think of it. It makes it all sound very businesslike—which is precisely what this is, when you get right down to it.

He had no idea about this part, of course. No reason for that.

No, this is strictly my own little scene.

Time to roll up the sleeves—and get to work.

The third floor is always stuffy at this time of year. Electric box fans in two of the windows do little to cool the sultry air.

Perched beside the third window in her wheelchair, Jeanne Remington longs for a genuine breeze as she gazes down at the darkening grounds of Oakgate.

Her late brother refused to have central air-conditioning installed in the old house, saying he didn't want to rip apart the walls to install the necessary ductwork. Nor would he even allow window units in the bedrooms; the wiring was so old the extra strain would be a fire hazard, and replacing it was, again, too much trouble.

Anyway, he liked to say, *generations of Remingtons got through Georgia summers without air-conditioning. We don't need it.*

Maybe *he* didn't . . .

But up here in the attic, there are only three windows that open, all of them small dormer-style. The others are even smaller: round bull's-eyes sitting high beneath the eaves, lacking even window treatments to block out the afternoon sun.

Gilbert never did spend excessive time worrying about anybody else's comfort, though. He was a difficult, self-centered man, to say the least.

A challenging boy, too, from what Jeanne can remember—when she chooses to remember anything at all about her childhood.

She was a few years younger than her brother, and frequently exasperated by his daring antics . . . when she wasn't feeling sorry for him as he endured his father's harsh punishment for sins real and imagined.

She probably should have been grateful that she never had to endure being locked in her room, or having her mouth washed out with soap, or, far worse, being beaten with a leather belt.

Oddly, though, along with pity, she felt a strange resentment whenever her brother suffered at their father's hands. Not just resentment toward the man who dealt the harsh punishment, but resentment toward her brother.

Sometimes she could almost convince herself that any attention from the man she called Father would be better than none at all.

But he ignored her. Totally. For as long as she could remember. He didn't discipline her, barely spoke to her, never even pretended to love her.

She didn't comprehend the reason until her eighth

birthday, when she found herself in tears, once again, because of something Father said—or, more likely, failed to say. That was when her big brother told her the truth: Gilbert Remington wasn't her real father, and he knew it. In fact, everyone in the household knew it. Everyone but Jeanne.

In retrospect, she and Mother were probably fortunate that Father didn't throw them both out of the house. His old-fashioned pride kept the family intact, if only for appearances' sake.

If Savannah was the most genteel of Southern cities, Father, with his impeccable manners, was the most genteel of its residents.

The first Gilbert Xavier Remington was an expert at keeping up the public charade. But in private, he had no use for Jeanne or her mother, Marie. He saw to it that neither of them would inherit a penny of the family fortune, and stipulated that if his son died without heirs, he was to leave his estate to a public trust—not to his sister.

That didn't happen. Gilbert II lost his wife and both of his sons years ago, but he has heirs: three grandchildren.

You can't resent them, or Gilbert, for that matter, Jeanne reminds herself. *Your brother did more for you than you ever could have hoped or expected.*

Unlike his father, Gilbert II had a heart. He must have. Because he clearly felt sorry for Jeanne. Especially when her mind started to go, just as Mother's did so many years ago.

Or so everyone believes.

Father isn't the only Remington who's an expert at charades.

* * *

"Let's go into town and have dinner," Royce suggests, giving Charlotte's hand a squeeze.

"Town," she knows, is not the Achoco Island's commercial strip but rather Savannah, about forty-five minutes' drive north of here.

"Here" is Grandaddy's vintage red brick, black-shuttered, white-pillared mansion.

Once a thriving plantation producing rice and indigo, Oakgate lies on the top third of the island, amidst the coastal marsh not far from the northernmost causeway. Its boundaries once encompassed several thousand acres of the island's narrower upper end, including a rice mill and brick slave cabins that now lie in ruins deep in the marsh. When the rice industry waned following the Civil War, the Remingtons sold off the southernmost parcels of land, traded for a prosperous paper mill.

Years before Charlotte was born, Remington Paper was swallowed up by an internationally renowned conglomerate, Global Paper Corporation; its operation moved to the Midwest, the paper mill was razed and a low-income housing development built on its site.

Grandaddy reinforced his position as one of the wealthiest men—and the family name among the most prominent—in coastal Georgia. As the local newspaper's social columnist once wrote: *Boston has the Kennedys, New York the Rockefellers, Delaware the Duponts, and Savannah the Remingtons.*

What the press failed to note is that unlike his Northern counterparts, Grandaddy wasn't exactly a philanthropist. The world never knew—or at least the press refrained from mentioning—his frugality. His children and grandchildren were provided with perfunctory trust funds, but he was determined to control the family purse strings until he died. His sons, who had been content with their figurehead positions in the mill, were equally content to live off the profits as long as they could afford their bon vivant lifestyles.

"What do you say?" Royce is asking. "Some seafood, a nice glass of Pinot Grigio . . ."

"The Pinot Grigio is definitely tempting. I wish there were a bottle in the house, though . . . That way we wouldn't have to go out." But there's no liquor here at Oakgate. Grandaddy didn't imbibe, or condone it in others, or allow the stuff to cross his threshold.

"Oh, let's go. Maybe we can even catch a movie after we eat. It'll get your mind off things."

"I shouldn't really be out socializing in public tonight," Charlotte reminds her husband. "It doesn't look right."

His brown eyes overcast with understanding, Royce nonetheless shakes his head and urges, "Come on, Charlotte. We're not staying on the island."

"Grandaddy wasn't exactly anonymous in Savannah, and neither am I. People will say, 'Look at her, out celebrating all those millions she just inherited.'"

That disapproving comment was uttered by Grandaddy himself about the widow of Dr. Silas Neville, his lifelong friend, when she showed up at the hospital ball in a red gown just weeks after the funeral.

"Who cares what people think?" Royce asks.

"Not me, but . . ."

Oh, who are you kidding, Charlotte?

The magnolia blossom doesn't fall far from the tree, or so Grandaddy liked to say. The Remingtons have always played by the rules of polite Southern society. Charlotte was raised to be a lady at all times.

That, in part, is why it took her so long to get out of her marriage to a man who was anything but a gentleman. If Vincent hadn't taken it upon himself to end it, she might still be with him.

What an abhorrent thought.

"I'm just not in the mood to go out," she tells Royce. "But you go, take Lianna. And maybe you should see if anyone else wants to join y'all," she adds as an after-thought, remembering the Remington relatives cur-rently staying with them at Oakgate.

"I barely know your cousins."

"That makes two of us. They were much younger, and I only saw them when they visited down here in the summers, remember?"

"Well, forgive me for saying this, but from what I do know, I'm not exactly anxious to spend the evening with them."

She smiles briefly. "It's all right. I don't blame you. But Lianna—"

"She won't come out of her room."

"Why not?"

"Who knows? She's refusing to talk."

Charlotte sighs. "Again?"

"She's probably just upset about your Grandaddy."

Charlotte shakes her head grimly. Her temperamen-tal daughter took to barricading herself in her bed-room in stony silence well before her great-grandfather's fatal heart attack.

If the doors in this old house had been updated in the last sixty years, Charlotte wouldn't hesitate to un-lock her daughter's and barge in whenever she pulls this. But Grandaddy, whose parents reportedly used to lock him in his room for days as punishment, had all the two-way locks removed when he became head of the household.

Now there are no keys; all bedroom doors lock only with latches on the inside. And Charlotte refuses to stand in the hall begging Lianna to open up, having en-dured that futile power struggle on more than one oc-casion.

Although handling Lianna's recent transformation from docile child to tantrum queen pales in comparison to other, far more traumatic maternal experiences Charlotte had faced in the past, it's distressing nonetheless.

With a rustle of her black-silk funeral dress, she stands and heads for the doorway.

"I already tried to talk to her," Royce warns. "She won't even answer. I think she's locked in for the rest of the night."

"I'm not going to try to talk to her. I'm going to change out of this dress so you can take me to dinner, just the two of us."

"Really?"

"Really." Suddenly, the last thing she wants is to spend a long evening in this house with a sullen teenager, a batty old aunt, and assorted relatives who came for the memorial service and obviously feel entitled to linger.

It's been a couple of years since Charlotte has seen Gib and Phyllida. Gib is presumably an attorney in Boston by now, and his sister moved to the West Coast years ago to pursue acting, before she was married. Charlotte hasn't seen Phyllida's husband, Brian, since their wedding, or glimpsed so much as a photo of their son, Wills.

But they all showed up for the funeral, and this is their house as much as anyone's—or so they seem to believe.

As the Remington homestead, Oakgate at times accommodated several generations of extended family. But for the better part of the last decade, only Grandaddy and his younger half sister, Jeanne, have remained in residence.

They were joined several months ago by Charlotte, Royce, and Lianna.

The Maitlands could have rented a place while their

new home in Savannah was being remodeled. But Grandaddy invited them to stay here, Royce thought it was a good idea to save money, and Charlotte reluctantly agreed.

Now Grandaddy's gone, and moving on won't be as simple as Charlotte had anticipated.

As she crosses the second parlor toward the large hall that runs through the center of the house, she can't help but notice that every time she thinks she's moved out of Oakgate, the old place sucks her back in.

Almost like the relentless grasp of a rip current at sea.

No, she admonishes herself, startled by the bizarre comparison.

Not like that at all.

Oakgate is just a house.

Just an inanimate pile of bricks and tabby and wood. It holds no power; it isn't dangerous.

Nor is it deadly.

Yet an odd chill of foreboding seems to follow Charlotte as she moves through its eerily still entry hall today, along with the flinty gazes of Remington ancestors forever caged in gilt-framed portraits.

Hearing footsteps approaching the second floor, Phyllida Remington Harper braces herself for yet another intrusion.

First came her husband, Brian, changing from his dark suit to a pink polo and madras slacks, and gathering the golf clubs he insensitively remembered to pack for this funeral trip back East.

"You won't mind if I hit the links, will you, Phyll?" he asked, and didn't wait for the reply.

Shortly after his departure came the housekeeper's

knock and the inquiry about whether Phyllida and her son planned to eat dinner this evening here at Oakgate or elsewhere.

Elsewhere?

As if there are dozens of restaurants in this god-forsaken place. One would have to go down to the southern end of the island to find a decent meal, or even the closest grocery store, as Phyllida pointed out to Nydia. With a sleepy, out-of-sorts toddler to care for and nary a nanny in the house, that's out of the question.

Nydia conspicuously avoided the unspoken invitation to babysit Wills for the evening—not surprising, since she never did seem to have a way with children. Phyllida distinctly remembers being intimidated by the woman's unyielding austerity whenever she and her brother visited, and finds it hard to believe that Nydia actually had a hand in helping to raise Daddy and Uncle Norris after Grandmother Eleanore died.

Soon after Nydia left the room, Phyllida's brother barged in to "catch up." Ah, Gib, with his swaggering comments, nosy questions, and barely gratuitous attention to his only nephew, who now lies sleeping in the ancient wooden crib across the room.

All right, not ancient. Charlotte claimed to have used it whenever she visited Oakgate when her own children were young. But safety standards have changed. For all Phyllida knows, the rails are far apart enough for little Wills to get his blond head stuck.

Being a responsible parent, unlike Brian, she doesn't dare leave the room. Not even for a moment.

Yes, she's a prisoner here; prisoner in an over-furnished, overly fussy cell awash in cherry antiques, Waverly wallpaper, and Laura Ashley linens. The room was once part of the much larger one next door, now occupied by Charlotte's daughter, and the dividing wall is thin. She can hear every word that's said in there, and no doubt vice versa.

Which means she can find herself serenaded, and not just by music, at all hours. Currently, Lianna's television is blasting some MTV show with a rap soundtrack. The throbbing bass grew so loud earlier that Phyllida tapped on the wall.

Lianna did turn it down that time. But not much, and subsequent knocks have yielded no response.

Yes, this is far from her favorite guest room in the house.

She and Brian spent their wedding night in the more spacious, elegant quarters down the hall.

But Charlotte and her husband occupy that room now, and apparently have for quite some time. Lianna's is the second-best location, a corner room with a private bath and fireplace, still spacious despite having been divided years ago.

Phyllida is hard-pressed to keep her envy at bay. Not that she wants to spend any more time in the dreary old mansion than is absolutely necessary. But it would have been nice to have seen more of Grandaddy in his final days.

At least, that's what she told Charlotte this afternoon, after their grandfather was laid to rest alongside his wife, Eleanore, and generations of Remingtons in Oakgate's cemetery.

"You're lucky, you know," she told her teary-eyed cousin. "I hadn't even seen Grandaddy in ages." Not since her wedding, in fact, three years ago. "I hope he knew how much I missed him. I think about him all the time."

Well, not *all* the time.

But she did, occasionally, think about her grandfather.

More often, she'd be willing to bet, than her brother ever did.

Leave it to Gib to show up at Oakgate mere minutes before the funeral started, with a mountain of luggage in the limo, requisite blonde on his arm—he apparently still dates only blondes—and chip on his shoulder.

Her brother never did get along with their father's side of the family. He preferred to mingle with the maternal Yankee relatives.

Now he knows as well as Phyllida does that it's going to take more than what's left of their Remington trust funds to see the two of them through the remainder of their adulthood, not to mention helping to care for their mother eventually.

Right now, Susan Remington is living in Providence with one of her sisters and working at a boutique. Someday soon, she's going to need financial help, and it will be up to her children to provide it. What else does she have? Her own family lost everything when their importing business went belly-up years ago; she'll get nothing from them.

Gib's law degree is mostly for show, as far as Phyllida can tell. When she pressed him, he admitted he has yet to join a firm.

"But don't tell Mother," he warned. "I let her think I accepted an offer last month—just so she won't worry about me," he added at Phyllida's frown.

As for her, the mere few million she received on her twenty-first birthday barely funded her move to California, a house in Beverly Hills, acting lessons, cosmetic surgery, and her wedding.

She chose Oakgate as the setting—not out of sentiment or Southern tradition, but because it was free—cost-wise and scheduling-wise. She was pregnant; the wedding had to be thrown together in a matter of months; there was no time to wait for an opening at a glitzy Beverly Hills reception hall.

Anyway, Oakgate was large enough to hold, and in close proximity to, hundreds of well-heeled guests who came bearing lucrative envelopes.

Hers was a fairy-tale wedding, the kind she'd dreamed about ever since she was a little girl, despite the fact that she was secretly well into her second trimester when she walked down the aisle.

But it hasn't been a fairy-tale marriage.

Well, whose fault is that? You could have married a rich husband, she reminds herself.

But back then she was still crazy about Brian. With his square-jawed, swoop-haired, preppy good looks and upscale wardrobe, she thought he came from a wealthy family.

Turned out he was probably a better actor than most of those trying to make it a profession in LA: he grew up in a blue-collar household in Long Beach. When Phyllida met him, he was a caddy at a fancy country club and a salesman in the men's department in Neiman Marcus, where he made good use of his natural charisma and his employee discount.

Infatuated, Phyllida was naive enough to believe they could indefinitely live a Beverly Hills lifestyle on his pay, her trust fund, and the wedding booty. But there was always the promise of Remington millions on the horizon—not to mention her acting paychecks once she hit it big.

So far, she hasn't, though she hasn't given up that dream. But at this point, Phyllida is banking on her inheritance from Grandaddy as optimistically as her brother is, if not as blatantly.

So, she's certain, is Charlotte. That second husband

of hers is some kind of computer technician. He can't possibly be supporting her and Lianna in the style to which they were accustomed.

Sorry, Grandaddy, but your death is a blessing.
For all of us.

Her palm skimming the polished wood banister as she goes upstairs, Charlotte is reminded of the time Grandaddy caught her sliding down it as a little girl.

"What on earth do you think you're doing, child?" he boomed, startling her so that she nearly toppled to the marble floor below. "That isn't a dime-store pony ride. Get down this instant! You know better."

She did, and it was the first—and last—time she ever broke that, or any other rule of the household. For years after, she would glance longingly at the inviting slope and remember those stolen moments of childish glee, so swiftly curtailed.

Back then, she was a mere visitor at Oakgate—and an occasional one, at that. Grandaddy's primary residence at the time was a Greek Revival mansion on Orleans Square in Savannah that had been in the family since the eighteenth century. Hardly the sentimental type, Gilbert sold it well before the revitalization of the historic district. Charlotte, who *was* sentimental, wistfully walked by it sometimes when she was growing up; saw it fall into disrepair, turned into tenements, and ultimately torn down.

Thank goodness her grandfather chose to keep the immediate grounds and gardens of Oakgate, including the forlorn little ancestral cemetery. The brick main house was built by Charlotte's great-great-great-grandfather, and its ownership has never strayed beyond the Remington family. It was constructed in typical antebellum style: symmetrical façade fronted by grand white pillars and a wide portico; hipped roof punctuated by third-floor dormers; distinctive raised basement walls constructed of tabby, a regional mixture of oyster shells, sand, lime, and water.

Oakgate didn't become Charlotte's official residence until the summer after she graduated from Duke, when she settled here rather than return home to live in Savannah with her recently widowed mother.

Daddy had been the bond that held the two of them together; without him, she felt out of place at home. She was closer to her grandfather than to her mother, and it seemed logical that she live at Oakgate with him.

It wasn't natural, on the heels of free-and-easy dormitory life, to settle into an old man's household with an old man's unbending rules and rituals. But somehow, they made it work. Charlotte eventually found herself looking forward to the rigid daily schedule of domestic events at Oakgate, in such stark contrast to her parents' chaotic nonroutines.

Every morning at precisely seven o'clock, Nydia served the same breakfast: grits, poached eggs, and slabs of thick country bacon that in the end probably contributed to Grandaddy's demise. The timing and menu didn't vary with the day of the week or the season; nor did it vary with the personal whims of the cook or diner.

It was grits, poached eggs, and bacon at seven. Always.

Grandaddy napped every afternoon after lunch, snoring peacefully in his recliner. A lifelong insomniac, he claimed it was the only place he could ever fall asleep—and stay asleep—without the prescription medication he often resorted to in the wee hours.

Every night, after supper and his bath, Grandaddy watched the *NBC Nightly News* at six thirty. Then, without fail, he would turn off the television and turn on the radio, the one on the mantel. It was always tuned to the same Oldies station, which ironically played swing music that was probably newer than the radio itself. Tommy Dorsey, Jimmy Dorsey, Count Basie . . .

That first Christmas she lived with him, Charlotte got her grandfather a brand new stereo system.

It still sits, unused from that day, in a cabinet in the far corner of the living room, along with the stack of golden oldies CD's she bought him to go with it. She has long since gotten over the hurt, having come to understand that Gilbert Remington was a creature of habit. He wanted to hear his old music on his old radio.

She stayed for almost two years, moving out only when she married Vincent.

But the Savannah condo and later the two-story, center-hall Colonial that she shared with her first husband never entirely felt like home. Not even when Adam was alive. Selling the house and returning to Oakgate after the divorce hadn't been a difficult decision, though Lianna had complained. But soon even she grew comfortable here.

It was Charlotte who couldn't quite settle in.

That had nothing to do with Grandaddy or the house. She was still mourning her losses. Initially, she thought being at Oakgate would make her feel closer to her little boy, buried in the family graveyard behind the house.

Instead, it was a constant reminder of all that she had lost; of what will never be.

She had already decided to buy a house of her own back in Savannah before that fateful Labor Day weekend three years ago.

It was shortly afterward that she met Royce, under the most horrific of circumstances.

The first time he showed up at the bereaved parents group she used to attend, she instantly recognized him from the beach.

She watched him running that day, screaming for his son. She saw him hurtling himself helplessly into the water, screaming for Theo, until the lifeguards dragged him out.

Lianna witnessed it as well.

As far as Charlotte knows, her daughter hasn't been back to the beach since.

But Lianna seemed to welcome Royce into their lives, when Charlotte finally got the nerve to bring him home.

Theirs was a whirlwind courtship that seemed inevitable from the moment they met. Each had found the only other person in the world who truly understood what they had been through.

Sometimes, even now, Charlotte finds it difficult to wrap her mind around the eerie, cruel coincidence that brought them together. She still wakes up every morning of her life wishing desperately that it had never happened, that Adam had never died. Yet if he hadn't, and if Royce hadn't lost his son, they wouldn't have found each other.

They've long since stopped asking why. It's far too painful to look back. They've both done their best to accept what is, to only look ahead toward their future and the fresh start they're building together.

But that isn't easy here at Oakgate, where the past exists hand in hand with the present.

Built on a slight knoll at the end of a long lane bordered by an arch of Spanish moss–draped live oaks, the red brick mansion's rooms remain filled with heirloom nineteenth-century furniture, and seem to echo with ghosts of a bygone era.

Charlotte has long harbored a curious mix of affection and dread for the old place, which, like many old Low Country homes, is rumored to be haunted.

She's never actually seen a ghost, but that doesn't mean they aren't here . . . And it doesn't mean she wants to continue living under this roof any longer than is absolutely necessary. Especially now that Grandaddy is gone.

But for the time being, with their own home in Savannah undergoing extensive renovations after having been gutted down to the studs, she, Royce, and Lianna are stuck here.

Everything will be brighter for all of us when we can get back home, Charlotte tells herself wistfully. *We just have to hang in there until then.*

Phyllida tosses a shrewd glance at the man in the framed photo on the nightstand.

The black-and-white image of her grandfather in his youth came with the room, of course. Though maybe she'll take it with her as a nice little memento when she goes back to California.

Yes, physical evidence of her loss will make her friends and neighbors out West even more sympathetic. She'll keep the picture on the mantel for a while and when people come to visit, she'll affectionately point out Grandaddy's cowlick, so like Wills's, and the bruise on his cheek undoubtedly caused by some youthful prank.

I'll tell everyone he got hurt rescuing the family dog from a burning house, Phyllida thinks dreamily. *I'll say that he used to take me on his knee and tell me that story when I was little.*

She smiles faintly at the image of herself as a wide-eyed little girl curled up on her grandfather's lap, almost believing, for a split second, that it really happened.

But, of course, it didn't.

Widowed when his sons were toddlers, Grandaddy was a tough old son of a bitch; tougher, even, than Phyllida's father. And unlike Phyllida's father, who didn't seem to care much for either of his children, Grandaddy played favorites.

Uncle Norris's daughter, Charlotte, was the only one Grandaddy ever really noticed. Not Phyllida, not even Grandaddy's own namesake, Gilbert IV.

Growing up, Phyllida couldn't help envying her Southern cousin. But not so much for their grandfather's attention. Nor for demure Charlotte's natural grace, her genuine kindness and goodness . . . nor for the fact that she always seemed to do and say the right thing without even thinking about it.

No, more than anything else, Phyllida was jealous of Charlotte's effortless beauty. Even as a child, she was lithe and long-limbed, with wavy black hair, porcelain skin, and unusual purplish eyes fringed with thick, dark lashes. She even inherited the "Remington chin," the same distinctive, comely cleft shared by Grandaddy and some of her ancestors, whom she's seen in old family portraits.

Today, Charlotte's striking face and figure remain unenhanced by cosmetic surgery—unlike Phyllida's.

But in the end, none of that matters, does it? In the end, everything equals out.

Phyllida has plain-old blue eyes, not aquamarine like those of her brother, father, and grandfather, nor Liz Taylor–violet like Charlotte's. She considered—and dismissed—the notion of wearing colored contacts, despite how authentic-looking they are these days. But thanks to Dr. Zach Hilbert of Beverly Hills, Phyllida is now easily as stunning as her East Coast cousin.

And Charlotte will be entitled to the same third of the family fortune Phyllida and Gib will get. No more, no less.

Financial fair-mindedness was a proud trait of Grandaddy's, and always had been.

Phyllida's father had always assured her of that. Grandaddy deplored his own father's decision to cut his daughter out of his will. Great-Aunt Jeanne got nothing; Grandaddy got everything—on the stipulation that he not leave a penny of it to his sister upon his death.

So Grandaddy's estate would be divided equally between his two sons, Gilbert Xavier III—always called by his nickname, Xavy—and Norris.

Nobody ever dreamed that neither son would outlive the father.

Now, presumably, what was meant to belong to Phyllida's father and his brother will be divided equally among their heirs.

Presumably.

Of course it will, Phyllida assures herself, watching her toddler's little chest rise and fall rhythmically in the questionable old crib.

In just a few days, when the will is read, she'll find herself tens of millions of dollars richer.

Then, to hell with the acting career, Hollywood, even Brian.

For once in her life, Phyllida Remington Harper will have everything she wants. Everything she needs.

But for now, there's nothing to do but bide her time in this spooky Southern relic of a house.

* * *

The huge plantation house kitchen reportedly once had a dirt floor and a fireplace big enough to walk into.

It's obviously been remodeled many times through the years. Royce doubts, however, that it's been touched in the last couple of decades, other than to add a fairly up-to-date dishwasher and wedge a microwave into a nook on the soapstone countertop.

Having spent the last few months pouring over design catalogues in the midst of redoing their new house in Savannah, he finds it fairly easy to identify each of the other upgrades with the era in which it was done.

The painted white cabinets with glass-front doors and fold-down ironing board have to be from the twenties. The enormous black cookstove is Depression era. And the floor—black-and-white tile set in a checkerboard diamond pattern—is as blatantly 1950s as a tuna casserole served by June Cleaver in a bib apron.

Retro style is all the rage in the Maitlands's social circle, but here at Oakgate, everything—including the appliances—is the real deal.

Standing at the vintage farmhouse sink, Royce pours his wife's untouched sweet tea—a remnant of her well-loved, late-afternoon ritual—down the drain.

"Better run some water," a voice says behind him, startling him so that he nearly drops the glass.

He turns to see the Remingtons's longtime live-in housekeeper standing in the doorway that leads to the maids' quarters off the kitchen. "Nydia! You scared me."

Her staccato laugh is free of mirth.

She's one tart old biddy, Royce thinks every time he finds himself interacting with her.

To Nydia's further discredit: she has a disconcerting way of slithering up behind a person when they least expect it. This isn't the first time she's caused Royce to jump out of his skin.

"Did you think I was a ghost, Mr. Maitland?"

"Of course not." *But you do look like one,* he can't help noting.

Nydia is a wisp of a woman, prone to wearing pastels, and her short hair and uninteresting features are as pale as the tiresome grits she dishes up every morning. Royce has no idea how old she is; she's one of those people who could be in her fifties or in her seventies, but is most likely somewhere in between. He does know she's been with Charlotte's grandfather since his children were young.

"Some people think this house is haunted," she comments, taking the glass from his hand and opening the dishwasher.

"Do *you* think it's haunted?"

"By the living as much as the dead," is her strange, prompt reply.

He waits for her to elaborate.

She doesn't, forcing him to ask, "What do you mean by that?"

Having placed the glass on the top rack, she closes the dishwasher in silence and turns to the sink, brushing him aside.

She turns on the water.

When she speaks, it's only to say, "Tea stains this old white porcelain, you know, Mr. Maitland."

Royce steps back, watching her wash it away, wondering if he should press her on that cryptic comment about the house. She's lived here for decades. She must know many things he doesn't.

Before he can speak up, she turns off the water, dries her hands, and faces him once again, dour as usual.

"There. A place for everything, and everything in its place."

"I was about to put away the glass and rinse the sink when you came in," he is compelled to inform her.

"I'm sure you were."

No, you aren't. You don't trust me, and you don't think I belong here, Royce thinks, not for the first time.

He can't help but notice, as he also has before, that Nydia owns the only pair of blue eyes he's ever seen that aren't the least bit flattering. They're close-set and small, the washed-out shade of the sky on a halfhearted summer afternoon, with a smattering of lashes the color of fresh corn silk.

What a far cry from Charlotte's rich, purply-indigo irises fringed by lush, dark lashes.

"Where is Ms. Remington?" Nydia inquires, as if she's read his mind.

He suppresses the urge to remind her that it's Mrs. Maitland now, not Ms. Remington, and has been for over a year.

"She's upstairs changing. We're going out to dinner."

"I was about to heat some soup for Mrs. Harper and the little boy."

And she's none too pleased about that, judging by her tone.

"What about you?" he asks, determined to be civil. "Did you eat?"

She shakes her head. "I'm fine."

"Can we bring something back for you from town?" he offers generously. "Pizza? Some pecan fried chicken?" *Sugar for that lemon you appear to have swallowed?*

"No, thank you."

Not only doesn't she trust me, Royce notes uneasily, taken aback by her utter lack of warmth, *but she doesn't like me. Not at all.*

Well, that's fine. The sentiment is definitely mutual.

He can feel her gaze following him as he leaves the room, and finds himself wondering if he should mention her to Charlotte later. Hired help, after all, is dispensable—especially now that the master of the house is gone. There's no reason in the world that Nydia should stay on at Oakgate. He and Charlotte and Lianna are capable of taking care of themselves for the remaining time they're here, and Jeanne has her visiting nurse . . .

Well, he won't bring up the idea of firing Nydia yet to his wife. It's too soon, her grief too raw. The last thing he wants is to upset her by suggesting any sort of change at Oakgate.

He'll take her out for a nice dinner, just the two of them, and do his best to get her mind off her sorrow.

That, Royce concludes, is all a loving husband can possibly do at a time like this.

As she walks up the curving staircase and crosses the wide balcony toward the second-floor guest bedroom wing, Charlotte considers what will become of Oakgate—and Great-Aunt Jeanne—now that her grandfather is gone. Obviously, the place will have to be sold. She certainly has no desire to go on living here, and she doubts her cousins would want to—or that Aunt Jeanne would expect to.

The plantation and the paper mill were strictly Grandaddy's, inherited from her great-grandfather, the first Gilbert Xavier Remington. Aunt Jeanne, the product of Great-Great-Grandmother Marie's shameful liaison with another man, received nothing.

Jeanne never married, and barely made a living as a bookkeeper in Savannah. She used to live in an apartment located, ironically, in one of the grand historic district mansions the Remingtons used to frequent. It, like Jeanne Remington herself, had discreetly fallen from grace over the years.

Grandaddy took her in years ago when her mental health began to fail just as their mother's had. He personally hired the finest visiting nurses available to care for her and made sure that her substantial medical and financial needs were met.

Charlotte assumes he would have expected his grandchildren to do the same after his death. She has no problem with that, though as the lone heir still living in Georgia, she can't possibly have Aunt Jeanne living under her own roof once Oakgate is sold. It's really time for her to have full-time care, and be surrounded by people her own age.

There are plenty of nice nursing homes in Savannah. Charlotte and her cousins will just set up her aunt in one of them, and she'll be sure to visit her often.

She's family. I have to keep her in my life, no matter what, she tells herself. *No matter how challenging it is, or how much time she has left.*

It's impossible to tell how long poor Aunt Jeanne will outlive her half brother. She's suffered from dementia for years, though she still has startlingly lucid moments.

Charlotte uneasily recalls the most recent of them.

This morning, Aunt Jeanne was transported by the creaky old elevator to the first floor where the rest of the family was assembled for the memorial service. It was an unusual occurrence, as the elderly woman rarely leaves her third-floor quarters.

But today, she seemed to know precisely where she was and who was around her. She even called several of the visiting Remingtons by name. The wrong names, in some cases, but at least she wasn't staring vacantly into space or hurtling angry accusations.

When Reverend Snowdon arrived he bent over Jeanne's wheelchair, clasped her gnarled hand, and said, "I'm so sorry, Miss Remington, about your brother's death. I know how difficult this loss is for y'all."

"Not *all* of us," Aunt Jeanne said darkly.

Taken aback, Charlotte laid a hand on her aunt's black crepe–covered shoulder and said gently, "We're all upset over Grandaddy's death, Aunt Jeanne. What are you talking about?"

The old woman seemed as though she was about to elaborate. Then, glancing around the room at those nearest, albeit not necessarily dearest, to her late brother, she shrugged. "Never mind."

Now, Charlotte hesitates slightly at the base of the stairway that leads to the third floor.

Maybe she should go on up for a few minutes, just to see how Aunt Jeanne is. And perhaps, to have her decipher that cryptic remark.

But Royce is waiting downstairs.

And she might be a bit hungry after all. She hasn't eaten since she picked at her dinner last night.

Charlotte continues along the hallway with its painted white wainscot, toward the remodeled master suite Grandaddy insisted she and Royce occupy during their stay. He said he preferred the smaller guest suite down the hall, anyway. That bathroom, he pointed out, had a bigger, deeper tub.

Grandaddy always did enjoy his nightly baths. He said they were a reprieve from daily stress, the one place he could ever truly relax in preparation for the ever-elusive full-night's sleep.

How ironic, Charlotte can't help thinking, that he had his fatal heart attack in the midst of an evening soak. If he had been anywhere else, somebody might have found him and helped him before it was too late.

But his body, like the water, was long cold by the time Nydia stumbled across him the next morning.

Charlotte pushes away the grim memory. Passing Lianna's closed door, she stops briefly and calls her daughter's name.

No reply.

The television is on, probably tuned to MTV or one of those reality programs she's always watching. Pressing her ear against one of the door's thinner inlaid-wood panels, Charlotte can hear background hip hop music and kids' voices whoo-hooing.

"Lianna?" she calls again.

Nothing.

Shaking her head, she proceeds down the hall, telling herself it's for the best. She isn't in any frame of mind to wrangle Lianna's latest mood.

As she turns down the narrower corridor that leads to the largest of the second-floor guestrooms, the one she shares with Royce, she sees a whisper of movement out of the corner of her eye.

Or maybe she just thought she did, because the hallway is empty.

And chilled.

Oddly chilled, given the midsummer season and the lack of air-conditioning.

"Grandaddy?" Charlotte calls in a whisper, standing absolutely still.

No reply.

Of course not.

Her grandfather is dead.

But she can't help wondering if Gilbert II, like other Remingtons before him, will continue to haunt the halls of Oakgate for years to come.

*   *   *

Catching a flicker of movement below, Jeanne leans closer to the window . . . just in time to see something dart into the shadow of a live oak at the front of the house.

Not something.

Someone.

Jeanne watches intently as the figure makes its way from tree to tree, away from the house.

Whoever it was seems to have just come from the house, and clearly doesn't want to be seen leaving.

Why not?

Does anybody know that that person was here? Or did they sneak in as furtively as they're now sneaking out?

"Jeanne? I'm back."

Startled by the cheerful singsong voice behind her, she realizes that Melanie, her home health care worker, has returned to the room.

Pushing aside her curiosity, Jeanne carefully reverts to her usual blank, wandering expression, taking up the charade once again.

CHAPTER 2

Approaching the nineteenth-century ramp that leads from Bay Street, Savannah's historic wide boulevard, to tourist-crowded River Street a story below, Charlotte finds herself reminded of the Long Island Sound beach she visited decades ago.

The sun was hot that day and the water still, lapping gently at the shore. She waded in barefoot to walk the length of the beach in ankle-deep water, as she often did back home. But here, there was no stretch of smooth, surf-washed sand. Beneath the water's surface lay a jumble of pebbles and rocks that made each step a precarious balancing act.

From a distance, the ramp to River Street is similarly misleading. It looks like a regular cobblestone path from afar, but is constructed of seashells and apple-sized rocks that jut irregularly from the mortar like clenched fists bent on toppling unwary pedestrians.

Tonight, Charlotte, in strappy high-heeled sandals, is wary of twisting an ankle as she walks down, clinging tightly to Royce's arm.

"Watch your step," he says needlessly.

She is, literally. Picking her way along, she keeps her eyes focused on her feet.

"Can you imagine having to run for your life on this surface?" she finds herself asking Royce.

"Run for your life?" He tightens his grip on her arm. "Why would you be running for your life?"

All right, it was an odd thing for her to say. For some reason, the image just popped into her head. And now that it's there, she can't seem to make light of it.

"I just mean, it wouldn't be easy if I had to," she tells Royce.

"Well, you wouldn't have to. I'd scoop you up and carry you away from whoever was chasing you."

"Who would be chasing me?"

"I don't know . . . a pack of ardent male admirers?"

She looks up to find him smiling at her—and promptly stumbles over a rock.

You really should have worn flats, she chides herself ruefully, returning her gaze to her feet as she resumes picking her way along the slope.

Yes, but these heeled sandals lengthen her bare legs, and they're a bright coral-red to match her favorite sundress. *Royce's* favorite sundress, really—which makes it, in turn, her own.

She usually doesn't like to bare her shoulders, because of an unsightly birthmark on her right shoulder. But sometimes, the oppressive summer heat allows comfort to outweigh concern about her appearance.

She still recalls the way his eyes lit up in appreciation the first time he saw her in this particular outfit, back when they were first dating. He didn't even seem to notice the birthmark.

"You look like a luscious lobster," he said with a low whistle, and she couldn't help but laugh.

"A lobster? Is that the best you can do?"

He nuzzled her neck and said, "Lobster is a well-known aphrodisiac."

"I thought that was oysters."

"Well, you don't look a bit like an oyster," was his response, and they shared a laugh.

A whirlwind courtship, a year of marriage, and still madly in love—*this*, she thinks often, in gratitude laced with relief, is how marriage should be.

Thank God, thank God, thank *God* for Royce.

Royce, who healed her in so many ways.

She emerged from her marriage to Vincent not just a bereaved mother, but a barren wife as well.

Her first husband lost interest in her sexually the moment she told him she was pregnant with Adam. Her gynecologist, when she reluctantly turned to him in despair, assured her that it was a fairly common syndrome in men, and that once the baby was born, and she regained her figure, and life settled back to normal, Vincent would want her again.

That didn't happen. Ever.

It wasn't until Royce came along that Charlotte discovered what it was to be truly desired, unconditionally. Truly loved.

Thank God, thank God, thank *God* for Royce.

With him, her life is complete.

As complete as it can ever be. Even a loving husband can't fill the hollow place left by Adam's death. But if Royce hadn't come along . . .

Who knows what might have happened to her?

Who knows how she would have managed to go on living?

There was a time, after she lost Adam, when she didn't want to. When she even considered seeing to it that she wouldn't have to.

She knew from experience that the world would go on spinning without her; that in time, she'd be just another scandalous skeleton in the Remington family closet.

After all, she wouldn't be the first young Remington mother to commit suicide.

Thank God she backed away from the edge of that precipice. But she's never forgotten what it felt like to teeter there, not even caring that her life hung in the balance.

If anything ever happens to Royce, or to Lianna—

She curtails the chilling thought with an oft-repeated reminder that she's endured her share of sorrow.

Nothing will happen to her husband or daughter.

They're both safe.

There will be no more tragedy in Charlotte's life.

Nagging fear is a natural result of all that's happened to her, and to Royce.

She can let it consume her, or she can ignore it.

I've got to ignore it, she thinks resolutely, lifting her Remington chin with conviction.

"Where are we going?" Lianna asks Kevin Tinkston when they reach the fork of the plantation road.

From here, there are only two choices: go pretty much straight west toward the northernmost of the two causeways leading to the mainland, or veer to the left toward the island's commercial district down at the southernmost tip.

All that lies north and east of Oakgate, beyond acres of alligator- and rattlesnake-infested marshland, is a narrow strip of sea oat–covered dunes and the Atlantic Ocean.

But why head south? Kevin knows they can't risk

being seen in public on the island, hanging around at the boardwalk T-shirt and surf shops, or the ice-cream place or café.

Which leaves the wide, miles-long stretch of sand along the southeastern coast.

She hasn't set foot back on that beach since that awful Labor Day weekend when Royce's son drowned. Though Theo was a stranger—and Lianna and her mother could never have known that his father would become a part of their lives—witnessing a tragic incident that echoed of her own family's worst nightmare left an indelible mark on her.

"Are we going to the beach?" she demands, trying to keep her voice from rising in panic.

"No."

"I don't believe you."

Kevin turns his gaze away from the road just long enough to wink at her and drawl, "It's a surprise. You'll see."

Some surprise. He's probably taking her to his family's ramshackle house down on the southwest canal, where they're among a handful of year-round residents. Most of the others are fishermen and Northern retirees.

Lianna has yet to meet the Tinkstons and she isn't sure what, exactly, Kevin's parents do besides drink beer and squabble with each other and their sons, according to local gossip.

"Local gossip" being her friend Grace, whose family has a summer house out on the island. It was Grace who first had the crush on Kevin, and dragged Lianna to meet him at the Mobil station, where he was pumping gas. But it was Lianna he noticed.

That was in June and he's been her secret boyfriend ever since. Her friendship with Grace is officially over.

She hasn't had any regrets about the whole thing, really . . .

Well, not until now.

"So are we going to your house?"

"What, are you sick? No!"

"Then where?"

Silence.

"I don't want to go to the beach," she warns Kevin. "If that's what you were secretly planning."

"No one will be down there to see us. Not where we're going."

Her pulse quickens. "So? My mother finding out isn't the only reason I don't want to go to the beach."

"Yeah, well, the sun's not out?"

Right. Now what? She's been using a fake sun allergy to avoid meeting him there during the day these last few weeks. That, and the threat that her mother might find out about it.

But she can't use either of those excuses now.

And she'll have to go back to the beach sooner or later, won't she?

Besides, anywhere is better than gloomy old Oakgate, especially tonight, with everyone moping around after Grandaddy's funeral.

Which is why she text messaged Kevin earlier and asked him to come get her. She didn't even have to tell him where to find her. After a few nights of sneaking out to meet him, the routine is set. He always picks her up just beyond the plantation gates, where she waits in her usual spot in the shadows of a towering live oak.

As far as her mother and Royce know, she's locked safely and sullenly in her room.

As far as Lianna knows, nobody—other than Kevin,

of course—is aware of the concealed panel leading to a secret door beside the fireplace.

Nobody alive today, that is.

"The wipers on the bus go swish swish swish," Mimi Gaspar Johnston sings for perhaps the twentieth time today. "Swish swish swish. Swish swish sw—"

"Babe, have you seen my keys?"

Unlike her son, Mimi welcomes the interruption. "On the hallway table," she tells her husband, who's standing in the doorway of the baby's room, wearing jeans and a T-shirt and clutching his travel mug.

Tow-headed, blue-eyed Cameron, who inherited his mother's coloring and his father's energetic personality, squirms in Mimi's arms as she tries to jam his arms into his blue and white striped pajama top.

Jed is speaking, but whatever he's saying is drowned out by Cameron shouting, "Sing, Mommy! Sing!"

"Just a second, Cam. What did you say, Jed?"

"I said, I already checked there."

"Milky, Mommy!"

"I promise you can have milk and cookies as soon as you're dressed, but you have to let me and Daddy talk," Mimi admonishes her son, then asks her husband, "Did you look under the pile of mail on the hall table?"

"No, but—"

"Look under the pile of mail," Mimi says above Cameron's howl as, top on at last, she attempts to stick one of his chubby, wriggling legs into the pajama bottoms.

"I don't think they're there."

She shoves aside a sweat-dampened tendril of blond hair that has escaped her ponytail. "They are."

"I don't think so." Jed turns on the heel of his steel-toed boot and leaves the room.

"Sing, Mommy!"

With an inner sigh, Mimi obliges. "The wheels on the bus go—"

"No. Wipers! Swish swish, Mommy!" orders the mini-tyrant who has recently possessed her sweet-tempered child.

Mimi sings about wipers swishing while getting his legs into his pajamas and his feet into the little suede-soled blue Padders. As she lets him squirm out of her grasp at last, she ruefully notes that Cam is rapidly outgrowing both the slippers and the pajamas.

How the heck are they going to squeeze more out of this month's already-exhausted budget? Mimi can't ask her mother to stretch her fixed income again—she already paid for Cam's last checkup at the doctor's.

"Y'all really need medical insurance," she recently admonished Mimi, as she often has. "If we hadn't had it when your father got sick . . ."

She always trails off at that point, but Mimi knows the rest of the story. Mimi knows her father had the best care possible after being diagnosed with lung disease; knows that the doctors bought him more time. Time enough to see his only daughter married and his first grandchild born.

"We'll get insurance, Mom." *Yes, and someday, we'll get to Europe, too.* "Just as soon as Jed finds a regular job with benefits."

God only knows when that will be.

Jed is back, standing in the doorway dangling his keys. "You were right."

She interrupts her singing and her private budget worries with a satisfied, "Told you so."

"Do you have to say that?"

"Yes," she replies with a grin as Jed steps over scattered DUPLO blocks to embrace her, "I do."

Her son tugs on the hem of her homemade cutoff denim shorts as her husband pulls her close. "Milky, Mommy."

"Hmmm?" Exhausted, Mimi rests her head on Jed's shoulder. She can't help wishing she was already in bed, rather than facing household tasks she's been meaning to get to all day—and wishing that Jed was in bed with her, instead of heading out to start the overnight road-crew shift he's been working since last October, when a hurricane all but destroyed the southernmost of Achoco Island's two causeways.

Now there's only one way on and off the island, whose burgeoning population makes for frequent traffic tie-ups, particularly during beach season. Jed and the crew are under a lot of pressure to finish the job.

"Milky, Mama," Cameron persists, tacking on an adorable, "Pwease?"

Stifling a yawn, Mimi recalls a line of an old Robert Frost poem:

> But I have promises to keep,
> And miles to go before I sleep . . .

"Hungry, Charlotte?" Royce asks, as they emerge on bustling River Street not far from the restaurant. The warm air is thick with the tantalizing aroma of deep-fried shellfish.

"Hungry—and homesick," she replies, longing for their new home on a leafy block facing Colonial Park Cemetery not far from here.

"Me, too. It won't be long now."

"Maybe we can come back home by the end of July," she tells Royce hopefully—though even if that's possible, she'll be facing almost a month at Oakgate without her grandfather . . . or *with* his ghost, depending on one's willingness to suspend disbelief.

"I doubt we'll be in before August. Even if the interior work is done, they'll still have to paint and paper, and finish the woodwork—" Catching sight of her expression, he adds reassuringly, "But I'm sure we'll be home before school starts, like I promised Lianna."

"I hope so." There will be hell to pay if the temperamental thirteen-year-old faces even another day of being driven forty-five minutes from the plantation to Savannah Country Day School by Stephen, Grandaddy's longtime chauffeur.

Lianna is embarrassed by the long black town car and, infuriatingly, by kindly old Stephen. She's conveniently forgotten that the chauffeur was her hero when he supplied her with pockets full of bubblegum back in the early days after the divorce, when they were first living at Oakgate.

These days, Lianna finds fault with everything about Stephen—from his being hard of hearing to his European formality.

"Does he have to wear that stupid uniform?" she frequently grumbled throughout the school year, always followed by her daily plea, "Why can't you just drive me, Mom?"

Because you'd have me so upset by the time we got to town, that's why.

But Charlotte would always manage to summon every bit of maternal patience she possessed and keep her thoughts to herself. She just shrugged and told Lianna that Stephen would be driving her for as long as they were staying at Oakgate, period.

Now, strolling along River Street, with its row of brightly lit restaurants and shops housed in former cotton warehouses, Charlotte so longs for her old life back that she's tempted to launch into a Lianna-style whine.

This, not Oakgate, is her home now.

Savannah, and the nineteenth-century architectural gem she and Royce bought this winter, with its dormered mansard roof, bracketed cornices, and lush gardens now fragrant with summer blooms.

It isn't far from where she grew up. But sadly, that Beaux Arts mansion on Abercorn Street—like its final owners—didn't live to see the turn of the millennium. A bank now stands where Charlotte's girlhood home once was; her parents lie miles away, in the cemetery at Oakgate.

Daddy went first: cirrhosis of the liver, courtesy of the same lifelong passion for Southern bourbon, of which his staunch Southern Baptist father didn't approve.

Alcohol probably had a hand in his own mother's death as well.

At least, Charlotte assumes it contributed to her paternal grandmother Eleanore's decision to kill herself. The topic of her death has always been as forbidden within the family as liquor was at Oakgate.

The official story is that Grandaddy's wife died in her sleep of some undiagnosed illness.

But local gossip, which invariably reached Charlotte's ears courtesy of insensitive childhood peers, claimed that one night, Eleanore tucked her two small sons into bed, then fixed herself a lethal cocktail spiked with barbiturates.

It was her younger son who reportedly found her the next morning, though Charlotte's father never affirmed that. No, Norris just wandered through life wearing a perpetually haunted expression that grew even more haggard when he was self-medicated with bourbon. The only time Charlotte ever really saw him looking at peace was the day she kissed him good-bye on one unfurrowed brow as he lay tucked into the white satin lining of the finest casket money could buy.

Mom followed him soon after, giving in to the cancer that had been recently diagnosed, and which she was prepared to battle valiantly as long as she had something to live for.

Without her husband, Connie June Remington apparently had nothing left to live for. He was her whole world. Raised on the island a stone's throw from Oakgate, Charlotte's mother was a spoiled, pampered only child. Her parents were middle-aged when she came along, and had thought they were infertile. Their daughter was the center of their world for the rest of their lives. The indulgent, laid-back Norris took over where they left off, coddling his wife until the day he died.

Nothing could fill the emptiness in the orphaned, widowed Connie June's life. Not even a daughter, no matter how Charlotte tried.

Not that she tried all that hard.

Her mother was never the doting parent Daddy was. Norris Remington showered his only child with both affection and material goods.

Now they're all gone, Charlotte thinks bleakly. Not just her father and her mother and Uncle Xavy, but her grandfather, too.

Yet none of those losses has had the shattering impact of another loss, the one that weighs most heavily on her heart.

The one she almost didn't survive at all.

You're supposed to bury your parents and grandparents.

Not your children.

* * *

Lianna discovered the cobweb- and dust-shrouded hidden stairway entirely by accident one night not long after moving into her temporary quarters at Oakgate.

Even with a flashlight and cell phone reassuringly in hand it took all her nerve that first night to descend the old wooden staircase into the depths of the house. When she realized where it led—to the basement, with its own exit to the outside world—she immediately recognized its potential.

Freedom.

Lianna had been feeling stifled by her overprotective mother long before they settled in at Oakgate. At least in Savannah, there was some reprieve from her mother's watchful eye. She could hang out occasionally at friends' houses, the squares, the mall . . .

But these days, her visits to Savannah require the orchestration of an overseas military invasion.

Basically, now that she's stuck out here in the marshes, there is no readily accessible escape.

At least, there wasn't. Not until she found the hidden passageway . . . and Kevin Tinkston.

Even he has no idea exactly how she gets out of the house for their forbidden rendezvous. She isn't about to jeopardize their relationship by admitting that the only way she can see him is to creep through an old tunnel in the night like a convict making a jailbreak. At eighteen he's five years older than her, but she told him she's almost seventeen and he apparently believes her, or doesn't care how old she is.

If her mother ever knew she was riding off into the night in a car with an older boy—a man, really—she would freak.

Look at how she went berserk just last week when she found out that Lianna hadn't spent the afternoon at the library with her friend Casey and her mother, but at the mall with her friend Devin and her stepfather. They were supposed to go to the library first, but it was closed, and Casey was supposed to be there too but she blew them off.

"You lied to me!" Mom screeched at Lianna, who denied it vehemently.

She didn't lie. She just deliberately failed to mention that Devin, whom her mother thought was a bad influence, was involved in the plans. Or that Devin's mother was staying out at their house on Tybee and Devin's stepfather, Ray, a long-haired, reportedly womanizing musician of whom Mom naturally didn't approve, would be chaperoning.

Lianna pushes away a renewed pang of guilt, reminding herself that she had no choice but to withhold the details that day. And that it isn't her fault that her mother is unreasonably protective.

But at least she wants you under her roof, she reminds herself.

Unlike Daddy, who decided not to fight for custody and moved away to Jacksonville.

Lianna can usually muster the resentment to blame her mother for all of that, and more. But not tonight. Tonight, on the heels of losing Grandaddy, maybe she's feeling a little sorry for her mother. There have been too many funerals in Mom's life, that's for sure.

And Mom has good reason to worry excessively about her safety—that much is definitely true.

But it isn't fair that Lianna has to suffer now for the tragedy that happened when she was a little kid. And it isn't her fault. None of it is her fault. Not her parents' divorce, nor her brother's death that triggered it.

Yeah, right. Sure it isn't, says a mocking voice she can never quite drown out with reason, no matter how she tries.

You know what you did.
You'll never tell, but you'll never forget, either.
And you'll never stop paying the price.

Royce squeezes Charlotte's hand reassuringly, almost as if he's read her mind and knows she's thinking about her lost son.

Thank God, thank God, thank *God* for this kind, loving man who descended to the bottomless pit of grief with her and brought them both back to life.

"What would I do without you, Royce?"

"I was just thinking the same thing about you." He opens the door to the Oyster Bar, one of their favorite restaurants on River Street. "I just wish I didn't have to leave tomorrow morning."

Charlotte's smile fades. "Then don't."

"I have to. But I'll be back before you know it. I have the first flight out Monday morning."

"You mean the flight that was late last time so you missed your connection and got stuck in Atlanta all day?"

"That wasn't because it was late—that flight always goes on time. It was a mechanical problem with the one from Atlanta."

"All I remember is that we were supposed to spend the day with the furniture designer picking out our new living room set—and I had to do it on my own."

"Right, and you got the one with the cabbage rose print that I never would have let you order, so count your blessings."

Her smile returns. "I'd have rather had boring beige and you with me instead of stuck in Atlanta."

"Well, this Monday morning I promise I'll be here before you set foot out of bed."

"Mr. and Mrs. Maitland! How nice to see y'all tonight," the hostess says in surprise when she spots them. She quickly adds, "I'm so sorry about your grandfather."

"Thank you, Lisa."

Charlotte shoots a glance at Royce, as if to say, *See? I shouldn't be out in a restaurant when the entire town must know today was Grandaddy's funeral.*

Royce shrugs as Lisa goes on, "I was so shocked when I saw the write-up about him in the *Morning News.* I thought he was going to live forever."

"So did we."

There's a moment of awkward silence. Then Lisa checks to see if a table is available and, luckily, one is.

As they settle in beside the large window facing River Street, Charlotte does her best not to pout about Royce's upcoming trip.

She should be happy that Aimee, Royce's nearly grown daughter, recently welcomed her father back into her life after a long estrangement.

And she *is* happy. She knows how tormented he's been, bearing his daughter's and ex-wife's blame for Theo's drowning death at Achoco Island Beach. Royce was in complete agreement with them. He blamed himself, too.

What parent wouldn't?

He was the one who had insisted on taking his son on vacation in Georgia, just the two "men" in the family, while he scouted business locations in Savannah.

Neither Aimee nor Karen wanted to leave New Orleans. It was Royce who wanted it. Royce who convinced little Theo that it would be a good idea.

Royce was the one who was there with his son on the beach that day. The only one. He was in charge. He turned his back . . . if only for an instant.

Having been in his shoes, Charlotte is glad that her

husband had finally made peace with his past. Really. She rejoiced with Royce when his only surviving child reached out at last.

It's just that he visited Aimee for Mardis Gras, for Easter in April, and again for her graduation, much to her father's pride, in Louisiana just last month. She had been working in a salon since high school, but after a catastrophic hurricane she had been inspired to go to nursing school. Royce was beaming from the front row at her graduation, presumably alongside his ex-wife.

Is it really necessary for him to fly back down there again just to spend Aimee's twenty-fifth birthday with her?

You're not jealous, are you? Charlotte asks herself, not for the first time.

All right, maybe she is, a little. But mainly, she's worried.

What if something happens to Royce while he's in New Orleans?

What if there's another terrible hurricane? It's the season . . . Did he even bother to check the Weather Channel?

Or what if he's in an accident?

Life is a series of accidents . . . some good, some bad . . .

That's what Josie, the counselor in the bereaved parents group, used to say whenever somebody grew despondent, asking why.

You can't look for reasons. You'll drive yourself crazy. There are no reasons. Things just happen.

There were times when Charlotte found those words oddly comforting. Now she just finds them frightening.

What if something "just happens" to Royce?

Stop it, Charlotte. He'll be fine. Why do you always have to do this to yourself?

Why, indeed?

Because I know what it is to be blindsided by an unimaginable loss.

Yes, so now what? Do you think that if you constantly dwell on the worst that can happen, it won't?

Perhaps.

Perhaps she's doomed to spend the rest of her life haunted by anxious what-ifs.

No. You have to stop worrying, Charlotte. Stop.

But what if . . . ?

What if these aren't mere worries?

What if they're . . . *premonitions?*

What if something really does happen to Royce?

No! Stop!

She has to let him go. This is the first birthday he'll be celebrating with his daughter since she was in her teens. The plane ticket was purchased long before Grandaddy's death.

But I need you, too, Charlotte longs to protest. *Especially now. Don't leave me alone in that house with a daughter who isn't speaking to me, an aunt who often doesn't recognize me, and those cousins . . .*

Not to mention the ghosts, which probably now include Grandaddy's.

If she says all that to Royce, he'll undoubtedly feel even more guilty than he already does. He'll quite possibly change his mind about leaving.

But whining to get one's way is a most unattractive characteristic, as Charlotte's mother liked to remind her.

There's nothing to do but hold her breath and let go.

This deserted stretch of beach is in a cove that lies, mercifully, a few miles north of the public beach where both Adam and Theo drowned.

But as Lianna watches Kevin spread out a blanket, it's all she can do to keep her feet firmly rooted in the sand.

Listening to the surf, breathing the warm salt breeze, it's all coming back.

"Thirsty?" Kevin asks, looking up as he pulls something from the backpack he was toting.

About to say *No*, and *Please take me home*, Lianna realizes what it is.

A bottle of wine.

She and her friends have snuck enough tastes from their parents' liquor supplies in the past year for Lianna to recognize a fortuitous escape route when she sees one.

"I'll have a sip," she hears herself say, as she sinks onto the blanket beside a smiling Kevin.

"Did you remember to put that leftover potato salad into the bag with your sandwich?" Mimi asks as, Cam in tow, she follows Jed to the tiny kitchen with its cracked linoleum, warped cupboard doors, and scratched laminate countertops.

"No, but I don't want it."

"Are you sure?"

"Positive. My stomach's a little queasy tonight."

"Again?"

"Not too bad. But I can't go around eating all that potato salad anyway. I'm getting a gut, see?" Jed pats his stomach.

"Where?"

"There." He pinches an imaginary inch.

She shakes her head. "I don't see a gut, but even if you had one, I'd think it's cute."

"Really? Then keep making potato salad and those

homemade biscuits you gave me yesterday. By Christmas I'll look like Santa." He leans in and plants a kiss on her cheek as she pours milk into a sippy cup for Cam.

"Daddy, is it Christmas? Is Santa coming?" the little boy asks as his father swings him up into his arms.

"Not for six more months, and only if you're good," Jed tells him. "Which means no more flushing things down the potty."

"What about pee pee?"

"Pee pee, yes. Anything else, no."

"What about—"

"Hey, you're about to sabotage the potty training, Jed," Mimi warns, taking Cameron from him with a laugh.

"Just trying to prevent having the plumber here twice in one week," he says, retrieving his brown paper bag lunch from the fridge and heading for the back door. "See you all in the morning."

"Be safe," Mimi calls after him, same as always.

"Don't worry," he replies, same as always, before he closes the door.

But she does worry. She can't help it. Safely sheltered in their cozy, two-bedroom canal-side home every night after dark, she doesn't like to think of him out there working on the damaged bridge under the glare of construction spotlights.

So many things can happen. There are deadly gators and poisonous snakes in the surrounding marshland, not to mention heavy equipment that can malfunction or tip and crush a person. Jed's seen that happen, and worse, in his decade as a construction worker. But he stopped telling her horror stories early on, realizing that what might entertain a casual girlfriend could scare off a potential wife.

Mimi can't bear the thought of anything happening to Jed. He's her whole world—he and Cameron.

Nor does she like to think about how close she once came to losing both of them.

But Jed doesn't know about that, or about the weighty secret she's determined to carry to the grave.

If he ever found out . . .

"Cookie, Mommy!"

"Okay, okay, Cam."

Hurrying to the cupboard for the package of store-brand chocolate-sandwich cookies, she forces away the terrible, haunting memories that are never far from flooding her thoughts.

Charlotte helps herself to the heaping platter of hush puppies the waitress has already set before them. She breaks open a plump, warm puff and slathers it with honey-sweetened butter.

Her husband smiles across the table at her. "I knew you had to be hungry."

"A little."

"Promise to eat while I'm gone?"

"I'll try."

"I'll be back before you know it," he says again. "It's only for the weekend. I got that first flight out on Delta Monday morning."

"I know. I just wish you had invited Aimee here instead. Or that I could be going with you. I'd love to meet her."

The smile fades from Royce's eyes. "I wish the same thing. But Aimee says she isn't ready to meet you yet. I'm lucky she even wants me."

Charlotte nods. She supposes she can't blame the

young woman for resenting not just the father she blames for a multitude of sins, both real and imagined by her bitter mother, but also the new wife and family in Royce's life.

"Well, sooner or later, I'll come with you and we'll get to meet. Not just Aimee, but your mom, too."

Her mother-in-law is in a New Orleans nursing home, too frail to travel. Royce usually makes an effort to see her when he goes back. Charlotte has never met her, and isn't in any hurry to, given Royce's tales of her mounting senility, near-deafness, and constant ill-temper.

"We'll make the trip," he promises. "Maybe for Mardis Gras. That's a good time to go."

"Well, be sure to tell Aimee she's welcome to visit any time," Charlotte reminds him, reverting automatically to her inherent Southern hospitality. "Especially once we're back home." *Oh, to be back home.* "And I hope she likes the brooch and earrings."

"She'll love them. Thank you for picking them out."

"It was fun. You know how much I love to shop."

"And you know how much I love you for being open-minded about my daughter." Royce picks up her hand and kisses away the crumbs that cling to her buttery fingers.

"I love you for the same reason, especially now that mine is such an insufferable little wench," Charlotte tells him with a grin.

"Oh, I remember Aimee at that age, before the divorce. Lianna will come through this stage just fine. Next thing you know, she'll be a gracious young lady fit for the Remington family portrait."

"Somehow I find that hard to believe."

"Trust me."

"I do."

And now that Grandaddy is gone, Royce is the only person left in Charlotte's world whom she *does* trust.

Certainly nobody else deserves it: not the daughter who lied just last week about where she was going and with whom; not the family members who might as well be strangers now in their midst; not the general contractor who repeatedly assured them they'd be back home in Savannah by February, then May, and now August.

Suddenly, Charlotte feels utterly consumed by exhaustion. She leans back in her seat, pressing a hand against her lips to mask a yawn.

"You're tired."

"I am. I feel like I want to crawl into bed and sleep for days," she tells Royce wearily.

"Well, then, go ahead and do just that when we get home."

"I wish."

"What's stopping you? You need to recover from all this. You should rest. Take some time for yourself."

She shakes her head, thinking again of Lianna, of the visiting cousins.

Both Gib and Phyllida are quite a bit younger than she is, and they lived up North, so she never really knew them as well as she'd have liked to. Her father always dismissed them both as spoiled brats, but Charlotte could imagine her Uncle Xavy might have said the same about her. He never seemed to give his only niece the time of day.

Then again, for all they had in common, he and Daddy weren't particularly close, either. The brothers were longtime rivals in everything from sports to acquiring fancy status symbols to garner their lone parent's meager affection.

"Listen, don't let your obnoxious cousins get to you while I'm gone," cautions the apparently clairvoyant Royce.

"They're the only family I have left in the world now that Grandaddy's gone," she feels obligated to point out.

"What about me?"

"Other than you and Lianna," she says hastily. "But you know what I meant. It's just kind of . . . strange. It suddenly feels like the Remingtons are . . . I don't know, a dying breed."

"I'm sorry. I didn't mean to be—"

"Oh, I know." She smiles up at him. "The fact that they're my only flesh and blood in the world, besides Lianna, doesn't make my cousins any less obnoxious."

Royce grins. "I just hope they're not planning to hang around for too long after I'm back."

"I doubt that. I have a feeling that once the will is read, they'll take their money and run."

"I wouldn't be surprised."

"And what about us?" Charlotte asks her husband.

"What do you mean?"

"We're about to inherit a life-changing amount of money, remember?"

He shrugs. "Frankly, I like our life just the way it is. Don't you?"

She flashes him a grateful smile. "Absolutely. And we always said that when the time came, we'd just tuck it away and go on the same as always."

"My thoughts exactly. I'm assuming that's still the plan?"

"That's still the plan," Charlotte assures him, aware, as always, how different he is from her first husband. Royce is as cautious financially as Vincent was a flashy spendthrift.

Both Grandaddy and Mother tried to warn her that Vincent married her for her money—they saw it from the start.

But Charlotte, still reeling from her father's death and her mother's cancer diagnosis, wouldn't listen— any more than she suspects her own daughter will listen to her.

But what can she do about that?

Nothing, Charlotte thinks helplessly for the second time this evening, *but hold my breath and let go.*

CHAPTER 3

"Want me to pick you up again tomorrow night?" Kevin asks hopefully.

Lianna pauses, her hand on the car door handle.

"I don't know," she hedges, needing to think about what just happened between them.

"Well I can, if you want me to. Or I can meet you somewhere, if you don't want to sneak out. You can tell your parents you're with one of your friends or something."

"You mean my mother."

"Huh?"

"You said my *parents*. My father lives in Florida—he's not the one with all the stupid rules. Royce is just my stepfather."

"Yeah," he says in a whatever tone, as if it doesn't matter.

But it does. It matters to her, a lot.

"So let me know, okay? I have to work at the gas station all day so I can't answer my cell if it rings, but you can text message me if you want."

"Okay. I'll let you know."

He leans over the console and kisses her one last time. She can feel stubble on his face, a tactile reminder that he's older than she is. Much older.

Perhaps too old, she allows herself to consider for the first time, as she closes the car door as soundlessly as possible.

Picking her way in the headlights' beam toward the stone-and-iron entrance to Oakgate, she wonders if she's in over her head.

If the wine hadn't smelled musty and tasted bitter, who knows what might have happened?

As it was, Lianna couldn't bring herself to drink more than that first tentative sip. She had tasted enough good wine pilfered from her friend Devin's parents to know that the stuff Kevin offered was either horribly cheap or horribly spoiled, perhaps both.

In the end, much to his disappointment, she managed to maintain her sobriety—and virginity. Not that she's particularly prone to clinging to either in the grand scheme of things.

But tonight, it wasn't meant to be. Or perhaps, just not there, on the island beach. Or with him.

Having reached the lowest spot in the stone wall surrounding the gated entrance to Oakgate, she waves at Kevin.

He blinks the headlights once before driving away, leaving her alone in the dark.

Royce reaches over to turn off the alarm a minute before it rings, not wanting to wake Charlotte.

She's sleeping soundly at last. Between her grief and the houseguests and Lianna's typical teenaged strife, his wife is on the verge of becoming a physical and emotional wreck.

And it doesn't help that you're leaving her for a few days.

Charlotte isn't the type to lay on a guilt trip. She really is upset to see him go.

Sorry, Charlotte, he thinks, rolling over to look at her, *but it can't be helped.*

The room is bathed in the soft glow of the night-light she insists on using. She was so embarrassed, back when they spent their first night together, to admit that she's afraid of the dark.

"I have been ever since I was a little girl," she confessed. "I know it's stupid, but . . . I can't help it. Even Lianna sleeps in a dark room, but I can't."

Royce lingers, watching her sleep, thinking that she really does look like a defenseless child, lying there with her beautiful face scrubbed clean, her hair tangled on the white pillowcase. The hint of vulnerability he glimpsed the first time he ever laid eyes on her is often swept behind a sophisticated façade during the day. Not so at night, especially when she's asleep.

Tempting as it is, he can't lie here watching her a moment longer. He sits up noiselessly on the new king-sized pillowtop Sealy that Charlotte's grandfather purchased when they moved into his guest room.

Nothing but the best for his favorite granddaughter— and, by proxy, her husband.

Royce yawns, wishing he could curl up beside Charlotte and catch some more sleep. But he can't. It's time to get moving.

He swings his legs over the edge of the bed and his bare feet make contact with the satiny hardwood floor walked on by countless Remingtons.

Sometimes he thinks, *If this old house could talk . . .*

Good thing it can't, Royce tells himself. Some things are better kept buried in the past, where they belong.

He bends over his wife's sleeping form and presses a gentle kiss on her exposed shoulder, just below a reddish, heart-shaped birthmark he once thought was an out-of-character tattoo.

"Are you kidding?" she asked laughingly the first time he questioned her about it. *"Grandaddy would have shot me if I ever got a tattoo!"*

She went on to reveal that she grew up calling the distinctive birthmark an "angel's kiss," one that was shared by a couple of other Remingtons. Grandaddy, for one.

Her late son, Adam, for another.

She sobbed when she told Royce how he looked when his body was pulled from the sea.

His face was . . . It was . . . That's how they knew it was him, Royce. Because of the birthmark.

Shhh, shhh, I know, he said soothingly, and hoped she wouldn't bring up the fact that he didn't know at all— that his own son's body was never found.

"Sleep well, darling," he whispers softly now, knowing she probably won't hear him. "I'll see you in a few days. Don't worry while I'm gone."

But she will. He's seen the haunted expression in her eyes, however fleeting; has caught her brooding when she doesn't realize he's watching her.

She's afraid. Of what, he doesn't know. But that comment she made earlier about running for her life . . .

He made light of it at the time, masking his uneasiness.

But it stayed with him, nagging at him all evening.

What if . . . ?

What if she's having some kind of premonition?

Maybe I shouldn't leave right now, Royce can't help

thinking, and he hesitates beside the bed, mulling it over. *Maybe it's not a good idea.*

But what about Aimee?

He has to go.

That's all there is to it.

Waist-deep in the rough sea, Mimi whirls around and around, flailing her outstretched arms in the water, grasping for the helpless child who vanished on her watch: a lifeguard's worst nightmare.

But it really happened to her.

And now she must continue to relive it, over and over, in her sleep.

She's aware that she's dreaming as the events unfold in numbingly familiar procession.

The fruitless, frantic search among the relentless breakers . . .

The hysterical father hurling pleas and, eventually, accusations . . .

The requisite paperwork and the endless verbal recounting, official and ultimately therapeutic, of what, exactly, happened on that beach beneath the hot September sun . . .

The shrill peal of the telephone . . .

The telephone . . . ?

Yes.

With that, the sequence is broken.

Mimi opens her eyes abruptly and finds herself looking at the illuminated digital clock.

Four thirteen AM, and a lifeguard's worst nightmare is instantly traded for a wife's worst nightmare.

Something's happened to Jed. Or her mother.

For no other reason would the phone ring at this hour.

Heart pounding with dread, she untangles herself from the sheets and hurries to answer it.

Lianna is uneasily aware of the rhythmic night sounds; the dank, humid smell of brackish water; the overcast night sky void of moon or stars.

She reaches into her pocket for her small flashlight, but comes up empty-handed.

Is it any wonder?

Kevin had her shorts halfway down her legs out there at the beach. The flashlight probably fell out into the sand as they rolled around.

Terrific.

Now she'll have to sneak back into the house in the dark.

It's not that she's a big baby about the dark . . .

Not like Mom.

No, but who wants to venture into a creepy old basement without even a flashlight?

The thought of that is bad enough; she can't imagine bringing herself to enter the tunnel and walk up two flights of the pitch-black hidden stairway. There are definitely spiders and mice. And probably even bats in there—what if one flies into her hair?

What if she loses her balance and falls? Several of the runglike steps have rotted away in the dampness; others are about to. With a flashlight, she can pick her way past them. In the dark, she'd be playing Russian roulette with every step.

Nobody would ever find her in there. Not with those fourteen-inch-thick tabby foundation walls that are probably soundproof.

Okay, so she obviously isn't going back into the house the same way she came out.

But maybe that's not necessary anyway. Glancing at her watch, she sees that it's well past four in the morning. Nobody will be stirring at this hour. She can slip inside through the back door, using the key Great-Grandaddy always kept hidden among the perennials that ring the base of an old stone sundial in the garden.

Her heart pounding, Lianna decides it's a brilliant idea.

It takes her quite a few minutes of rooting around for the key in the dewy, overgrown bed that contains more weeds than flowers. Something pierces her fingertip, probably a spider's bite, and she thrusts her stinging finger into her mouth.

This is a stupid idea. Really stupid. What if the spider was poisonous? There are lizards in here, too, and God knows what else. A dark, rodent-infested tunnel is now almost more appealing than reaching back into the weeds again.

But when she does, she finds the key almost immediately.

All right, so this was a good plan after all.

The big door opens silently and the rooms are deserted, just as she knew they would be. She pockets the key, hoping she'll remember to replace it later, in broad daylight.

It isn't until she reaches the door to her bedroom that she realizes she's made a huge mistake.

It's latched . . . from the inside.

How could she have forgotten?

Now what?

Before she can plot her next move, she hears a movement behind her.

A voice drawls, "Well, look who's prowling around at this hour."

*   *   *

Charlotte sits straight up in bed, heart racing wildly.

Then she realizes it was just a dream.

No, not a dream. A nightmare.

Not even that.

It really happened.

But it isn't happening now, she reminds herself, pressing her hand against her pounding chest. It's over. Long over.

She lies back slowly against the pillows, closing her eyes as if to block out the images that have haunted her for eight years. But they're still there, more vivid than ever.

She can see the foaming ocean; can feel it, sunwarmed and saltily stinging her newly shaved legs; can feel her hands swirling helplessly through it, coming up empty again and again.

She can hear screams, her own screams, as she bellows her son's name over and over again in futile, exhausting effort.

A sob escapes her throat even now.

She shudders and rolls toward Royce's side of the bed, needing to feel his warm body against hers. He alone understands. He's been there, too.

Even on their honeymoon, when they found themselves standing at the brink of Niagara Falls, he knew instinctively what she was thinking as she gazed down at the churning blue-gray water. He was thinking it, too. "Come on," he said, and quietly led her away.

Charlotte needs him now as she needed him then.

But the covers are thrown back on his side of the bed; his spot as cold and empty as her arms that ache for a child who will never come home.

*   *   *

Even in the dim light from a distant sconce, Gib can see the panic in the kid's eyes.

"What are you up to, Leigh Ann?" he asks, reminded suddenly of a childhood fishing expedition with his maternal grandfather in Narragansett Bay: the empowering sensation of gazing down at a helpless cod trapped in his net.

"Lianna," she says, lifting her chin, and it takes him a moment to realize she's correcting him about her name.

"Lianna," he repeats, amused by the insult that now mingles with panic in her gaze. "Sorry about that."

She shrugs and tries to seem casual as she inquires, "What are you doing up?"

"I asked you first."

"Well, I'm going back to bed."

"So am I," he tells her, though it's not entirely true.

He hasn't yet been to bed in his assigned guest room. But he's willing to bet Cassandra has long been asleep beneath the old-fashioned eyelet canopy. He can feel his loins tighten at the mere thought of her, naked, between the sheets.

He'll get to her momentarily.

For now, he can't resist toying with Charlotte's daughter. Poor thing clearly didn't inherit the Remington genes when it came to looks. Perhaps she looks like her father, although he can't seem to conjure an image of Charlotte's first husband. Gib saw him only rarely, and hasn't in years.

Lianna isn't unattractive, yet hardly possesses her mother's beauty, or Phyllida's, or even Gib's. Maybe she'll get there one day, but for now, she's on the scrawny side, with sharp features and a slight overbite. Braces would help, Gib concludes. Braces, and longer hair. Highlights in her hair would be good, too—or even if she was a brunette like her mother . . .

Instead, her hair is a dull, sandy shade that could, Gib supposes, pass for blond—just not to a connoisseur, like him.

"I'd be willing to bet," he says, leaning in, "that your mother doesn't know you're locked out of your room at this hour."

"What makes you think I'm locked out?"

"I saw you try the door and I heard you curse when it didn't open."

There's little she can say to that, of course. To her credit, she remains silent, glaring up at him.

No stranger himself to adolescent prowling in the wee hours, Gib can't help but admire her spunk. As he recalls, Charlotte wasn't the kind of girl who would be caught dead disobeying her parents' rules. How interesting that this apple fell hard and rolled quite a long way from the tree.

"So what are you going to do now?" he asks Lianna, folding his arms. "Wait it out until morning? Break the door down?"

Before she can answer, his ears pick up the sound of a door creaking closed down the hall. Footsteps approach.

"Please don't tell," Lianna hisses at him, before slipping into a shadowy nearby nook.

It takes three attempts before Mimi's violently trembling hands are successful in fastening the carseat buckle snugly across her son's chest.

By then, Cameron is asleep again, as blissfully unaware of his mother's growing panic as he was before she plucked him from his bed five minutes ago.

Mimi slides into the driver's seat, manages to get the

key into the ignition, and says a brief prayer as she backs out into the street.

Please, dear God, don't let anything happen to Jed.

Then she shifts into DRIVE and races off toward the highway that leads to Savannah, and the hospital emergency room.

Moments after Gib watches Charlotte's daughter disappear into the shadows of the hall, her stepfather appears.

Royce is fully dressed, carrying luggage, and striding briskly, though he stops short at the sight of Gib standing before him.

"Hey, what's up?" Gib asks, as though they're casual acquaintances running into each other on the street in broad daylight.

"I'm leaving to catch an early flight. What are you doing . . . ?" The remainder of Royce's sentence trails off, as though he isn't sure whether to conclude it with an "*up*" or a "*here.*"

"I'm going to bed after a late night," Gib says truthfully. He adds, at Royce's doubtful look, "I couldn't sleep so I drove down to the other end of the island for a nightcap at the Reef. That always was my favorite beach bar—It sure looks a lot different these days, though. It used to be a dive."

He just hopes Royce isn't, say, friends with the owner or something. The last thing he needs is to be caught in a lie.

"Where's your girlfriend?"

Gib resists the urge to correct the terminology. Let Royce think whatever he wants about his relationship with Cassandra. It'll be much easier that way. "She's probably asleep. She stayed here."

Royce frowns.

"What's the matter?" Gib asks.

"Nothing, I just . . . I thought you were talking to someone. I heard voices."

Gib hesitates, weighing his options.

Should he tell Royce about his stepdaughter sneaking around in the middle of the night? How will he react? Gib doesn't know what kind of guy he is—they never even met before this week. But he seems like a decent fellow, unlike Charlotte's first husband. He couldn't stand Vince, and the feeling seemed mutual on the few occasions they were thrown together for family functions.

Anyway, Royce would probably go tell Charlotte that her kid is up to something. Why get the kid into trouble? Gib has to give her credit, having this much spunk with such a Goody Two Shoes for a mother.

So he shrugs and tells Royce, "I don't know what you heard . . . maybe it was just me, talking to myself. I do that sometimes."

"We all do, I suppose." Royce barely cracks a smile.

"Have a good trip," Gib calls after him in a whisper as Royce walks off down the hall, unwittingly passing within a few feet of his stepdaughter's hiding place. "See you when you get back."

"Maybe not. I'll be gone for a few days."

"Oh, I'll be here," Gib replies, relishing the stiffening—just barely visible—of the other man's spine at the news.

Yes, he'll be here. Where else is he going to go? Oakgate is as much his home as anybody else's, and at this point, it's the only one he has. Not that he's about to let on to his sister or cousin or even Cassandra.

Cassandra.

Stirred by renewed lust, he hurries off down the hall, leaving Lianna to resolve her own dilemma. She'll undoubtedly be grateful he didn't rat her out to the old man. It might have been tempting if Charlotte's second husband didn't seem to have the temperament of a tree stump.

The kid will just have to owe me a favor, Gib decides, smiling as he lets himself into his room.

A big favor that he has every intention of collecting at some point. But for now there are other things on his agenda.

Slipping into his room, he steals across the carpet to the canopy bed.

There, instead of a slumbering beauty, he finds a note impaled on the pillow with an antique hat pin.

He has to turn on the bedside lamp to read it, but he probably shouldn't even have bothered.

Gib,
I decided to go back to Boston.
Sorry,
Cassandra.

For a moment, he stands there staring at it.

Then, with a smirk, he plucks the paper from the pin, wads it into a ball, and tosses it in the general direction of the wastebasket. The pin he stabs into place on the cushioned top of a dusty sewing box that rests on the nearby bureau, a forgotten relic of some bygone Remington spinster.

Easy come, easy go, Gib thinks as he crawls into bed alone.

Phyllida is awakened by Brian's prodding hand in her side, his stale, boozy breath wafting beneath her nostrils.

She yawns, opening her eyes to darkness. "What time is it?"

No reply, just an urgent, "Come on, Phyll," as he tugs at her cotton nightgown.

"Come on, what?" She rolls away—or tries to. This isn't their California King. There's little room to escape him on a full-sized mattress that butts up against the wall on her side.

"You know . . ."

She knows. And she isn't in the mood.

"Did you just get home now?" she asks, flinching beneath his cold touch on her bare skin.

"No! I got home hours ago. You were asleep." He moves closer and nuzzles the back of her neck with his razor stubble.

Phyllida endures it for a few moments, wondering if he might actually be able to arouse her for a change.

Nah. Try as she might, she can't even pretend he's somebody else. There are occasions when that works, but not this time.

"Stop, Brian. We can't," she tells him softly, nudging his probing fingers from her hip.

"Sure we can."

"No. The baby is right here."

Baby? Wills is no more a baby than Brian is the man of her dreams.

Yet her son is sleeping in a crib again, and right here in the room, a mere few feet from their bed, just as he was as an infant.

Back then, of course, it was with great reluctance that Phyllida warded off her husband's advances.

"He's asleep," Brian protests, just like old times.

Unswayed, Phyllida whispers, "If he wakes up, he'll be traumatized for life."

"Yeah, right." He resumes his neck-nuzzling.

She brushes him away. "Seriously, Brian, cut it out."

"Jesus, you're no fun anymore, you know that?"

"Yeah, I know. You keep reminding me."

He rolls onto his back, the bedsprings creaking loudly beneath his weight.

She wonders if he really was here, asleep beside her, for hours as he claimed.

She wouldn't know. As Brian likes to say, she sleeps like the dead.

"What time is it?" Phyllida asks again.

"Who knows? Four? Five?"

She groans. "I'm going back to sleep."

So leave me alone.

The unspoken words linger in the darkness between them.

Back in her room at last, Lianna goes straight to the antique dressing table, turns on the lamp, and looks into the slightly wavy looking glass that has undoubtedly reflected countless other—and much prettier—Remington females before her.

Her nose wrinkled in distaste, Lianna leans into the mirror, checking her straw-colored hair for cobwebs.

None are visible, though she swears she can feel them lingering.

The trip back up two flights of stairs in total darkness was almost as much fun as running into her mother's creepy cousin in the upstairs hall. She shudders, as much due to thinking about Gib as at the memory of hearing something scamper in her wake on the return trip to her room.

Is it really worth all this, just to be with Kevin?

No, she concludes with little deliberation. He's kind of a jerk. Cute, but a jerk.

Still, it's not just about Kevin.

It's about freedom. It's about evading her mother's constant stranglehold, about being in charge of her own life for a change.

Lianna turns away from the mirror and changes swiftly into pajamas, tossing her shorts and T-shirt in a heap on the floor.

Hearing a clattering sound, she realizes that it's the key to the back door. She forgot to return it to its hiding place in the garden.

Oh, well. She'll do it some other time.

She tosses it into a drawer, turns off the lamp, climbs into her bed, and wearily decides she's had enough of sneaking out into the night . . . for now.

But the secret stairway will beckon again. Of that, she has no doubt.

And it's comforting just to know it's there whenever she feels the need to escape.

Dawn creeps gray and rainy over the Atlantic sky, washing away the remains of a strange, restless night.

At last, the players are in place for Act Two, the first act having drawn to a satisfying close.

Soon enough, the residents of Oakgate—past and present, permanent and temporary—will find themselves playing out a drama nobody could have seen coming.

Nobody but me.

The stage must be set for the next act.

And life must go on normally.

Rather, as close to normally as possible after a death. Even when that death claimed an old man who had long overstayed his welcome.

Interesting, how many ways there are to make death seem accidental.

The right poisons, administered in the right doses, can approximate any number of fatal illnesses without leaving a readily discernable trace.

Or, an electrical device thrown into a tub of water can result in fatal cardiac arrhythmia that leaves no outward signs, giving the appearance of a heart attack.

All you have to do is remove the device from the water, and nobody will be the wiser.

But it has to be the right kind of device. These days, household appliances have ground-fault circuit interrupters that turn off the power instantly in the case of immersion.

Years ago, there were no such precautions. Toasters, lamps—and yes, *radios*—lacked breakers that would prevent accidental electrocution.

Oakgate's closets, attic storage room, and cellar are as cluttered with antique appliances as they are with family secrets.

But the weapon of choice was right out in the open, and carefully, deliberately, chosen.

After it served its purpose, Gilbert Remington II's prized radio was carefully replaced on the mantel, right out in the open where it has always been.

Such a shame, in a way, that the delicious irony was lost on the victim. The old man never knew what hit him.

Neither, should the time come, will anyone else who dares to get in the way.

PART II

THE SECOND
VICTIM

CHAPTER 4

"It's just that I missed you while you were gone, and you've only been back twenty-four hours," Charlotte wistfully tells Royce, opening the top drawer of her bureau. "I wish you could come with me today, that's all."

"I wish I could, too." He vigorously rubs a towel over his shower-dampened hair. "We could play footsie under Tyler's conference table while the will is being read."

She can't help but smile at that. "Yes, and I wouldn't feel so uncomfortable around my cousins if you were there."

The weekend, her first without Grandaddy, was a difficult one—especially with Royce gone, her cousins here, and Lianna more remote than ever. Charlotte did her best to keep it together, even spending two full days at the beach with Phyllida and her son while Brian and Gib were out golfing.

But it was nerve-wracking for her in the end. Every time the lifeguard blasted a whistle, or little Wills tried to squirm out of his mother's arms in the surf, Charlotte endured a stab of uneasiness.

And it isn't as though she and her cousin have much in common. Phyllida's world seems to revolve around the gym, shopping, filling out preschool applications for Wills—reportedly a complicated, competitive process— and occasionally going to an audition.

Several times, Charlotte welled up with tears over their grandfather, but she kept her grief hidden behind her sunglasses, knowing its intensity isn't shared.

It isn't that Phyllida and Gib didn't love Grandaddy. Of course they did, despite their apparent indifference. Although disconcerted, Charlotte has repeatedly assured herself of that. They just aren't as emotional as she is, that's all. They haven't lost all that she has.

She was relieved when Royce got home early Monday morning, his flight right on time, as he had promised. He even took the day off, and they spent most of it at their new home in Savannah, checking on the progress of the renovation. The contractor and Royce seem satisfied that they're on track again, but the job isn't going quickly enough for Charlotte.

And she doesn't want to go without him today.

She removes a new package of pantyhose from her drawer. Ordinarily she doesn't wear stockings; she hates the constricting feel on her legs. Now, she's forced to don them for the second time in a week. The funeral, of course, was the other occasion.

Oh, Grandaddy.

"I'm sure it'll be fine. Your cousins seem nice enough," Royce points out, oblivious to the tears welling in her eyes as he stands before the full-length mirror to expertly knot his tie.

She swallows the lump in her throat. "They might

seem nice, but I keep feeling like they resent me—and Lianna, and you, for that matter."

"Me?" he echoes incredulously.

"I think so." She sits on the edge of their bed and gingerly pulls the dark stockings up her legs.

"Why would they resent me?"

"Who knows? Because you get to sleep in the nicest guest bedroom? Or because you've spent more time with Grandaddy than they have these past few years?"

"Oh, come on. It isn't as if your grandfather and I ever went palling around together, Charlotte. In fact, I'm not all that convinced he even liked me."

"He did," she assures him, standing and smoothing her tailored navy blue skirt over her legs. "He's gruff with everybody, even me. I mean, he *was*."

She pauses to regain her composure. There are those tears again, ever ready to spring to her eyes and spill down her cheeks. She probably shouldn't have worn mascara today. "But if he didn't like you, Royce," she goes on, "he'd have let me know about it."

"I wouldn't be so certain about that."

She shakes her head. "Are you sure you can't cancel your meeting and come with me?"

"I wish I could, but this could be a major new corporate client for me."

"Yes, but after today . . ." She trails off, but he must know what she's thinking. After today, they'll be millions of dollars richer. The income from his computer-consulting business will be even less necessary than it is now.

"It isn't about the money for me, Charlotte," he reminds her. "I love what I do, and I'm good at it."

"Of course you are. I didn't mean—"

"I know you didn't." He smiles as if to show her that his pride isn't wounded.

"Nothing is going to change, Royce. After today. I remember what we said about tucking it away and going on. So don't worry."

"I'm not worried."

Then why, Charlotte can't help but wonder as a nagging uneasiness takes over, *am I?*

"How about a little more pudding, Jeanne?" Melanie asks. "It's tapioca. You love tapioca."

Jeanee hates tapioca, but what does it matter? They've been bringing it to her for years, assuming she enjoys it because she eats it all.

She supposes she could ask for vanilla pudding instead, or even chocolate, but that would mean striking up a conversation, and potentially inviting other topics.

It's much easier, much safer, to just eat the tapioca, and whatever else the nurse brings to her.

Today it was sloppy joes, overcooked carrots, and pudding; yesterday, creamed beef, limp string beans the color of jarred olives, and stewed peaches.

Institutional food. If you're hungry enough—and Jeanne invariably is—you'll eat it.

Jeanne eats it, and she remembers . . .

Remembers beans freshly picked off the vine: stem ends snapping easily beneath her fingers; their vibrant, grassy shade of green retained even after they were slightly steamed; delicious buttered and salted—the crisp burst of flavor on her tongue . . .

Remembers peaches plucked from the orchard out back, so ripe your fingertips could rub the skin from the flesh at the slightest touch, revealing luscious, pink-tinged, orange-yellow fruit that always reminded Jeanne of a Low Country sunset . . .

"Jeanne?" Melanie persists. "More tapioca?"

She shakes her head vehemently.

Now her peaches and her beans come from cans, plopped in compartments of thick beige paper trays and delivered by young women who speak to her with the measured simplicity of a preschool teacher and merely bide their time here, their thoughts on their otherwise fascinating lives.

Petite blond Melanie is Jeanne's favorite by far of all the nurses who have come through here over the years; she, at least, doesn't seem particularly eager to leave when her shift is over. She doesn't seem to have much of a life away from Oakgate. Often, she arrives early or stays longer than she needs to, bustling around reassuringly, often humming.

She's always, always cheerful. Too cheerful, almost. Never before has Jeanne ever encountered another human being who doesn't seem to have a bad day—or even a so-so day—*ever*.

But she doesn't only sing and hum and, on occasion, whistle jauntily. She talks, too, ostensibly to Jeanne, but sometimes, it seems, to herself, often *about* herself. She reveals in disarming detail a childhood spent in one foster home after another, abusive parents who willingly signed away their rights. She spent years praying she'd be adopted, and realized in her teens that the prayer would never be answered.

You'd think a person like that would grow up to be a glum, pessimistic adult. But not Melanie.

She even wound up on the streets for a few years, and has alluded to doing whatever was necessary to stay alive. Then, she said, along came a wealthy older gentleman who took her under his wing, got her an apartment, put her through nursing school.

"If it weren't for him, Jeanne, who knows where I'd be?" she likes to ask. She also likes to answer. "I know where I'd be. *Dead.*"

Jeanne would be very interested to know more about the mysterious benefactor who saved her. Whenever Melanie mentions him, Jeanne notices that she fails to reveal even his first name—and senses that the oversight is deliberate. Jeanne can't help but sense an uncharacteristic reticence that hints there might be pertinent details Melanie isn't sharing. But asking about the man would open the door to reciprocal interaction—and perhaps, emotional complications—that Jeanne just doesn't need.

Certainly not now, when she has a difficult decision weighing on her mind.

Decision?

What decision?

You know what you have to do, Jeanne. You always knew what you'd do if it came down to this . . .

But not yet.

Not when there's still a chance.

"Would you like to get back into bed now, and take a nap?"

She shakes her head at Melanie's query, preferring to remain here in the window, where she can watch the driveway below.

They all left a short time ago, separately, in pairs. First Charlotte and her daughter, then Phyllida and Gib, followed shortly by Phyllida's husband whose name Jeanne can't recall, toting their young son and a beach umbrella.

Charlotte's husband, Royce, left hours earlier in his

silver Audi, dressed in a suit and carrying a briefcase as he does most mornings—probably going to his office if it's a weekday.

Is it a weekday?

Where is Royce's office?

What does he even do?

If Jeanne ever knew, she can't remember.

Nor is it important.

"What day is it?" she asks the nurse, bustling somewhere behind her.

"Did you say something, Jeanne?" Melanie is instantly at her side, eager to be engaged in conversation.

"What day is it?" Jeanne is careful to maintain a monotone this time.

"The date? Let's see, it must be July—"

"No, the day. What day? Saturday, or . . . ?"

"Oh, it's Tuesday."

Tuesday.

A weekday.

Her grandnephew and both grandnieces were dressed in dark-colored, professional-looking suits.

They're going to the lawyer's office, Jeanne concludes, momentarily pleased with her detective work.

Then, as she acknowledges what that means—Gilbert's will is about to be read—the tapioca pudding goes into a spin cycle in her stomach.

In all his years as an attorney, Tyler Hawthorne has never faced the reading of a will with as much trepidation as he does now, as he paces his Drayton Street office.

It isn't just because he and Gilbert Xavier Remington II had been friends since childhood. When they lost

Silas Neville—the third member of the close-knit group formed in a boarding school dormitory almost eighty Septembers ago—Tyler was mostly just sorrowful.

Then again, Silas's will was straightforward; no surprises there. He left everything to Betsy, his fourth wife, who spent more time fluttering around Savannah than she did at Silas's bedside during his last months on earth, after the stroke that paralyzed just about every function but his speech. As Betsy so eloquently phrased it, "I've always been a little squeamish. Those hospice nurses are much better at this kind of thing than I am."

If Tyler had any anxieties about the prospect of reading Silas's will, they were based on the fear that Betsy might put her hand on his thigh beneath the table, as she was reputedly inclined to do even when her husband was alive.

It didn't happen. The will was read without a hitch—and Betsy went on to get rehitched just six months later, to a man her own age—or perhaps a decade younger. As Gilbert dryly stated at the time, he probably needed someone to pay his college tuition.

I miss you already, Gilbert.

And you, too, Silas.

This world seems to get lonelier with every passing week.

Tyler is acutely aware of his status as a widower himself, and as sole survivor of a lifelong threesome referred to back in their boarding school days as the Telfair Trio. He sinks into his leather swivel chair behind the mahogany desk at which two previous generations of Hawthornes practiced law.

The days of standing weekly golf games and lunches at the club with Silas and Gilbert were long gone well before his friends died. But despite having drifted with old age from their social and recreational rituals, the bond forged four score—give or take a year or two—ago, remained.

The trio staged some risky schoolboy pranks and escapades in their days at Telfair Academy—always knowing they had each other's backs.

That loyalty—that willingness to cover for each other, even if it meant lying to an authority figure, or a spouse—lingered into adulthood. They knew each other's deepest and, in some cases, darkest secrets.

Thanks to Silas and Gilbert, Tyler's beloved Marjorie went to her deathbed never knowing of his foolish, youthful indiscretions.

And thanks to Silas and Tyler putting their own careers as doctor and lawyer on the line, Gilbert's family fortune remains intact—and, perhaps even more importantly, the Remington name untarnished.

Perhaps it was the Telfair Trio's final escapade, that ultimate test of their allegiance, that pushed them all too far. After that, things were never quite the same. On the surface, yes. But deep down, Tyler suspects, guilt had finally caught up with all three of them.

Perhaps Gilbert most of all.

But it all happened years ago. Another lifetime, it seems.

Tyler drums his fingertips on the green blotter and turns a nervous eye toward the swinging pendulum of the wall clock opposite.

In about five minutes, Gilbert Remington II's descendants are going to walk through that door, fully anticipating that they will walk back out set for life, millionaires many times over.

One won't be disappointed.

*   *   *

"Remember, you need to be ready when I come back here to get you." Parked at the curb in front of Casey's house on Bull Street in Savannah's historic district, Mom taps the steering wheel of her white Lexus SUV with both hands for emphasis.

Lianna almost wishes old Stephen had driven her into town instead of her mother. But the chauffeur has gone to visit his daughter in Atlanta for a few weeks, and Great-Grandaddy's shiny black car sits unused in the carriage house until he gets back.

"I'm going to call your cell phone when I'm on my way," Mom goes on, "so you'll have plenty of warning, and I swear, if you're not ready—"

"I will be," Lianna says, wishing her mother would stop talking to her, and frowning over at her in the passenger's seat, as if she's a naughty little girl. It's enough to make her add, snippily, "Just don't call and say you're coming back a half hour from now and expect me to be happy to see you."

"Don't use that tone with me." Mom's violet eyes darken ominously.

Lianna can't help but notice, jealously, that her mother is strikingly pretty even when she's angry. It isn't fair. Why can't Mom look like a regular person, the way her friends' mothers do? Or, if she has to be so beautiful, at least Lianna could have inherited her looks.

Lianna apparently resembles not her father, with his dark good looks, but his side of the family, though she doesn't know firsthand. Her paternal grandparents died long before she was born, and she hasn't seen her father's only sister in years. For that matter, she doesn't see a whole lot of Dad himself—but only because Mom won't let her. That's what he says, and Lianna believes it wholeheartedly.

Mom wasn't even nice to Daddy at the funeral, after he drove all that way to offer his condolences.

Too bad that he couldn't stay longer or that Lianna couldn't go home with him. He said his apartment is too small, but he's working on getting a bigger one, so she can start spending every other weekend with him, the way she's supposed to—and never has.

"You heard what I said, Lianna." Mom is still glaring at her. "When I get back, you'll be ready to come home with me."

"Yeah, well . . . Oakgate isn't home. Just so you know. In case you forgot."

Shut up, Lianna tells herself. *Why are you making things difficult? Why don't you just get out of the stupid car before she decides to take you with her to the stupid lawyer's office?*

Why?

Who the heck knows?

She just can't seem to help herself. Lately, whenever she's talking to her mother, she opens her mouth and harsh, spiteful things fall out of it.

To her surprise, her mother doesn't have an angry retort. This time, anyway.

"I know Oakgate isn't home, Lianna," Mom says, sounding almost sympathetic. "It really won't be much longer till we come back to Savannah. I promise."

Lianna is tempted to point out that the new house in Savannah isn't home, either. Not to her. No place feels like home to her anymore.

Poor, poor child of divorce, she tells herself—mockingly, yet the words sting.

Struck by a sudden, fierce longing for her father, she wishes she had told Mom earlier that before he left the funeral reception last week, he promised to visit next weekend . . . and that Lianna wants to stay with him while he's here. He always stays at the same place: the

Shark's Tooth Inn on the southernmost tip of the island.

She figures he won't mind having her stay there, too. Especially since that will mean he won't have to keep dealing with Mom and her rules.

Now isn't the time for Lianna to bring it up to her mother, but she will, first chance she gets.

Right, and Mom will have that tight-lipped expression she gets every time Lianna brings up her dad.

Why does Mom hate him so much? Why can't she see that her nasty attitude keeps her ex-husband away, not just from her—which is how she wants it—but from his daughter as well?

It isn't fair.

I need him. He's my dad.

Lianna turns to look out the car window at the dense, graying sky beyond the rooftops. Raindrops threaten to fall any second now, as do her own tears.

"Listen, go have fun with your friend," her mother tells her unexpectedly, and leans over to peck her on the cheek.

Lianna doesn't mean to brush away the kiss as if it was a pesky fly.

But she does. She can't help herself.

The instant hurt in Mom's expression sends Lianna scrambling for the door handle.

As luck would have it, Tyler happened to be recuperating in the hospital from a car accident when Gilbert Remington changed his will last winter. His grandnephew, Jameson, a new partner in the firm, handled it in his absence.

By the time Tyler realized what had happened, the new will was completed and signed.

At that point, it wasn't necessarily Tyler's place to question a client's decision to all but disinherit two of his three heirs. He did so anyway, in part because Gilbert was a close friend; but mostly because Gilbert was always adamant that his estate be divided equally among the remaining Remingtons, regardless of his feelings for them.

Something drastic must have happened to change his mind. Tyler couldn't deny being curious about a possible rift in Savannah's most prominent family.

So he picked up the phone and called.

He fully expected Gilbert to brush him off in his usual brusque manner, but his friend seemed oddly subdued as they exchanged initial niceties that day.

When Tyler brought up the will, he drawled, "I knew I'd be hearing from you about it, Tyler. If you didn't croak, that is."

Ah, that zinger was more like the cantankerous old SOB.

"No, I'm alive and well—for the time being, anyway, according to my doctor. And thank you for the fruit basket." A personal note, let alone a visit, would have been nicer, but Gilbert never was the warm-fuzzy type.

"I don't plan on going anywhere anytime soon," Tyler went on, "and I'm sure you don't either, Gilbert."

No reply.

"But when you do . . . I see that you're essentially leaving everything to—"

"Don't question me, Tyler. You didn't give me grief when I eliminated Xavy's wife after he passed away."

"No," Tyler told him, "but that was different, Gilbert."

"How?"

"This involves your own flesh and blood."

It was no secret that Gilbert wasn't particularly fond of his daughter-in-law Susan. He never did take kindly to "Yankees," and he merely tolerated her from the moment his son brought her home.

Not that he ever had much use for his other daughter-in-law, a fragile, petulant Southern belle who grew up on Achoco Island. He'd probably have gone to the trouble to write out Connie June as well, if she hadn't already been terminally ill at that point.

In fact, Tyler recalls that at the time he was touched by Gilbert's concern over her health, particularly toward the end. Gilbert flew in specialists to treat her and when that failed, hired the best private hospice nurses his money could buy. He arranged for fresh flower arrangements to be delivered daily to her bedside, and ordered in bulk any foods she could manage to keep down.

As Tyler saw it then, the overly solicitous behavior was most likely in deference to Connie June's daughter.

Either that, or in his twilight years the old man was starting to soften . . . a suggestion he'd have taken as an accusation, not a compliment, should Tyler ever have brought it up.

Which he wouldn't.

Even if he hadn't eventually learned the real, and shocking, reason for Gilbert's solicitous behavior toward Connie June, the final change Gilbert made to his will would certainly have ultimately proven he wasn't softening with age.

Rather, it would seem to indicate the opposite.

"You know it's my job as your attorney to ensure that you were of sound mind and body when you made these latest changes," Tyler told Gilbert.

"Your nephew must have decided that I was, because he didn't have a problem with the new will when he drew it up."

"He doesn't know you the way I do."

Gilbert snorted at that.

As if to say, *You don't know me at all, Tyler.*

Still . . .

"Why didn't you wait for me to come back before you made the changes?"

"At our age, Tyler, who has time to wait?"

"You could at least have consulted me."

"You were lying in a hospital bed." Gilbert's tone was surprisingly subdued. "How could I do that to you?"

"What did your family do to piss you off, might I ask?"

"You might," Gilbert shot back, his lapse into kindly consideration unsurprisingly temporary, "but I don't have to answer, you nosy son of a bitch."

It was hardly the first time in Tyler's life that Gilbert had called him that—usually with utmost affection. But this time, it was hardly a term of endearment.

What on earth could have happened? Obviously, something earth-shattering enough to cause Gilbert to set aside his typically pragmatic approach to family finance.

"You have to know all hell is going to break loose when your family finds out what you've done."

"I won't be there to see it," was Gilbert's succinct response.

"No, but I will."

"Look on the bright side, Tyler. Maybe you'll get lucky and check out after I do."

"I doubt that. I've always thought you were going to live forever," he replied, only half-kidding.

"Then neither of us has anything to worry about, do we?"

Maybe you don't, Tyler thinks now, gazing at the legal document waiting on his desk. *But I most certainly do.*

The will is bound to be messily contested.

What the hell was Gilbert thinking?

* * *

The Magnolia Clinic is conveniently located in the shadows of Highway 16, just off the exit ramp. Mimi has no problem finding it, just as Dr. Redmond's nurse promised when she called this morning to summon them.

Everything about this place is depressing, from the unadorned, yellow-brick façade to the rusty chain-link and barbed wire fence that rings the parking lot. There is narry a magnolia in sight. Most of the cars here, including those with MD license plates, are older domestic models, many in some form of disrepair, mute testimony to the economic level of clientele and staff.

But this is where the Johnstons have landed, courtesy of a nonexistent insurance plan and a virtually empty bank account.

"I'm going to have to park pretty far away from the door. Do you want me to go get a wheelchair?" she asks Jed, when they find themselves circling the lot a second time.

"No. I'll walk."

She opens her mouth to protest, but thinks better of it. He hates being treated like an invalid. He's been through enough of that lately, and who knows what lies ahead?

After collapsing at work and being rushed to Candler General's ER with unbearable stomach pain, poor Jed spent a miserable week in a hospital bed. He was hooked up to an IV, injected and scanned and drained of various fluids as gastroenterology specialists attempted to determine the cause of his illness.

Now, presumably, they know.

And it's news that needs to be delivered in person.

Which means it can't be good.

This is just like what happened with Daddy . . .

No, don't go there, Mimi warns herself, turning into a fortuitously vacant spot beneath the parking lot's lone shade tree, a straggly-looking oak.

Don't think ahead. Don't even consider that. Daddy was a time bomb; he smoked three packs a day. Jed doesn't even—

"Stop!" Jed calls sharply.

She slams on the brakes and looks at him in hopelessness, wondering how on earth she's going to coax him into going in to face the prognosis. He didn't want to come, doesn't want to know.

When he's spoken at all in the hours since the doctor's nurse called to summon them here, it's to voice his intent to steal a boat and hurtle himself overboard far out in the Atlantic the next time a storm blows in.

I swear, Mimi, if that doctor tells me something's really wrong with me, I'm not going to sit here and die a slow death . . .

"Jed, I know this is hard," she says gently, her hands trembling on the steering wheel, foot frozen on the brake, "but we can get through it, whatever—"

"Broken glass," he interrupts.

She stares at him. Now he's incoherent. How on earth is she going to get him to—

"There." He points to the parking space she was about to take. Shards of a brown glass bottle are strewn with other litter between the parallel white lines. "Don't pull in. You'll slash the tires."

"Oh." She swallows hard, shifts into REVERSE.

Slashed tires can be patched, replaced. Slashed tires are so easy, really, in the grand scheme of things; ridiculously simple to remedy.

"I'll find another spot," she manages to say around the lump in her throat as she eases the car back into the midday sun's full glare on the asphalt.

"Or we could just leave. We could go pick up Cam from your mother's and get the hell out of here."

"And go where?"

"Who the hell cares? California. Hawaii. Europe. You've always wanted to go to Europe. You would have, if it weren't for me."

"Don't say that!"

"Why not? It's true. If you hadn't stayed on the island and married me, you would have eventually found your way back to college and finished your degree."

"Stop it. That's not true!"

Yes, it is. You know it is. But it doesn't even matter. You never second-guessed your choice.

The sunny parking lot disappears behind a watery haze of tears. "Jed, we'll go to Europe. Maybe next spring. We'll plan a trip."

He's silent.

Next spring.

Please let us have next spring.

And the one after that . . .

Please let us have time.

Heart pounding in dread, she pulls blindly into a parking spot and turns off the engine.

"Ready?" she asks—and instantly regrets it. What a foolish thing to ask.

He merely shrugs.

Slowly, hand in hand, the way they used to toddle down Achoco Beach as children, they walk toward the clinic to hear the doctor's verdict.

"'Bye," Lianna calls over her shoulder, bolting from the car, her own guilt, and mainly, her mother.

She half-expects Mom to take off as well, tires shrieking. She wouldn't blame her.

But the car remains, engine idling, as Lianna scurries up the walk leading to Casey's family's red brick

Colonial. Why? Is Mom going to come after her to apologize, or yell at her some more? Or, uh-oh, is she suspicious?

Liana forces herself to turn and give a quick wave to show that everything is all right. Looking into the bright sunlight, she can't see into the car. Which is fine with her.

Go on, Mom. Leave, would you? Just get out of here.

It isn't until Lianna has disappeared through the wrought iron side gate that leads along a shade-dappled path, and slammed it firmly behind her, that she hears the Lexus pull away.

Good riddance. Geez.

Dry-eyed again, thank goodness, she makes her way beneath a canopy of centuries-old trees toward the back of Casey's house.

It's peaceful here in the old-fashioned garden; the grounds as deserted as the house itself.

Birds sing from overhead branches. Fat bumblebees hum lazily above magenta hibiscus blossoms. A steady trickle of water flows into the little lily pond Casey's father built for her mother last Christmas. Lianna's steady footsteps crunch on the white gravel path.

Then she hears something else . . .

The slightest rustling from behind a blooming shrub.

Her heartbeat quickening, Lianna breaks into a run—toward, not away from, the sound.

Rounding a bend in the gravel path, she smiles.

Kevin is waiting here for her.

Just as he promised.

"It's good to see you again, Phyllida. You're looking lovely as always."

"Thank you." As Tyler Hawthorne ushers her into the conference room with a hale handshake, she can't help but think that her grandfather's attorney would be a casting agent's dream should a role call for a stately Southern businessman. The elderly attorney comes complete with three-piece suit, well-tended thatch of white hair, and a booming accent thicker than peanut soup.

She hasn't seen him since her wedding day. He invited her to waltz, chatted charmingly and flirted harmlessly, then handed over an envelope that contained a card, with a sentimental, cliché-ridden rhyme, and a thousand-dollar check.

"I hear you and your husband have a little boy now. How are they?"

"Fine—they're at the beach today." She can't help but notice that Tyler seems oddly reluctant to look her in the eye.

Is it because this is official business, and not a social event?

Or because he's torn up over Grandaddy's death?

She doesn't even want to consider what other factor might have rendered him uncharacteristically reticent. Not now. Not when financial salvation is as much within her grasp as Tyler Hawthorne's cold hand.

"Have a seat, won't you?" He releases his grip abruptly and turns to her brother, who's wearing, as usual, a custom-made suit, custom-made dress shirt with French cuffs, silk tie—and, today, the greenish pallor of one who has had a few too many bourbons the night before.

"Gib, my boy, I see life is treating you well."

Is it Phyllida's imagination, or is there a hollow ring to Tyler's jovial words?

"Settled somewhere up North now, are you?"

"Boston. I passed the bar a while back."

"Congratulations. Which firm are you with?"

An invisible crank tightens Gib's polite smile just a notch. "I haven't joined one yet. I'm still, uh, entertaining some offers."

"All in good time," is Tyler's response, after an awkward silence.

Maybe, Phyllida thinks, as she settles into one of the leather chairs at the conference table, *he thinks we're underachievers. Maybe he was expecting me to be a big movie star by now, and Gib to be a partner in some fancy firm.*

Well, it doesn't matter what Tyler Hawthorne thinks of them. His role here isn't to judge Grandaddy's heirs, but to present them with Grandaddy's money.

She notices a limp in Tyler's gait as he walks to his own seat, and he winces visibly as he sits down.

He looks up and sees that she's watching him, so she politely asks, "Are you all right?"

"I will be. I was hurt in an accident a while ago."

"What kind of accident?"

"I was in the crosswalk right out here on Drayton, in front of the building. It was raining, and a car came flying around the corner at top speed . . ."

"Was it a young kid? They're the worst."

"I have no idea. Whoever it was kept right on going. Either they didn't see me, or didn't care."

"Probably a kid."

"Probably. Anyway, I broke my leg and a couple of ribs, but the doctor said I'm lucky it wasn't worse. At my age, you don't bounce back as quickly as you'd like."

Phyllida murmurs an appropriate comment, and sneaks a glance at her watch.

"I trust your cousin Charlotte is on her way?" Tyler asks, somewhat anxiously.

As if on cue, the door to the conference room opens. The receptionist announces, "Mrs. Maitland is here."

"Wonderful." Tyler's tone is hearty. "We can get started."

But Phyllida can't help but notice that he looks far more apprehensive than he does relieved.

Dr. Maurice Redmond has garlic breath and a splash of something tomato-orange on his white shirt, just below his collar.

But that isn't why Mimi dislikes him even more intensely today than she did when they first met in Jed's hospital room.

The man has zero bedside manner. He greets them with all the warmth of the security guard who validated their parking ticket downstairs.

Now, after brusquely ordering them to take two hardback chairs pulled up to his battered metal desk in an office with all the ambiance of a public restroom, he reaches unceremoniously for a manilla folder.

Watching him scan the report inside, Mimi fantasizes about bolting from the clinic with Jed in tow. Europe . . . They really should go to Europe, like Jed suggested. Right this second. They should grab Cam and get on the first plane the hell out of here.

Never mind that there are no direct overseas flights from Savannah, that they don't have passports, that they can't afford a pack of gum, let alone airline fares. None of that matters. All that matters is escaping.

Before it's too late.

Before this unpleasant man tells them his horrible news.

And Mimi has no doubt that it will be horrible.

Nothing positive can possibly transpire in a place like this: scarred linoleum and fluorescent lights. Concrete-block interior walls painted mustard yellow. The perva-

sive scent of Pine-Sol that doesn't quite mask the under-
lying odor of vomit.

"Mr. Johnston, I have your test results here."

Dr. Redmond has begun.

God help us.

Jed squeezes Mimi's hand.

Not reassuringly.

No, it's as though he's holding on for dear life, terrified that whatever the doctor is about to tell them is
going to change their lives forever.

"I'm afraid . . ." The doctor pauses, takes a deep
breath and seems to hold it indefinitely.

He's *afraid?* Mimi thinks incredulously. *He's* afraid?

"I'm afraid," Dr. Redmond repeats, "the tests indicate a rare malignancy."

"I direct that all my debts and funeral expenses be
paid as soon after my death as may be practicable. I further direct . . ."

The document trembles in Tyler's hands as he
pauses in the reading, just for a moment. Just to gather
his nerve for the gathering storm.

The only sound in the conference room is the distant wail of a siren somewhere up by the river. The
three heirs of Gilbert Xavier Remington II are focused
on him, their collective silence and unwavering stares almost as unnerving as the prospect of what comes next.

He continues to read the standard language involving estate and inheritance taxes, conscious that nobody
in the room has moved a muscle, or made a sound.

Is it because they sense what's about to happen?

No.

It's because they continue to erroneously anticipate
what is not.

Tyler can stall no longer. "I give, devise, and bequeath all of my estate of whatever kind and wheresoever situated . . ."

Tyler clears his throat and adjusts his reading glasses one last time. He knows they're expecting him to continue with the phrase "in equal shares."

But that was in the old will.

Tyler's voice somehow holds steady as he delivers the explosive language of this one—"to my granddaughter, Charlotte Remington Maitland, provided she survives me."

Royce welcomes the blast of dim, cool air as he steps into the small café a stone's throw from the loft space he rents for his computer-consulting business.

Beyond the plate glass windows, Broughton Street is awash in relentless noonday sun and teeming with hot, sticky pedestrians.

Ella Fitzgerald croons a bluesy ballad on the café's retro soundtrack as he waits his turn behind a middle-aged couple. If their Yankee accents didn't give them away as tourists, their order would: two large "iced" teas, unsweetened.

Here in the South, it's sweet tea, sugary as gumdrops. Even his wife, who always drinks diet soda and sweetens her coffee with Splenda, enjoys her daily glass of sweet tea before dinner.

Royce orders his from Sheryl—or is it Sherri?—the multipierced, college-aged Goth Girl he finds behind the register every weekday about this time.

Her black-polished fingernails clack on the keys as she rings it up. "We have your favorite eggplant sandwich on whole grain bread as a special today, Mr. Maitland."

"That sounds tempting, but I can't have lunch today.

I've got a meeting to get to down the street in fifteen minutes." He checks the Breguet watch Charlotte gave him on their wedding day, and amends, "Ten minutes."

"Maybe tomorrow."

"Maybe," he agrees, opening his wallet to remove two dollar bills, fully aware that Sheryl or Sherri is checking him out, as usual.

He probably should be flattered that a girl more than half his age finds him attractive—and some days, he is. Especially with his fiftieth birthday looming in just a few months.

Fifty? How can it be? Royce doesn't feel that old, nor, he's certain, does he look it. Those who don't know his true age—and very few in this world do—would most likely think he's in his mid-thirties.

Nevertheless, the milestone birthday sits squarely on the horizon like an oppressive charcoal storm cloud over the sea.

But Royce doesn't want to think about that at the moment. Nor is he in the mood for casual banter with the counter girl, who fills a clear plastic cup with ice, then pours the tea from a tall metal dispenser.

Moments later, he's back out in the steamy Southern sun, gulping the translucent brown beverage he tends to find far too syrupy to effectively quench his thirst. Regardless, he drains his cup quickly and deposits it in a trash can as he strides toward the intersection of Broughton and Bull.

He checks his watch again as he waits to cross. When Charlotte gave it to him, he protested that it was far too extravagant a gift.

"Oh, come on," she said, laughing, "you deserve a little bling bling."

"Bling bling?" he echoed with a grin. "Have you been hanging around with Jenny from the block again?"

It's been a while since they've been that lighthearted, he notes grimly.

And it's not as though their lives will brighten anytime soon.

Not with Charlotte mourning her grandfather even more deeply than he'd anticipated.

She really loved the cranky old guy, Royce realizes now.

Sweet Charlotte, with her gentle soul and kind, forgiving heart, might just be the only person who ever did.

And she, in turn, might truly have been the only person the aging curmudgeon ever really loved.

Royce pictures his wife, who at this very moment, a mere fifteen blocks south of here in Tyler Hawthorne's law office facing Forsyth Park, is witnessing the reading of her grandfather's will. He wonders whether her inheritance is official yet.

We always said that when the time came, we'd just tuck it away and go on the same as always . . .

Well, Darling, Royce thinks, wiping a bead of sweat from his forehead, *it looks like the time is here.*

So.

There it is.

Malignancy.

Not just any malignancy, but a rare one.

In other words, a fluke.

A cruel twist of fate, like being struck by lightning, or attacked by a great white shark—either of which would be preferable to the excruciating pain of slowly rotting away from the inside out.

Which is what is going to happen to Jed.

There's no cure for the disease, known as Kepton-Manning Syndrome. Dr. Redmond delivers that information with all the emotion of a meteorologist predicting rain.

"What about some kind of treatment?" Mimi asks, when she can push past the choking grief to find her voice.

Jed remains frozen beside her, still crushing her hand in his grip. She doesn't dare look at him.

"There's no cure," Dr. Redmond repeats robotically.

"I know," she snaps. "There's no cure for lung cancer, but there are treatments. More every day. So what I'm asking is, what kind of treatment is available for my husband?"

Dr. Redmond pauses briefly before saying, "There is no effective treatment."

That slight hesitation is enough to spark hope, however futile, in Mimi.

"There must be something that can be done. Y'all can't just send him home to—"

Die.

She won't say it. Saying it would make it real, and it isn't. None of this is actually happening. It can't be.

But she'll go along with the new nightmare for now, until she opens her eyes and finds herself safe in her own bed. Just like she always wakes up to comforting reality after the recurring nightmare of having a child drown on her watch.

Except . . .

That really happened.

Dear God, is this really happening, too?

"I'm sorry, Mrs. Johnston, but there really is no effective—"

"But there is *some* kind of treatment?"

The doctor shakes his head, looking puzzled.

"You said there was no *effective* treatment. What kind of treatment is there? An ineffective one?"

"I'm afraid I don't follow your logic. You're seeking an *ineffective* treatment?"

"It's better than nothing at all!" Her tone is bordering on hysteria. "It's better than sending my husband home to—"

Die.

"Mrs. Johnston," Dr. Redmond says calmly, "as I said, this is a rare disease. Very little research has been done. There's one physician, in Europe . . ."

Europe. That can't be a coincidence. Just minutes ago, she and Jed were longing to run away to Europe, and now . . .

"What?" she persists anxiously, realizing the doctor has trailed off and is tapping the stack of lab reports on the desk, lining up the edges in preparation for replacing them in the file and dismissing the patient and his pesky wife. "What is he doing in Europe?"

"She," Dr. Redmond corrects.

"She." *Whatever.* "Who is *she*, and what is she doing?"

The doctor doesn't sigh in resignation, but he clearly would like to as he says, "Her name is Petra Von Cave and she's spent decades conducting what amounts to highly controversial clinical trials."

Mimi seizes that information like a drowning victim grabbing a buoy. "I need to get in touch with her."

"Mrs. Johnston . . ." Dr. Redmond reaches across the desk and rests a hand on her wrist. His fingers are warm; his grasp almost gentle. So he's human after all. "Your husband is uninsured, and even if he had the best policy in the world, Dr. Von Cave's 'treatment,' as it were, wouldn't be covered."

"We'll find a way to pay for it," Mimi says frantically, shaking off his hand.

"Do you have any idea what kind of money you're talking about?"

"So what? It's a chance to save him. I don't care what it costs. We can—"

"Mrs. Johnston, please take this." The physician opens a desk drawer and pulls out a stack of business cards. Removing one, he thrusts it into her hand.

She looks down, expecting to find Dr. Von Cave's contact information.

What she finds is the address and phone number for Baywater Hospice.

"Make no mistake about it, Mr. Hawthorne, this will is going to be contested."

Gib delivers his parting shot from the doorway of the conference room, then turns to follow his sister, whose Oscar-worthy sobs are audible from the reception area.

As rattled as the plate glass windows in the wake of Gib's reverberating slam of the door, Charlotte looks across the table at Tyler Hawthorne. He is rhythmically tapping the bottom edge of his sheath of papers on the polished mahogany surface, but she can see that the movement is more frenetic than productive.

He, too, is shaken.

Charlotte leans back in her chair and kneads her forehead with her thumb and fingertips. The migraine she felt coming on in the car after the scene with Lianna is full blown now.

"Tyler," she says, still dumbfounded, as much by what was in the will as by her cousins' reflexive, melodramatic responses, "what on earth just went on here?"

"Your grandfather left most of his money to you."

"Most?" she echoes, shaking her head. "Tyler, he left all of it."

"Not all."

"You're right, I forgot . . . He did include my cousins." The corners of her mouth twist sardonically.

Yes, he left both Phyllida and Gib the same token sum he had bequeathed to his maid and his chauffeur.

Turning the stack of papers horizontally, Tyler continues his fidgety pretense at efficiency. "Face it, Charlotte, you were always Gilbert's favorite. You were the only one who ever gave him the time of day. And he knew you much better—You lived down here; they didn't."

"Come on, you know that never mattered to Grandaddy. Anyway, Gib lived here, too, when he was in high school."

She was married to Vince by that time, and rarely saw her cousin, who attended Telfair Academy.

"Your grandfather liked you best, Charlotte."

She doesn't bother to argue the point with Tyler. He's right. Still . . .

"Both my cousins were in the will as equal heirs all these years. Why would he change it now?"

"Maybe they said or did something he didn't like."

"Both of them together?" She dismisses that notion with little consideration. "They live on opposite ends of the country, and they never visit Oakgate. I can't see them teaming up to do or say something drastic enough to get cut out of the will."

Tyler shrugs. "I'm sure Gilbert had his reasons. In fact, I assumed the three of you must know what they were."

"I'm clueless."

"I'll bet your cousins aren't."

Charlotte isn't so sure about that. Gib and Phyllida

seemed as stunned as she was to learn that they had been relegated to the inheritance level of mere household help.

Gib did come out slightly ahead of his sister: Grandaddy bequeathed to him a pair of heirloom platinum monogrammed cufflinks that had belonged to the first Gilbert Xavier Remington.

But the gesture was probably more practical than sentimental on Grandaddy's part: who but a man who shares his unusual initials—and is similarly inclined to wear French-cuffed shirts—would have any use for the cufflinks?

"Now what?" she asks Tyler, pressing her thumb and middle fingertip into her temples to somewhat ease the throbbing.

"Now your cousins hire a lawyer and contest the will."

"Are they going to be successful?"

"If they can prove that Gilbert was under duress when he made the change, yes. Or that he was senile. Or that the will is invalid due to some legal technicality—trust me, it isn't. My nephew oversaw the change, but I went over everything."

"Well, Grandaddy wasn't senile, either."

"No," Tyler agrees, offering a half-smile at the notion, "he wasn't."

"So chances are, Gib and Phyllida aren't going to overturn the will."

"People rarely manage to do that. But it doesn't stop them from embarking on drawn-out, expensive legal battles. It happens every day."

"I'm sure that when things settle down a bit, they'll come to their senses."

"Don't be so sure. Greed is a powerful driving force."

"You've seen my cousins. Phyllida has a beautiful

home and a nanny and a career in California. Gib went Ivy League all the way and now he's a lawyer in Boston. They—"

"He hasn't joined a firm yet."

"He isn't hurting. Those clothes he was wearing today cost more than a year's tuition at Lianna's school."

Tyler shrugs. "Maybe there's more to them than meets the eye."

"Maybe . . . But I've known them my whole life. They're family. I don't think they'll want an ugly, endless battle over this."

"Do you know what physiognomy is, Charlotte?"

She shakes her aching head.

"It's the ancient art of face-reading: studying physical features to determine temperament, character, personality . . . I've done some reading on the subject. Some trial lawyers—not me—consult physiognomists about their clients, witnesses, prospective jurors . . ."

Unsure what he's getting at, she murmurs, "It sounds fascinating."

"It is—not that I'm inclined to put much stock in such a subjective 'science.' Anyway, a Swiss essayist named Johann Kasper Lavater was the father of modern physiognomy. There are a number of well-known quotes that are attributed to him, but my favorite is: *'Say not that you know another entirely, until you have divided an inheritance with him.'* You'd be wise to keep that in mind, Charlotte."

She nods, pushing back her chair. "I will. I just wish I knew why Grandaddy did what he did."

"I'm afraid his reasoning was buried with him," Tyler says with a shrug. "All we can do now is see that his final wishes are carried out."

* * *

Mimi hurls the white rectangle toward Dr. Redmond, only to have it flutter benignly onto his desk. She wishes it had been something jagged, and heavy . . . something that would injure him the way he had just ripped into her.

"Mrs. Johnston, please take the card. You're going to need it."

"I know where that office is." It's located on the mainland, between the Achoco Island causeway and the interstate, housed in a renovated ranch house painted in deceptively cheerful tulip shades: yellow clapboard with red shutters and trim. "I've been there."

She squeezes her eyes closed, remembering that awful August day three summers ago. It was she who had to go make the arrangements for her father. Neither of her parents was able to accept the inevitability of his death. Maybe that lingering hope is what helped him to survive for as long as he did—much longer than the specialists and even the hospice workers anticipated.

Well, this time, with Jed, it's Mimi who will refuse to give up hope.

"Mrs. Johnston, I understand how difficult this is—"

"Difficult?" she shrieks. "You sit there handing out death sentences and call it 'difficult'?"

"Mimi, for God's sake, stop it!"

Startled, she closes her mouth and looks at Jed at last.

She immediately wishes she hadn't. Tears are streaming down his cheeks.

"We don't have money for any kind of treatment, and the treatment doesn't work anyway, and I don't have a chance. Okay?"

"No, Jed. Not okay." She's crying, too. "We're not going to walk out of here and give up."

"What choice do I have? I'm going to die."

"We're not going to let that happen. We have to fight." She chooses the pronoun deliberately, refusing to let him shoulder his fate alone.

We. Not *I.*

We're in it together, Jed, until death do us part.

And death, as far as Mimi is concerned, isn't an option.

Money.

It all comes down to money.

A vast sum.

A sum that, unbeknownst to Jed, may not be out of reach at all.

CHAPTER 5

"You've reached Royce Maitland Network Consulting. Please leave a detailed message at the tone and we will return your call."

There's a long pause before the tone—too long. Why hasn't Charlotte ever noticed that before?

Maybe it just seems endless today, because she's so anxious—desperate, really—to speak with her husband.

"Royce, it's me. I already tried your cell but it went right into voice mail. Are you still in your meeting? Or are you there working? Pick up if you are . . . Royce?"

She waits for a click and her husband's reassuring voice.

It doesn't come.

"Okay. Please call me as soon as you can. I need to talk to you."

It takes three stabs at the cell phone's keypad with a shaky index finger before she manages to press the END button.

She stashes the phone back in her purse.

Now what?

Her migraine is growing worse. The car is stifling: doors closed, windows rolled up. She reaches for the keys she tossed onto the passenger's seat when she got in.

She can't just sit here in the parking lot of Tyler Hawthorne's law firm all day, trying to digest what just happened.

But she isn't particularly anxious to go home, either.

Not with Phyllida and Gib inevitably waiting there to pounce on her.

She fumbles with the key ring, pushing aside a plastic-framed souvenir photo: of herself and Royce, posing before a picture-perfect artificial backdrop of the Grand Canyon. They were there in May, for their anniversary. In reality, the canyon was shrouded in mist that day.

It seems like a lifetime ago.

Finding the right key, she pushes it into the ignition.

"Grandaddy, what have you done?" she whispers, resting her forehead against the steering wheel.

Unable to bear another moment in the suffocating heat of the car, Charlotte at last turns the key. Her sweat-dampened forehead is struck by a welcoming blast from the vent.

Okay, good.

Now what?

Of all the days for Royce to have an important meeting. If she could just see her husband, talk to him, she'd feel better. She always does when he's around.

But she'll just have to wait.

Right now, there's nothing to do but pick up Lianna and go home to face her cousins.

* * *

"Will you please just shut up so I can think straight?" Gib rakes a hand through his blond hair and paces across the small second-floor sitting room, shuttered against the strong afternoon sun.

"Don't tell me to shut up."

"I'm sorry," he tells Phyllida, if only to prevent a petty argument with the drama queen. "I'm just trying to figure out what the hell could have happened to cause this."

"Nothing *I* did, if that's what you're thinking."

It is what he's thinking. He doesn't trust his sister. Never has. As far as he's concerned, Phyllida is a lying, scheming diva whose only interest is herself.

And maybe her kid, he allows. To be fair.

Remingtons are nothing if not fair.

Yeah, right.

"I haven't even talked to Grandaddy in months," Phyllida informs him, to further prove her innocence.

"Well, neither have I."

"Maybe that's the problem."

"Oh, please. Do you really think he cut us out because *she* gave him more attention than we did?"

"Do *you?*" Gib shrugs.

"Why did he do it, Gib? This is crazy."

It is crazy. What can their grandfather possibly have against them?

Grandaddy was a pretty staunch Southern Baptist. Unreasonable, in Gib's opinion, at times. Did he and his sister somehow offend the old man's morals?

What if . . . ?

No, Gib tells himself sternly. *There's no way he knows about you. No way on earth.*

It had to be something else. Something that involves Phyllida, too.

"Maybe it's because he didn't like Mother," he suggests.

"What does she have to do with anything? Grandaddy cut her out years ago, after Daddy died. You know that."

"I know, but maybe he knew that if we got the money we'd use some of it to help her, and he didn't like that idea."

"You're really reaching here, Gib," Phyllida tells him. "I doubt Grandaddy has even thought about Mother in ages. And you saw him waltzing with her at my wedding. I think he decided to let bygones be bygones."

"I think he was senile and had no idea who she even was."

She snorts. "Grandaddy might have been old, but he wasn't senile. He knew it was Mother. He was laughing and talking to her."

"Yeah, well, he didn't write her back into the will after that, did he?"

"No, but I don't think he wrote us out because of her."

"I guess not." Gib is quiet for a moment, thinking. "Maybe if she convinced him to do it . . ."

"Mother?"

"No! Charlotte. Maybe she talked him into giving it all to her."

Phyllida shakes her head. "She's too damned nice. I honestly don't think she cares about the money all that much."

"Nice people like money too."

"I don't know . . ." Phyllida toys with the edge of a tabletop lace doily, rolling and unrolling it. "Don't you think she seemed as surprised as we were?"

"Maybe she was faking it."

"She's no actress."

No, but you are, Gib can't help thinking. He wonders again if his sister could be hiding something.

Then again, who isn't?

He, at least, is more skilled at it than most.

Anyway, even if Phyllida did do something to upset Grandaddy, why would Gib be cut out of the will as well? That doesn't make any sense.

No, it seems far more likely that the one person who benefitted from the change in the heirs apparent would be the person responsible for it.

"At least you got the cufflinks," Phyllida tells him pettily.

He knew that was coming.

"Only because nobody else can use them," he's obliged to point out. "You know how much he hated to see anything go to waste. Remember when we were kids? He saved twist ties off bread bags."

"The cufflinks are platinum. They're worth something if you sell them."

"I'm not going to sell them, Phyllida." Not right away, anyway.

"You're going to wear them?"

He shrugs. "Why not?"

"Oh, right, I forgot. You're a fancy lawyer with fancy shirts."

He chooses to ignore that, as he does her other, frequent comments about his wardrobe.

He also ignores his sister's catty, "I'm surprised Grandaddy didn't also leave some jewelry to Nydia."

At least, until she adds a provocative, "Considering what people have been saying about the two of them."

"What have people been saying?" Gib asks with interest.

"You know . . . that Grandaddy had been . . ."

"What?"

She bobs her perfectly waxed eyebrows provocatively.

"You think he was doing the housekeeper?" he asks with perverse delight. The thought had never entered his mind. So much for old-fashioned Southern Baptist morals.

Well, good for the old geezer, getting regular action at his age. That's more than anybody can say about Gib at the moment.

It's been over a week since Cassandra took off, meaning it's more than a week since he's been with a woman.

He actually called her in Boston to see why she'd left, hoping he might be able to persuade her to come back, at least for the weekend.

No such luck.

Her reason: *Sorry, Gib, funerals and families just aren't my thing.*

Yeah, like funerals and families are *his* thing?

Anyway, she knew why they were coming down to Georgia. She didn't have to accept his invitation to come down here with him—not that she was entirely sober when she did. And not that they had known each other for twenty-four hours at that point, having met in a bar at Logan Airport after getting off separate but equally turbulent flights home to Boston.

She claimed to be returning from a business trip—not that there was anything remotely corporate about her skimpy outfit.

Then again, he told her the same thing. But at least he looked the part, in his custom-made suit and silk tie.

He was well into his second Dirty Martini—his mind filling with significantly dirty thoughts as his hand made its way from Cassandra's arm to her bare knee—when his cell phone rang with the news about Grandaddy.

He didn't cry.

It was a call he'd been waiting for. He knew it would eventually come. He just didn't know exactly when, or who would make it.

As it turned out, it was Charlotte, and she sounded pretty broken up over Grandaddy's death.

Gib tried to at least sound sorrowful, but it was hard for him to carry on much of a conversation with the noise in the lounge and the announcements over the airport PA system. In the end, he simply told her to hang in there and promised her that he'd catch the next plane down to Savannah.

"What happened?" Cassandra asked when he hung up, watching him quickly drain what was left of his drink.

So he told her.

He wasn't entirely serious when, fueled by too much gin, he asked her to come to Savannah with him.

Nor was he entirely surprised when she said, "I might as well—my bag is already packed and I really don't have plans for the weekend."

Several hours and several cocktails later, they were landing in Savannah. Cassandra didn't bat an eye when he suggested that they spend that night in a hotel and wait until the next day to go to his family's place.

That was some night. The room had a king-sized bed, a Jacuzzi, and a dazzling view of the riverfront. Not that Gib and Cassandra spent much time looking out the window.

Too bad about her. Really, it is. She was Gib's kind of woman.

At this point, however, pretty much any halfway attractive female would be his kind of woman . . . She might not even have to be a blonde.

"So how do you know about Grandaddy and Nydia?" he asks his sister, his curiosity piqued.

"I overheard a couple of his old cronies talking about it at the funeral. They said she was probably in the tub with Grandaddy when he had his heart attack. That she was *why* he had the heart attack, actually."

"No way." Gib finds it hard to imagine a skinny, housefrau like Nydia nude, giving anybody a heart attack . . . not in a good way, anyway.

Still, maybe there's some truth to the theory. After all, Nydia *is* the one who found his body . . .

"We need to call Mother, Gib," Phyllida says, effectively curtailing his titillating thoughts.

"Mother? Why?"

"Because she's counting on this money as much as we are. She doesn't want to live with Aunt Rosemary the rest of her life, and work in some store waiting on people who used to be her friends."

"I know, and she won't have to. We're going to contest the will. Why upset her?"

Phyllida shrugs. "I just think she needs to know."

No, you just need to go crying on her shoulder, as usual, he thinks, aggravated.

"Don't tell her, Phyll. Don't."

He can tell by the look on her face that she isn't planning to heed his warning. God, she's as pathetically needy now as she was when they were growing up. She always ran to their mother with the slightest problem, whining and wailing for attention.

She always got it, too.

Mother might have coddled his sister, but she admired and respected Gib. He's always been content in that knowledge.

And he sure as hell isn't going to burst her bubble now.

"Don't tell Mother," he tells Phyllida one last time. "I mean it."

"Well, I definitely think we should confront Charlotte about Grandaddy when she comes home, Gib."

"About him getting it on with the housekeeper?" he asks facetiously, just to get on her nerves.

"About the will!" Phyllida is suitably exasperated. "Don't you think we need to talk to her?"

"Not really." He paces across the room, then back again. "What do you think she can possibly tell us?"

"Who knows? We need to put her on the spot."

"Frankly, I'd rather avoid her for the time—"

Gib stops pacing abruptly, struck by something that hadn't occurred to him until now.

He was wrong earlier.

Charlotte isn't necessarily the *only* person who benefits from the changed will.

"Kevin, I'm totally serious. Cut it out."

"Why?"

"Because!" Lianna slaps his hand away before it can creep beneath her T-shirt again. The glider they're sitting on groans beneath her shifting weight as she moves away from him.

He moves closer. "It was okay five minutes ago."

"So? It's not okay now."

"Why not?"

"Because . . ." She juts her lip to blow her own hot breath on her face in a futile effort to cool off. "I'm all sweaty."

"Who cares? So am I."

Yeah, no kidding. The faint, pungent, unfamiliar odor of masculine perspiration mingles with the heady scent of Casey's mother's climbing roses that cover a nearby arbor.

Kevin reaches for her again.

"Come on, stop it! I mean it! My mother's coming."

His head jerks around to examine the garden path beyond the glider's canvas awning.

"She isn't here *now*, you idiot," Lianna says with a laugh, tucking her shirt back into the waistband of her shorts. "Do you think I'd just be sitting here with you if she was?"

"Nope." Undaunted at being called an idiot, he smirks. "You'd be running away to hide."

"So would you."

"You know it." He glances at his Timex. "Anyhow, I thought you said she wasn't coming for at least another hour."

He's right. She did say that.

But that was before he tried to go further than she expected. Again. It's getting to be a pattern with them over these past few weeks—yet, one she doesn't necessarily want to avoid.

After all, Kevin's cute, and a good kisser, and he really likes her.

She just isn't comfortable making out with him outside in broad daylight, that's all.

Things might be different if they could really be alone together, in private. Sometimes, she thinks she's ready for that. Other times, she knows she's not.

Being Kevin's girlfriend is confusing.

"Listen, I have no idea when my mother's going to show up, actually. You need to go, so I can get out front and wait for her on the steps." Lianna inches away from him on the green and white vinyl cushion, feeling around with her feet in the grass for the rubber flip-flops she kicked off earlier.

"Won't she think something's up when you're outside and your friend's not around?"

Maybe she will, come to think of it. But the plan to use Casey's house while her friend's family is away on vacation seemed like a good one when Lianna came up with it last night.

"I'll make up something," she tells Kevin.

"Like what?"

"Like Casey was eating this cinnamon taffy and she broke a bracket and had to go to an emergency orthodontist appointment."

"That's pretty good," Kevin says admiringly. "Cinnamon. How'd you think of that? Telling the flavor, I mean."

She shrugs. "You've got to use details. That makes it real."

"Wow. You're a great liar."

"Thanks."

"You're so beautiful, too."

She so *isn't*. She has buck teeth and knobby knees and it's taking forever for her to grow out her hair from that layered cut she got last spring that her mother thought would look good on her.

But Kevin really must think she's irresistible, because he slides close to her and the next thing she knows, he's pulling her into his strong arms again, pressing a hot, wet kiss on the damp skin of her neck, beneath her hair.

Lianna finds herself stirring with an unfamiliar longing despite her resolve to get the heck out of here. She manages to squirm out of Kevin's grasp, only to have him grab her and kiss her again, this time on the mouth. She immediately kisses him back.

Later, she'll go over and over the moment, analyzing everything about it.

How his hand was slipping under her shirt again, and this time, she didn't bother to stop it . . .

How her own arms circled up around his neck almost against her will, like they belonged to somebody
else . . .

How her heart must have been pounding too loudly
for her to hear footsteps approaching on the gravel
path . . .

How it must have looked to her mother when she
came around the corner of the house and saw them.

Lianna will analyze the moment because she'll have
little else to do, having been grounded—without her
cell phone—for the rest of the summer.

"Mr. Remington?"

Gib stops short, halfway down the second-floor hall
to his bedroom. He looks over his shoulder to see
Great-Aunt Jeanne's nurse, Melanie.

"Yeah?" he asks, his gaze flicking with interest from
her blond hair pulled back into a becoming ponytail to
her ample breasts straining the floral fabric of her
nurse's smock. Even in the frumpy uniform, she's hotter than the blazing Georgia sun.

"Your aunt asked me to come down and find one of
you."

"One of me?" he asks, fixing her with a lazy grin, his
troubles momentarily forgotten. "You can have all of
me."

She smiles at the flirtatious comment. "I mean, she
asked me to find you, or your sister, or your cousin
Charlotte."

"I'm the most interesting of the bunch . . . I promise
you that."

He sees the pink flush coloring her cheeks before
she ducks her head, charmingly flustered.

"All right, so let's go on up and I'll talk to the old gal. What's it about? Does she need me to move a piece of furniture? Or stop all those annoying devil voices in her head?"

He laughs at his own joke.

The lovely Melanie seems to lack a sense of humor. "Don't make fun of her . . . She's a sweet lady."

"I know she is. Sweet and," he can't resist leaning so close he can smell her fresh herbal scent—lotion, not perfume, "you have to admit, just a little bit . . ." He rotates an index finger alongside his ear.

To her discredit, Melanie again fails to crack a smile. She turns on the heel of her sensible white shoe and heads down the hall in the opposite direction of the third-floor stairway.

"Hey, where are you going? I thought we were going up to talk to Aunt Jeanne!"

"You are," she calls over her shoulder without a backward glance. "I'm going to get her some hot tea."

Your loss, Gib thinks with a shrug as he takes the stairs up two at a time.

And Aunt Jeanne's, he adds, as a wall of heat hits him.

Hot tea? Is Melanie trying to kill the old bat?

"Cripes, it's a sauna up here," he comments to the old woman, who's facing the opposite direction in her wheelchair. "You need to open some windows, Aunt Jeanne."

He strides toward the nearest dormer, deciding the lovely Melanie lacks a sense of humor *and* common sense.

"They are open," Aunt Jeanne tells him, and he realizes she's right. Several electric fans are whirring as well.

But with the late-afternoon sun beaming in through

the glass and baking the roof overhead, there is little that can be done to sufficiently cool the large space.

Why central air was never installed in this old house, Gib will never understand.

Maybe these crazy Southerners are accustomed to the heat, but he personally can't wait to get back to Boston.

Literally "*crazy* Southerners" in Aunt Jeanne's case, he notes as she turns her wheelchair to face him, looking somewhat wild-eyed.

"I need to know, Gilbert."

For a moment, hearing the cryptic demand and the formal name nobody *ever*, ever calls him, he wonders if she thinks he's her dead brother.

Then, her gnarled old hands rolling the chair closer to him with surprising speed, she says, "I need to know what was in that will."

The will.

It comes crashing back with a vengeance; all the angst of the calamitous session in Tyler Hawthorne's office.

"Do you mean what was in it for you?" he asks the expectant Aunt Jeanne. "Because that would be the same thing that was in it for me. Nothing."

"Nothing?" Her voice is tremulous, yet there seems to be a curious lack of expression in her wrinkled face.

"Nothing. He left everything to dear cousin Charlotte."

Aunt Jeanne is nodding. For a moment, he isn't sure she even heard what he said.

Then she says, her jaw set in what seems to be resignation—or even, oddly, acceptance, "That's just as I expected."

* * *

People really shouldn't play favorites.

It isn't nice.

Who was it who once said a little healthy rivalry never hurt anyone?

Probably your mother . . . who else?

Well, she was wrong. About a lot of things.

But now isn't the time to worry about that.

Now is the time to make the final preparations of the cabin that continues to look for all the world like a vine-covered nursery rhyme cottage—or some lucky little girl's adorable playhouse.

Lucky little girl . . .

Pammy Sue.

Now *there* was a lucky little girl. With her blond ringlets and big green eyes, she was the apple of everybody's eye: Mama's, and Aunt Chessie's, and Pastor Brigham's . . .

Everybody's but mine.

But Pammy Sue never figured that out, not as a child, not even now, all grown up. It would simply never occur to her that one of her nearest and dearest could possibly dislike her.

Dislike?

Hah.

Even *loathe* is an understatement.

Yet nobody in all those years ever seemed to suspect the pure hatred expertly concealed by a mask of benevolent affection.

Pammy Sue might have won the lead in every school play, but her so-called acting talent didn't hold a candle to mine.

It's ironic, even now, to recall that the spotlight and the applause always belonged to Pammy Sue when the truly masterful performance was unfolding right before everyone's eyes, undetected. Unappreciated.

Blind, smitten fools.

Yes, and you were right there in the front row every time, beaming, clapping for Pammy Sue along with those blind, smitten fools.

Ah, well, the perpetual deception was certainly good practice for all that lies ahead.

And it won't be long now before the ultimate curtain call is carried out in vengeful perfection.

The marsh after dark isn't a particularly appealing place to be . . . not even with a couple of kerosene lanterns. Their flames flicker eerily on the brick walls, casting the lone human shadow larger than life.

Which is as it should be.

At least I'm the master of this domain.

Yes, but what good is that? taunts an inner voice. *It's still empty.*

Although not for long.

Just outside the door lies a brown carton, its sides damp and pungent with absorbed humidity.

Inside are the last few items necessary to turn this little house into a home.

First, a large flattened cardboard box must be lain across the mud floor like a fine carpet. The new door came inside it.

Next, the pieces of furniture are arranged one by one on the makeshift rug: a small wooden table and three small chairs.

Finally, the family materializes.

Three small dolls—a blonde, a brunette, and a red-head—perfectly scaled to occupy the furniture, their plastic lips frozen in garish smiles, unblinking eyes unable to witness what will unfold within these walls.

*   *   *

The lush, landscaped grounds at Oakgate might be inviting during the day, but at night, even with a three-quarter moon hovering above the oaks, it's the opposite.

Phyllida is glad she thought to stop in the kitchen and hunt down a flashlight—she found it in the utility drawer—before slipping out the back door; she wouldn't want to be alone out here in the dark.

She doesn't want to be alone out here at all, but she has to make this call. Brian and Wills are asleep in her room upstairs and she doesn't want to disturb them. Nor does she want to risk being overheard by anybody in the house.

So here she is, clad in a filmy summer nightgown, making her way through the shadowy back garden. The wet grass brushes against her bare feet in hastily donned flip-flops. She tries not to think about snakes, or anything else that might be slithering nearby, as she heads as far away from the house as she dares to go.

The night is still and moist; the live oaks form a canopy overhead, although it's anything but protective. Phyllida won't imagine what creatures might be tucked amid the foliage webbed in dry Spanish moss, poised to drop on her head at any moment.

She comes to a halt when she reaches the small cemetery surrounded by a low ironwork fence.

Gravestones of her ancestors loom eerily in the night. Some are thin, leaning slabs whose etching is all but worn away, glowing white beneath the moon. Others, like the large one belonging to Grandaddy and the grandmother Phyllida never knew, are elaborate monuments carved in polished black granite, rising from the earth like formidable warriors standing guard over fallen comrades.

Phyllida takes a few more tentative steps forward, until some winged creature abruptly departs an overhead branch with a rustling flutter.

She stops short, her heart pounding.

That's it. Phyllida won't venture any closer to the graveyard, and she certainly has no desire to venture past it.

Night sounds reverberate from the thicket on the far side of the iron fence: crickets, frogs, owls, an ominous, occasional rustling in the undergrowth, a distant splashing sound from the marsh and tidal creeks.

The current property line extends a little ways in. Beyond that line, to the north and east, are acres upon acres of woods and wetlands that were once a part of the Remingtons's plantation. Grandaddy sold the entire parcel years ago to some developer, who had planned to build a sprawling condo community, until a vocal environmental group successfully challenged the plan. Now it's a wildlife refuge, protected in its natural state from further development.

When Phyllida was a little girl and Daddy would bring them down to visit his family on the coastal island, she and her brother loved to explore the abandoned portion of the property, especially the remnants of slave cabins.

It's hard to believe nobody kept a closer eye on them. But then again, Mother wasn't here to do it because she rarely came South. She said she didn't like the heat and humidity, but Phyllida suspected that in reality, she didn't like Grandaddy any more than he liked her.

Back then, the undergrowth didn't seem this dense— or maybe it was, and Phyllida and her brother brazenly pushed their way through it anyway, not caring about things like mud, or rattlesnakes and gators.

Charlotte cared. She never came with them. She might have been older, but she was always squeamish, not to mention afraid of everything, even the dark.

Wanting to get this over with so she can go back to bed and maybe get some sleep at last, Phyllida flips open her cell phone, presses a speed dial button, and holds it against her ear, listening to it ring.

"Hello?"

Her throat clogged with emotion, she manages to say, "Mom? It's me."

"Phyllida?"

"Yes . . ." She's crying, then. She can't help it.

"What's wrong, Darling? What is it?"

"He cut us out of the will. Both me and Gib. He left everything to Charlotte."

On the other end of the phone, Susan Remington gasps. "Oh, no!"

"I'm afraid, Mommy," Phyllida sobs. "What are we going to do now? We were all counting on that money . . . all of us."

"I know, I know . . ." Her mother's voice is soothing. "Don't worry, sweetheart, we'll survive. We always have."

"I know, but . . ." She sniffles. "I don't know how."

"What does your brother say about this?"

"That we're going to contest the will."

"That's my brilliant attorney son. That's exactly what you'll do."

Still sniffling, Phyllida wipes her eyes with the back of her hands, feeling better already. She knew she would, if she could just talk to her mother.

Mommy always makes her feel better.

"There, now, Darling, you just calm down and get some sleep. It's late."

"I know."

"Where's your brother? Is he there? Can I speak to him?"

"He went out someplace," Phyllida says truthfully, then adds, "please don't tell him I told you about the will, okay, Mom? He didn't want to worry you with it."

No, but I did. Because I'm a big baby, incapable of dealing with anything on my own.

Or so her brother liked to tell her, when they were younger.

"That's my son," her mother says with affection. "Always protective. I wish he wouldn't worry about me."

Phyllida bites back a comment.

If her mother hasn't figured out by now that Gib worries about nobody other than himself, she never will.

What on earth is *she* doing out here at this time of night?

The arc of her flashlight swings dangerously close to the nook beside the back steps. Any second now, it might expose this hiding spot.

And then what?

That won't happen. Don't even think about it.

Just hold your breath and don't move.

Yes, but it's nearly impossible to stay motionless when mosquitos hover about one's exposed skin, landing and stinging in a frenzied blood feast.

Giving in to the almost overwhelming desire to slap at an insect would cause quite a stir in the quiet evening, and undoubtedly make it necessary to extinguish the human pest as well, with considerably more bloodshed.

That might be infinitely satisfying in the moment, but would pose an unnecessary risk, overall.

Why is she out here?

Why am I out here?

I'm exhausted after all that work on the cabin.

This wasn't a good idea—this last-minute improvisation, courtesy of the unexpected codicil.

Oh? It will be a good idea if it works.

Yes, but . . . There had to be another way to do this.

Her footsteps are coming ominously closer, each one marked by the distinct slapping of a rubber sole against her heel.

What if she sees me?

What then?

Then, whatever has to happen, will happen. That's all there is to it. She's certainly expendable.

Yes, but all in good time. Don't get overly anxious.

Just stay still.

She'll be gone momentarily.

The flopping sound made by her shoes masks the sound of a long-held breath necessarily expelled in a hushed, quavering rush.

Then she's gone, up the steps and disappearing into the darkened house with a faint creak of the outer screen door, and a quiet click of the lock on the solid inner one.

She must think she's safe, turning that deadbolt.

They all do, including Charlotte.

None of the residents of Oakgate would dream that mere locks can't keep predators at bay. Not *this* predator, anyway.

But now is not the time to prowl through the quiet house unnoticed.

Now there's nobody outside to hear the soft padding of footsteps in the dewy grass, or the satisfying slapping of a carnivorous insect, or the probing of fingertips along the rough, wide ledge atop a raised basement window.

There, tucked among the oyster shells that rise deceptively from the tabby surface, is the reason for this risky late-night sojourn.

And once the items are tucked safely in hand, there's no further reason to linger in the shadows of the old plantation house.

Not tonight, anyway.

Around front, one last glance shows that all is still within; the windows that punctuate the façade are darkened, shades and draperies drawn.

Then, high overhead, something flashes in the night.

It takes a moment to realize that a light has come on, way up on the third floor.

A shadow passes in front of one of the dormer windows; somebody is prowling about up there.

Charlotte isn't surprised to find that she can't fall asleep.

What *is* surprising is that her cousins have steered clear of her for the remainder of the afternoon and evening. She fully expected an ugly confrontation when she got home from Savannah, but there was no sign of Phyllida or Gib, though Gib's rental car in the driveway meant they were in the house somewhere.

The ugly confrontation, for that matter, had already occurred—with Lianna.

"I still can't believe it," she murmurs, mostly to herself, as she stares at the outline of the antique furniture across the room in the night-light's glow.

Beside her, the bedsprings creak in response to her voice. Royce is still awake. She thought he'd drifted off when he stopped commenting earlier, as she went over and over what happened this afternoon.

"I'm sorry," she tells him. "You should sleep. That's why we came to bed early . . . I know you have to get up early tomorrow for work. And here I am, keeping you up all night."

"It's okay. I'm here." He yawns deeply.

"I didn't even ask you how your meeting went," she realizes belatedly.

"That's okay. You've got a lot going on."

"That's the understatement of the year."

If she didn't have so much on her plate before this mess with Lianna, she would have remembered to call Lianna on her cell phone this afternoon to tell her she was on the way to Casey's house. Then she never would have stumbled upon that scene in the garden.

Which, in some ways, would have been a blessing.

Not that she isn't glad she nipped that little rendezvous in the bud when she did, but . . .

It's just that life was much better before she realized that her only child lies to her face and does God knows what behind her back.

"So how was it?" she asks Royce, knowing that he deserves her attention now that she's kept him awake for hours. "The meeting, I mean."

"Oh, it was fine."

"Did they like you, Royce?"

"Who doesn't?" he asks with a chuckle, then adds, when she remains silent, "I'm just kidding. You were supposed to laugh at that."

"Oh, sorry . . ." She mentally backtracks over the last exchange, realizes what he said, and tells him, "It wasn't a joke, as far as I'm concerned. I've never come across anyone who doesn't like you."

"That's because you've never met Karen."

His ex-wife.

"And if I had to guess, I'd say Vince isn't all that crazy about me, either," he adds good-naturedly. "But as I was saying, these guys I met today seemed to like me, so I'm hoping I might get their on-site business."

"That would be great."

"It would."

She's glad he doesn't elaborate. Normally, she takes an interest in his business dealings, but tonight she can dwell only on her own disastrous day.

"How could she do that to me, Royce?"

"If it's any consolation, I really don't think she meant to do anything to *you*."

"She lied. She snuck around with that boy behind my back. And judging by the looks of things, this isn't the first time they ever laid eyes on each other. Or *hands*." Charlotte shudders, wishing she could block out the image of Lianna, her baby girl, with that trashy Tinkston boy pawing at her.

"The only consolation is that she isn't pregnant," she adds darkly, rolling onto her side to face him. "That I know of, anyway."

"Of course she isn't pregnant." Royce touches her arm. "Charlotte, don't blow it up into anything it isn't. You said yourself that they were just kissing."

"She was kissing. He was groping."

"They're teenagers. It happens."

"She's barely a teenager, and it's not allowed to happen to my daughter." Her voice has risen above a hysterical whisper, but she can't help herself.

"Sweetheart, what she did was wrong," Royce says soothingly, "but it's over, and it's not going to happen again. We'll make sure of that. So don't obsess about it. You've got enough to worry about right now."

She sighs. "Did you have to remind me?"

"Sorry."

Charlotte remains silent, turning her head restlessly on the goose down pillow, which seems to be deflating by the second. If she could just get comfortable, she might be able to fall asleep.

No, you won't. You're wired. You're not going to sleep tonight unless you take one of Grandaddy's pills.

She doesn't want to resort to that, though it's been tempting to sneak into his medicine cabinet on the sleepless nights that followed his death. She probably would have, if she could bring herself to walk into the bathroom where he died.

"For what it's worth," Royce says around a yawn, "I don't think you should worry about the money, Charlotte. Your Grandaddy wanted *you* to have it, not your cousins. He must have had his reasons."

"I can't imagine what they were. And I honestly don't think Phyllida and Gib have any idea, either."

"Oh, I don't know about that."

"They were as shocked as I was, Royce. I saw the looks on their faces. And they both swore up and down to Tyler they had no idea why Grandaddy would have done this."

"Do you honestly think they'd admit it if they did know?"

"I don't know." She pauses, mulling that over. "I'd like to think so, but—"

"But you're willing to believe they might not be telling the whole truth?"

Reluctantly, she says, "I guess so. I mean, obviously, I'm not terrific at spotting a liar. Look at the way my own daughter pulled the wool over my eyes. Maybe my cousins are doing the same thing. Maybe they know exactly why he changed the will, but they're not admitting it because they're planning to have it contested."

"Which is going to be hard on everyone," Royce points out grimly.

"No kidding." Charlotte sits up, plumping the pillows in a frustrated effort to get comfortable. "Everyone in Savannah is going to know about this before they're through. Do you know what people are going to be saying about Grandaddy? And me?"

"And your cousins, for that matter."

"Right. Oh, Lord, I wish I could just pay them two-thirds of my inheritance, and make this whole mess go away."

"What's stopping you?"

Charlotte immediately goes still. "What do you mean?"

"Just write them each a check and get it over with, if that's what you want to do."

She remains silent.

"It would make the mess go away," Royce tells her. "Which is what you want. And we both said before, the money isn't going to change anything for us. We were doing just fine without it."

"I know—"

"So take your third of it, and we'll put it away, and give the rest to Phyllida and Gib. Or give them the whole damned fortune if you want. It's only money. It'll save everyone a whole lot of trouble."

She contemplates the suggestion. It can't be that easy.

"What's the matter?" Royce asks, after a long minute. "Don't you want to make this go away?"

"It's tempting, but I don't think it's a good idea," she tells him, unable to put her finger on just why.

"Because it isn't what your grandfather wanted, right? He cut your cousins out of the will for a reason, and you want to respect his wishes."

"That's exactly right," she exclaims, relieved that he put it into words for her. "How did you figure that out before I even did?"

"Because I'm a very wise man," Royce says, rolling so close she can smell minty mouthwash lingering on his breath. "And you're a very wise woman. That's why you'll probably do the right thing, no matter how hard it is on you. On all of us."

"Things could be worse, considering that the right thing happens to be accepting my grandfather's entire fortune."

Royce laughs, folding her into his arms. "Don't get any big ideas. We're not going on any spending sprees in the near future . . . unless you've changed your mind?"

"Why? Do you need a little more *bling bling*?"

"I've got plenty of bling, thank you very much, Jenny from the block." He kisses her neck. "But I can think of something else I need . . ."

In her husband's tender embrace, Charlotte allows herself to relax at last.

Royce is right.

It's only money.

And, as Phyllida and Gib have yet to learn, money can't buy the things that matter most in life.

Royce's mouth is moving down, trailing kisses over her collarbone.

Grandaddy didn't withhold her cousins' inheritance in order to teach them a lesson—of that, Charlotte is certain.

He must have had a more compelling, much darker reason.

And I'm going to find out what it was, she vows silently,

before giving in to her husband's quest to take her to a place where she can forget everything for a blissful little while.

Jeanne lifts the items out of her top middle bureau drawer one by one. Nearly all of them once belonged to her mother.

The stack of lace-embroidered handkerchiefs.

The crocheted woolen shawl for winter mornings when a cold draft permeates the third floor as effectively as does the summer heat.

The precious journals filled with poetry, day-to-day household events, and family secrets—all of it jotted in mother's spidery handwriting.

The album filled with sepia-toned photos of unsmiling ancestors, some of whom played a role in those very secrets.

At the very bottom, beneath a locked wooden case that contains her last-resort salvation, is a stack of birthday cards from Gilbert, banded together with a faded, blue-satin ribbon that once adorned Mother's hair.

The cards didn't start coming until after Father and Mother had passed away, and Jeanne's mind started to go. Perhaps they were sent out of nostalgia, perhaps out of pity. Or, just maybe, out of guilt.

In any case, each card contained a crisp twenty-dollar bill.

Twenty dollars a year.

From a man worth tens of millions.

Twenty dollars, cash—as if she could take it right down to the mall and treat herself to a little something.

Ah, well, it will come in handy after all, this nice little wad of "mad money" . . .

In the truest sense of the phrase, Jeanne thinks, a sad smile grazing her lips.

"Don't you worry, Gilbert," she whispers into the empty room as she begins to count the bills. "I'll be sure and put it to good use."

CHAPTER 6

"I guess I just don't understand why you aren't flying home with us," Brian Harper tells his wife on Saturday morning, as she tucks another small T-shirt into the Vuitton suitcase that holds their son's clothing.

"I keep telling you," she says wearily. "It's because I have to see this through."

"Contesting the will? It's going to drag on for months, Phyll. You're not planning on staying here for that long . . . are you?"

"Not *months*. Weeks, maybe."

"You'll be trapped in this house without a car."

"Gib has one, and I can always rent something if I need to. Anyway, I'm sure Grandaddy's chauffeur will be back from vacation soon. He can drive me anywhere I need to go."

She closes the top of the suitcase—or tries to. It seems to contain more than it did when they came, which is impossible. It's not as though she's been out shopping for clothes lately.

Far from it.

When she isn't taking care of an increasingly irritable toddler, the last few days have been spent with Gib, talking to attorneys. Being a lawyer himself, her brother isn't content with just any legal representation.

We need the best if we're going to win this, he keeps telling Phyllida.

Right. Still, she can't help wondering if he's stalling his efforts a bit. Gib doesn't seem to be in any hurry to get back home to Boston. Which makes her wonder just what kind of life he left behind there.

She, on the other hand, would like nothing more than to return to the West Coast, with its ubiquitous central air-conditioning, utter lack of humidity . . . and Lila, her longtime live-in nanny for Wills.

Pushing aside her guilt for sending her son home without her, Phyllida reminds herself that he'll be in good care. Once they land at LAX, Lila will be perfectly capable of keeping Wills happy until her return.

It's just a shame his own father isn't more attentive. Brian has his limits. Which is why he's been virtually useless here. All he's done is golf, complain about the muggy weather, and express his outrage over Phyllida's token inheritance.

"Do you need me to help you, Phyll?"

She looks up in surprise at her husband's unexpected offer, then realizes Brian is talking about the suitcase, not the unfortunate state of her life in general.

"Go ahead." She steps aside and allows him to deftly rearrange the clothes inside. He quickly manages to get it closed.

As he does, she can't help wishing he was this efficient when it comes to other things. Household help—the nanny and maid and gardener—can do only so much. They don't provide emotional, intellectual, or financial support—and neither does her husband.

You're on your own, she tells herself, not for the first time.

A few minutes later, on the circular drive before the white-pillared portico, she presses her child in a tearful embrace, then offers her husband a perfunctory kiss good-bye.

"Come home soon," he tells her. "Wills isn't the only one who's going to miss you."

Watching Brian climb behind the wheel of the rental car, she wishes she was still in love with him. Life would be so much simpler if she was.

He starts the engine and glances at the gas gauge. "Hey, it's full."

"I know. I took it down to the Mobil station by the causeway last night."

"*You* pumped gas?" he asks incredulously.

"No! A very nice young man did. It's full serve."

"But why even bother?"

"Because it was almost on E."

"So? I can just bring it back to the rental place empty and they'll add the gas charge to the bill."

Right. At some ridiculous price per gallon.

Does Brian not grasp that they can't afford to squander money now?

She, who has never pumped gas in her life, was almost tempted to pull up to the self-serve pump. But she isn't that desperate—yet. Anyway, it was kind of flattering to flirt with Kevin, the obviously smitten surfer-boy attendant, as he pumped her gas.

"Okay, then," Brian says, shifting into DRIVE. "I guess we're off."

"'Bye," Phyllida calls, blowing kisses at Wills and jogging after the car a little ways as it heads slowly down the dappled drive beneath the verdant arch of towering oaks cloaked in silvery Spanish moss.

Then it disappears through the gates, leaving her alone.

It's a beautiful day. They should have a nice flight—at least, the takeoff portion of it, she thinks, looking up at the clear blue sky beyond Oakgate's familiar brick silhouette.

Her eye follows a white trail to a distant plane buzzing along, until a shadow passing directly overhead captures her attention.

She trains her eye on it and realizes that it's a circling vulture. Within moments, it's been joined by several others, swooping gradually lower, toward the gabled roof.

Phyllida knows that the ill-fated prey must be somewhere in the thicket behind Oakgate, but from this vantage, it almost seems as though the prey lies in the house itself.

It's some kind of omen, she thinks, as goose bumps rise on her bare arms.

I'm never going to see my baby again.

The thought darts into her mind with all the premeditation of the stray orange butterfly flitting among the hibiscus blooms along the drive.

Of course she's going to see Wills again.

But . . .

What if Brian turns his back in the airport and a stranger snatches him?

What if his plane crashes?

What if hers does?

Oh, God.

Chilled despite the ninety-degree heat, Phyllida wraps her arms around herself in an effort to keep a sudden, inexplicable panic at bay.

It's normal to worry, she assures herself. *And those vul-*

tures don't mean anything. They're just looking for a meal in the marsh.

Probably every single person who ever sends off a loved one on an airplane wonders, at least just in passing, about the possibility of a crash.

And of course she's uncomfortable with the prospect of her irresponsible husband transporting their child across the continent, not to mention the lengthy separation to follow. Who wouldn't be?

Calm down, Phyllida. Everything's going to be just fine.

Gradually, the chill subsides. The winged black predators have disappeared from sight, no doubt to feed on some hapless swamp creature.

Walking on toward the portico, she once again feels the warm sunlight on her bare shoulders; becomes aware of the pleasant, rhythmic hum of insects in the tall grass that lines the drive, punctuated by occasionally chirping birds.

Then Phyllida hears another sound, spilling from a window somewhere overhead, on the side of the house.

Female voices.

And they're arguing.

Her own anxiety conveniently forgotten, she smiles thoughtfully.

Sounds like Charlotte and her daughter are at it again.

"So how's the house coming along?" asks John Hirsch, the architect who designed the Maitlands's renovation, as he and Royce walk off the tennis court at the sprawling Achoco Island Club overlooking the shimmering blue Atlantic.

"Slow and steady." Royce mops his forehead with a

towel, then gulps the rest of the lukewarm water left in his bottle before saying, "Charlotte and I are heading over there today to take care of some finishing details."

John's mouth quirks. "Fun stuff."

"*She* thinks so." Royce shakes his head. "I have a feeling I'm going to spend the rest of the day comparing shades of paint."

"Trust me, you are."

They've arrived at the white-clapboard men's locker room complex. Royce holds the door open, then follows John into the welcoming blast of air-conditioning.

"You have no idea how anxious I am to get this whole renovation thing over with and move into the house," he tells John. "Especially now that—"

"Now that what?"

Royce hesitates. "You know . . . now that this whole thing happened with her grandfather, and we have all these people staying with us."

They're in the locker room now; the place is bustling as always on a Saturday morning. Men linger in the dim, climate-controlled quarters, some chatting amiably in pairs and threesomes.

"Getting a little crowded over at Oakgate, is it?" John asks as he and Royce make their way past others in various stages of undress to two lockers at the far end, where they stashed their belongings earlier.

"It's not that . . ."

"What is it?"

Royce shrugs, conscious that others might be listening to their conversation. "Nothing, really. Nothing specific, anyway."

"You don't sound so sure about that. Did something happen?"

"I don't know."

"You don't know?" John echoes, glancing up at him

over the door of his locker on the bottom row. "What do you mean?"

"Just . . . I think somebody might have gone through my stuff," Royce says in a low voice as somebody slams a locker door in the next aisle.

"What?"

"I don't want to broadcast it, okay?"

"Sorry, but I didn't hear you." Looking over both his shoulders, Royce sees several club members who are apparently absorbed in their own business.

He repeats what he told John, and his friend's eyebrows shoot toward his sweat-dampened forehead.

"Is something missing?" he asks Royce.

"I don't know. I couldn't tell. But everything in my bedroom drawers and closet was moved around, just slightly. Just enough so that I could tell somebody had gone through it like they were looking for something."

"Cash?"

"Who knows? I leave money in my pockets all the time. I wouldn't know if any was missing."

"What about Charlotte? Did somebody go through her drawers, too?"

"I have no idea. I didn't mention it to her," Royce confesses.

"Don't you think you should? What if one of her relatives is a kleptomaniac?"

"It doesn't have to be her relatives," Royce is quick to point out. "There's a housekeeper, and a nurse who comes in to take care of her aunt, and then there's her daughter—"

"You don't think her kid is snooping around your room?"

"No, but she has friends. Maybe one of them—"

Noticing a surreptitious glance from the towel-clad stranger standing a few lockers down, Royce breaks off.

He shakes his head slightly at John, to let him know that they're being overheard.

"Sounds like you'd better get moving, my friend," John advises, shaking his head as he strips off his tennis whites. "The sooner y'all get that house finished and get the hell back to Savannah, the better."

Royce nods. "My thoughts exactly. Just—don't tell Charlotte about any of this if you see her. Okay? She's got enough going on with losing her grandfather and— well, you know how it is. She's really stressed. I don't want to worry her about something like this."

"I don't blame you. But watch your step. I wouldn't leave anything valuable lying around that house. And I absolutely wouldn't trust anybody around there, including your wife's kid."

"Don't worry," Royce says with conviction. "I absolutely don't."

"I wasn't sure you were going to show up," Gib remarks lazily from beneath dark sunglasses, as Mimi hurries toward the shady bench in Reynolds Square, their designated meeting place. "I've been waiting more than twenty minutes and it's hot as blazes out here."

"Sorry I'm late. It took me longer than I thought to get out of the house."

"You mean, to *sneak* out of the house without your husband figuring out what you were up to."

She chooses to ignore that comment, as well as the tall plastic cup of sweet tea he offers as she sits down.

"I don't have germs, you know," he persists, prodding with the straw beneath his lips.

She pushes it away. "I'm not thirsty."

"Suit yourself." He shrugs and sips the tea, watching her. "You look tired, Mimi."

"I am tired."

"Not sleeping well these days?"

She shakes her head.

He shrugs. "Who is?"

"I don't know . . . *You* look pretty well rested."

She can't help but resent him, sitting there casually in his Tommy Bahama sport shirt and pressed khaki shorts, his shaggy blond locks carefully, stylishly tousled. Of course she can't see his eyes, but she'd be willing to bet there are no dark circles beneath them.

"Looks can be deceiving," he points out.

Don't I know it.

"So what can I do for you this fine morning, Martha Maude?"

"It's Mimi."

"You don't look like Mimi anymore. And you sure don't act like her."

No comment from her. There's no arguing with that.

"Whatever happened to that girl?" Gib asks, reaching over to casually brush her hair back from her face.

She died with Theo Maitland on the beach that day.

That's what happened.

No . . .

No, it isn't.

She died in your arms, Gib, on the beach that night.

Aloud, she says merely, "She grew up," and flinches as his fingers brush her cheek.

"Happens to the best of us."

Not you, Gib. You'll never grow up.

He shifts his position on the bench, moving his hand away from her hair at last. "As much as I'd like to talk about the good old days, surely you didn't ask me to meet you here for that."

"No," she admits, "I didn't."

"And you didn't want to invite yourself along with me tonight, either . . . did you?"

"Where are you going?"

He hesitates slightly, as if still trying to make up his mind—not just about inviting her, but about where he's actually headed.

"There's a gallery opening on River Street," he says. "Want to come?"

"No."

"I didn't think so." He's watching her intently. "What *do* you want?"

She takes a deep breath and holds it. Once she plunges ahead with this part of the plan, there will be no turning back.

This is crazy. I should get out of here, she tells herself frantically, even as she maintains her outward composure. *I should tell him to go to hell, and I should run back to my normal life as fast as I can.*

Except . . .

That normal life—that precious, precious normal, everyday life—is no longer waiting for her.

She has no choice but to muster every bit of courage she possesses and tell Gib Remington exactly what she wants—*needs*—from him . . . and why.

"I don't care what the judge said, you are not leaving this house this weekend . . . or until school starts, for that matter," Charlotte hurls at Lianna, who stares sullenly from the haven of her unmade bed.

"That *so* isn't fair."

"It *so* wasn't fair of you to break the rules by lying and sneaking around."

"At least I didn't break the *law*, like you are. Daddy is supposed to get to see me every other weekend."

Charlotte bites her lip to keep from retorting that Vincent has been free to see his daughter every other weekend for the past five years, per their custody agreement, and he's never bothered to uphold it.

She swore during the divorce that no matter how bitter things got between her and Vince, she wouldn't say a bad word about him to Lianna.

Charlotte's ex-husband might be a snake, but he's her daughter's father nonetheless. Someday, Lianna is bound to figure out on her own what kind of man he really is. Until his inevitable free-fall from the pedestal, Charlotte intends to keep her opinion to herself.

That doesn't make it easy to see Lianna constantly upholding him as her hero, with Charlotte perpetually cast in the roll of shrew—and now, jailor.

"If your father is in town and he wants to see you, he can come here to Oakgate," she manages to say, quite reasonably, as she stoops to pick up a rumpled pair of shorts from the floor by the hamper.

"He doesn't want to come here."

"How do you know? Did you ask him?"

"I don't have to. He hates it here. He knows he isn't welcome."

"That's not true," Charlotte protests, fighting the urge to cross her fingers against her own white lie. "He can come here anytime he wants. Nobody's stopping him."

"You are."

"Lianna, I never said—"

"Maybe you didn't say it, but he can tell you hate him. Everyone can tell."

Charlotte shrugs, not quite sure who "everyone" is, but not about to argue, either.

"This room is a mess," she tells her daughter, "so you can get busy cleaning it now."

"I'm still sleeping." Lianna's voice is muffled by her coverlet as she rolls over, toward the far end of the bed.

"You sound wide-awake to me," Charlotte says, looking at her watch. It's getting late. She still has to change out of the gray jersey shorts and white Nike T-shirt she threw on this morning after her shower, and it would be nice if she had an extra few seconds to do something with her hair. She's had it stuck in a careless ponytail the last few days.

Royce should be back any minute now from his tennis game at the club, and then they're planning on heading to Savannah. The contractor has been nagging them for the last few days to pick out paint shades for their new master bedroom and the trim in the walk-in pantry off the remodeled kitchen.

"It's past noon. You need to get out of bed. Now." She pulls the coverlet off Lianna. "And be sure to make it this time."

"Isn't that Nydia's job?"

"No, it isn't Nydia's job. It's yours."

"She's the housekeeper."

"She's your grandfather's housekeeper, not yours. You can make your bed here just like you do at home. Got it?"

"Got it," Lianna grumbles, swinging her long, bare legs around to the floor. "What about Dad?"

"I'll call him and tell him to come here."

"He won't."

"He will if I tell him that's the only way he gets to see you," Charlotte says with more conviction than she feels.

She'd be willing to bet Vince isn't just here to see Lianna this weekend. He probably has some kind of real estate business in the area. He's been involved the last couple of years in flipping houses down in Florida—another of his get-rich-quick schemes, no doubt, but one that might actually have some merit.

"Can I call him instead?" Lianna asks, and adds, "Since talking to *you* won't put him in a good mood."

You just had to get in another dig, didn't you? Charlotte thinks wearily.

"You can call him, but remember what I told you. You aren't to leave this house, Lianna. Not for any reason."

"I know." Lianna seems to choke on her next words: "And you don't care if that means I don't get to see my dad."

Struck by a sudden hint of vulnerability in her daughter's tone, Charlotte longs to take Lianna into her arms and rock her, the way she used to. She can't help but notice that she looks like a little girl again, sitting there in shorty pink pajamas, her hair tousled and her face puffy with sleep.

It's almost enough to make her relent, just this once, about the grounding.

Then Lianna sees her mother looking at her, her expression hardens, and the moment is gone.

Charlotte turns to leave the room, stepping over several magazines, a pair of sneakers, and one pink flip-flop.

"Nydia will be around if you need anything," she tells Lianna. "And she knows you're grounded, so don't try to pull anything."

Her cousins might be around, too, but she wouldn't know their plans, and she wouldn't expect them to keep an eye on her daughter. They've given her a wide berth, and vice versa, ever since the confrontation in the lawyer's office.

Royce is incredulous when he comes home at night, asks whether she's had any contact with them, and is told that she hasn't.

"They're living under this roof, for God's sake, Charlotte. How can you not interact with them?"

"It's a big house," she pointed out. "Aunt Jeanne lives here, too . . . How often do we see her?"

"That's different. She's an invalid. But your cousins— I just can't believe y'all have managed to avoid each other completely."

"Considering that we all share the same goal—stay the hell out of each other's way—it isn't all that difficult, Royce."

Plus, they're all on completely different schedules. Phyllida and her family are still on West Coast time, so they sleep late and stay up late, while Charlotte tends to do the opposite. Gib might live in the same time zone, but he seems to be on his own laid-back inner clock. Anyway, he's gone a lot, doing God knows what. Probably out in the clubs, prowling for women, if history serves.

Charlotte has made little headway in figuring out why Grandaddy disinherited them—in part because of what's gone on with Lianna.

But it will be her first priority just as soon as things settle down enough so that she can think straight, and start looking more closely into Grandaddy's papers.

"Where are you going?" Lianna calls after her as she opens the door to the hall.

"To Savannah with Royce, to take care of some things with the house. We'll be back later tonight. And make sure you clean up this mess."

"I *said* I *will.*"

"And Lianna?" Charlotte pauses with her hand still on the knob, one foot in the hallway.

"Yeah?"

"If your dad does come over today, have a good time with him."

Silence from Lianna.

Then, "He won't come."

No. He won't.

I'm sorry, Charlotte silently tells her daughter, and closes the door quietly behind her.

Alone at her third-floor window, Jeanne watches Melanie drive away, just as Charlotte and Royce did earlier, following the separate departures of Gib, and Phyllida's husband and son.

Earlier, Jeanne strategically complained of an upset stomach and asked if there was any ginger ale in the house.

Melanie checked. Surprise, surprise: there wasn't.

"Do you want me to go out and buy some for you, Jeanne?"

"No, don't go to all that trouble. If I still don't feel good tomorrow, you can bring some then."

"It's no trouble. And I won't be here tomorrow, so here's your big chance." She smiles cheerfully.

"You won't be here tomorrow?"

"It's a Sunday," Melanie reminds her gently. "I don't come on Sundays, remember?"

"Oh. Well, it's all right. I don't want to make you go out in the heat."

"Come on, Jeanne . . . Your wish is my command."

"Really?" Jeanne asked.

"Really. You know I'd do anything for you, hon."

If Jeanne had any doubt about that, it's been erased.

And if ever she needed that crucial assurance, it's now.

So Melanie left, leaving Jeanne alone in the house

with just Nydia, Lianna, and Phyllida—and she hasn't heard any of them stirring below for quite a while.

Now is the time.

She rolls her wheelchair over to the door, expertly steering around the obstacle course of furniture that has found its way up here over the years, just as if it was still an attic.

Which it isn't.

It's her room now, and has been for years. Gilbert had it finished off nicely for her: whitewashed walls, carpeting, a slight drop ceiling to conceal the rafters.

Most of the family's unused junk—household clutter, dusty photograph albums, vintage clothing heaped in steamer trunks, forgotten correspondence from forgotten people—is relegated to one windowless, unfinished storage room beneath the eaves.

She really should ask somebody to move some of this extra furniture in there—if there's room. Which there probably isn't.

She expertly steers her chair around a café table and chairs that once stood in the first-floor atrium, before Charlotte's husband moved in with his exercise equipment.

"Isn't this nice, Aunt Jeanne?" Charlotte asked, when Royce carried the table and chairs up to the third floor. "Now you'll have a place for people to sit and eat lunch with you."

Yes, but nobody, except Melanie, ever does.

I'd do anything for you, hon . . .

God bless Melanie.

Having reached the door at last, Jeanne stops rolling and listens intently for some movement below.

All is silent.

Still, maybe it's too risky.

What if she gets caught?

She weighs the chances of being seen by each of the three current occupants of the second floor.

There's Nydia, whom Jeanne has never liked, not from the very start. She has a feeling the sentiment is mutual. The housekeeper comes and goes like a cat, as if she's sneaking around the place, whether she is or not. For all Jeanne knows, she's lying in wait at the foot of the stairs, hoping to catch Jeanne up to something illicit.

Then there's Lianna. Charlotte's daughter leaves her room almost as infrequently as Jeanne leaves hers. At least, Lianna doesn't come and go by traditional means. So, odds are against Jeanne running into her in the second-floor hall.

As for Phyllida, there's no telling what she's doing with herself now that her husband and son have abandoned her at Oakgate, without a car. But she's the least aware of the household's normal rhythms, and the least likely to realize that Jeanne doesn't belong where she's about to venture.

The elevator is out of the question—it's so creaky it would alert the entire household to Jeanne's movements.

She opens the door and pauses once more, the wheelchair's tires aligned with the threshold.

Silence below.

Aware of the danger if she goes too far, she inches painstakingly forward to the head of the steep flight of stairs before setting the brake.

Then she stands and makes her way quickly down the steps to the second floor . . . and her late brother's private quarters.

CHAPTER 7

Jed has been sleeping ever since Mimi got home around lunchtime. Now, as she sits on the couch reading *Are You My Mother?* to Cameron for at least the tenth time in a row, she hears a movement in the doorway.

Looking up, she sees her husband standing there.

"Hey . . ." She lowers the book. "How are you feeling?"

"Great," he says, either out of sarcasm, or a valiant effort to put up a good act in front of Cam.

Mimi can't tell which, as the inflection is contorted by a flinch of pain.

"Here, sit down." She tosses the book aside, to Cameron's immediate protest, and rises to help him.

But Jed shakes off her supportive hand beneath his elbow, grunting, "I'm fine," as he makes his way toward the nearest chair.

Mimi gazes helplessly at him. He isn't fine.

"You need to take a Hydrocodone, Jed."

"I took one earlier."

"It wore off."

"How do you know? Are you psychic?"

Ignoring the definite sarcasm that time, she says, "I can tell you're in pain, and you don't have to be. That's why the doctor gave you the drugs."

"They mess with my head, and they knock me out." Jed eases himself into the chair. "Plus, we can't afford them. You know that. They're costing us a fortune."

So that's why he's taking the prescription pain pills so sparingly. Tears spring to her eyes as she says, "Jed, you have to take your medicine. Please . . . I can't stand seeing you tossing and turning in bed all night long."

He looks up, studies her face for a moment. Then he says simply, "I'm not taking it during the day. Just at night, so I won't keep you awake."

"Jed, that's not what I—"

"I know, Mimi. Come on, let's drop it." He tilts his head meaningfully in their son's direction. "I'll be all right. Cam, buddy, come over here."

Swiping a hand across her moist cheeks, Mimi watches the little boy reluctantly climb off the couch and cross the carpet to his father's side.

"Hi, Daddy," Cam says warily.

Gone is the exuberant child who once wrestled in his father's arms and showered him with kisses. Gone is the big, strong Daddy who carried his son effortlessly on strong shoulders and made him feel safe.

They haven't told Cameron about Jed's disease, but it's obvious, even to a toddler, that something has changed.

In the past few days alone, Jed has lost even more weight, and his face has taken on a gaunt look Mimi's seen before. She saw it settle over her father's features not long before he died of lung cancer.

That look scares her.

It scares her to death, but she hasn't given up. Not by a long shot.

"How's it going?" Jed asks Cam in an effort to be cheerful. "Are you reading books with Mommy?"

"One book."

"It's his favorite," Mimi says softly, going to kneel beside Cam, hoping to ease the stilted conversation between father and son.

"I thought *Mike Mulligan and His Steam Shovel* was his favorite."

"That was last month," Mimi says, and belatedly realizes she shouldn't have.

Jed was the one who got that book for Cam from the library; the one who read it to him nonstop, pausing to answer Cam's questions about construction machinery he uses in his own job.

Now Jed hasn't worked in days and the book sits, untouched and overdue, collecting fines and dust on a shelf in Cam's room.

"Do you want me to go get *Mike Mulligan* so you can read it to him, Jed?"

The question hangs in the air.

Jed's face is contorted in pain once again—physical pain, but the emotional pain lurks, too, just beneath the surface. She can sense it.

Mimi turns fervently to Cam. "Honey? Do you want Daddy to read *Mike Mulligan* to you?"

Cam's only response is a blank stare.

He's forgotten, she realizes in despair. *He's forgotten all about the book.*

But how could he? It was his favorite. He spent every day carrying it around . . .

He's so young. They forget so quickly at this age.

Cam has forgotten the book his father shared with him, and one day, he might forget . . .

No, Mimi thinks fiercely, *he won't. I won't let him. He'll never forget his father any more than I've forgotten mine. Not even if Jed . . .*

Once again, she refuses to allow the unthinkable into her head.

Today, difficult as it was, she set things into motion with Gib.

His reaction wasn't quite what she had hoped for . . . but there's still time. Not a lot, but time enough.

If all goes according to plan, Jed will be reading *Mike Mulligan* to his son for years to come.

"How are we all doing today, guys? Or should I say *ladies*?"

One by one, the flashlight's beam illuminates three faces framed by nylon hair. One blonde, one brunette, one redhead, all of them grinning.

"No wonder you look so happy. You must know that you're going to be getting some compan—"

An ominous rattling in the shadows over by the fireplace cuts the word short.

A swing of the flashlight reveals the source: a large diamondback rattlesnake is clearly visible on the mud floor.

"Did you know, ladies, that some of the largest rattlesnakes in the country live out here on Achoco Island? That's right. They're a protected species out here."

The reptilian intruder slithers its way closer.

"Protected means you aren't allowed to kill them."

The snake weaves its way through the maze of tiny chair and table legs, its menacing rattle reverberating in the small cabin . . .

Until its head is neatly sliced off with a blade it never sensed coming.

"But sometimes, you have to kill them anyway."

The snake's body ceases to writhe as its head is kicked aside, to rot in a far corner.

"And sometimes, it's sad to say, it's exactly the same way with people."

Hmmm . . .

Charlotte steps back to examine the parallel stripes of paint she rolled on the bedroom wall, careful not to spill any on her pale-yellow linen sleeveless shift and white sandals. Had she realized she'd be doing more than just shopping for paint, she would have left the shorts and T-shirt on.

It was Royce's idea to haul the samples over to the house when she couldn't make up her mind, after stops at the hardware and tile stores. Once they got here, of course, they got caught up in countless details.

Royce wanted to remeasure the master bathroom to make sure they'd have enough tile for the back-splash.

Then he decided to install the new switch plates they'd just picked up, not trusting the workers to figure out which styles went in which rooms.

While she was waiting for him to do that, Charlotte started lining the cupboard shelves with the cute con-tact paper they'd just bought. Naturally, he would end up helping her, insisting on measuring each shelf pre-cisely and cutting each piece himself with a razor blade he had to keep changing because it kept getting gummy with the paper's backing.

She should probably respect his perfection—and she usually does—but she never expected them to be here

into the night. She's tired and hungry and rapidly losing interest in anything related to home décor.

Just when they were ready to leave an hour ago, the
sky opened up in a late-day thunderstorm. They came
up here to kill time, and the next thing Charlotte knew,
Royce was caught up in something all over again.

Still, she tries to keep her irritability at bay, remembering that Royce was exceedingly patient with her in
the hardware store. He was even more patient at the tile
place, where he allowed her to spend an hour going
back and forth among three kinds of marble for the
backsplash around the new clawfoot tub.

When she finally made her decision, he decided to
buy it and haul it back here himself, rather than wait for
the contractor to do it.

"The fewer steps we leave to him, the less chance for
further delays," he pointed out. "This way, they can get
the installer here with a wet saw first thing Monday
morning."

"What do you think?" she asks her husband now, as
she tilts her head to look at the shades of paint.

Royce looks up from the box of tumbled marble
squares he's been counting. "Very good, honey. I think
you're great at making nice, straight lines."

She grins. "I mean, what do you think of the colors?
Which do you like better?"

"They're different colors?"

"One is antique blue, one is colonial blue."

"They both look plain-old blue-blue to me," he says
with a shrug, and goes back to the box of tiles.

"You're a lot of help," she grumbles good-naturedly,
and steps away from the wall, around both roller trays
and a stack of sample-sized paint cans on the floor, to
get a better look.

"Is there going to be enough tile?" she asks now, hoping they aren't going to come up short.

"Shhh, you'll make me lose count again."

"Sorry."

She crosses all the way to the far side of the room, coming to a stop beside the window overlooking the street. From here, the blue paint stripes really do look identical.

Oh, well.

Maybe she'll be able to tell which she prefers tomorrow, with natural daylight coming in.

Right now, there's only the light from a bare bulb protruding from the ornate plaster medallion in the middle of the ceiling, where a light fixture will hang—which they really do need to pick out before this weekend is over, according to the message the general contractor left earlier on her cell phone's voice mail.

There's so much to do before the renovation can be completed. Mostly just finishing touches, but they combine into a series of daunting tasks.

Today, despite her physical exhaustion and all she's been through this week, Charlotte welcomes the distraction.

Still, she wonders in retrospect if they would have taken on the project had they known how complicated and drawn out it would be. She might have been content to buy a newer home, outside the historic district, in the suburbs, maybe.

But there was something about this house, an original Greek Revival that was later remodeled in the Second Empire baroque style. Its architectural quirks appealed to her, even in its former state, with peeling paint, broken windows, and overgrown shrubs.

There was a time, at least a decade before Charlotte's

own childhood, when the historic district was riddled with such neglected places. Then came the revitalization that transformed the mansions, one by one, to their former glory.

This frame structure on East Oglethorpe Avenue was one of the last historic homes in the district to have escaped preservation—or the wrecking ball. Its longtime owner had been placed in a nursing home years ago and refused to sell, clinging to the hope that she would go home again one day. That wasn't to be.

The owner's sole surviving heir, a distant cousin living in Chicago, couldn't wait to wash his hands of the place. Charlotte and Royce snagged it for a song—only to spend hundreds of thousands of dollars on the renovation.

Not that it matters, in the big picture.

They can afford it.

Especially now, she thinks, her heart sinking as she remembers the inheritance.

What she and Royce spent on the house is a tiny percentage of the fortune she's about to receive from Grandaddy.

She again considers, and quickly dismisses, her husband's suggestion that she give away two-thirds of the money to her cousins.

She hasn't come up with a likely motive for Grandaddy's decision, though she spent most of yesterday combing through his papers, searching for a clue.

Nothing yet.

But sooner or later, something is bound to turn up. And until it does . . .

Don't worry, Grandaddy. I won't give away your money to anybody who doesn't deserve it.

* * *

"Hey. You've reached Vince's cell phone. Leave me a message, and I'll get back to you as soon as I can."

Lianna ends the call in frustration, unwilling to leave yet another message for her father, who is apparently missing in action.

He called this afternoon to say he was looking at a couple of commercial real estate properties in Brunswick, but would be by later to take her to dinner.

"I made a reservation for us at a nice upscale place," he told her. "It's called the Sea Captain's House. Ever hear of it?"

"Oh, yeah."

The Sea Captain's House is the fanciest place on the island. Lianna has eaten there lots of times with her mother and Royce, but never with her dad. It killed her to tell him she couldn't go because she was grounded.

Naturally, he wanted to know what she'd done to deserve that.

When she told him, all he said was, "Well, that's your mother's rule and you have to live with it."

But she could tell he thinks Mom is too strict. She was about to ask him to intervene on her behalf when he said, "Listen, it wasn't easy to get that dinner reservation, so . . . You won't care if I go myself, will you?"

"Of course I won't care," she said, masking her disappointment. "I just wish I could have seen you tonight, that's all."

"I'll come by and visit after dinner, okay?"

But here it is, long after dinner, and he has yet to appear. Nor is he answering his cell phone. In fact, it must be turned off, because it goes right into voice mail every time she calls the number.

Missing her own cell phone, Lianna replaces the receiver in its cradle on the wall opposite the kitchen sink.

It wouldn't be so bad if this old house at least had a cordless phone she could carry back upstairs to her room, not to mention more than just three phone jacks in the whole place.

One is located in the kitchen, one in the far parlor, one in the second-floor study. All of them have old-fashioned telephones with curly cords, which makes it very difficult for a person to carry on a private conversation.

At least the house is pretty deserted tonight, with Mom and Royce still out. That jerk Gib has gone off somewhere, too. She assumes Phyllida is in her room, watching television—Lianna could hear it through the door when she passed. As for Nydia, she must be in bed asleep, because there's no sign of light or sound from the maid's quarters adjacent to the kitchen.

Now would be a good time to try and reach Kevin again, she decides, glancing at the stove clock. She tried him earlier, but he didn't pick up his phone, and when she tried him at home one of his brothers said he was out.

"Do you know where he is?" Lianna asked him.

"Nope, do you?"

"Um . . . Do you know when he'll be back?"

"Nope, do you?" The guy laughed and hung up.

What a loser. Lianna isn't particularly anxious to talk to him again.

Maybe Kevin's working down at the Mobil station tonight. He isn't allowed to take phone calls on the job.

If she had her cell, she could text message him.

Maybe she should go look for it in Mom and Royce's bedroom . . .

But even if she finds it, she doesn't dare use it. Knowing Mom, who seems to think she's working for the CIA these days, she'll probably check the records when she gets the bill next month.

She picks up the phone again and dials the number for Kevin's house.

The same brother picks up the phone.

"Is Kevin there?" she asks tentatively.

"Nope. Who is this, his girlfriend checking up on him or something?"

"Actually, yes it is," she finds herself retorting. "Have him call Lianna when he gets home, will you? Oh, and tell him not to use my cell number. Just call Oakgate."

There's a moment of silence.

Then Kevin's brother says, "Oakgate? You mean the Remington place?"

"That's the one."

"Yeah? Who are you, the maid's daughter or something?"

She contemplates that.

It's not like her mother doesn't already know she was seeing Kevin. And it's not like she's ashamed of it, or anything like that. Still, Achoco Island is like a gossipy small town, and she isn't exactly anxious to broadcast their relationship. That's bound to happen if the Tinkstons get wind of it.

"Yeah," she says, "I am. Just have him call, okay?"

Gone is the slightest bit of interest from his brother, who hangs up with a brusque, "Whatever."

Kevin probably won't even get the message, she thinks with a sigh.

"Done counting yet, hon?" she asks Royce, giving up on the paint selection for tonight. "I think we should go down to River Street and get some fried oysters and beer."

He holds up a finger. ". . . fifty-six, fifty-seven, fifty-eight . . ."

"Sorry," she says again, trying to be patient.

She can't help feeling vaguely uneasy, though, and anxious to get the heck out of here, at least for tonight.

The house is so different by day, its tall windows flooding the place with light. Now those same windows are foreboding black rectangles and the high ceilings trap eerie shadows, especially without lamps and fixtures to brighten the large rooms.

It doesn't help that it's so darned stuffy in here, she thinks, and the whole place smells strongly of paint fumes and sawdust. The house is sealed shut; the construction guys blast the central air when they're working, then turn it down before they leave.

"Do you think I should open this?" she asks Royce, examining the latch on the newly installed window. "Just to get some ventilation while we're here?"

He shakes his head, still counting. "Almost done," he murmurs. "Hang on. Sixty-three, sixty-four . . ."

Restless, her stomach rumbling, Charlotte perches on the freshly sanded built-in seat beneath the window. She presses her nose against the glass to shut out the glare of the room behind her so she can see out.

The pavement is shiny from the storm earlier, and glistening puddles pool in the street along the gutter on the far side, near Colonial Park.

Why the heck do we have to live across from a creepy old cemetery?

That was Lianna's first—and predictably dour—question, when they initially brought her to see the house.

Because live neighbors are noisier and a heck of a lot more trouble, that's why, was Royce's easy-going response.

Now, as Charlotte peers into the night, she decides Lianna might have had a point. The cemetery might resemble a beautiful park by day—indeed, it was long ago designated one by the City of Savannah—but at night, the place is definitely creepy.

Along the black wrought iron fence that marks the perimeter, tufted palm trees rise like towering sentinels amid leafy oaks whose boughs weep silvery Spanish moss. Within the fence lies the seemingly infinite stretch of granite slabs. Some seem to glow an eerie white in the moonlight, others lean at awkward angles, seeming to defy gravity. The whitest, most tilted stones mark the graves of Savannah's earliest—and most illustrious—residents.

Okay, so an eighteenth-century burial ground doesn't exactly provide a picturesque view from the master bedroom.

Throw in a little midnight mist, or creaking branches and a scary thunderstorm, and Charlotte can imagine being too spooked to go to bed in her own house, night-light or no night-light.

Oh, come on, don't be ridiculous, she admonishes herself. *You're a grown woman, not a young—*

Her eyes widen.

A black-clad figure just darted behind a raised rectangular crypt in the foreground, directly in her line of vision.

Still puttering restlessly in the kitchen, wishing the phone would ring, Lianna glances over the contents of the refrigerator, looking for a snack. Not much here, she thinks, pushing things around on the shelves: the ever-present cut glass pitcher of sweet tea Nydia prepares almost daily for Mom, some bottled water, condiments, salad stuff, ham . . .

The boring sandwich Nydia made for her dinner was a far cry from the feast she would have had at the Sea Captain's House with Dad.

She loves their grilled scallops, and the lobster risotto, too. Oh, and they have the best triple chocolate cake on the dessert menu—almost as good as the one Mom used to make every year for Adam's birthday . . .

Yeah, and after he died, she stopped making birthday cakes altogether. Whenever Lianna's rolls around, she always lets her pick out whatever she wants from Baker's Pride on DeRenne Avenue. Their Georgia River Mud Cake is her favorite, but she'd still rather have her mother's homemade triple chocolate.

Yeah, like that'll ever happen again.

Thinking about cake is giving Lianna a fierce sweet tooth, but all she can find in the refrigerator that tempts her in the least is a cup of strawberry Dannon yogurt, the kind with the fruit on the bottom.

Adam always liked this stuff, too, she recalls as she carries it up to her room.

She can remember arguing with her older brother over who got to eat the blueberry kind, their mutual favorite, and who had to have the peach, their mutual least favorite.

Lianna invariably got stuck with peach.

"No fair, Adam!"

How many times did she whine those words, growing up?

No fair, Adam—you got the good flavor.

No fair, Adam—you got the best seat.

No fair, Adam . . .

You left me all alone here with Mom, and Dad is gone now, too.

Tears spring to her eyes.

I know . . . I know it wasn't your fault. It was mine.

Maybe Mom knows, too.

At least it would explain why she hates me so much.

Lianna stops short on the threshold of her room, hearing the shrill ring of the telephone from the extension down the hall, in her grandfather's study.

It must be Dad or Kevin, she thinks in relief, her troubles instantly forgotten as she hurries to answer it.

Startled, Charlotte strains to see the spot beside the cemetery crypt, telling herself that it's probably just kids . . . local teenagers, up to mischief.

"Ready?" Royce asks, directly behind her, and she jumps.

"Oh! You scared me!"

"I didn't mean to . . . Hey, are you okay?"

"I'm fine." And more than ready to get out of here. She turns away from the window. "So do you want to go eat?"

"You bet. And you'll be glad to know that we'll have just enough marble, as long as the tile guys are careful and they don't crack any while they're installing them."

"That's great . . ."

She glances again at the window.

"Charlotte . . ." Royce puts his hand on her arm. "You look like you've seen a ghost."

"I think I just did. Across the street, in the cemetery," she elaborates at his doubtful expression.

"Let me guess . . . a filmy white figure was out there floating among the headstones?"

"It wasn't floating, and it was wearing black, actually."

His grin doesn't quite hide the shadow of concern in his eyes, though his tone is playful as he says, "Bad guys wear black, you know. It must have been an evil spirit."

"Terrific."

"I'm just teasing you."

"I know. But I'm not kidding about seeing something out there."

"Like what?"

"Like a real person."

"Real people walk through cemeteries, you know. Even at night."

"This one wasn't just walking—it was more like, I don't know, hiding."

Realizing how ridiculous that sounds, she forces a laugh that sounds hollow, and not just because of the echo in the room. "I guess hanging around this empty house is starting to creep me out."

"Come on, then, let's go." Royce crosses the room and flicks off the wall switch.

A reassuring wedge of light from the hall spills across the floor, not quite reaching the window where Charlotte still stands.

She turns back to look through the glass again. With the room's overhead bulb extinguished, she can see the cemetery much more clearly.

There's no sign of the person she spotted earlier lurking near the crypt. Whoever it was must have taken off to catch up to his friends, probably tossing beer cans or cigarette butts along the way.

Right.

A teenager, up to no good. But not in a threatening way. And he's long gone, for sure.

It's just . . .

He isn't gone.

Charlotte has the oddest sense that somebody's still there . . .

Watching her.

She takes a quick step back from the window, still feeling exposed.

Shades . . . and draperies.

Yes, that's what they need, as soon as possible. She won't move in here until the windows can all be covered.

She'll order the treatments first thing tomorrow. Before the light fixture, before deciding on paint, before anything else . . .

From the doorway, Royce asks, "Coming?"

Her anxiety must be contagious; now he, too, seems a bit apprehensive as Charlotte hurries toward him. Clearly, she isn't the only one who's grateful to be getting out of here.

"I hope this place seems less spooky after we move in, Royce," she comments, "because if it doesn't . . ."

"I'm sure it will be fine." But he doesn't sound so sure at all.

He flicks off two more light switches as they walk the length of the upstairs hall, plunging them into pitch blackness by the time they reach the stairs.

Below, the first floor is completely dark as well; they had come up to the second floor well before dusk and didn't think to turn on lights.

"Isn't there a switch up here to light the stairs?" Charlotte asks, feeling like a frightened little girl as she clutches the back of Royce's shirt.

"I thought there was." She can hear Royce feeling around on the wall beside them.

"Here it is," he says finally, and she hears a clicking sound.

But there's no reassuring burst of light.

"There must not be a bulb in the fixture yet," Royce tells her, sounding as apprehensive as she feels, and he's not the one with an irrational fear of the dark.

"Do you think there's a flashlight up here somewhere?"

"I doubt it."

"Maybe we should look."

"Let's just get out of here," he says, sounding as antsy as she feels. "Come on, just watch your step."

Together, they descend in utter darkness, picking their way down the unfamiliar flight of stairs to the front entrance hall.

There, at last, she can literally see the light . . . beyond the pillared arch that leads to the front door. A golden glow from the porch light—on a timer to come on at dusk—falls through the arched transom and the narrow windows beside it.

"Do you have your purse and everything?" Royce asks belatedly as they reach the front door.

"Yes."

And if I didn't, Charlotte thinks to herself, *there's no way I'd go back up there in the dark to get it.*

"Okay, then, let's go." Jangling his car keys impatiently, or perhaps nervously, Royce opens the door.

Sultry moonlight seeps in to meet them, tinged with the scent of blooming flowers and the dank odor of the river blocks away.

Charlotte steps out to the small wooden porch perched six feet above street level; the house sits on a raised basement like so many others in Savannah.

She inhales the heady perfume of blooming Confederate jasmine that twines over the trunk of an ancient oak tree beside the house, then exhales audibly, feeling better already in the comforting splash of light from the overhead fixture.

In a few weeks, she tells herself, this place will surely feel like a safe haven, rather than a haunted house she can't wait to escape.

Of course it will.

Look at Oakgate.

If one wasn't familiar with the old home, it, too, would seem gloomily foreboding. In fact, it does even now, sometimes. Even to her.

Royce pauses on the doorstep, fumbling with his keys, attempting to insert first one, then another, into the unfamiliar deadbolt.

"Do you want fried oysters?" Charlotte asks, eager to go on to the restaurant, "or should we go all out and get a pizza with extra cheese and pepperoni?"

His reply is lost in a sudden, deafening burst of sound.

"Lord, that scared me," Charlotte gasps, pressing a hand to her violently pounding heart.

A car must have backfired, so close by she swivels her head to see if it's parked right at the curb in front of the house.

No car . . .

But there's a flash of movement in the cemetery across the street.

It's the same black-clad figure, running, fleeing into the heart of the cemetery.

"Royce, look!" she exclaims, reaching back for her husband's arm—and encountering thin air.

The spot where he stood just a moment before is empty.

Or so she believes . . . until she looks down and sees Royce crumpled at her feet in a spreading pool of his own blood.

PART III

THE THIRD VICTIM

CHAPTER 8

At last, the first rays of light appear in the eastern sky, bringing to a close what has felt like the longest night of the year . . . but, in terms of sunrise and sunset, was among the shortest.

This July Sunday dawns almost eerily still above the maritime woodland on Achoco Island, the air already warm. By late morning, it's bound to be hot and humid; the oppressive afternoon will undoubtedly usher the threat of thunderstorms.

What else is new?

The Low Country is hardly the ideal place to spend the summer months. Not unless one enjoys wading through soupy air while fully clothed, every time one steps outdoors.

Yes, but next summer at this time, I'll be someplace cool and comfortable.

Someplace where the air is crisp at night and the sea is refreshing. New England, or the Northwest Coast . . .

Or perhaps the mountains would be a nice change of

scenery. The Canadian Rockies are supposed to be beautiful.

Yes, the mountains. Definitely. The high altitude would be welcome after drowning in summer days at Southern sea level.

Perfect. Next year, the sky will be the limit, quite literally.

Next year? It won't be that long.

If all goes according to plan, it won't be long at all.

Last night brought an important challenge that was met without complication.

It was tempting to stick around for the aftermath, but nobody in their right mind would take that risk.

Anyway, it isn't hard to figure out what came on the heels of an expert aim that easily found its target, and the resonant crack of gunfire.

Here is what happened: Charlotte Maitland watched her husband drop at her feet like an arcade pin.

She had to be utterly shocked and terrified.

Indeed, her screams echoed faintly, and yes, quite satisfyingly, for quite some distance across the dark expanse of Colonial Park Cemetery.

Ah, sweet Charlotte, it's only just begun.

"But first, I have places to go . . . people to see. Right, ladies? You're finally going to get that company we've been talking about. Won't that be fun? . . . What's that, Pammy Sue?"

The blond doll gazes mutely from its little wooden chair.

"Why don't you like visitors? Are you afraid they might be prettier than you are? Are you afraid that Joe will find somebody he likes better than he does you? Well, don't worry. Because Mama always says it isn't nice to play favorites. Don't you, Mama?"

The redheaded doll is wrenched from its seat.

"Why, Mama, it isn't nice to say that. You're supposed to like everybody just the same, just the way Daddy did. You're going to hurt poor Odette's feelings. And so is Joe."

Birds nesting in the makeshift roof overhead chirp their early-morning song.

"Don't worry, Odette." A gentle hand strokes the dark nylon hair of the third doll. "Joe loves you best, and so does Mama. Yes, she does. Don't you, Mama?"

A rustling sound disturbs the thicket outdoors. Probably a deer. Or maybe a wild hog.

"Shut up, Mama. That isn't kind. You shouldn't talk like that . . . Stop it, Mama!"

With a brutal, satisfying twist, the red head snaps off the doll's body.

"Oh, Mama, look what you made me do. Just like the snake."

With a sigh, the head is tossed into the corner to join that of its reptilian counterpart.

"It's okay, girls. I'll go get your visitor. But you'll have to wait until I have a chance to get her down here. You're going to be so surprised when you see who it is . . ."

"So that's all we have to go on, Ms. Remington? The person who shot your husband was wearing dark clothes?"

"That's all I saw—and it's *Mrs. Maitland*," she wearily corrects him for at least the third time since she sat down to face two uniformed officers from the Savannah-Chatham Police Department.

They're conducting the witness interview, which feels more like a suspect interrogation, in a private employee breakroom not far from the operating room where the doctors are working on Royce.

"I'm sorry, *Mrs. Maitland*. I'll make a note of the

name." Detective Williamson—who is, in Charlotte's opinion, a fat, balding, gruff cliché—scribbles something on his report. Considering his less-than-apologetic tone, it could just as easily be a reminder to bring home milk.

"Thank you," she says stiffly.

He doesn't reply. No, he's not the most pleasant guy in the world, but these are far from pleasant circumstances.

Being called by her proper name and title should be the least of Charlotte's concerns at a time like this, but she can't help it. She's been the object of blatant curiosity ever since somebody on the hospital staff recognized the Oakgate address on the paperwork and asked— with the other ER waiting room occupants in earshot— whether she's one of *the* Remingtons.

As in, one of the Remingtons for whom the entire ambulatory wing of the hospital is named.

Like his father and grandfather before him, Grandaddy never was much of a philanthropist—not, that is, until fairly recently. But in Charlotte's opinion, the state-of-the-art addition to the hospital could hardly be considered too little, too late.

She just wishes Royce had been brought to some other hospital, or that she hadn't been recognized.

As word spread, some of the nurses seemed more curious about her pedigree—and the potential scandal of her husband being gunned down on a city street—than they were concerned about her husband's well-being.

Oh, how the mighty have fallen, she can imagine people thinking as they stare at her: unkempt, her rumpled linen shift covered in dried blood, her cheeks mascara-stained.

She was a crying, quivering mess, perpetually on the verge of hysteria before she found out Royce is going to pull through.

But even now . . .

Somebody shot my husband. Dear God, this can't be happening . . .

"What about the perp's build?" The question comes from the other officer, Detective Phillip Dorado, who's about twenty years younger and a hundred pounds lighter than his hulking partner. With his Latino good looks, he could be playing the role of a cop on one of those television dramas Royce likes to watch. And there's a shimmer of kindness in his rich mocha-colored eyes when he speaks, as though he, unlike his partner, realizes Charlotte is a victim, not a perpetrator.

"His build? I don't know . . ." Charlotte closes her eyes, trying to remember. "He was so far away from where I was in the window . . ."

"Was he tall? Short?" Williamson prods impatiently.

"About medium-sized . . ."

Hearing his snort in response, she keeps her eyes shut, not wanting to see his expression as he jots that down on his report.

He's already all but berated her for not having any idea who could possibly want to hurt Royce. He questioned relentlessly, as though if he asked enough times, she'd pull a likely suspect out of thin air—or confess to the crime herself.

"Was he fat?" Dorado continues. "Skinny?"

"About medium weight, I guess," she reluctantly says again, and opens her eyes in time to see the look that passes between the two men.

"Listen, I know I'm not much help, but I'm doing the best I can." Her tone is as steely as she can muster, and she clasps her hands on her lap beneath the table so they won't see how badly she's still shaking even now, a good eight hours after Royce was shot.

"We're trying to help you, Ms. Rem—Mrs. Maitland,"

Detective Dorado tells her. "We're going to do everything we can to find whoever did this to your husband. We just need every detail you can possibly come up with."

"Okay."

"Is there anything else you can tell us about his appearance?"

"Just that I know the person was small enough and agile enough for me to think he might be a teenager. You know—he wasn't big and bulky." *Like you,* she adds silently to Detective Williamson.

"Can you estimate his height?" Williamson asks.

"Not really." Sensing by the look on his face that her answer isn't sufficient, she offers, "I guess somewhere between five-foot-five and six feet."

He writes it down. "And weight?"

"I don't know . . . under two hundred pounds, I guess."

There's a moment of silence as the detective finishes writing. Then he closes his pad, a cue for him and Dorado to get to their feet and thank her.

"What do y'all do now?" Charlotte asks them.

"Now that the sun is up, we'll be conducting a more thorough investigation of the cemetery," Williamson informs her.

"Let me know what y'all find." She, too, stands, and realizes her legs feel as though they're going to give out.

Well, what do you expect after a night without sleep and at least eighteen hours without food?

She can't imagine eating anything right now, but she could probably force down a cup of coffee. She needs the caffeine. It's been a long night and it's going to be a long day.

Royce won't be out of surgery for at least another

hour. She'll go make a couple of phone calls, then stop in the cafeteria for coffee to bring back up.

"We'll be back to check in with you as soon as we know something, Mrs. Maitland," Dorado says, and both men shake her hand. Williamson's beefy grasp is sweaty and it's all she can do not to wipe her palm on her dress. She's not exactly unsullied herself.

After the detectives leave, she checks in with the head OR nurse to make sure there's no news about Royce. There isn't.

Clutching her cell phone in her hand, she hurries to the nearest exit, past signs indicating the turnoff toward the Remington Wing.

The first call she places is to Oakgate, hoping someone will answer before the ringing wakes Lianna. Grandaddy had never bothered getting an answering machine or voice mail.

As the phone rings on and on with no answer, she remembers that it's Sunday, the housekeeper's day off. But Nydia usually doesn't leave until late morning, and it's still early, so maybe—

"Hello?"

"Nydia?"

"Yes?"

"Have you heard what happened?"

There's a pause. "What do you mean?"

Charlotte fills her in as quickly as she can. "I know this is your day off, but—"

"I'll stay right here," Nydia offers without hesitation. "I didn't have any plans for today, anyway."

Grateful, Charlotte doesn't argue with her. "This news is bound to get out, and when it does, reporters might call the house. Can y'all please make sure you don't give out any information? And whatever you do, don't let Lianna find out. She shouldn't hear this from anyone but me."

"I won't say a word."

"Are my cousins there?"

"I don't know. Do you want to hold on while I check?"

No, she doesn't want to hold. She wants to do something else, anything else. She wants to be someplace other than this hospital; longs to flee the concrete walkway leading up to the surgical wing where her wounded husband lies unconscious and ripped open.

"Yes," she tells Nydia, "I'll hold."

She's gone several minutes. Charlotte listens to silence on the other end, watches a couple of doctors step outside and light cigarettes, joining a group of other employees on a smoking break. She turns her back on them, not in the mood to witness their easygoing, upbeat, meaningless chatter out here in the sunshine.

The ER doctor told her Royce was lucky. The bullet lodged in the muscle tissue of his upper thigh. If he had been hit as little as an inch in any other direction, things might have been very different. He should regain full use of his leg after surgery, recuperation, and physical therapy.

Lucky.

The irony of that word choice keeps coming back to haunt Charlotte. Lucky, to be chosen at random by a sniper?

"Mrs. Maitland?" Nydia is back on the line. "Mrs. Harper is here. I told her what happened and I'm handing her the phone now."

Phyllida is on the line instantly, asking one fervent question after another. It takes a while for Charlotte to even get to the point of the call and ask her to bring a change of clothes and her toiletry bag to the hospital.

There's a moment of silence. "I don't have a car, Charlotte."

"Isn't Gib there?"

"No. I don't know where he is, but I'll try to reach him on his cell. We'll be at the hospital with your things as soon as I find him."

"Thanks."

It isn't until she's hung up that Charlotte realizes this is the first conversation she's had with either of her cousins since the meeting in Tyler's office the other day. Now she'll be forced to come face-to-face with them as well.

But Phyllida and Gib's lingering animosity and contestment of the will are the least of her worries.

Right now, all she cares about is Royce.

She reaches into her pocket and finds his cell phone, which the nurses gave her along with the rest of his personal belongings. For the second time since the shooting, she searches the phone's memory base for his daughter's cell phone number, then presses SEND.

It takes a few rings for Aimee to answer, with a fumbling sound as she does.

"Sorry, Charlotte, I'm at the airport trying to get to the gate," she says, sounding a little breathless.

"I'm glad you got a flight." Charlotte can hear the noise from the terminal in the background.

"I'm on the next plane out of here, but I have to connect through Atlanta so it's going to be a while. How's Daddy? Is he out of surgery yet?"

"Not yet. What flight are you on, Aimee? Do you want me to have somebody meet you at the airport?" Even as she asks the question, she hopes her stepdaughter will say no. Who, after all, could Charlotte possibly send to the airport?

The chauffeur is away, she wants Nydia to stay at

home with Lianna, and she isn't comfortable asking her cousins for yet another favor. Nearly all of Charlotte's friends in Savannah are traveling this summer, and she hasn't been in close contact with them, anyway, since moving out to Oakgate. Not close enough to involve them intimately in something like this.

But it doesn't matter, because Aimee tells her she'll just take a cab to the hospital when she lands.

"Make sure you tell the cab driver that it's the hospital off the expressway . . . Are you at all familiar with Savannah?" Charlotte asks.

"No—hang on a second, they're making an announcement . . ."

In the background, Charlotte hears, *"The aircraft that will make up Delta Airlines Flight 640 to Atlanta is now at the gate and will begin boarding momentarily. Please have your tickets ready so we can board the plane for an on-time departure."*

"I have to go," Aimee says in a rush. "I'll get there as soon as I land."

"Have a safe flight."

Delta Airlines flight 640 . . .

That's the one Royce always takes home to her from New Orleans, first thing in the morning. Ironic that just days ago, Charlotte was sitting in the Oyster Bar, worried about something happening to him.

Maybe it really was a premonition.

And maybe the next time you have one, you should listen.

Remembering to stop in the cafeteria, she waits in line for coffee with yet another group of casual, chatting staff members, along with a smattering of patients' loved ones. They're easily identifiable, not just by their street clothes and hushed conversations, but by their drawn faces etched with telltale concern.

To the workers, who seem disconcertingly oblivious

to the life-and-death domestic dramas unfolding around them, this is just another morning on the job.

As Charlotte flips a black lever and watches steaming, aromatic liquid pouring into her white foam cup, a long-forgotten detail flits into her exhausted mind.

She remembers being huddled in the sand on the dusky beach off Achoco Island, some distance from the cluster of divers that had just emerged, empty-handed, from the depths of the sea.

She couldn't hear what they were saying as they removed their equipment.

Then the wind shifted abruptly and the unmistakable sound of laughter reached her ears. As she listened in disbelief, it became clear that they were discussing bets they had placed on the weekend's opening games of the NFL season.

Somebody's son had been lost in the treacherous Atlantic, and the men responsible for finding the child were engaged in lighthearted, meaningless conversation.

She never forgot it.

Nor did she ever tell Royce.

The divers were human. They were doing their job. Their cavalier talk of football wagers had nothing to do with the fact that they didn't retrieve Theo Maitland's body.

Intellectually, she knew that. Of course she did.

She just never got over that feeling of betrayal—or the realization that the immediate family, despite the hustle of activity by the many helping hands that materialize in their time of need, is unalterably isolated in any loss.

Feeling lonelier than she has in years, Charlotte pays for her coffee, grabs a couple of creamers and a packet of Splenda, and makes her way back to the elevator.

Upstairs, the nurse spots her coming toward the station and shakes her head. "Nothing yet, Ms. Remington."

"Thank you."

And it's *Mrs. Maitland*.

Toting Cameron on her hip, Mimi steps into the kitchen of her mother's small tract house in Tidewater Meadow to find Maude Gaspar seated at the table with a cup of coffee, utterly fixated on the small portable television on a metal stand in the corner.

"Good mornin', Honey Buns. How's Jed today?"

"Still asleep. He had another restless night." *And so did I.*

"I lit a candle for him down at church this morning." Maude's eyes remain fastened to the screen even as she holds out her arms for Cameron. "Where's my precious grandson? Come here to Granny, sugar, and let me give you some lovin'."

"Is there coffee?" Mimi asks, placing her son in her mother's embrace.

"Is the sky blue?"

She glances out the window above the sink, framed by limp, once-white curtains trimmed with red rickrack. "Today, it is."

"Gonna stay that way till about noon, accordin' to the weatherman."

Mimi crosses to the counter, and the electric percolator her parents received as a wedding shower gift three decades ago. Her mother has used it faithfully every morning, but Mimi wonders now how much longer it can possibly last without Daddy here to tinker with it the next time it goes on the fritz.

Behind her, Cameron squeals, "Bob!"

"Bob?" Maude bounces him on her lap. "What does that mean?"

"He wants to watch *Bob the Builder*. On TV. It's his new favorite show."

"I thought you didn't like him to watch television."

"I don't." *I didn't. But that was before I needed to distract him from the misery our lives have become.*

"When is it on?"

"It was starting when we left home just now, and I promised him he could finish watching it here."

"Oh, all right, sweet pea. Let Granny change the channel for you."

"You don't have to do that, Mom." Mimi pours steaming coffee into a chipped mug from the plastic drying rack beside the sink.

Using the remote to change the channel, much to Cam's delight, Maude says, "I was just watchin' the news, but all that's left now is the sports and your daddy is the only one who liked to watch that part. I just like the news. Have y'all seen what happened in Savannah?" She rises from the chair and sets Cam on it, in front of his program.

"No, what happened?" Mimi turns to the refrigerator for creamer.

Thus, her back is turned to her mother when Maude informs her, "Charlotte Remington's husband was shot right on Oglethorpe Avenue last night. You must know her, don't you? From when you used to run around with that Remington boy? What was his name? I know it was Gilbert, after his daddy and Grandaddy, but what did they used to call him again?"

Gib.

"I know Charlotte—I mean, I knew her a long time ago." Ignoring the other question, Mimi lifts the carton

of half-and-half from the shelf with a trembling hand. "I
don't know her husband, though. Is he . . . ?"

"Serious condition in the hospital is all they're sayin'
on the news."

"Do they say who shot him?"

Maude shrugs. "It's just like those snipers that go
around shootin' up cities up North. Can't believe it's
startin' down here."

"I can't, either." Mimi fumbles for a spoon in the
drawer, then stirs her coffee so violently that it spills
over the top of the mug.

"Everybody always thought those Remingtons had it
all," Maude muses, stooping to pick up a little truck
from the collection of toys she purchased at yard sales
and keeps in a plastic laundry hamper for Cameron.
"I'm startin' to think all they really have is a whole lot of
money. I wouldn't trade places with any one of 'em.
How 'bout you?"

"Of course not," Mimi murmurs, watching her son
happily grasp the used toy in his chubby little hands.

Tucked into the pocket of his lightweight black-wool
dress pants, Gib's cell phone rings just as he reaches the
Bryan Street parking garage where he left his rental car
the night before.

He contemplates not answering it, hardly in the
mood to talk after the night he just had.

But curiosity gets the better of him and he reaches
for the phone to see who's calling.

The number on the caller ID screen isn't local, and it
takes Gib a moment to place the area code.

Oh. California.

He flips the phone open. "Yeah, Phyllida."

"Where are you?"

"Why?"

"Because I want to send you flowers," is the sarcastic response. "What do you think? For one thing, it's Sunday morning and I'm assuming you never came home last night and I have no idea where you are."

"Save the worrying for your kid, Phyll. I'm a big boy. Sometimes these things happen."

"Trust me, I'm not all that worried about *you* right now, Gib. But I need you to get back here as soon as you can, and . . ."

"And what?" he asks edgily when she trails off.

"And I hope you can account for every second of the last twelve hours."

"Why?" he asks, his heart pounding.

"Because somebody shot Charlotte's husband."

Pacing the narrow aisle between two short rows of uncomfortable chairs, Charlotte instantly recognizes the slender young blonde who bursts into the private surgical waiting room, pulling a rolling suitcase.

Royce's daughter.

At last.

"Charlotte Maitland?"

"That's me. You must be Aimee."

"Yes." Her stepdaughter rushes over to her, grabbing her in a tight embrace.

Caught off guard by the fervent greeting, Charlotte returns it gratefully. These have been the longest, loneliest hours of her life, and Aimee feels less a stranger to her than her own cousins did when they were here earlier.

"I'm so glad you're here," Charlotte tells her, but the words sound more strained than she intended.

Probably because I've never met her before in my life, and here I am clinging to her like she's my long-lost best friend.

She releases Aimee from her grasp.

"My luggage," the girl says, turning to the suitcase she left behind in the doorway.

"I'll get it. Sit down." Charlotte hurries over to grab the bag, noticing the airline tag around the handle. "You had to check it?"

"Too big for carry-on. I didn't know how long I'd be here, so I just threw everything into the biggest bag I had."

"That's good." Charlotte nods, trying to think of something else to say, and missing her husband more than ever. This wasn't how she was supposed to meet Royce's daughter for the first time.

"When I didn't see you in the big waiting room I was worried that something went wrong and he was still in surgery, but I can tell by your face that Daddy's okay. He is, isn't he?" Aimee adds anxiously.

"He's out of the OR but still in recovery. They told me I could wait in here instead of going down to the big waiting room."

"Why?"

The question is perfunctory, yet Charlotte doesn't want to answer it.

She suspects the nurses allowed her to remain in this small, empty waiting room rather than mingle with the masses because she's a Remington, a VIP. Or maybe it's because of the commotion caused earlier down the hall when a couple of pesky reporters tried to question her, before a stern nurse ordered them out.

It doesn't matter why she's here. She's far more comfortable in seclusion, where she can weep and pace and worry away from the prying eyes of strangers.

"How did the operation go?" Aimee asks.

"The surgeon said we're lucky it didn't shatter the bone, or hit an artery . . ." She shudders at what might have been.

"Oh, God." Tears spring to Aimee's eyes. "I've been so worried . . . I tried to call you when I landed but I got your voice mail. Is Daddy awake? Has he said anything?"

"I don't know, I haven't seen him. The doctor said they were able to remove the bullet and repair the damage to his leg."

Charlotte can't help but feel as though she's methodically reciting a report she's given before, and in a sense, she is. She repeated the same information to both her cousins when they were here earlier.

It took at least two hours after she called Phyllida for her to show up with Gib. They both seemed shaken, and asked if there was anything else they could do.

There are probably a lot of things they could do, if Charlotte was capable of thinking straight—and willing to ask.

But she is neither. Not under the circumstances.

"So Daddy will really be okay?"

"They said he will."

"Thank God." Aimee's voice is ragged; she sinks into a chair. "It must have been awful . . . You must have been so scared."

"I was."

Charlotte closes her eyes tightly, trying to block out the barrage of memories.

The deafening report of what she didn't even realize was gunfire . . .

The shocking sight of Royce lying at her feet, bleeding . . .

Cradling her moaning husband in her lap on the wooden porch floor, pressing the open wound in his leg with her bare hand . . .

It seemed as though she sat that way forever, fearing the worst, reliving the frightful moments on the beach that day as the lifeguards searched for her lost son in the surf. But that took hours; this couldn't have been very long at all.

No, she heard sirens screaming through the night even as the 9-1-1 operator she had reached on her cell phone told her to stem the flow, keep him alert, and stay on the phone—that help was on its way.

They let Charlotte ride in the back of the ambulance with him, and she watched as the paramedics stabilized him and stopped the bleeding. Royce was conscious, moaning, but unable to respond to the questions the medics were asking.

Mostly the questions were about his pain, but one of them did ask if he had any idea who could have shot him.

Royce could only groan in response.

At the time, Charlotte was irked that the medics would even ask such a question at a time like that.

Now she understands that it was necessary; that they were probably trained to do so.

And when Aimee asks almost the same thing now— "Did the police get whoever shot him?"—Charlotte is less irked than she is reluctant to reply.

"I wish I could tell you they'd found him, but they haven't. They think it might have been random, a sniper attack."

"Oh, my God." Aimee digs her fingertips into her scalp beneath a thick mane of flaxen hair. "Poor, poor Daddy."

Struck by a wave of renewed longing for Royce, Charlotte fumbles in her purse for a tissue, finding only a clump of damp used ones.

She turns her back, hoping Aimee won't hear her sniffling, and wipes her eyes with the back of her hand.

Royce. I need you, Royce.

"Here . . ." Aimee is pressing a packet of Kleenex into her hand. "Take this."

"Thank you," she manages to say, before her voice gives way to sobs.

CHAPTER 9

"Jeanne?"

It takes her a moment to wake from a sound sleep. When she does, she opens her eyes to find Gilbert's housekeeper standing above her bed.

It's late morning—she can tell by the angle of the light coming in the bull's-eye window above her bed.

"I'm sorry to wake you, but I thought you should know."

"Know what?" Her brain still fuzzy with sleep, she sits up, rubbing her eyes.

"Mr. Maitland was . . . injured last night. In Savannah."

"What happened to him?"

Nydia hesitates.

"Was it a car accident? Is he all right? Was Charlotte with—"

Jeanne closes her mouth abruptly, remembering belatedly not to appear too lucid, even in front of Nydia.

The housekeeper seems to falter a bit—unusual for her—before admitting, "It wasn't a car accident. He was shot by a sniper."

Jeanne gasps in horrified dismay. "No! Oh, no. Charlotte . . . ?"

"She was with him, but she's fine. And Mr. Maitland is in surgery, from what I understand."

Jeanne nods, pressing her fist against her quivering mouth.

"I just thought you should know." Nydia turns to leave.

"Thank you. Will you . . . tell me how he is? When you know more?"

"Of course."

Jeanne watches Gilbert's housekeeper make her exit.

She waits until the door closes at the foot of the stairs before slipping from beneath the covers.

It takes a minute for her bare feet to grow accustomed to standing. Gradually, the circulation returns to her wobbly old legs beneath the cotton summer nightgown, and they feel sturdy enough to carry her across the room, careful not to let the floorboards creak.

At the bureau, she opens the top middle drawer and reaches beneath the stack of handkerchiefs, the shawl, the journals and photo album.

Taking out the locked wooden box, she sets it on the bureau top, and glances over her shoulder as if she's going to find somebody watching her.

There's nobody up here, Jeanne, don't be silly.

Nobody but the ghosts . . . And they know all about this.

They know everything.

Jeanne reaches into the lace-edged neckline of the nightgown and retrieves a long gold chain that once belonged to Mother. Dangling from it are a locket that contains a picture of Marie Remington in her youth, and a small silver key.

With a quivering hand, Jeanne removes the chain

from her neck and inserts the key into the lock on the box.

She opens the cover and glances down at the contents.

This, too, belonged to her mother.

This small pistol with the mother-of-pearl handle that was Marie Remington's protection—and may prove to be her daughter's salvation.

"I can't believe this is happening," Aimee says yet again, as she and Charlotte wait side by side for word about Royce.

Dry-eyed at last, Charlotte nods, too numb to say much. She just wishes the nurses would come and tell her something about Royce's condition, but there's been no word for quite some time now.

"I can't believe just a few hours ago I was happy-go-lucky, hanging out in New Orleans with my friends." Aimee pronounces it the same as Royce does, like a true native: *N'Awlins.* Her accent is even thicker than his—of course, since she still lives there.

With her mother.

Charlotte wonders idly whether Karen, Royce's ex-wife, is aware of what happened. Not that it matters. They're never in contact, as far as she knows.

But if something violent ever happened to Vincent, she would want to know. He's the father of her child.

Surely Aimee told her mother why she was leaving town abruptly.

"I'm just glad you found a seat on a plane," Charlotte tells Aimee. "I was worried you wouldn't be able to, on a weekend."

"After I got your message last night, I went straight to

the airport. But I missed the last flight that could have possibly connected to Savannah before this morning. I was in such a panic. I called the main line for the hospital a few times during the night, but nobody would tell me anything. It was horrible." She buries her face in her hands, sounding as though she's on the verge of breaking down in sobs.

"I'm sorry." Charlotte wishes she felt comfortable enough to just reach out and give Aimee a reassuring hug.

But it might not be welcome now that their initial, emotion-driven physical contact has been broken.

For all she knows, Aimee resents her father's second wife. She wouldn't be the first stepdaughter to feel that way. And she's certainly capable of resentment, considering that she refused to speak to her father for so long after her brother's death.

But when Aimee looks up at her again, Charlotte sees immediately that there's nothing but genuine concern in her gaze. Her eyes, Charlotte notices, are a beautiful shade of light green, not brown like Royce's. She must have inherited them from her mother.

Charlotte rarely gives Royce's first wife much thought, but for the second time in as many minutes, she finds herself wondering about her. Wondering if she's as beautiful as Aimee, if she has the same willowy build, fair hair, and tawny complexion . . .

"I need to get a hotel. Is there one near the hospital?" Aimee asks, cuting into Charlotte's thoughts.

"Not right here, no . . . But there's a beautiful Marriott right down on the River Walk, though. Your dad and I . . ."

Stayed there on our wedding night, before we left for Niagara Falls.

No, she shouldn't say that to Royce's daughter; it might

be insensitive, considering the romantic, intimate honey-moon images it evokes.

"Is it expensive?" Aimee asks a bit apprehensively, seeming not to notice Charlotte's unfinished sentence.

"Not very," she replies, and, seeing the look on the girl's face, quickly thinks better of it. Her idea of what's expensive is probably very different from that of a girl who just graduated nursing school and doesn't have a job yet. "But of course, we'll pay for your room, Aimee. And we'll reimburse you for your plane ticket."

"Oh, no, Charlotte, I wasn't hinting for y'all to—"

"I know you weren't hinting. But of course we'll pay for it. In fact, I can give you the money for the ticket right now," she offers somewhat awkwardly, reaching for her purse. For all she knows, Aimee spent her last dollar on the flight. "How much was it?'

"It wasn't much at all, and I can't let y'all do that. Really. I can afford it."

"It must have been a fortune at the last minute like that."

"It wasn't bad. Really. And I'm a big girl. Y'all don't have to pay for my room. Just . . . Maybe there's a Super 8 around, or something?"

"I'm . . . not sure. But we'll check."

I should just ask her to come back to Oakgate with me, Charlotte thinks. But with her cousins occupying the other guestrooms, where would Aimee even stay?

There's Grandaddy's room . . .

Charlotte hasn't ventured there since he died, but Nydia has been cleaning it regularly. And it isn't as though he was the type of man who collected clutter and had personal effects scattered about.

In fact, it's one of the few rooms in the house that re-mains free of framed photographs and other remnants of the past. Anyone glancing through the doorway might mistake it for a guest room: all it contains are a bed, a chair, and several bureaus and a nightstand whose tops contain only table lamps. Plus, there's a private bathroom.

But that's where Grandaddy died. Does it really feel right to turn it over to a stranger?

Not a stranger. My husband's daughter. My stepdaughter.

Unaware of Charlotte's inner turmoil, Aimee says, "Thank you so much again for calling me last night."

"Of course! Of course I would call you."

"I don't know . . . You didn't have to."

Before Charlotte can interject a protest, Aimee goes on, "But you did call. And I appreciate your thinking of me right away."

Charlotte hesitates, then, because she has to say *something*, tells Aimee, "You must know that I totally respect your relationship with your dad . . ."

She trails off, aware that this isn't the time or place for this conversation.

Never in her wildest dreams did she imagine that her first meeting with Aimee would be in a hospital waiting room, with Royce lying unconscious.

She always pictured flying with him to New Orleans; shaking hands with Aimee in the airport, or maybe even giving her a motherly, polite embrace. Then they would all go someplace for a nice dinner . . .

But it wasn't meant to happen that way.

Life is a series of accidents . . . some good, some bad . . .

And some, Charlotte can't help but think with trepidation, perhaps not accidents at all.

Lianna is sitting on the bottom step on the stairs in the front hall at Oakgate, willing the doorbell to ring, when a voice from above startles her.

"What on earth are you doing down there?"

She looks up to find Nydia peering down at her. "Geez, do you *have* to sneak up on people like that?"

The housekeeper narrows her eyes as she walks down the stairs, a can of furniture polish and a rag in her hand. "I wouldn't go around accusing other people of sneaking around, if I were you."

Lianna scowls. Obviously, nobody's business is private around here.

"Hey, isn't this your day off?" Lianna asks. When she got up at twelve thirty, she figured the housekeeper must have been long gone.

"Your mother asked me to stay. All this company in the house makes extra work."

Judging by the disdainful look on her face, Nydia doesn't appreciate that.

"Do you know where my mother and Royce went this morning?" Lianna asks, changing the subject.

Nydia stops to wipe something, probably a microscopic fleck of dust, on the wooden stair tread as she answers, "I haven't seen them. Why?"

"I just wondered, that's all. When I got up, they were already gone somewhere."

She waits for the inevitable comment about sleeping late. Not that Nydia has said anything about it in the past, but Lianna can tell by her usual attitude that she disapproves of anyone lying around in bed past noon.

"You still haven't told me why you're sitting here all dressed up," is all Nydia says.

Lianna is wearing the sundress Mom bought for her at the beginning of the summer, the one Lianna said was too fancy to wear.

She changed her mind when she tried it on. It made her look longer, leaner, more grown up.

More like Mom, in fact.

"My father's coming to see me," she informs Nydia.

"How do you know that?"

"He told me yesterday. He was supposed to try and come last night but he got hung up at the restaurant with some business clients."

What he said when he called her at Oakgate was that he had invited a couple of people to come to dinner with him since he didn't want to eat alone.

Of course he didn't. Who would blame him? If it weren't for Mom, he wouldn't have to, because Lianna would have been with him, instead of his having to eat with some stupid people who took their time over dinner, then wanted to go somewhere else after, for drinks.

"I just got back now, and it's getting late," he told Lianna, *"and I figure it won't make much sense now for me to drive all the way to the opposite end of the island just for a quick visit. So I'll come tomorrow, honey. At noon. I'll bring lunch. Okay?"*

She sneaks a glance at her watch and notes that Dad is now almost two hours late.

"I hope you don't think you're going out with him," Nydia tells her, "because your mother said—"

"Don't get all worked up. I'm not going out with him. He's just coming to see me and bring me some lunch." *And I wish he'd hurry up, because I'm starved.*

"That's nice," Nydia says, and looks like she wants to add something else.

But she doesn't, just steps around Lianna as she reaches the foot of the stairway.

Lianna sticks out her tongue at the housekeeper's back as she disappears toward the rear of the house, then immediately feels guilty. Nydia isn't that bad. She usually has very little to say, and keeps to herself. She can't help it if Mom makes her enforce the prison rules—and, most likely, regales her with tales of her daughter sneaking around with the local riffraff.

Resting her chin in her hand, Lianna stares at the door, wondering where her father is. Not that this is the first time he's ever been late. Not by a long shot.

But he usually calls to let her know he's on his way, at least.

Come on, Dad, Lianna sends a silent message. *I'm waiting. Where the heck are you?*

"Are you okay? You don't seem it."

"I'm fine, really." As Charlotte brushes away the desolate tears that trickle from her eyes, it's Aimee who reaches out with an almost maternal hand, patting Charlotte's shoulder.

"You know, I'm kind of surprised you're here all by yourself, Mrs. Maitland."

"Oh, you can call me Charlotte."

"I will. I thought you had a lot of family here."

"My grandfather passed away a few weeks ago."

"I know, and I'm so sorry—I should have said so sooner. I know how hard it is to lose somebody you love."

"Thank you. It is." Charlotte watches a cloud of sorrow cross Aimee's face. She's thinking about her kid brother, Theo.

"I have a daughter," she says quickly, to keep the conversation from venturing to a place she can't bear to go. Not right now. Not with all her emotions on edge.

"Her name is Lianna, right?"

"Yes. Lianna."

I once had a son, too—Adam.

"Where is she?"

"Back at home, probably still asleep."

"You didn't tell her about my father?"

"No, I don't want to wake her up with news like this, especially when I can't deliver it in person."

"Of course not," Aimee murmurs. "Poor thing. She's going to be upset when she finds out. I know Daddy is close to her. He talks about her a lot."

Charlotte marvels at Aimee's utter lack of resentment. It wouldn't be unnatural for Aimee to be jealous of Lianna, given the circumstances.

But she isn't.

She's a sweetheart, Charlotte concludes, giving her stepdaughter's hand a squeeze. Thank goodness.

"So you've been here all alone all night, just waiting, Mrs. Maitland?" Aimee asks sympathetically.

"It's Charlotte—please just call me Charlotte."

"Oh, I'm sorry—old habits never die. I was raised with old-fashioned Southern manners, I guess."

Charlotte smiles. "Me, too."

"So . . . You've been all alone here?" Aimee asks again.

All alone. God, yes.

"My cousins came earlier, but . . . They couldn't stay."

To their credit, both Phyllida and Gib were properly alarmed and concerned—and relieved to learn that Royce was out of immediate danger. They both asked a lot of questions and gave Charlotte an obligatory hug before departing, asking to be kept apprised of Royce's condition.

And they both wanted to know who could have done such a thing.

It's the same question Charlotte was repeatedly asked by Williamson and Dorado. She supposes a good detective has to be persistent . . .

But what if they were hoping she'd trip over her own words and implicate herself?

She remembers reading somewhere, long ago, that the primary suspect in any murder is the person's spouse. Royce is still alive, thank God, but the police would have to consider her a possible candidate—as a matter of routine, if nothing else.

The mere idea that she could shoot Royce is ridiculous . . . But then, the detectives don't know her. They aren't aware that she loves her husband more than anything in the world. They don't know that she would never, ever, harm him—that she has no reason whatsoever to do so.

But what if somebody did?

What if it wasn't a random shooting after all?

Try as she might, Charlotte can't shake the memory of whoever was hiding behind the crypt in Colonial Park Cemetery. If the gunman really was a sniper with no specific victim in mind, wouldn't he have chosen a more populated place to commit his act?

That stretch of Oglethorpe Avenue is mainly residential. At the hour of the night when Royce was shot, pedestrians were few and far between.

So why there?

Why then?

Why Royce?

Charlotte is almost looking forward to her next meeting with the detectives, though it won't be fun to sit through another session like the one she endured earlier.

Maybe Aimee will be here with me, she thinks hopefully.

Of course she will. Where else does she have to go? Unlike Gib and Phyllida, her main concern is for her father's well-being.

Relieved to be in the company of a kindred spirit, Charlotte lets out a deep, quavering breath.

"You know, everything is going to be okay," Aimee says. "I just really feel like he's going to be fine."

"I know he is . . . But why Royce? Why did this happen to him?"

"The police really don't know who did it?" Aimee asks again.

"No."

"Well, they're right about it probably being random . . . I know that for sure."

"How do you know?"

"Because Daddy didn't have an enemy in the world."

I wouldn't say that, Charlotte can't help thinking.

And I don't think Royce would, either.

It's no secret that Vince holds a grudge against his daughter's stepfather.

Still, for everything Vince is, Charlotte is fairly certain of what he *isn't*: a cold-blooded killer.

But Vince isn't the only one who isn't fond of Royce.

He has frequently mentioned how much his ex-wife hates him. He said it just the other night, when Charlotte told him she'd never encountered anyone who didn't like him.

That's because you haven't met Karen.

Could his ex possibly hate him enough to come here and gun him down?

Again, Charlotte thinks of the person she saw in the cemetery. She gave as thorough a description as she could to the investigators, which was a challenge, considering that she didn't see much.

As she told the detectives, all she knew for sure was that he was wearing dark clothes, and agile enough to be mistaken for a teenager.

In other words, it was no hulking, six-foot tall hit man . . .

Or woman.

After all, the shooter *could* have been a female.

Oh, come on, Charlotte. You're not really thinking Royce's ex-wife hates him enough to try to kill him, are you?

No. Of course not. It's just . . .

Well, as she learned in the bereavement group that literally saved her life, grief can do strange things to people. It can put ideas into their heads they might otherwise never have conceived—or seriously considered.

Why else would Charlotte have fantasized about taking her own life after her only son lost his? If it wasn't for Lianna, she would never have gone on.

Karen doesn't have a small child at home who needs her. Aimee just graduated from nursing school; she'll be out on her own from now on. And, more importantly, she's forgiven her father, forged a new bond with him.

How does Karen feel about that?

On Charlotte's best days, despite her best intentions to be adult about the situation, she can't help but resent Vince's relationship with Lianna.

She should be glad, perhaps, that her daughter doesn't see him for what he really is, but she isn't always. Not when she herself gets the brunt of Lianna's moodiness and has the sole responsibility for disciplining her, while Vince is the lone recipient of whatever shred of respect a troubled adolescent is capable of showing anyone.

Surely Karen has mixed feelings, at the very least, about Aimee welcoming Royce back into her life?

The door to the waiting room opens, and a nurse in green scrubs peers in. "Mrs. Maitland?"

"Yes?" Charlotte gets immediately to her feet, pulse racing.

"You can see your husband now. He's awake."

"Thank you." She practically flies across the room, and is halfway to the door before she remembers.

Aimee.

"This is his daughter," she tells the nurse, turning back. "Can she come, too?"

"Of course. But only one of y'all in the room at a time. The other can wait outside the door."

Aimee smiles gratefully at Charlotte, who grasps her hand tightly as the two of them hurry down the corridor after the nurse.

"You don't think she did it herself?" Phyllida asks her brother in disbelief, staring at him over the rim of her coffee cup.

"Shhh!" Gib looks around as if to make sure the other patrons of the Bull Street Café haven't overheard. "I didn't say *she* did it . . ."

Phyllida lowers her voice to a whisper. "You just said—"

"What I meant was that she could have hired somebody to do it."

"I can't think of anything more out of character than prim-and-proper Charlotte sneaking around interviewing hit men. Sometimes I think you're losing it, Gib."

"And sometimes *I* think that prim-and-proper thing she does is an act."

"I don't know . . . I think she was really shaken up by this," she tells Gib. "I felt sorry for her at the hospital."

"So did I," he admits. "Do you think one of us should have stayed with her for a while?"

So Gib suddenly has a conscience? Talk about out of character . . .

Phyllida watches him douse his scrambled eggs with another hefty dose of Louisiana hot sauce, then take a huge bite without wincing or washing it down with water.

She shakes her head and nibbles a green grape from her fruit plate, remembering that he always did like things hotter and spicier than anyone else could stomach. Their mother always said his taste buds just aren't wired to be as sensitive as most people's.

Phyllida sometimes wondered if the rest of him might not be wired that way as well. In that way, her brother reminds her of their grandfather. Nothing bothers him, really. Physically, emotionally . . .

Financially, yes, she acknowledges. Money, he cares about.

"Do *you* think we should have stayed at the hospital?" she asks him.

"I guess not. I don't think she really wanted us there."

"No, probably not." She spears a fat red strawberry with her fork before asking casually, "So where *were* you last night, anyway?"

His head jerks up. "How did I know you weren't going to let that drop?"

"Come on, Gib. You were out all night. Where did you go?"

"To an art gallery opening."

"Where?"

"In Savannah. On River Street. You want the address and a bunch of witnesses? Because I promise I can give you both."

Ignoring that, she asks, "You were there all night?"

"No. I hit a couple of bars after."

"Who were you with?"

"Nobody you know."

"So do the bars still close at three AM around here?" she asks.

He shrugs. "I wouldn't know. Maybe you should call City Hall and see if they do."

"I'm just wondering," she says succinctly, "where you were between three in the morning and when you came home to pick me up."

She bites into the strawberry, conscious of her brother's gaze on her.

"You actually think I had something to do with trying to bump off Charlotte's husband, don't you?" he asks flatly.

"Or course *I* don't think so, Gib. But I hope you have a good alibi. Because you know they're going to ask."

"The police?"

She nods.

"What about you?" he asks in return. "Where were you?"

"Where else? Stuck at Oakgate."

"Doing what?"

"Mostly watching TV in my room. And sleeping."

"You were there all night? You never left?"

"How could I leave? I don't even have a car. I had to wait for you to get home before I could even go to the hospital, remember?"

"You could have taken Grandaddy's Town Car out of the carriage house."

Phyllida sets down her fork, having lost her appetite. She forgot all about that.

"How would I even know where the keys were?" she asks Gib defensively.

"Nydia would have known."

"Oh, please. She goes to bed at eight o'clock."

"How do you know?"

"Because I tried to find her to see if she knows if there's an Internet connection on the computer in Grandaddy's study, and her door was closed. There was no light on in there. I could tell by the crack under the door."

"Why the computer? Trying to hack into the financial files?" Gib asks, looking momentarily amused.

"No, Brian took the laptop back with him and I wanted to read *Variety* online. I'll leave the financial hacking to you," she adds with a smirk.

"Don't kid about that. We might have to resort to it. So did anybody at Oakgate see you last night so they can vouch for you? Nydia? The kid?"

"No." This isn't good. The police might do some snooping around, find out about the will, and realize she or Gib would have had a pretty good motive to get rid of the Maitlands.

"I wonder if I can possibly get Nydia to say she saw me around the house," she muses aloud, then dismisses the idea with a flat, "Nah, I can't see her helping out of the goodness of her heart. She never liked me—or you, either. She thought we were the wild kids compared to Miss Perfect."

Gib doesn't argue with that.

"Maybe she won't help out of the goodness of her heart, Phyll," he says, "but she might if you give her some incentive."

"Like what?"

"What else? Cash."

"She never struck me as being the least bit materialistic," Phyllida points out.

"Yeah, well, maybe she's secretly longing for a mink coat."

"How much money are we talking about, here?" Phyllida asks.

"A lot. This is serious, Phyll. You need an airtight alibi as much as I do."

"Well, I can't imagine Nydia agreeing to lie to the police for anyone, at any price."

"You're probably right." Gib polishes off the rest of his eggs in a single gulp, then eyes the remains of her fruit plate. "Are you going to eat that?"

Wordlessly, she slides her plate across the table and wonders how he can possibly eat at a time like this. Her own stomach is in knots.

But then, that's Gib. She doubts he's ever missed a meal, or lost a moment's sleep, because of stress.

It must be nice to go through life that certain you're going to land on your feet. Somehow, Gib always does.

But the odds are that sooner or later, he's going to fall flat on his face.

Phyllida just hopes—for his sake, and her own—that time isn't upon him now.

"Royce? Royce . . . Are you awake?"

Drifting along through heavy fog on a delightful cushion of tranquility, he wonders, *Royce? Who's Royce?*

Then somebody shakes his arm, ever so gently, and the cloud of medication lifts enough for him to remember.

Me! I'm Royce.

And that's Charlotte's voice, calling me.

He opens his eyes to see his wife leaning over him, smiling tearfully. The light is so bright. Why is it so bright?

"Where . . . Where am I?" he murmurs, and tries to roll over, his effort halted by a fierce stab of pain in his leg. He goes still, trying to find his way back to the calming fog . . .

"You're in the hospital."

The hospital?

Why—? Oh!

A fleeting memory slams into him like a bullet, and his eyelids fly open again.

"Shot," he manages to say, and Charlotte nods.

She's been crying, he realizes. Her eyes are black with mascara smudges that track faintly toward her jaw.

"You're going to be fine, Royce . . . Are you in pain?"

"My . . . leg." He tries to move it again and winces.

"Does it hurt?"

Like hell.

She must have read his mind, because she says, "They've got you on some heavy stuff to relieve it. The nurse said it might make you confused and that you might not remember things at first."

He's silent, searching his muddled brain for details.

"Do you remember what happened, Royce?" Charlotte asks gently.

"I don't know . . . not . . . everything."

"They just upped the dose. It'll probably knock you out again. But that's good. You should just sleep."

He nods, searching his muddled memory for details, coming up with the right question. "Who . . . shot me?"

"They don't know. Whoever it was got away." She leans over to kiss his forehead. "I'm just glad you're okay, Royce. And there's somebody else here to see you. Aimee flew in from New Orleans this morning."

Aimee? New Orleans?

"Aimee!" he exclaims, as the light dawns. "Yes. Where is she?"

"I'll send her in." Charlotte brushes his cheek with the back of her fingers. "I'm so thankful you're okay, Royce."

"Yeah." He tries to shift position slightly, and grunts in pain. "My leg."

"I know. But the damage was repaired in surgery, and you're going to have full use of it again after you recover. You'll be playing tennis again in no time."

Tennis. Good. That's really good. He likes tennis, doesn't he? It's all so fuzzy . . .

"I'll go tell Aimee it's her turn," Charlotte says.

"Yes. Aimee."

"She's wonderful, Royce."

He smiles, relieved that the two women in his life have met and everything is apparently fine between them.

"Wish I could have been there to introduce y'all," he tells Charlotte.

"We did just fine on our own. And I'm going to ask her to stay with me at Oakgate. She had said she'd get a hotel, but . . . She's family."

This is more than he ever could have hoped for.

Feeling the tide of weariness sweeping toward him, he closes his eyes contentedly to wait for Aimee.

CHAPTER 10

"Nydia!" Lianna shouts, plunking the telephone receiver back into its cradle in her grandfather's study. "Nydia! Where are you?"

She hears footsteps pounding up the stairs and decides the housekeeper sure can move pretty fast for an old person.

"What? What is it?" Nydia asks breathlessly, bursting into the room.

"Did you take this telephone off the hook? I came in here to make a call and I found the receiver dangling on the floor."

The woman averts her gaze, telling Lianna that she correctly guessed the culprit.

"Why did you do this? My father has probably been trying to reach me!"

Silence, although Nydia looks directly at her now, and seems to be weighing some kind of decision.

"How long has it been off the hook?" Lianna demands.

"Since this morning," the woman confesses, without the decency to look the least bit apologetic. "And I did it because your mother asked me to."

Fury churns in Lianna's gut. How dare her mother go to such deliberate lengths to make it impossible for Dad to reach her?

That does it.

This is the last straw.

Lianna turns her back on the housekeeper and reaches for the phone again. She has to get ahold of her father. He must have been trying to call her all day to tell her why he hasn't shown up. Wait till he hears what Mom did. He's going to be livid.

Before she can pick up the receiver, the phone rings.

"Don't answer that!" Nydia says sharply.

"The hell I won't!" Lianna snatches it up with a breathless hello.

"Who is this?" an unfamiliar voice asks.

Disappointment courses through her as she answers, "It's Lianna."

"Lianna? Charlotte Maitland's daughter?"

"Yes."

"I'm calling from the *Chatham Gazette* for a comment on the shooting of your father last night, Miss Maitland."

A river of icy panic floods Lianna's veins. *"What?"* she shrieks. "Somebody shot Daddy? Oh, my God, is he—"

A pair of firm hands take hold of her shoulders from behind, and Nydia's stern voice commands her to hang up the phone. When Lianna is too frozen in panic to move, she grabs the receiver and does it herself.

Then she turns the whimpering Lianna around to face her.

"Look at me. It wasn't your father, Lianna . . . Do you understand me?"

It wasn't your father . . .

I'm calling from the Chatham Gazette *for a comment on the shooting of your father . . .*

Lianna stares up at Nydia, shaking her head in mute confusion.

"It was Mr. Maitland who was shot," Nydia tells her, and it falls into place.

Royce.

Royce was shot.

Royce . . .

"Did he die?" she manages to ask, forcing the words past the lump of dread rising in her throat.

"No, he was shot in the leg, and he's going to be just fine."

"Where's my mother?" Lianna asks shrilly, suddenly needing to feel her mother's arms around her, hear her reassuring voice. "What happened to my mother?"

"She's fine."

"Where is she!"

"Shhh, you'll frighten your aunt Jeanne. Your mother is still at the hospital with your—with Mr. Maitland."

Your father.

That's what she was about to say.

Even Nydia, who knows their domestic situation better than anyone, almost called Royce Lianna's father.

Why do people always do that?

Why don't they remember that she already *has* a father?

Bitter longing courses through her; longing for her dad, her mom . . . and Adam.

We were a family. A *real* family, all of us with the same last name, all of us living under one roof.

Doesn't anybody remember that but me? Doesn't anybody care?

"I need to call my father," she informs Nydia curtly. "And my mother, too. Which hospital is she at?"

"I don't know."

"Yes, you do. Y'all just don't want to tell me."

"Your mother asked me to protect you, Lianna." Nydia looks Lianna in the eye and rests staunch hands on her shoulders.

It isn't a hug—far from it. Lianna can't imagine this woman being capable of showing affection.

But she senses that the gesture is meant to comfort her.

And for some reason, it actually does.

"Mrs. Maitland didn't want the news to get to you before she did," Nydia tells her. "She wanted to let you know about it herself."

"When?"

"Whenever she gets home—I'm sure it'll be soon."

Never in her life has Lianna felt more alone.

"Can I call my father?" she asks in a small voice. "Please? He must have heard about this if reporters are calling, and he's going to be worried about me."

Nydia seems to mull that over. "Go ahead," she says reluctantly, releasing her hold on Lianna.

She dials the number hurriedly, wondering why, if he tried to call and repeatedly got a busy signal—or, more importantly, if he heard about the shooting—he hasn't shown up at Oakgate to check on her.

He must have a good reason, Lianna thinks.

He always does.

Mimi can't help but find it ironic that police headquarters is located on the corner of Habersham and Oglethorpe—just down the street from the spot where last night's shooting occurred.

In fact, she has to walk by the Maitlands' new home on her way there after leaving her car in a parking garage several blocks away.

No, you didn't have *to. You* wanted *to.*

All right. So she could have parked someplace else, or walked a different route.

She *wanted* to come this way; *needed* to see the crime scene, if only to make what happened last night—and her own involvement—a reality.

But she doesn't allow herself to stop and stare, like other curious onlookers milling around the sidewalk.

No, she keeps right on walking, allowing herself only a cursory glance at the tall frame house beyond its yellow crime scene tape.

She takes in the light green paint and dark green shutters with contrasting ochre trim, the looming mansard roof adorned with three arched dormer windows, the small pillared porch half a story above the sidewalk.

It was there, she knows, that Royce Maitland was gunned down.

Turning her head, she sees that the cemetery, too, is ringed in yellow tape. Several uniformed officers are visible among the tombstones, undoubtedly looking for clues to the shooter's identity, unaware that the person who holds the key is right here beyond the black iron fence.

Mimi takes one last look at the house. It's not as grand, by any means, as the Remingtons' plantation house on the northern end of the island. But it's an elegant home just the same, certainly suitable for one of Savannah's most prestigious families, and located in the heart of the city's most sought-after—and expensive—neighborhood.

She can't help noting as well that this house is a far cry from the Johnstons' modest Low Country cottage.

But that's home, and she doesn't have any regrets. Not about giving up college and Europe and marrying Jed and having Cameron, anyway.

If only she could take back some of the other decisions she's made in her life . . .

Specifically, decisions involving Gib Remington.

Then again, if she hadn't gotten involved with him all those years ago, she might have altered her destiny in every way. Some of them positive, but others too heart-wrenching to even imagine.

As a rule, she tries not to.

She tries to forget what happened between her and Gib, not just in high school, but that night on Achoco beach.

It's just that sometimes the past roars into the present like a tidal surge in a hurricane's wake, and it's impossible to escape its path.

Mimi quickens her pace, shoulders hunched and her hands buried deep in the pockets of her khaki pants.

"Where are you going?" Jed had asked drowsily, stirring on the couch when she'd looked in on him.

She gathered her thoughts quickly before answering, and hated herself for lying to him. But there was no other way. "I have to run to the store. Do you need anything?"

"Nothing you can buy at the store."

Those words pierced her heart.

"Do you want something to eat before I go?" she managed to ask.

"Eat? No. No way."

"Maybe just some Jell-O? Or broth?" He managed to keep both of those down yesterday, as far as she knows.

"No, thanks." He shifted his position on the cushion, wincing as he did so. "Where's Cam?"

"At my mother's. She offered to keep him for the day." That, at least, is the absolute truth.

Mimi has reached the intersection of Habersham and Oglethorpe at last. There's the precinct building, kitty-corner from the northeast perimeter of Colonial Park Cemetery.

She forces herself to cross the street and walk directly inside, knowing that if she falters for even a moment, she'll risk losing her nerve altogether.

Long shadows fall through Lianna's second-floor windows, but she doesn't bother to reach over and turn on the light. Huddled on her bed, her arms wrapped around her knees, she can't seem to do anything but sit here crying and feeling sorry for herself.

It isn't just because her mother seems to have abandoned her and her stepfather was shot by some lunatic.

Part of it is utter frustration that her father was so close by for an entire weekend, and she didn't even get to see him.

For that, she blames her mother, and Nydia, too. If the phone hadn't been off the hook for the better part of the day, Daddy would have been able to get through.

When she reached him on his cell phone, he was already back in Jacksonville. He told her he kept trying to call and tell her that he had gone out sailing earlier with some friends, and wouldn't be over until later, on his way home. When he got back from sailing and the phone was still busy, he left for home.

"You know how it is, with Sunday-night traffic on I-95, honey," he told Lianna, when she asked why he didn't just stop by, since he had to drive north to get to the causeway.

"I had to get moving or I never would have gotten back here. I have to work in the morning."

He was making excuses, she could tell by the way he sounded. He didn't drop by because he was afraid of what Mom would say if he did that.

"It's okay," she said, trying not to cry.

Especially when she told her father what happened to Royce.

He sounded shocked, and really upset. He asked her if she was okay about fifty times.

All right, so it was only a few times.

Her friend Devin called her, freaking out, about a minute after she hung up with her father.

"Oh my God, Lianna, are y'all okay? I've been trying to get you all day. I heard about Royce and I thought maybe something terrible happened to you, too!"

"No, just my stepfather . . . And he's okay. I mean, he will be."

"Is he, like, unconscious and all bloody and everything?"

Lianna was forced to admit that she hadn't even seen him, let alone talked to her mother, since it happened. Hearing that, Devin felt as sorry for her as she felt for herself.

"I can't believe your mother would totally leave you alone out there when some crazy lunatic is going around shooting at your family."

Lianna, who hadn't even thought of it that way, grew even more upset at her mother, who sure seemed to be taking her sweet old time coming home.

Seated beside his sister in the last row of the dark-ened movie theater, Gib stares unseeingly at the screen. This is their second movie in a row, and the summer's biggest blockbuster. But it could be a thrice-viewed 1980s B-flick for all the interest Gib has in the heroine's involvement in the assassination plot on-screen.

He has his own problems right now. Problems that, for all he knows, are escalating back at Oakgate even as he and Phyllida hide out at this multiplex off the interstate.

We aren't hiding out, he admonishes himself. *We're just . . .*

Lying low.

That's how he phrased it to his sister, when he outlined the plan for the evening, which included dinner at Chili's just off the exit—which turned out to be jammed—and will entail one more film after this one. By the time they return to Achoco Island, everyone in the household should be asleep.

There will be no accusatory stares or probing questions. No insinuations that Gib and Phyllida are anything but sympathetic about what happened to Charlotte's husband.

"Is that the guy who was in that car before?" Phyllida whispers, and it takes Gib a moment to realize she's talking about—and actually focused on—the movie. Leave it to the would-be queen of Hollywood.

"Yeah, that's him," he tells her, though he has no idea.

"But I thought he was the one who shot—"

"Shhh!"

Grateful to the annoyed patron behind them, Gib returns in peace to his own thoughts.

No, not in peace.

He's feeling anything but peaceful at the moment.

In fact, he had to force himself to stick to his own plan, rather than go rushing back to Oakgate to take care of unfinished business.

That, he keeps telling himself, can wait.

It's not as though anyone is likely to go searching his room.

And even if they did, they wouldn't find it.

Reassured, Gib finally helps himself to the tub of popcorn he bought earlier in the hope that he'd appear—to anyone who might happen to notice him, let alone recognize him as a Remington—for all the world like a relaxed moviegoer . . .

And not like the on-screen fugitive to whom he can suddenly, disturbingly, relate.

A bright swoop of approaching headlights reaches Jeanne's attic room before the sound of tires on crushed shells drifts through the open window.

She rolls over to see who it is, and is surprised to see two cars pulling up to the portico. One is the familiar white SUV; the other a sedan Jeanne doesn't recognize.

Charlotte climbs out from behind the wheel of the first; an unfamiliar woman—at least from this perch, with Jeanne's failing eyesight—emerges from the other.

Or maybe I do know her.

Jeanne squints into the twilight, searching her memory.

As happens with increasing frequency, the search yields nothing.

She isn't particularly surprised. This day has been more difficult than most. Perhaps if Melanie had been here . . .

But as fate would have it, Sundays are her days off. Jeanne has spent the day alone, without anyone to bring her meals. Gilbert or Charlotte always took care of that on Sundays.

One would think Nydia might have taken pity on

her, considering that her car has remained in the driveway all day. She, too, is usually off on Sundays; she may be unaware that Jeanne has been left here to starve.

But you would think she might have checked in, at least.

You would think she might have updated Jeanne on Royce's condition as she promised . . . and let her know whether there are any suspects yet in the shooting.

Through the screen, Jeanne watches the younger woman heave a large suitcase from the car trunk, with Charlotte rushing to help. Together, they pull it toward the house.

Just before they disappear from view, the sound of laughter floats up to Jeanne's ears.

Her mouth tightens with disapproval.

If they're laughing, she concludes, *then Royce Maitland must still be alive.*

At long last, Lianna's mother shows up, bursting into the room without even knocking, and rushing over to the bed.

"Lianna! Nydia said you know . . . Oh, sweetie, I've been trying to get back here to you all day, but I couldn't leave Royce."

Unexpectedly overcome by a wave of emotion that sweeps the anger away, Lianna allows herself to be hugged fiercely. Her mother rocks her back and forth, crying into her hair.

What a relief. A relief to have Mom back here with her, a relief to feel Mom's arms around her.

She hasn't hugged me in so long, Lianna realizes, with tears streaming from her own eyes. *She hasn't been nice to me in so, so long . . .*

"Is he okay, Mom? Is Royce all right?"

"He will be . . ."

"Who did this to him?"

"Nobody knows . . . The police say it was random."

Mom releases her, takes a deep breath and lets it out, then plucks a couple of Kleenex from the box on Lianna's nightstand. She hands one to Lianna, who wipes her eyes as her mother does the same.

Lianna crumples the tissue and turns to pitch it into the wastebasket across the room.

That's when she sees the stranger standing in the doorway.

"Hi, Lianna." The woman waves.

She knows me. Who the heck is she, and why does she know me?

"Oh, Aimee . . . I'm sorry, come on in. I guess I lost my composure when I saw my baby girl there for a second. Lianna, this is Aimee."

Aimee? Who the heck is Aimee?

Mom is acting like she should know, and so is the stranger, who crosses right over to the bed and reaches down to give her a hug.

Lianna stiffens.

Confused, she looks up at her mother.

"I told Aimee she should stay here with us," Mom says—as if that explains everything.

"Yes, and y'all have no idea how grateful I am, Mrs. Maitland."

Wow, Aimee's accent is really thick.

"I keep telling you," Lianna's mother says with a good-natured laugh. "It's Charlotte. If you don't figure that out soon, your wicked stepmother is going to insist on being called Mom."

Aimee laughs, too.

Zebra Contemporary

Whatever your taste in contemporary romance — Romantic Suspense... Character-Driven... Light & Whimsical... Heartwarming... Humorous — we have it at Zebra!

And now Zebra has created a Book Club for readers like yourself who enjoy fine Contemporary Romance written by today's best-selling authors.

Authors like Fern Michaels... Lori Foster... Janet Dailey... Lisa Jackson...Janelle Taylor... Kasey Michaels... Shannon Drake... Kat Martin... to name but a few!

These are the finest contemporary romances available anywhere today!

But don't take our word for it! Accept our gift of FREE Zebra Contemporary Romances — and see for yourself. You only pay $1.99 for shipping and handling.

Once you've read them, we're sure you'll want to continue receiving the newest Zebra Contemporaries as soon as they're published each month! And you can by becoming a member of the Zebra Contemporary Romance Book Club!

As a member of Zebra Contemporary Romance Book Club,

- You'll receive four books every month. Each book will be by one of Zebra's best-selling authors.

- You'll have variety — you'll never receive two of the same kind of story in one month.

- You'll get your books hot off the press, usually before they appear in bookstores.

- You'll ALWAYS save up to 30% off the cover price.

SEND FOR YOUR FREE BOOKS TODAY!

To start your membership, simply complete and return the Free Book Certificate. You'll receive your Introductory Shipment of FREE Zebra Contemporary Romances, you only pay $1.99 for shipping and handling. Then, each month you will receive the 4 newest Zebra Contemporary Romances. Each shipment will be yours to examine FREE for 10 days. If you decide to keep the books, you'll pay the preferred subscriber price (a savings of up to 30% off the cover price), plus shipping and handling. If you want us to stop sending books, just say the word... it's that simple.

THE BENEFITS OF BOOK CLUB MEMBERSHIP

• You'll get your books hot off the press, usually before they appear in bookstores.

• You'll ALWAYS save up to 30% off the cover price.

• You'll get our FREE monthly newsletter filled with author interviews, book previews, special offers and MORE!

• There's no obligation — you can cancel at any time and you have no minimum number of books to buy.

• And — if you decide you don't like the books you receive, you can return them. (You always have ten days to decide.)

Be sure to visit our website at www.kensingtonbooks.com.

Zebra Contemporary Romance Book Club
Zebra Home Subscription Service, Inc.
P.O. Box 5214
Clifton NJ 07015-5214

PLACE
STAMP
HERE

Huh? Wicked stepmother? Who's that?

"I'll find Nydia so she can help you get settled down the hall," Charlotte says.

"Are y'all sure it's no trouble?"

"Positive. Royce is so glad you're staying here—and so are we."

We? As in Lianna?

Who the heck—

Oh. It hits her, then, and she realizes who this Aimee is.

She's Royce's daughter.

Mom must have called her.

She called her, but she didn't call me.

"When did you get here?" she asks, trying to sound friendly.

"First thing this morning. I had to fly in from N'Awlins, where I live."

It takes a moment for Lianna to decipher that—at least, most of it.

"From *where?*" she asks.

"N'Awlins."

"New Orleans," Mom clarifies with a laugh. "And you must be exhausted, Aimee. I know you didn't sleep any more than I did last night, and you spent the whole day with me at the hospital."

Lianna looks at the newcomer, further resenting her. Not just for the obvious closeness between the two of them after a day spent together, and a shared tragedy.

But also for her looks. Aimee is as beautiful as Mom is, with same kind of long, thick hair—except hers is golden—and the same perfect figure.

Lianna is conscious that her own hair is matted to her head—thanks to Mom and her sloppy tears—and that she's still wearing the ratty T-shirt she threw on when she found out Dad wouldn't be coming. Her beautiful sundress lies in a heap somewhere on the floor at the foot of her bed.

But Mom didn't say anything about that, or about the general mess in the room she told Lianna to clean yesterday.

Naturally, Lianna forgot about that until just now.

"Aimee is a nurse," Mom informs Lianna, as if that matters in the least.

"I started out as a hairdresser," Aimee says wryly, "but then I got caught up in an awful hurricane, and I realized what really matters. So now I can save people's lives, instead of just fixing their hair."

Lianna's hand goes instinctively to her own head, even as she notices that Mom is looking at Aimee as though she's some kind of superhero.

"Have you eaten dinner, Lianna?" Mom asks, patting her hand, then her head, like she's a very young child, or a cute pet. Or maybe she's just trying to fix Lianna's hair without Aimee noticing.

"No," she says glumly.

I haven't eaten lunch, either.

She thinks longingly of her father.

Daddy, I wish you were here.

I wish you were here, and this Aimee person wasn't.

"I'm going to ask Nydia if she can make something for the three of us while I go take a shower and get cleaned up," Mom says, getting up off the bed.

The three of us?

Does *she* have to eat with them, too?

"I'm really not hungry," Lianna says, folding her arms across her chest.

"I'm not either, but we have to eat," Mom tells her.

"And you can get to know Aimee. You always said you wanted a sister."

"I never said that."

Mom gives her a look that says *don't be rude.* Now she looks more like her usual self—the self she's been lately, anyway.

Lianna feels more like her usual self when she insists, feeling ornery, "Well, I didn't."

"You did. Maybe you don't remember." Mom laughs the nervous laugh she does whenever Lianna is embarrassing her in front of someone. "When you were little, it's all you used to talk about. You wanted me and your father to have another baby, a girl, so that you could have a sister."

"I don't remember that."

No, all I remember is wanting my big brother back.

Lianna looks away, toward the collection of antique dolls that line a bookshelf, and blinks annoying tears out of eyes.

But her mother is reaching out to touch her chin, forcing her to turn her head back.

"What?" she asks, humiliated to be caught crying, especially in front of an outsider.

To her credit, Aimee has drifted closer to the door again, and seems to be caught up in examining the fringed shade of an old lamp.

"Come on downstairs for dinner," her mother says in that kind tone again. "I want to spend some time with you. I've missed you all day."

I've missed you, too, Lianna thinks sadly. *And for a whole lot longer than just a day.*

The police station is bustling on this summer Sunday evening.

Mimi waits to speak to the jolly-looking desk sergeant, meanwhile nibbling her lower lip so fiercely she tastes blood.

Finally, it's her turn. She gives her name, feeling as though she's going to faint any second.

"How can we help you, Mrs. Johnston?"

"I need to speak to, um, somebody. About a case."

"About a report you filed?"

"No . . ."

He waits. Beneath brows raised in obvious question, his eyes are kind.

Nonetheless, she's paralyzed with fear, barely able to draw a breath.

This is it.

If she reveals anything to the police, she'll officially be involved. She doesn't need this complication in her life. Not right now.

But what else can she do?

Run out of here?

What if the sergeant comes after her, demanding that she talk?

Come on. That won't happen.

He doesn't even know which case I mean.

All right, so she can probably get away, if she flees the station right now, and nobody will ever be the wiser.

But how will she be able to live with herself?

You won't.

Besides, don't you remember what he did to you?

Don't you remember that day in the dormitory at Tellfair Academy?

Yes.

She remembers.

Sorry, Gib, she thinks now, steeling her nerve, *payback can be a real bitch . . .*

And so can I.

She leans toward the officer and confides, "I have some information about the shooting last night on Oglethorpe Avenue."

"Goodness, I'm so smart to have thought of picking up this hand truck at Home Depot the other day, don't you think? Oh, I forgot . . . you can't say anything. For a change. Well, silence is golden, as Mama used to say. Shoo!"

Another pesky insect is buzzing around the corpse lashed to the hand truck as the tires become bogged down, once again, in mud.

"Shoo . . . go away."

It takes a good five minutes to free the cart and its grisly cargo. The process entails repeatedly swatting at insects and juggling the flashlight from hand to hand, accidentally dropping it, several times, into the muck.

At last, the cart is on its way again, following the now-familiar path through the marsh, well lit by the flash-light's glare.

The brick cabin isn't all that far from the main house, really—but it remains as much a world away now as it did back in slavery times. God forbid the Remingtons find it necessary to associate with the household help.

"Here we are, home sweet home . . . what do you think? Oh, I keep forgetting . . . you can't tell me what you think anymore. Well, that's a darned shame but I have to say it was inevitable."

The handcart drops with a thud beside the old brick

doorstep. The flashlight's beam pivots wildly over the darkened landscape, the flashlight itself clenched ear to shoulder, leaving both hands free to work the padlock.

"Yoo-hoo, ladies, I've brought a visitor, just like I promised."

At that, the corpse is cut loose from the hand truck and dragged over the threshold.

Rigor mortis has set in; it takes quite a bit of effort to get it propped just right in the place of honor at the small table, positioned between the redheaded doll and the brunette. The blond doll sits across, seeming to stare at the newcomer, whose wide green eyes are frozen in an expression of eternal horror.

"It's like looking into a mirror, isn't it Pammy Sue? Oh, wait . . . there are two Pammy Sues now. And isn't it ironic? Neither of you can say a word!"

Laughter fills the old cabin.

But with it drifts the echo of a long ago voice. Mama's voice, scolding.

You naughty, naughty child. What have you done?

But Mama isn't here. She can't be here. Mama is dead.

The flashlight's beam bounces around wildly, revealing one reassuringly empty corner after another.

"See? Nobody here but me. And you, Pammy Sue. One, two, Pammy Sues."

Another wave of hysterical laughter.

Then the flashlight bounces from the redheaded doll to the brunette. "Oh, no, I didn't forget. You're both here, too. Now we can have our little doll tea party. Just like old times."

The tea set, delivered to the cabin on an earlier trip, is retrieved from its shopping bag and lain out on the table. It's the one that was purchased two decades ago at the Pigeon Creek five and dime, an extravagant birthday gift for Pammy Sue.

Those familiar green eyes seem to be following the action with unnerving intensity, almost as though they recognize the childhood relic.

But that's ridiculous, of course. They aren't really watching.

Pammy Sue is dead. She can't see any more than she can speak.

Which is why I get to do all the talking from now on. And that's just fine with me.

"Oh, look . . . one of the cups is chipped. How on earth can that have happened? Oh, wait, I remember!"

Yes, it happened on Pammy Sue's birthday, when she left the room to get her favorite doll, leaving the tea set spread out on the kitchen table. It was so pretty, the white china sprigged with little pink roses. It must have been expensive.

I never got such an expensive, beautiful birthday gift in my life. Not in that *life, anyway.*

That was why it was so tempting, that day—Pammy Sue's birthday—to snatch the nearest cup. It was hurtled to the floor in a sudden burst of rage, so hard that it should have smashed into tiny shards.

But it didn't. It hit the edge of the thick braided rag rug and bounced gently onto the linoleum.

Only a sliver of porcelain splintered off the rim, so slight a break that Pammy Sue didn't even notice it when she came back into the room with her doll.

And when she finally did see the chipped spot, days later, she thought she must have done it herself somehow.

Stupid, stupid girl.

"Here you go." The chipped cup is placed in front of the corpse. "You won't mind. You probably won't even notice."

What fun this is. Just like old times.

"All right, now, we'll have to pretend there's tea in the cups." The little china spout is positioned over each of the four rims and the pot is tilted as if to dispense its steaming beverage. "And we'll pretend there are cookies on the plates, too . . . what's that, Pammy Sue? You don't like to pretend?"

Silence.

Of course.

Because Pammy Sue can't speak.

And she can't see.

Really, she can't.

But I can't help it. I need to make sure . . .

Rage sweeps in, the same as it did on Pammy Sue's long ago birthday. This time, it's a little silver teaspoon that is snatched abruptly from the table.

Then the corpse is grabbed roughly by its blond hair, now matted with coagulated blood.

The edge of the spoon is jammed into the socket beneath Pammy Sue's motionless right eye. It gouges mercilessly, in a seemingly futile effort until suddenly, the eyeball is severed.

Ah, there.

The gory orb plops, oozing, onto a small china plate. Its counterpart follows after another brief struggle with the spoon.

Then the corpse is returned to its position and the plate is set in the middle of the table like a gruesome centerpiece.

"There . . . I'm afraid we're all out of cookies, but

here's a delicious treat just for you, Pammy Sue. Go ahead, dig in. I'm sure you won't mind if I don't stay . . . I've got to be going now, before somebody misses me. But I'll be back soon for another visit. I promise."

CHAPTER 11

First thing Monday morning, Charlotte finds herself facing Detectives Williamson and Dorado once again.

But this time, it's on her turf: in the second of the double parlors at Oakgate, with the doors closed.

And this time, Aimee is at her side.

When the detectives showed up unannounced, Charlotte was just about to leave for the hospital with her stepdaughter.

They initially asked to speak to Charlotte in private. She quickly spoke up and told them she would feel more comfortable with her stepdaughter there.

"Aimee should hear anything y'all have to say—Royce is her father. She flew in yesterday from New Orleans and she's as concerned as I am."

To her relief, and frankly, her surprise, even Williamson didn't oppose her request.

"Do you know who did this?" Charlotte asks the moment they're all seated—on a cluster of circle-backed nineteenth-century chairs upholstered in yellow silk;

Williamson's ample girth overflowing beneath the wooden arms on either side of his.

"Not yet." He doesn't elaborate.

Frustrated, Charlotte snaps, "Well, what did you find out?"

And why are you here? Don't you realize that I have to get back to my husband's bedside?

Dorado takes over. "Mrs. Maitland—and Miss Maitland, is it?" At Aimee's nod, the detective goes on, "Have y'all been here all night?"

"Ever since we left the hospital at around seven," Charlotte tells him, bristling at the question. Surely he doesn't consider her a suspect at this point, does he?

"Can you just tell us what you did here, and who all was in the house?"

Suppressing a sigh, Charlotte recounts the evening step-by-step: she talked to her daughter, spoke to the housekeeper about dinner, then took a shower while Aimee settled into Grandaddy's room with Nydia's assistance . . .

"Nydia? She's the housekeeper who let us in just now?" Williamson interrupts, jotting something on his pad. "The one you mentioned yesterday when we asked who was living in the house?"

"Yes."

"We'll want to talk to her."

"Fine, but I don't know what she can possibly tell y'all."

Keeping her gaze focused on the pair of antique andirons at the far end of the room so that she won't have to look at Williamson, Charlotte goes on with her account of last night. She fails to mention that Nydia was silently disapproving when Charlotte asked her to put fresh sheets on the bed; clearly, she doesn't think anybody should be moving into the room so soon after Grandaddy's death.

Charlotte still isn't so certain about it herself, but she made the offer spontaneously, and Aimee is grateful for a place to stay.

Anyway, Nydia seemed to get over it pretty quickly, because she cooked them a hot meal. But they were too exhausted to touch it. They all went to bed early.

"Was anybody else here?"

"Just my great-aunt up on the third floor. She has a visiting nurse during the day, but not at night."

"What about your cousins? Were they here?"

"Not when we went to bed, no."

"Where were they?"

"I don't know. Gib's rental car wasn't here and I'm pretty sure they were both out."

"Pretty sure?"

"They keep to themselves, Detective. And they don't live here; they're houseguests."

"I realize that. I'm just trying to figure out whether they were here or out when y'all got back last night."

"Out. When I asked Nydia about them, she said she hadn't seen either of them since yesterday morning."

"What about this morning?"

"You'll have to ask her. I haven't seen them. Gib's rental car is parked out there now, though."

"All right." Dorado seems to be finished taking notes. He looks up at Williamson, who gives a slight nod, cue-ing his partner to say, "We've turned up a couple of in-teresting things in our investigation of the cemetery."

It's Charlotte and Aimee's turn to exchange a glance.

"We found footprints in the mud in a number of spots, which we think belonged to the shooter," Dorado announces.

"Men's shoes?" Charlotte asks, and holds her breath for the answer.

"Yes."

All right. So it couldn't have been Karen.

Of course it wasn't Karen!

Right. She knew that all along, really.

She just couldn't help getting paranoid earlier, thinking about the people in Royce's life who might have a vendetta against him.

But Karen isn't any more likely to have shot him than Vince is. Or so she tried to convince herself last night, when Lianna told her that he was supposed to have visited Saturday night, but didn't—and couldn't be reached.

That isn't unusual. It wasn't the first time Vince had failed their daughter. Nor should it make Charlotte wonder if he really was where he claimed to be, dining on Achoco Island.

But she isn't about to bring up his name or voice her suspicion, however slight, to the police.

Not yet, anyway.

Dorado goes on, "The soles in the footprints we found indicate that these were men's dress shoes."

"Dress shoes?" Charlotte echoes, frowning.

That doesn't fit her image of an anonymous sniper at all.

It's Aimee who asks Dorado, "What do y'all think that means?"

"We're looking into it."

"So you don't have a suspect in mind yet?" Charlotte asks. "That's all you have to go on? Footprints?"

Again, the two men exchange a glance.

"We did find something else, a few yards away from where the shooter was standing." Williamson reaches into his pocket and takes out a small envelope.

He opens it, removes a small object, and holds it out in the palm of his hand.

"Do either of you recognize this?"

Aimee, seated closer to him, leans over, then immediately shakes her head. "No."

Williamson swoops his hand forward, bringing it to rest directly in front of Charlotte. "How about you, Mrs. Maitland?"

She gazes in disbelief at the heirloom platinum cuff-link emblazoned with the initials *GXR.*

"Yes, may I please speak to a Dr. Petra Von Cave?" Mimi asks the person who's come on the line at last, after a lengthy wait while the foreign receptionist apparently scrambled to find someone who speaks English.

"Dr. Von Cave has left for the day," the voice tells her in a thick accent, and Mimi is taken aback until she remembers that it's already midafternoon overseas.

Still, you'd think a world-renowned scientist would at least stick around the office—or is it a lab?—until five or six.

"May I ask who's calling?"

"Maybe y'all can just tell me where I can reach her?" she asks, remembering to keep her voice low.

Jed is asleep in the bedroom, and Cameron is completely absorbed in a *Bob the Builder* video—a gift from his grandmother—in the living room.

"I'm afraid I can't do that. Who is this, please?"

Mimi hesitates. "I'll . . . I'll call her back, if y'all will just tell me when I would be likely to find her at this number."

"That's hard to say. You might try her tomorrow, but

Dr. Von Cave can be difficult to reach. Are you certain you wouldn't like me to take a message?"

"No, that's all right."

Mimi hangs up, frustrated.

What message could she possibly leave?

My name is Mimi and I live in America and I need you to save my dying husband out of the goodness of your heart.

She'd have a better chance if she knocked on the door of Trump World Tower and asked The Donald if he can spare a few million.

Still, she'll try again later. And tomorrow. For as long as she has to.

Because now that Gib will be behind bars, her only option is to give up and helplessly watch Jed waste away in agony.

Damn you, Gib.

How could you?

Restless, she paces the length of the small kitchen, then back again, and returns to refill her coffee cup. God knows she needs the jolt after yet another sleepless night.

She did the right thing, telling the police what Gib said . . .

Didn't she?

It's not as if she has any proof that he's the one who shot Royce.

Still, after what he said Saturday morning when they met on that bench in the square, after she asked—no, shamelessly *begged*—him to help her . . .

"I'd love to loan you some money, Mimi, and it's for such a good cause. But I just don't have it."

He was lying.

That's what she thought at the time, anyway. She thought he *had* to have money. He's a Remington, for God's sake.

"My trust fund is ancient history, I've got student loans, credit cards, borrowing against future earnings—all that, and nothing coming in."

"What do you mean?"

"I don't have a job yet," he claimed.

She should have stopped right there, but she couldn't. Not with Jed's life hanging in the balance, and money being the only way to save him.

She had to go and bring up the fact that Gib's grandfather had just died.

Well, who wouldn't assume he had inherited millions from the old man?

"No, he left everything to my cousin Charlotte," Gib informed her, so venomously that she realized he had to be telling the truth.

There was no mistaking the authenticity of that vengeful glare in his eyes as he went on, "So it looks like I'll be a pauper for at least a while longer, until Phyllida and I are successful in contesting the will—unless something god-awful happens to Charlotte and her husband and kid."

He said it carelessly, or so she thought, tossing the words from his tongue as easily as he asked her, in the next breath, if she was sure she didn't want to join him that evening for a night on the town.

"I'm married, Gib," she pointed out. "Remember?"

"Oh, yeah," he said flatly, in a tone that told her he hadn't forgotten, even for a moment. Far be it from Gib Remington to let a little thing like another man—or a wedding ring—stop him from making a move.

She couldn't help but be reminded of that awful day back in high school, when she let herself into his dormitory room to find a live tableau of the world's oldest boarding school cliché: there was Gib, in bed with Miss Lucas, the blond, buxom young English teacher.

Mimi's favorite teacher, in fact, and the one who helped her fill out all those essays on her scholarship-application forms.

To her credit, Miss Lucas was mortified.

To Mimi's utter disgust, Gib was not.

No, he had the nerve to be vexed that she had invaded his privacy and used her key—the key *he* had pressed on her just weeks earlier, when he hinted that it would be a nice birthday surprise if he came back from physics class and found her waiting for him, naked, in his bed.

So much for physics class.

So much for Miss Lucas being Mimi's favorite teacher.

And so much for Mimi being Gib Remington's girl-friend.

She vowed then that she would never speak to him again.

And she kept that vow . . .

Until that the day on the beach.

The day that forever altered the course of her life—just as Gib Remington's eighteenth birthday had years earlier and the Magnolia Clinic would years later.

"Why would Gib shoot Royce?" Charlotte asks in dis-belief, still trying to absorb what the detectives have inferred these last few minutes, after she told them that the cufflinks belonged to her grandfather, and were bequeathed to Gib.

But if Gib did take them, there's no telling when, and that would mean that he helped himself from Gran-daddy's jewelry box. At least, that's where the cufflinks were the last time Charlotte saw them, along with his prized gold watch, on the day her grandfather died—

when she was gathering it and the burial suit he had chosen long ago.

"Could money have been a motive?" Williamson suggests. "It often is."

Seeing her cousin in a whole new light, Charlotte pushes aside a renewed rush of speculation over why Grandaddy might have disinherited Gib and Phyllida.

"Royce doesn't have money," she tells Williamson. "He runs a computer-consulting business."

"And he's married to you."

She shrugs. "Why him, then? Why not me?"

For a moment, the only sound is the chirping of birds beyond the tall screened windows, and the hum of the paddle fan as it turns overhead, failing to stir the sultry morning air.

Then Dorado says, "We aren't entirely sure that your husband was the shooter's intended target, Mrs. Maitland."

With a sigh, Mimi remembers her coffee, growing cold in her hand.

She shoves the cup into the microwave and presses REHEAT, with a silent pledge to put Gib out of her thoughts for the remainder of the day.

Her regret that she had even approached him in the first place mingles now with relief that she wasn't forced to take things a step further.

She had been prepared to do whatever she had to, if it meant she'd have a way to get the money from Gib.

But in the end, that wasn't necessary.

Gib might have revealed *his* shocking little secret— his own unlikely poverty—but hers is still safe.

Yes, but at what cost?

Shaking her head as if to rid it of that distressing thought, Mimi opens the refrigerator to look for the half-and-half.

Staring unseeingly at the contents of the fridge, she reminds herself it wasn't meant to be. She wasn't meant to tell. And now, she knows she never will.

But what about Jed? How can I help him now?

Sorrow, swift and raw, settles over her once again.

At least she did the right thing, going to the police. If Gib had anything to do with the attack on his brother-in-law . . .

"Unless something god-awful happens to Charlotte and her husband . . ."

Mimi shakes her head.

Why did you have to go and say that, Gib?

Amazing that there's still a part of her that wants to protect him, even after all the lousy things he did to her.

She should be remembering being disgraced that day in his dormitory. She should be thinking payback is a bitch.

But she isn't.

She only feels sad for him.

That's because he's an expert manipulator. He knows just how to get what he wants.

Don't I know it.

There's another part of her, thank goodness, that doesn't give a damn about Gib Remington anymore. Yes, and she'd just as soon see him thrown in jail if he really did take a shot at Charlotte and her husband Saturday night.

If he didn't, the police will figure out his innocence quickly enough.

Detective Williamson certainly was grateful for her

information. He was no teddy bear, but he did shake
her hand warmly and thank her for coming forward.

So she did do the right thing.

Definitely.

Realizing that the microwave is beeping, she grabs
the half-and-half. The cardboard carton is weightless
when she lifts it from the shelf; she realizes it's all but
empty.

Terrific. They're out of everything. Milk, bread,
eggs . . .

I have to buy food, she thinks dully. *And I have to pick up
Jed's prescriptions from the pharmacy, and drop off Cam's library books and duck out before I have to pay a fine we can't
afford, and pay the electric bill . . .*

Life goes on.

It has a way of doing that.

It did after Daddy died.

It is now, with Jed so sick.

And it will even if something happens to him.

For the first time, Mimi allows herself to imagine life
without her husband.

What will happen to me and Cam?

Who will love us?

She sinks into a chair, buries her head in her arms,
and cries at last, long and hard.

"Y'all mean, Gib might have been aiming for Charlotte?" Aimee rests a reassuring hand on Charlotte's
trembling arm as she sits in silence, shaken by Dorado's
ominous theory.

"There's no way of knowing exactly where the
shooter was aiming."

Charlotte notices that Detective Williamson is careful not to implicate Gib directly. Of course not, because there's no way he can actually be a suspect in this. That's crazy.

Gib, with all his swagger, isn't her favorite person in the world, nor, to be honest, is he the most upstanding citizen she can think of. But that doesn't mean he would try to kill his own flesh and blood over money.

There has to be some other reason—a logical reason everybody's overlooking—for the cufflink to have turned up in the graveyard.

As she told the detectives, for all she knew, Gib didn't even have them in his possession yet. He certainly hadn't asked her about them, so unless he did take it upon himself to go through Grandaddy's things and help himself . . .

The thing is, it isn't all that difficult to imagine her cousin doing just that. Especially since the two of them haven't exactly been on speaking terms.

And . . .

Well, Grandaddy had some reason for writing him out of the will. What if it was because he thought Gib was . . . dangerous?

It seems ludicrous.

It is ludicrous, she assures herself. *Whatever Grandaddy's reason for doing what he did, Gib being some kind of threat wasn't it.*

"All right," she tells the detectives, "then, if I was the real target, why didn't he just finish the job? Why not gun down both of us, and shoot until we were dead?"

"Who knows? That's easier said than done. Especially from that distance, unless the shooter were an expert marksman . . . which by all accounts, the suspect is not."

"But why not just keep shooting until he hit something?"

"Maybe the barrel jammed. Maybe there was no more ammunition," Williamson says. "Maybe he realized he misjudged the distance after he started and that he'd have to be at a closer vantage point to finish."

"Right," Dorado puts in, "or maybe he was spooked by the first shot, or when he saw Royce fall and realized he'd missed, or when it hit him that he was trying to take a human life. The truth is, Ms. Remington, if you're dealing with an amateur, and not a professional hit man, things are bound to get messy."

"It's Mrs. Maitland," she says wearily.

"I'm sorry."

Dorado's tone is sincere, and Charlotte gets the impression that he, at least, is sorry about a lot more than using the wrong name.

It's Williamson who rubs her the wrong way; Williamson whose bemused expression rankles.

"I honestly don't think my own cousin would try to hurt me," she says firmly, mostly to him. "I mean, why would he?"

"Charlotte, you said yourself that he seemed really angry when he found out about the money," Aimee points out gently, and Charlotte's heart sinks.

She shouldn't have said anything to Aimee about that. But during the long drive back from the hospital last night, she found herself baring her soul to her stepdaughter about her loss, her cousins, the will . . . even her troubles with Lianna.

Naturally, both detectives are all ears now, asking questions.

"He's angry at you? Why?" That's Williamson, practically growling at her. "And why didn't you mention this until now?"

Dorado, his brown eyes focused unwaveringly on Charlotte, chimes in to ask, "What money are we talking about?"

Reluctantly, she tells them about her grandfather's will. She does her best to be brief, but they're asking countless questions and taking notes.

In the end, she's forced to admit that she has no idea why her grandfather cut out her cousins and that the will is most likely to be contested by both of them.

That clinches it. Charlotte can see the decision in their eyes before she's ended with a trite-sounding, "But none of that has anything to do with Royce being shot."

The detectives have obviously concluded that it does.

"Where are your cousins now, Ms. Remington?"

"It's Mrs. Maitland," she bites out through a clenched jaw, "and I have no idea where they are. Probably upstairs, still asleep."

"Really." Williamson looks at Dorado. "Let's wake them, shall we?"

"Lianna? Are you in there?"

She sits up in bed, rubbing the sleep from her eyes, trying to place the unfamiliar voice on the other side of her door.

"Lianna? Can I come in?"

Oh. It's Aimee, Royce's daughter, and, technically, her stepsister.

But as far as Lianna is concerned, she's a total stranger. A stranger who was with her mother all day yesterday, while Lianna was stuck here all alone.

I don't like her, Lianna decides. *Who cares if she tried so hard to be nice to me last night at dinner?*

Lianna can tell Aimee is a total brownnoser. But Mom can't see that, so no wonder she's crazy about Aimee. She seems like the perfect daughter.

Unlike me.

"I'm sorry. Were you sleeping?"

"Ye-ah," Lianna intones to show her annoyance. "I like to sleep late in the summer."

"Actually, it isn't that late," Aimee says apologetically.

Lianna sneaks a peek at her bedside clock and is surprised to see that it isn't. What the heck is Aimee doing waking her up at eight thirty in the morning?

"Your mom asked me to take you over to one of your friend's houses."

Okay, that's even crazier.

She opens her mouth to inform Aimee that she's grounded, but thinks better of it. Maybe Mom forgot about that, considering everything that's gone on.

Instead, she asks Aimee, "Which friend's house?"

"She said it was up to you. I'm on my way to the hospital in Savannah, and she told me to tell you to call and make arrangements so I can drop you off."

"Mom isn't going to the hospital with you?"

"No, she's . . ." Aimee hesitates. "She's coming later."

That's odd. None of this adds up. Why wouldn't Mom rush off to the hospital first thing? That's what she said she was going to do last night, before they went to bed.

She had kissed Lianna's forehead and said, "I'll probably be gone when you wake up in the morning, but I'll call to check in during the day, okay?"

Oh, well.

Far be it from Lianna to question any change in plans that allows her to be sprung from this prison.

She swings her legs around the edge of the bed and tells Aimee, "I just have to take a shower, and get dressed, and eat breakfast. Then I'll call my friend . . . Devin."

She almost said Casey, but that would be pushing it. Tempting as it is to try and sneak a chance to set up a meeting with Kevin, she'd better not risk it.

Mom might be distracted, but she'd probably remember that Casey and her family are still away on vacation, which is the root of Lianna's being grounded in the first place.

No, she can't pull that again.

Kevin will just have to wait.

Even though he whined, when he called Saturday night, about not being able to see her any time soon, which definitely made her feel wanted. Naturally, she promised she'd sneak out of the house some night after everyone is asleep. Just not for a few more days, after her mother calmed down about last week's incident.

"Wait, Lianna." Aimee holds up her hand. "You don't have that much time."

"For what?"

"You know . . . a shower . . . Just throw on some clothes and we'll go. I'll take you someplace for breakfast on the way, and you can call your friend Devin from my cell phone in the car if you want."

Lianna narrows her eyes. "What's the big rush?"

It sounds like her mother's trying to get rid of her.

"I'm sorry . . . It's just that I want to get to my Dad," Aimee replies. "I had a hard time sleeping last night, I was so worried about him."

"Oh."

Who is Lianna to argue with that?

Especially with imminent freedom hanging in the balance?

"Just let me find something to wear and brush my teeth, and I'll be right with you."

CHAPTER 12

Standing in the window of the front parlor, Charlotte watches Aimee drive away in her rental car with Lianna in the passenger's seat.

Thank goodness.

It was all she could do to act as though everything was normal when she gave her daughter a hurried kiss good-bye in the hall just now.

"Have fun at Devin's," she said. "I'll call later about picking you up when I'm through at the hospital."

"Thanks, Mom."

Lianna, who can be especially prickly in the mornings, was surprisingly docile. Charlotte was glad to see her leave, and grateful to Aimee for hustling her right out of here.

She heard her daughter ask Aimee, as they walked down the wide front steps, about the black sedan parked in the shade of a towering oak.

"I don't know whose it is," Aimee said convincingly. "Probably the nurse who comes to see your aunt."

"She drives a Honda."

"Well, maybe she sent somebody else today." Without missing a beat, she said, "Hey, you know what? I saw a Bojangles off the highway on the way back from Savannah last night. Maybe we could stop there for breakfast on the way. Do you like biscuits?"

"They're okay," said Lianna.

Just okay? Charlotte thought in irritation. Bo-Berry Biscuits happen to be Lianna's all-time favorite thing to eat.

Obviously, she isn't going to go out of her way to be accommodating today. At least, not to Aimee.

Lianna's resentment of her stepsister was palpable at dinner last night. She barely spoke two words, and Charlotte spotted her sneaking a jealous glare at Aimee when Lianna thought she wasn't looking.

Oh, well. She'll come around sooner or later. Charlotte hopes so—for Aimee's sake, anyway.

What matters most now is that she's out of here.

Charlotte doesn't need to have her teenaged daughter involved in what's about to happen in this house.

She sighs, pressing her forehead against the screen, wishing she could go, too.

Royce will wonder why she isn't there. She told Aimee to tell him that she had some things to see to at home first and that she'll be along shortly.

"If he asks what they are, make up something," she cautioned her stepdaughter. "Tell him I . . . I had to pay bills, or something."

She hates to lie, or have Aimee do it on her behalf, but there's no reason to alarm Royce by letting him know what's going on around here. Not right now, when all he should be focused on is recovering from his ordeal.

A floorboard creaks, and Dorado reappears in the

doorway, a questioning look on his darkly handsome face.

"My daughter's gone," she tells him.

He nods. "All right."

She sees a flicker of sympathy in his eyes and wishes he would say something, anything, to make this less disturbing.

But he simply turns to leave the room, undoubtedly going to alert Williamson that the coast is clear.

The backup officers are already on their way, she knows. As soon as they arrive, Charlotte is certain, chaos will prevail.

Gib and the others will be questioned, and the detectives will be free to execute the search warrant they obtained before they arrived.

If Grandaddy really is haunting Oakgate, he's got to be furious about this, Charlotte thinks, shaking her head in dread as she hears heavy footsteps going up the stairs already.

"I still have no idea why you left everything to me and not to my cousins, but I really don't think Gib is guilty, Grandaddy," she whispers to his ghost. "I want to help him somehow. But there's nothing I can do for him now."

Then it comes to her, as if her grandfather's spirit really does exist, and is channeling thoughts into her head.

There is one thing she can do.

She hurries out of the parlor to make the necessary phone call.

Perched in her wheelchair before the oval mahogany cheval mirror, Jeanne stares vacantly at her reflection.

One story below, she can hear heavy footfalls, creaking floorboards, doors opening and closing, and the rumble of unfamiliar voices.

"Something is going on down there." Melanie's voice is an octave lower than usual and she frowns as she runs the brush through Jeanne's long white hair. "I don't like the sounds of it, Jeanne, do you?"

"No . . ."

The bristles tug at a snarl; Jeanne winces.

Melanie's reflection reveals that she doesn't even notice; her eyes dart expectantly toward the door with every stroke.

"What do you think is happening?" Jeanne asks nervously.

"I have no idea. Do you want me to go down and check?"

"I don't know. I'm afraid . . ."

The distinct crunch of rubber tires on the crushed-shell driveway floats up through the open window at the front of the house.

"Do you hear that? Somebody else is here," she informs Melanie, who has already lowered the brush and is hurrying over to peer out.

"It's definitely a police car," she reports. "This time, it's marked. But I knew those others were cop cars, too. One, two, three . . . Why are all these police here, Jeanne? This isn't good. It isn't good at all."

Gnarled hands clenched into fists in her lap, Jeanne remains silent, staring at herself in the mirror—this time, really seeing what is there.

A sad, lonely old woman.

There was a time, in her youth, when she was quite beautiful, almost as great a beauty as her grandniece Charlotte, minus the distinctive Remington cleft chin, of course.

The first time Jeanne laid eyes on Charlotte the day Norris and Connie June brought her home as a newborn, that chin of hers surely put to rest any doubt that Charlotte was a Remington, through and through . . .

More importantly, that her father was, before her.

Unlike his older brother, Xavy, Norris never did favor his father's side of the family. He had the same long, lean build, but his coloring was different, lighter. He looked so little like a Remington, in fact, that outsiders occasionally teased Eleanore about the mailman.

She never laughed.

Within these tabby and brick walls, there was no teasing about Norris's looks. Gilbert managed to treat his second son the same as he did his namesake. But Jeanne knew her brother had his doubts about his paternity.

More importantly, Eleanore knew as well. Nothing would convince her stubbornly suspicious husband of her faithfulness.

Nothing during her lifetime, anyway. Eleanore didn't live to see the granddaughter whose birth put the question to rest.

Before Charlotte came along, Jeanne herself used to stare at Norris, looking for any resemblance to Jonathan Barrow, the handsome financier Eleanore met at one of her own dinner parties not long after Xavy was born.

In the wake of Gilbert's accusations, Mr. Barrow was banned from Oakgate forever.

Jeanne longed to come right out and ask her sister-in-law, point-blank, if it was true she'd had an affair. Jeanne would have understood—in fact, wouldn't have blamed her sister-in-law if she had packed up the babies and left Gilbert altogether.

Nor would she have been surprised if Eleanore had threatened to take Gilbert's life—and her own—just as

Jeanne's mother, Marie, had threatened, decades earlier brandishing a mother-of-pearl-handled pistol.

One would think that her brother—after watching
his own mean-tempered father drive his mother into
the arms of another man—would have learned. One
would have expected Gilbert Remington II to do everything in his power to make his own marriage work.

But then, Gilbert never did see the worst of what had
happened between his parents. Only Jeanne was here,
cowering in her bed, on the night when the gun was
drawn. Gilbert was safely off at Telfair Academy.

Thus, the sins of the father were passed to the son,
along with the alma mater, the Remington millions—
and the widower's curse.

Life went on . . . for everyone except Eleanore.

Jeanne wonders to this day whether her brother secretly blamed himself for his wife's suicide.

Just as she wonders whether her own mother's fatal
fall from a horse while out riding alone was truly an accident—or instead a murderous reprisal for drawing a
gun on her own husband.

Marie feared her husband's fierce temper. That much
is clear in her journals.

But Jeanne will never know the whole truth.

And whatever her brother Gilbert might have known,
or suspected, about their parents' dark past was buried
with him in the grave he shares with Eleanore.

Only the pearl-handled pistol and the journals remain—in Jeanne's possession—as evidence that any of
it ever ever, happened at all.

Now, listening to the police moving through the
floors beneath this one, Jeanne knows that she must get
to it before they do.

She turns to Melanie. "Can you push me over to the
bureau, please? Hurry."

* * *

"I *said* I'm not answering any questions without my attorney present," Gib insists, fixing the pair of detectives with a flinty stare.

"And we just asked where you were on Saturday night. If you don't have anything to hide, Mr. Remington, there's no reason why you should have a problem answering that simple question."

"I have absolutely nothing to hide," he lies, hoping his narrowed gaze masks his inner turmoil. "But I happen to be a lawyer myself, so I know better than to tell you anything that might be used against me."

The door to his room was left slightly ajar when the detectives came in to rouse him from a sound sleep. Now he can hear activity in the hall and beyond; scurrying footsteps, the rumble of unfamiliar voices, even what sounds like furniture being moved about.

Obviously, the police are searching the house. They must have a warrant.

It's only a matter of time before they make their way in here and start going through Gib's things.

And when they do . . .

Feeling sick, Gib watches Williamson idly lift his cell phone from the dresser. The detective examines it, turning it over and over in his beefy hands as though he's never seen such an object before. Then he sets it down again, wearing a thoughtful expression.

My phone . . .

Even if their search of Gib's room somehow neglects to turn up anything incriminating, the police are going to go through his telephone records.

Gib's heart beats faster, his thoughts careening wildly through a mental roster of potentially damaging calls he's made lately.

There are plenty, should the detectives go to the trouble of tracing the numbers.

But none that can prove I had anything to do with what happened Saturday night.

"If you won't tell us where you were," the other detective, Dorado, says casually, "maybe you can just tell us whether you're going to have somebody who can vouch for you. That way, we can start making calls."

"I told you, I'm not saying anything until I can get a lawyer."

And that's going to take quite some time. Enough time to allow him to come up with a suitable alibi . . . and cover his tracks.

There's a knock on the door.

"Yeah? What is it?" Williamson asks in the same brusque tone he uses for interrogation.

The door opens wider.

A uniformed officer pokes his head in. "Mr. Remington's attorney is here, Detective."

Startled, Gib raises an eyebrow.

"You already called an attorney?" Williamson asks, equally startled.

"No . . ."

"I did." The door opens wider, and Gib sees Charlotte standing there.

Behind her is Tyler Hawthorne.

"Oh, my God, I'm so happy to see—hey, who's she?" Devin is standing on the elevated stoop of her parents' house on East Jones Street, watching Aimee wave as she pulls away from the curb.

"Royce's daughter." Reaching the top step, Lianna gives her friend a quick hug.

"I didn't know he had a daughter."

"Yeah, she doesn't live around here. She's here because . . . well, you know."

"Right. How is he?"

"Fine, I guess. I mean, he will be."

"What's *she* like?"

"Aimee?" She rolls her eyes. "She's a major pain in the butt."

"Why?"

"She talks too much. I swear to God, my ears are ringing after being with her for the past hour."

All right, maybe that's a slight exaggeration, Lianna admits, but only to herself.

Aimee does talk a lot, though it wasn't necessarily nonstop chatter. She asked a lot of questions on the way to Bojangles, about what music Lianna likes, and which TV shows she watches, and where she goes to school, and what her favorite subjects are.

They're the same basic, boring questions all grownups ask when they're trying to make conversation, and Lianna grudgingly answered them all.

Until Aimee asked, just as casually as she posed the others, "So do you have a boyfriend?"

In the passenger's seat, Lianna instantly went from sprawled to stiff-spined. Did Mom tell Aimee about Kevin? Did she instruct her to try and get Lianna to spill the details about him? Is that why she relented on the grounding, and asked Aimee to drive her to Savannah?

When Lianna didn't answer, Aimee glanced over at her, and she must have seen the look on Lianna's face, because she said, "Not a good topic, huh?"

Lianna shook her head, turned up the radio, and remained silent all the way to the restaurant.

She wasn't planning to order anything when they got

there, out of spite. But when she smelled food, her appetite returned with a vengeance. She realized she hadn't eaten much of anything since the yogurt late Saturday night. When it was their turn at the register, she found herself ordering a big biscuit with sausage gravy, and fried chicken on the side.

"Fried chicken for breakfast?" Aimee asked dubiously. "Does your mother give you that at home?"

"My mother would probably spoon-feed me Gerber strained peaches from a little jar if she had her way," Lianna retorted.

Aimee laughed. "Parents are tough, aren't they? I'm twenty-five and my father still calls me 'Baby Girl.' Order what you want. I just can't believe they really serve fried chicken at this hour."

Aimee just ordered a cup of coffee, saying she never eats breakfast. "If I did, I'd look like . . . well, like her," she said with a tilt of her head toward the large woman adding napkins and condiments to her loaded tray of chicken and fries.

Lianna told herself that that was really mean, even though it was the kind of thing her friends would say, and she would giggle at.

The truth is, she doesn't want to like Aimee. She never wanted a sister, older or younger, step or otherwise, no matter what her mother likes to think.

Now, with Devin apparently waiting for her to go into detail about Aimee, she just shrugs and asks, "Are we going inside, or what?"

"Nah. My mother and Ray are still sleeping. They were out late at some party, and I bet they're really hungover. Let's just get out of here."

Lianna's first thought is that her mother probably thinks she's spending the day safely at Devin's house.

Her next thought is, who cares what her mother

thinks? If she was so eager to unload Lianna for the day that she doesn't even remember she's been grounded, that's *her* problem.

"Where do you want to go?" she asks Devin.

"Do you have any money with you?"

Aimee asked the same thing, just before she pulled up at Devin's.

When Lianna said no, she reached into her purse and pulled out a couple of twenties. "Here," she said easily. "Take it. You know . . . in case you and your friend want to do something later."

"Like what?"

"Like go to a movie, or shopping, or something. I don't know, what do y'all usually do when you hang out?"

Wondering again if she was being baited by a nosy stepsister on behalf of a nosier mother, Lianna just shrugged.

But she took the money with mumbled thanks.

When she nods, Devin decides, "We'll go to the mall, then. I need to get some stuff for school."

"It doesn't even start for weeks."

"Whatever. It's an excuse to buy new clothes, right?"

Lianna grins. "Right."

"Your mother's not going to show up here looking for you any time soon, is she?"

"No way. She's going to the hospital. Trust me, she won't even think about me for hours."

"That's great."

Yeah, Lianna thinks, following Devin back down the steps to the street. *Just great.*

Tyler closes the door to Gilbert's private study with a quaking hand, trying not to remember what transpired the last time he crossed this particular threshold, with Silas Neville on his heels.

He pauses to gather his composure before turning to face his late friend's grandson.

Gib has taken a seat—or rather, collapsed—on the couch across from the antique desk where generations of Remington men have conducted their very successful business dealings.

Never, Tyler thinks, would any of them have imagined that one day, the lone remaining Remington son—the only hope for carrying on the family name—would be sitting here accused of an unthinkable crime.

Tyler can't help but acknowledge the bitter irony. After the extraordinary lengths Gilbert went to in order to preserve the legacy, this young, cocky successor has seemingly destroyed the whole damned thing.

He knew plenty of brash young men like Gib Remington in his days at Telfair Academy. Arrogant offspring of wealthy families, believing that the rules didn't apply to them. They started out breaking curfews.

Some—like, perhaps, Gib Remington—went on to break laws.

I was one of them, Tyler thinks, a wave of nausea swishing through his gut.

But that was long ago. Too long ago to dwell on now—or here.

This is about a new generation—not the Telfair Trio.

Gib's face is drawn; he's obviously quite shaken.

"Is there anything you want to tell me?" Tyler studiously avoids Gilbert's tidy desk as he pulls a chair adjacent to the couch and sits down to face his would-be client.

Gib shrugs, refusing to meet his gaze. "Just that I haven't done anything wrong."

Tyler nods. It's not as though he expected a confession. He crosses his legs and leans forward, his chin resting on his fist as he studies Gib's face.

If he subscribed to the theories of Lavater's physiognomy, as some trial lawyers—and, subconsciously, jurors—do, he would deem Gib Remington innocent just based on his looks. With that shock of blond hair, wide-set eyes the shade of a summer sea, and strong jaw, he's a mirror image of his grandfather at that age, right down to the cowlick. In other words, Gib, like Gilbert before him, is the polar opposite of the beady-eyed, unshaven caricature of a criminal.

So what does that tell you? Tyler asks himself wryly.

All right, then, when it comes to nonverbal indications of possible guilt, he's far better off considering demeanor—and Gib's is telling, particularly in response to the next question.

"You might as well tell me now: is there any chance at all that those detectives are going to turn up anything of interest when they search your room?"

Gib doesn't reply, but the answer is plain to see in a pair of fists that clench and unclench in his lap.

Then he looks up, but not at Tyler—and not in resignation. Gib's gaze shifts directly toward the window, where a slight breeze stirs sun-dappled boughs. "Why are you here, Mr. Hawthorne?"

Irritated by the indolent tone—or perhaps, by the realization that it echoes his own, and Gilbert's, in their own youthful era of entitlement—Tyler snaps, "Well, it's not because I have ESP, that's for damned sure. You heard what your cousin told the detectives in there, didn't you? She called me."

"No, I mean, why did you agree to come rushing right over here? You're Charlotte's lawyer, not mine."

"No, I'm not her lawyer, either. I'm your Grandaddy's lawyer." *And his oldest, most faithful friend, dammit.*

"As you may recall," Tyler can't resist adding with a tinge of sarcasm, "I represent his estate."

"Which he didn't leave to me."

"Which has nothing to do with this." Tyler deliberately inserts a significant pause before asking, "Does it?"

"No!" Gib raises a hand to thrust his blond cowlick farther away from his forehead, a gesture Tyler noted repeatedly in his office last week, as the tension mounted after the will was read.

But Gib's current level of stress doesn't necessarily mean he's guilty. Anybody would be uptight under these circumstances, Tyler acknowledges.

Nor has Gib Remington been formally accused of any crime . . . yet.

"Do you want me to leave?" Tyler asks, entirely poised to do so. "I'm not about to waste my time here, or yours."

"With any luck, this is going to turn out to be a waste of everyone's time," is the surly reply.

Tyler uncrosses his legs and begins to stand.

"Wait!"

The word is spoken sharply—almost desperately.

He looks at Gib to see a row of perfect teeth—professionally whitened, no doubt—descend over his lower lip and bite down, hard. When they lift, a bead of blood appears.

Then, for the first time, Gib Remington looks Tyler in the eye.

"Don't go," he says heavily. "I think I'm going to need you."

Charlotte leans in the doorway of Gib's room, arms folded across her middle in as laid-back a posture as she can manage. Inside, she's a mess, her thoughts racing with possibilities she never before would have willingly entertained.

She watches the detectives seize stacks of carefully folded clothing from his drawers, tossing them on the bed. They do the same with the contents of the small closet, not pausing to remove them from their hangers. Each garment is thoroughly examined, creases and pockets and shirt cuffs checked, before it is unceremoniously tossed to the floor.

Gib would be cringing, Charlotte thinks, if he could see this.

Hopefully cringing only because of what they're doing to his cherished wardrobe, and not trepidation over what they might discover.

She breathes an inner sigh of relief when half a dozen pairs of shoes are swept up from the closet floor, their soles scrutinized before they're tossed into a heap in the corner.

Gib's brown Italian-leather Dopp bag is emptied on the floor, with a cursory inspection of his toiletries. Charlotte doesn't miss the snorts and derisive comments from the macho cops about the many hair products "pretty boy" uses.

A more thorough perusal is made of the contents of Gib's matching leather jewelry case. Charlotte's pulse quickens, as she waits to see if the heirloom cufflink's missing partner will turn up.

It doesn't.

Furniture is pushed and pulled from place to place, draperies yanked from their rods, the rug rolled, lifted, propped upright in a corner. The bedding is removed, the mattress patted and probed, then slid away altogether and leaned against a wall.

Poor Grandaddy must be turning over in his grave,

Charlotte thinks, shifting her weight but not her gaze as the men inspect the box spring. Thank goodness they're almost finished in here, and so far, nothing—

"There's a slit in this cover. Look at this!" Dorado plunges a hand through the box spring's gauzy lining and pulls something out.

In the immediate flurry of activity around the bed, Charlotte can't see the object, but whatever it is seems to be incriminating.

A swift, further probe into the hole in the box spring yields several other items as well.

Steeling herself in dread, she stands on her tiptoes to look over Williamson's imposing shoulder to see what the fuss is about.

In that instant, her worst fear materializes.

Lined up on the floor as a police photographer snaps pictures from every angle are a pair of muddy brown dress shoes and a rumpled, yet still-starched white dress shirt, one French cuff still studded with an unmistakable heirloom platinum cufflink—the other empty.

CHAPTER 13

"Here, Royce . . ." Leaving his left elbow in Aimee's capable grasp, Charlotte releases his right and scurries ahead to shove the coffee table away from the couch in the front parlor. "Sit right here."

Royce groans slightly as he lowers himself, with his wife and daughter's help, into the cushions. "That's better."

Charlotte and Aimee exchange a worried glance. Maybe it is too soon for him to be home from the hospital, less than a week after his ordeal began. They both thought so, especially since the old elevator at Oakgate stopped working sometime this week. It would have come in handy, getting him to and from the second floor.

But Royce was determined to get out of there regardless, and the doctors agreed to release him Friday afternoon, just in time for the weekend.

Longing for privacy, what with the media going crazy over the scandal of Gib's arrest, Charlotte nevertheless can't help being jittery about the prospect of caring for

Royce at home. She wanted to hire a full-time visiting nurse, but Royce wouldn't hear of it.

"I'll be good as new in a couple of days," he proclaimed heartily.

That bravado disappeared somewhere during the painstaking journey through the gathering dusk, up the front steps and across the portico.

Charlotte and Aimee both urged him to agree to let them bring a wheelchair along, but Royce is determined to go on his own steam from here on in.

Thank goodness Aimee has agreed to put her resume and post-graduation job hunt on hold for a while longer, to stay and help. As she pointed out to Royce, she's an RN now. Who better suited to handle the task?

"You're not still feeling dizzy?" Charlotte asks, resting a hand on Royce's cheek.

Aimee warned her they'd better keep an eye on him for possible fever and infection, but he doesn't feel unusually warm. The doctor wouldn't have let him leave without making sure he was fine, and it hasn't even been an hour since he left the hospital to return to Oakgate.

"No, I'm fine now. Really. Walking all that way just took a lot out of me, that's all." He sighs. "Maybe I can sleep down here tonight."

Charlotte looks dubiously at the nineteenth-century couch, with its low arms and back, and wood moldings bordering the cushions. It wouldn't make the most comfortable bed in the world.

Aimee speaks up as if she's read Charlotte's thoughts, "I bet we can arrange to rent one of those hospital beds for a few days, Daddy. Until you can make it upstairs to your bedroom again."

Sensing Royce is about to protest, Charlotte quickly

agrees, "That's a great idea—and I can sleep right here on the couch in case you need anything."

"No way am I making you sleep on this thing," Royce tells her. "We'll both sleep in our own bed. I'm sure the stairs will be no problem."

Aimee shakes her head, looking at Charlotte as if to say, *He's too stubborn for his own good.*

Charlotte, who wishes Royce hadn't repeatedly pushed aside the elevator issue in his eagerness to spring himself from hospital care, nevertheless isn't particularly anxious to spend another night in bed without her husband beside her.

"Is it good to be home?" she asks, plumping a throw pillow behind his neck as he settles back with a sigh of relief.

"I'm not home," he reminds her with a faint smile. "Not yet."

It takes her a perplexed moment to figure out what he means.

Oh. Of course. He's referring to *their* house: the one on Oglethorpe Avenue.

The house where he was gunned down.

She murmurs her agreement and turns her back to flip on a table lamp so he won't see her expression.

How can he even want to go back there after what happened?

It's like the beach all over again . . .

Except Royce lived.

And Adam's death was an accident.

What happened to Royce was not.

Now Gib is in jail, thus far unable to raise the sizeable bail. Apparently, he doesn't have a penny to his name. His bank accounts are all but empty, and he had liquidated all his investments a few years ago.

He turned to his family for help, but Phyllida claims to be incapable of coming up with the money and their mother doesn't have it, either.

Charlotte knows because she overheard Phyllida's end of a long-distance conversation with Aunt Susan.

It started out in a fairly composed manner, with Phyllida saying, *"No, my house is already mortgaged up to the hilt, and even if it weren't, I wouldn't risk losing it . . . I know he's my brother . . . I know . . . No, we can't do that . . . Because I don't trust him not to take off and leave the country, that's why."*

Knowing how Aunt Susan always doted on her son, Charlotte wasn't surprised by the obvious argument that ensued. It wound up with Phyllida tearfully saying, more than once, *"I know, Mommy, but I can't"* and *"We just don't have that kind of money."*

Whether Phyllida was telling the truth and whether her regret was real remained unclear to Charlotte until the call ended with a slammed receiver. Phyllida's quiet sobs were barely audible, which convinced Charlotte that for once, her cousin's emotional display was real.

But Charlotte didn't go in to comfort her. The two have kept a cordial distance all week, ever since Gib was taken out of here in handcuffs.

Phyllida cried then, too. But when her brother turned to beg her to help him, she literally turned her back as he was led out the door.

"Do you honestly believe Gib could have done something like this, Charlotte?" she asked afterward, more than once, in disbelief. *"Do you honestly think he's guilty?"*

Charlotte's answer is always the same.

Yes.

What else is there to think? What other conclusion can be drawn from the evidence that was found in his room?

He admitted that the shoes were his, but denied wearing them on the night in question.

He also vehemently denied ever having removed the cufflinks from his grandfather's jewelry box, much less having worn them. No, he had no idea how one landed in the cemetery and the other on a shirt that was, indeed, his own. But he didn't know how any of that stuff got into his box spring.

The detectives don't believe him, and neither does Charlotte.

She's certain now that Grandaddy's reason for disinheriting Gib, and Phyllida, too, stemmed from something he must have found out about them. And she's going to find out what it is.

Now, however, she's just trying to focus on Royce, on getting him settled here at Oakgate so he can heal.

As for Phyllida . . .

Charlotte couldn't bring herself to ask her lingering cousin to leave, though that's what she wanted.

But Phyllida is going anyway. She announced this morning that she's booked a flight out for tomorrow night.

"I wanted to get out over the weekend," she told Charlotte. "They're saying there's a tropical storm coming this way early in the week, and it could turn into a hurricane."

Charlotte was cordial, hoping to mask her relief with a pleasant, "That's a good idea. You'll be home safe and sound before the storm hits."

"Right, and—well, I wanted you to know I've realized there's no point now in contesting the will. So I might as well go."

Good. Just leave me alone, Charlotte thought when she said it.

She wants nothing further to do with either of her

cousins, regardless of Grandaddy's reasons for disinheriting them. Charlotte is more than ready to move on . . . if not, necessarily, *out*.

The prospect of preparing Oakgate to be sold is a daunting one. In her exhaustion, she can't imagine finding the motivation to start sorting through the house, packing things up, bringing realtors through, making arrangements for Aunt Jeanne . . .

Anyway, there's no rush.

The house on Oglethorpe isn't ready yet, thank goodness. The renovation has ground to a halt, with the finishing fixtures and paint as yet unselected. On Monday afternoon, Charlotte instructed the contractor to just go on to his next project, promising she would call him to finish when things settle down.

"Are you sure you don't just want me to wrap things up for you now, Mrs. Maitland?" Don asked, as she pulled out a pen and her checkbook. "If you just had a few hours to go over the paint and the other couple of things, I could—"

"No," she said firmly. "Right now, my time is devoted to my husband. We'll call you when we need y'all again, after he gets out of the hospital."

The contractor left with a doubtful *suit yourself* shrug and a hefty check.

Now that Royce is out of the hospital, the last thing Charlotte wants to think about is that house.

Gone are her visions of cheerful, sun-splashed rooms and laughter; all she remembers is that awful night in the dark, and fumes, and gunshots, and blood . . .

How can that house ever be home?

Maybe in time . . .

That's what Aimee keeps telling her.

"You know, I hate that this has robbed you of your

spirit, Charlotte," she said just last night, when Charlotte halfheartedly said she didn't care where they stopped for dinner on the way back from the hospital, or what they ate. "Don't let him do this to you."

"Who?"

"Gib!" Aimee said, in a *who else?* tone. "He hasn't won yet. Daddy is alive, and so are you. And Gib is in jail. He can't hurt y'all anymore, and he can't win, unless you give in and let him."

Aimee is right.

Charlotte has no intention of letting Gib ruin the life she's worked so hard to rebuild. She just needs time.

Time for Royce's wounded leg to heal.

And time for Charlotte's wounded soul to do the same.

It has become increasingly difficult for Phyllida to leave her room. Every time she ventures out into the house, she feels like an interloper, disgraced by association to her brother.

Anyway, it's no longer as though she has as much a right to be here as Charlotte does.

The house, and everything in it, belong to Charlotte. It's a wonder she hasn't come right out and asked Phyllida to leave, though the unspoken invitation has been obvious all week.

Well, she'll be out tomorrow. With little else to occupy her, she's been watching the Weather Channel, and she has no desire to top off this horrendous visit East with a hurricane. All she wants for the next twenty-four hours is to be left alone to pack her things and gather her courage to return to the wreckage of her life.

Now, as she rounds a corner of the upstairs hall on her way to find something to eat in the kitchen, Phyllida is dismayed to hear movement on the stairs below.

She pauses to consider fleeing back to her room, but hunger gets the better of her and she continues on.

To her relief, it's only Melanie, Aunt Jeanne's terminally cheerful nurse, starting back up the stairs carrying a tray filled with food.

"How are you?" Phyllida asks, because she has to say something, conscious of the younger woman's curious gaze from the foot of the steps.

"Fine," Melanie says, and makes a tremendous effort to adjust a steaming cup on the tray with one hand.

That's so she won't have to look at me, Phyllida notes.

She'd be amused at the transparent ploy, if she weren't so darned . . .

Well, weary.

Not so much physically tired, though she can't remember the last time she slept through an entire night.

She's just . . . depleted. Utterly depleted, in every way. She has nothing left to give to anyone.

Not even her own child.

That's part of the reason she's lingered at Oakgate this long. How can she bring herself to fly home to her son when she can barely get through each day without falling apart?

Brian asks countless questions and goes on and on every time he calls about how much he misses her. Translation: everything is falling apart around the house without her there to keep it together. There are bills to be paid, and calls to be returned, and appointments to be kept . . . It's all so overwhelming.

Then there's Lila, who keeps telling her how happy Wills is going to be when his mommy comes home to take care of him.

Lila. She'll have to be let go. If not immediately, then as soon as Phyllida can bring herself to do it. There's no money for household staff, not now. She's been scraping together the nanny's salary every two weeks as it is.

Not to mention the way she and Brian have been living off their credit cards for a couple of years now, undaunted by the mounting interest and finance charges.

Phyllida always knew that even if Grandaddy lived to be a hundred—and well he might—her inheritance would come along eventually to bail them out and guarantee that Wills's college tuition will be paid, no matter where he wants to go.

There was never a need to worry about what they owed; never a reason to stop spending. What's a few hundred thousand dollars in debt when you're worth millions?

Not anymore.

She's never going to be wealthy.

She's never going to be an actress.

She's never going to be anything she dreamed of.

As she passes Melanie on the stairs, she wonders what on earth she's going to do. How are she and Brian going to pay off any of that debt now that the promise of a vast windfall has been whisked from their future? How will they survive?

These last few days, as her anxiety escalated, she could only assume that Gib, too, must have felt this . . . desperate. This hopelessly trapped, facing a lifestyle unfit for a Remington.

Unfit for poor little Wills, whose toddler cronies and their nannies will continue to meet a few times a week at one palatial Beverly Hills spread or another while Phyllida pushes him on a swing in the park. Parks are still free, right? Swings are free?

Hell, some of his friends have yards that are bigger

than parks; their parents rent carousels and petting zoos for birthday parties. Where will Wills have his? Chuck E. Cheese?

"Um, Mrs. Harper?"

"Yes?" Having reached the bottom of the stairs, she turns to look back at Melanie, up at the top.

"I just wanted to ask if there's anything I can do. If you need to talk, or anything. You know . . . You just look so upset, and . . . I know what it's like."

Oh? Your brother was arrested on attempted murder charges, too?

Phyllida curbs her tongue. She might not buy the woman's all-chipper, all-the-time act, but she shouldn't be rude to her. Maybe she really is just trying to help. At least somebody around here is.

"Thank you," she says awkwardly, wishing Melanie would just continue on to the next flight of stairs and leave her to her own business.

But the nurse goes on, "I just know that you're far away from home, and your little boy, and you might feel like you're all alone, and you might really need a friend. Really, I've been there."

Phyllida nods and offers what she hopes is a pleasant smile even as she thinks, *Go away, will you? Just go away.*

But when Melanie gets the hint and does moves on, Phyllida finds herself feeling vaguely abandoned.

Which is ridiculous.

Because she doesn't want to talk to a nurse about her problems. She doesn't want to talk to anyone.

She just wants . . .

What? To go home? That isn't it. Not with the mess waiting for her in LA.

All right, so what does she want?

All I want right now, she thinks grimly, *is to curl up and die.*

* * *

In her room, Lianna pulls on the dress she wore last weekend in anticipation of seeing her father.

He's coming back to Oakgate to take her to dinner tonight. It was his idea, to make up for the disappointment of last weekend.

She begged her mother to let her go, and to her surprise, Charlotte relented. Apparently, Lianna is no longer grounded.

Mom never said anything about her earlier punishment when she picked her up at Devin's Monday night after a long day at the hospital. She was more cordial than usual to Devin's parents, and thanked them for keeping Lianna all day and seeing to it that she ate lunch and dinner.

Naturally, Mom couldn't have known that lunch was nachos at the mall food court, dinner was three Krispy Kreme donuts, and that Devin's mother and stepfather didn't even know she was around until right before Mom showed up to get her.

The last few days, Lianna has been trying to work up the nerve to ask her mother for her cell phone back. But she's afraid to even remind her mother that she took it away, just in case she also forgot she grounded Lianna.

She's also skittish about sneaking out to meet Kevin, though he keeps urging her to do it. She will, eventually . . . just not yet. It isn't just that she's afraid she'll get caught—it's that she's afraid of what will happen between the two of them when she's alone with him again.

So she's spent an entire week hanging around Oakgate, bored out of her mind, unable even to speak to her friends and Kevin, unless she calls them from the main line—usually with zero conversational privacy.

There was nobody to talk to around the house but

Nydia. Oh, and Aunt Jeanne's chatterbox nurse, Melanie, who likes to drift downstairs whenever Aunt Jeanne is napping.

But anything, even total social isolation or listening to Melanie chirp on and on about her life story, is better than going back and forth to the hospital in Savannah every day with her mother and Aimee.

Her stepsister actually had the nerve to offer to fix her hair before dinner tonight. She's taken on the annoying habit of knocking on Lianna's door in the evenings to see if she wants to go to a movie, or shopping, or whatever.

"No, thanks," Lianna said curtly in response to her hair makeover offer. "I like it the way it is, and so does my dad."

"Oh, Lianna, I didn't mean . . ." Aimee was immediately all flustered. "I just thought it might be fun, you know . . . I never had a little sister."

You still don't, Lianna wanted to retort, but she managed to hold her tongue.

That was last night.

She hasn't seen Aimee all day, but she's beginning to feel a little guilty. Maybe she really was just trying to be nice, and not critical about Lianna's appearance.

Still, who needs another grown-up hanging around the house, trying to be all girly-buddy? You'd think Aimee would go back home to New Orleans now that her father is out of the hospital, so things can get back to normal around here.

But apparently she's not, because Lianna overheard her and Mom talking this morning about how Aimee's going to stick around awhile longer to help.

Why doesn't Mom ask me *to help?* Lianna can't help but wonder. *Why doesn't she treat me like a real person, instead of some annoying kid who's just in the way?*

Thank goodness for Dad. He should be here any second.

Lianna surveys her reflection in the mirror.

The dress is a little wrinkled, from being on the floor overnight before she rescued it and replaced it on a hanger. Maybe she should have at least ironed it.

And her hair isn't that great. She really needs to have it cut, or . . . something.

But she doesn't need Aimee. They aren't going to be a happy little family together, no matter what Mom would like to think.

The odd thing is . . .

Well, Mom really likes her. It's almost as if, in Royce's daughter, she's found something that's been missing in her life ever since . . .

Adam.

Yes.

It's almost as if Mom has allowed Aimee to fill that gaping void left by his death; as if she's finally found a second child again.

Well, no way is Lianna going to consider Aimee a replacement for the older sibling she lost.

Just as Royce isn't a replacement for her real dad, and never will be.

With a resolute nod and a silent prayer, Lianna hurries to finish getting ready for her dinner date.

Please, don't let anything keep my dad from showing up this time.

Please.

"Alone at last," Royce murmurs, as Charlotte settles on the couch beside him.

Aimee has gone off to make some calls about renting a hospital bed for the parlor, or so she claimed. According to Charlotte, she probably just discreetly wanted to give the two of them some privacy after a trying week.

Charlotte sighs. "I'm so glad you're back . . ."

Home.

This time, however, she doesn't add that part. She probably doesn't want to get into that again.

Good. Neither does he.

"So am I." He stretches an arm along the back of the sofa. "Come here."

"I don't want to bump your leg."

"Don't worry about it. My leg is fine." He pats the cushion right beside him. "I miss cuddling with you. That's not all I miss," he adds suggestively, "but the other part's going to have to wait."

She smiles and slides close to him, leaning her head against his chest.

For a moment, they just sit contentedly.

Royce senses that Charlotte's muscles are beginning to unclench for the first time all week. She feels more tightly wound than the antique clock on the mantel.

Its steady ticking is the only sound in the room, besides a soft chorus of crickets that drifts through the open window as dusk settles over the grounds.

"It's so quiet," Royce murmurs, leaning his head back and closing his eyes. "That hospital was so noisy, all the time."

"It was pretty noisy around here, too, until the new unlisted phone number kicked in yesterday."

That's right, Royce remembers, she mentioned this morning that she was forced to abruptly terminate the old one, thanks to incessant calls from the press. The Remington scandal has enveloped the regional news for days now.

There was even a news van parked out beyond the stone gateway when they arrived here. Aimee—who has no use for the nosy press and is quite vocal about it—said it was worse the other day, when they returned from the hospital to find reporters broadcasting live from the lawn.

Charlotte had forgotten to close the gate when they'd left that morning—it isn't a habit anyone has been in for years. Of course, the news crew had no qualms about trespassing.

"I swear, they're like cockroaches—all they need to do is find a tiny crack in the foundation, and the next thing you know, whole armies are streaming in."

Royce had to laugh at that. She always did have a way with colorful metaphors.

Well, at least the main house isn't visible from the gate, which they have been careful to keep closed ever since. The brick plantation home is well screened by the long lane and all those Spanish moss–draped live oaks, safe from prying eyes—and cameras.

"Are you in any pain?" Charlotte asks, idly studying the label of an orange prescription bottle. "Because it says you can take this again in an hour."

"No, I'm fine." He watches her set the bottle back on the table beside the couch, aligning it with the other medication they brought home. "Charlotte, maybe you should put those away somewhere."

"Oh, no you don't, Mister," she says lightly. "No way are you going to start in again about how you're just fine, and you don't need anything for the pain. There's no reason for you to suffer. You're taking these, Royce, until the doctor tells you to stop."

"No, that's not what I meant." He hesitates, trying to phrase it correctly. "I just don't know if y'all should leave them out here where anyone can . . . you know . . . find them. Some of those are narcotics."

"What are you getting at, Royce? You don't think that Nydia or Phyllida—"

"No," he cuts in, "I don't."

She stares at him.

He gives a slight nod.

"Royce, she might have lied and snuck out to see an older boy, but you're talking about drugs, here. I really don't think—"

"You said you didn't trust her after what happened. I don't, either. And why leave the slightest bit of temptation in her path?"

Charlotte sits in moody silence, staring into space.

"I'm sorry," Royce tells her after a minute. "You're right. There's no reason to think Lianna might help herself to my medication. That's ridiculous."

"It *is* ridiculous."

"I guess after seeing how they kept the narcotics in the hospital under such tight control, I couldn't help but think anybody could just stumble across these and help themselves."

"Lianna would never do that. I know she's done some awful things, and I don't trust her as far as I can throw her when it comes to boys, but I know my daughter. She wouldn't touch drugs."

"I'm sorry."

"Don't be. You were right to consider it. But you don't have to worry about it, or anything at all, for that matter. Why don't you just rest now?"

Charlotte strokes his cheek gently, sounding, and looking, just as exhausted as he feels. Her face is drawn; her lovely violet eyes underscored with dark crescents.

"I'm afraid I'm going to fall asleep," he tells her, allowing his own eyelids to droop, just for a moment.

"Go ahead. You need it."

He shakes his head, forcing his eyes open. "Not yet. I haven't been alone with you in a week; I'm not going to waste this opportunity by being unconscious."

She smiles. "How about if I put on some music?"

"That sounds good," he says around a yawn, fighting sleep. "I'll just close my eyes for a few seconds while you . . ."

Hearing Melanie climbing the stairs, humming to herself, Jeanne quickly slides the bureau drawer closed. No need to have the nurse catch her checking and rechecking her possessions. When the police made it up here, they gave her room only a cursory once-over. They never thought to search beneath the woolen shawl spread over an old lady's lap on a sweltering afternoon.

By the time Melanie reenters the room bearing an aromatic tray of food, Jeanne's wheelchair has been turned and she's once again facing the window, wearing an absent expression.

"I heated up your dinner, Jeanne," Melanie announces in her buoyant way. "I even put it on a regular plate for you for a change, and I brought real silverware, too."

Yes, she did. And the meal looks even skimpier on the good china than it would have in the compartments of a cardboard tray.

"Look what we have tonight, Jeanne! Turkey and gravy, mashed potatoes, asparagus. Doesn't that sound good?"

It sounds *good,* Jeanne thinks morosely, *but it won't be.*

Melanie chats about the weather as Jeanne inspects her tray.

"Big storm brewing," she says in the same manner in which she'd inform a small child that a carnival is coming to town. "It's called Douglas. Everybody's been talking about it on TV. They're saying it could turn into a hurricane. But don't worry, Jeanne, I'll make sure you're safe. And it's not for a few more days, anyway. Tomorrow we're just going to get some plain-old summer rain."

Jeanne nods. The turkey appears to be reheated sliced cold cuts doused with canned gravy, the potatoes are instant, and the asparagus has been reduced to green slime she could eat with a spoon . . . if she had one.

She usually gets a set of three white plastic utensils shrink-wrapped with a paper napkin and salt and pepper packets.

Not tonight.

For whatever reason, Melanie has decided to go all fancy on her. Jeanne suppresses the urge to ask her where she found the fancy table service. Did she take it upon herself to go through the cupboards?

It's been years since Jeanne has laid eyes on this white china with the gold rims. It belonged to her own mother first, and then to Eleanore.

She gazes down at the plate, eyes blurred with a flood of renewed disillusionment that it was Gilbert's wife, and not Jeanne, who inherited Mother's china.

It wasn't Eleanore's fault, of course. Nor was it her husband's. No, it was Father who decided that the china, and everything else that had ever belonged to Mother, would be given to his son and daughter-in-law.

Without his father's knowledge, Gilbert allowed Jeanne to take a few of their mother's possessions that had only sentimental value. The handkerchiefs and shawl that bore Mother's meticulous stitchery. The photograph album. The hair ribbon.

Gilbert never knew about the journals—or about the gun.

How proud Eleanore was to have service for sixteen.

She even threw a couple of dinner parties back when she and Gilbert were first married.

In fact, that's how Eleanore met Jonathan Barrow in the first place, beginning the downward spiral that eventually ended in her death.

But, of course, nobody knows about that. Nobody alive today, other than Jeanne, can truly appreciate the peculiar manner in which history tends to repeat itself, generation after generation, at Oakgate.

Jeanne doesn't believe in coincidences, however. There are reasons for what happened to Eleanore, just as there were reasons for what happened to her own mother . . .

And what is soon to befall yet another Remington woman who lives under the old plantation's dormered roof.

"Jeanne?" Melanie asks, hovering at her elbow. "Aren't you hungry?"

She is. She's famished. She picks up her fork and knife, relishing their pleasant weight in her grasp. She notices that Melanie has also provided her with a cloth napkin this evening, and a pair of salt-and-pepper shakers she remembers her mother using years ago.

After taking a predictably disappointing bite of the turkey, Jeanne moves the plate around, checking beneath the rim.

"What's the matter, Jeanne?" the nurse asks, hovering at her elbow. "What are you looking for?"

"A spoon . . . I need it for mashed potatoes, and the gravy . . ." She doesn't want to waste a drop—especially since there's barely enough to cover the rubbery turkey in the first place.

"Oh, no problem. I'll go back down and get one for you. Is there anything else you need?"

Yes, Jeanne thinks glumly, staring at the dismal meal, *but not yet. Not tonight.*

Soon, though, very soon.

Charlotte slips out from beneath Royce's arm and crosses the parlor to the mantel, where Grandaddy's radio has sat mute for weeks now.

It'll be good to have music in this house again, Charlotte thinks as she reaches for the dial. *Maybe I'll even leave it tuned to the Oldies station.*

She turns the knob with a click, but nothing happens. Not even a burst of static.

Oh—the volume must have been turned all the way down. She twists the dial all the way around clockwise, but the radio remains silent.

Ah, Nydia must have accidentally unplugged it while she was winding the clock.

Charlotte follows the dangling cord, but finds that it's still plugged into the outlet on the wall beside the mantel.

"That's odd," she says softly.

"Hmmm?" Royce asks, stirring on the couch behind her.

"Nothing, it's just . . . Grandaddy's radio doesn't work anymore for some reason."

"It's old," he murmurs. "Must be broken."

"First the elevator, and now this. After all these years. I'm going to have it fixed."

"The elevator?"

"The radio," she decides aloud. "Aimee already called the elevator guy. He's coming next week. I'll take the radio to Mr. Goldberg."

"Who's he? The radio guy?" Royce looks amused.

"Pretty much. He has the little repair shop down by the canal—he tinkered with Grandaddy's television last winter and got it running again. I have to go down to the South Shore tomorrow or Sunday, anyway, to pick up some things at the supermarket."

"Why do you have to go running all the way down there? Let Nydia do the shopping."

Normally she does, but she wants to pick up the ingredients for the complicated French seafood dish she cooked for Royce back when they were first married and she had vowed to become more domestic.

He loved it, and she'd promised him she'd make it every week.

Has she bothered with it since?

Um, no you haven't. So much for Super Wife.

Royce never really seems to mind that she rarely cooks, but it will be nice to surprise him with dinner tomorrow night.

And she'll get a chance to get the radio fixed.

Hearing a footfall beyond the parlor door, she looks up expectantly, expecting Aimee to return, or maybe even Lianna, who has yet to come down and greet her stepfather. Charlotte realizes she must be upstairs getting ready for her dinner out with Vince, but it would be nice if she spared a few minutes to see Royce before she leaves.

But nobody emerges from the next room.

Frowning, Charlotte calls, "Lianna? Is that you?"

The only reply is a creaking floorboard.

Irritated, Charlotte crosses to the French doors, which Aimee left ajar, and peeks into the larger parlor.

It's deserted, but she glimpses a shadow disappearing around the corner into the hall beyond.

"Lianna!" she calls.

No reply.

"Lianna?"

She hurries to the door, and finds the hall deserted as well.

A moment later, Nydia appears in the doorway leading toward the back of the house. "Is something wrong, Mrs. Maitland?'

Frowning, Charlotte asks, "Have you seen Lianna in the last few seconds? Or anyone?"

"I haven't seen her, but I did knock on her door and tell her that her father is here waiting for her. I sent him into the parlor to wait."

"Well, he isn't there."

"Maybe they left."

"She better not have left without letting me know," Charlotte says, and strides quickly to the window to see whether Vince's car is still here.

Sure enough, it's parked right out front—and there's Vince on the portico, settling himself into a wooden rocker just beyond the pool of light shining from the sconce beside the door.

"Thanks, Nydia." She peers out the door beyond the portico. A light rain is falling. "Vince?"

Her ex-husband looks up. "Oh, hi. How's it going?"

How's it going?

What she wants to say is, *My husband was just shot by my cousin and the whole world is buzzing about the scandal . . . How do you think it's going?*

Instead, she merely asks, "Were you in the parlor just now, waiting for Lianna?"

"No."

"Are you sure?"

"Of course I'm sure. I decided I'd rather wait out here. Why?"

"No reason," she says, not certain she believes him. Maybe he was eavesdropping on her and Royce. He must be nosy about all that's gone on, especially given the media's attention to the topic.

It would certainly explain why, for once in his life, he's actually shown up on time to see Lianna.

Or rather, shown up, period.

God only knows, it would make more sense if there was something in it for him. He probably wants to ensure his bragging rights as a "Remington insider." For all she knows, he'll sell an interview to some reporter tomorrow.

"Listen," Charlotte says, pushing aside her suspicions, "make sure you have Lianna back here at a reasonable hour, will you?"

"What's reasonable?" is the maddening reply.

"Just have her back here by eleven, okay? It's supposed to pour all night and I don't like her out late in bad weather." *Or with you.*

He salutes.

"Oh, and Vince? You should know I had to change to an unlisted phone number yesterday," she remembers to say. She hasn't even had a chance to tell anybody in the house, including Lianna, about that yet. Not that there's any hurry. Another day or two of silence after the constant ringing will be welcome, especially with Royce home, resting.

"What's the new number?" Vince asks, reaching into his pocket.

"Do you have a pen and paper?"

"No, I'll program it into my cell," he says, holding it up. "That way, I'll be able to call without having to look it up."

As if he's really going to suddenly start phoning their daughter on a regular basis. Yeah, sure.

Frustrated, Charlotte gives Vince the number, and reminds him again to have Lianna back by eleven.

Then she slowly returns to the parlor, and Royce.

"What's going on?" he asks drowsily.

"Nothing, I just . . . I think I'm hearing things. And seeing things," she adds, almost positive she had glimpsed a figure disappearing around the corner into the hall.

"Maybe Grandaddy really is haunting this place," she muses, glancing again at the radio. She read somewhere once that ghosts often use electronic devices to make their presence known.

Maybe Grandaddy's spirit has silenced the radio.

Maybe he's trying to tell her something by doing that.

Yes, she thinks wryly as she snuggles beside her husband once again, *and maybe you've finally gone off the deep end, Charlotte Maitland.*

For the second time this month, Mimi is awakened by the piercing ring of a telephone.

It's four thirty AM.

She seizes the cordless receiver from the nightstand and bolts from the room with it, not wanting to wake Jed. He had a terrible time earlier, restless and moaning in agony. It was only after she gave him another round of pain meds—too soon after the last dose, but she couldn't stand to see him suffer—that he finally fell into a deep sleep.

"Hello?" She clutches the receiver hard against her ear, praying it's not about her mother this time. She wouldn't be able to bear it.

"Yes, is this Mrs. Johnston?"

"Yes . . ."

"This is Dr. Von Cave," a distant, European-accented

voice announces. "I apologize if I've woken you . . . I'm afraid I have, haven't I? I didn't even think to consider the time difference before I dialed . . ."

Stunned, Mimi stammers that it's all right.

She never expected a return call when she at last poured out her heart to the doctor's receptionist a few days earlier. She didn't even entirely believe at the time that the woman truly took down her name and telephone number.

"Thank you so much for calling me back," she says in a rush. "I honestly . . . I didn't really expect it. I thought you must get countless desperate messages from people like me . . ."

"To be quite honest, Mrs. Johnston, I do. But yours caught my eye when I noticed the familiar area code."

"Familiar?"

There's a pause. "Mrs. Johnston, you do live in Georgia in the vicinity of Achoco Island, don't you?"

"Yes, I live on it," Mimi replies, wondering why that's relevant—and not really caring. All that matters is that the only woman on earth who can possibly save Jed's life is on the other end of the telephone line at last.

But before she can beg her to help, Mimi finds herself listening in growing disbelief to the precise reason Dr. Von Cave returned her call.

Jed, she realizes in shock, may be ensnared in a malignancy whose lethal tentacles extend far beyond his own life-and-death race against time.

Careful not to make a sound, Phyllida slips down the shadowy hallway toward the stairs. The treads, she's taken care to note in the past, creak only on either side; not down the middle.

She descends directly along the center in swift,

feather-footed silence, gracefully balanced without needing to grasp the rail. All those ballet lessons she took as
a girl come in handy when it comes to sneaking through
a sleeping house.

It's near dawn here, but only past one on the West
Coast. Brian will be up watching *Conan* or *Baseball Tonight*
or whatever it is he stays up late to watch. She wouldn't
know. Wouldn't care, either.

What matters is that she doesn't have to wait until
noon tomorrow to call and tell him about the decision
she's made.

In the kitchen, she pauses, clutching her cell phone
and the flashlight she retrieved from the utility drawer.
Then she peeks through the window and realizes that a
steady rain is falling.

Okay, so she won't make the call from outside.

But she can't do it right here in the kitchen. Who
knows what time Nydia begins to stir, considering the
ungodly hour she goes to bed, and the even more ungodly hour she's been serving breakfast all these years.

Nor should she go back to her room; the dividing
wall between her room and Lianna's is one of the few
that isn't made of plaster, and the last thing she wants is
to be overheard.

No, she's better off going to the far parlor, where
she'll be ensured of a private conversation behind
closed doors.

It's not one she's looking forward to, but now that
she knows what she has to do, she owes it to Brian to tell
him right away. Doesn't she?

It wouldn't be fair to wait until she gets back tomorrow night.

No, her flight gets in late, and by the time she gets
home from the airport and looks in on Wills . . .

Face it, Phyllida. You want to break it to him over the phone

right now so you won't have to wait and do it in person. That
way, you won't have to see his face when you tell him.

All right, that's true.

But what's wrong with that? This is easier, on both of
them. She'll just deliver the news gently.

Yeah, sure.

How do you gently drop a bombshell on your husband that you're planning to leave him, sell the house
and cars and every material possession you own, and
then take your young son and move to the opposite end
of the country?

I have to do it. That's all there is to it, she assures herself yet
again.

It's the only possible solution to her predicament.

This way, she can leave behind the mess in
California, abandoning once and for all her dreams
that weren't meant to come true. She'll start a new life
in Rhode Island; her mother can help her with Wills
while she goes to school, or gets a job, or does whatever
it takes to get back on her feet.

As she tossed and turned in her bed, thinking things
through, she briefly entertained the thought of asking
Brian to come back East with them. But there's no way
he'd agree to that. He's a native Californian; he hates
the very notion of cold winters as much as he hates
summer humidity. Not to mention the fact that he also
hates her mother.

He's bound to make a fuss when she first tells him
her plan, but she has a feeling he'll get over it pretty
quickly in the end. He'll come to realize what she already has: that he'll be free to golf whenever he wants,
and lounge around watching television, and spend his
money on expensive clothes and toys. He'll see that she
and Wills will be better off without him—and that he'll
be happier without the burden of a wife and child.

Eager to make her call now that her mind is made up, Phyllida leaves the kitchen.

Back in the shadowy hall, she realizes she's still clutching the flashlight. Rather than putting it back, she flicks it on and uses its beam to guide her through rooms that open onto each other from the center hall. That way, she won't have to leave a trail of lamplight that Nydia might follow if she awakens.

The floor plan is fairly familiar; the cluttered furniture layout, not as much. She moves slowly, taking stealth care to shine the light on every table and chair in her path. Outside, she can hear the patter of raindrops and the rushing sound as it pours from the downspouts along the portico. A cool gust stirs the lace curtains at the open windows in the first parlor as she moves past.

It's a good night for sleeping. Maybe, after she's made her call, she'll actually be able to do just that.

Yawning, Phyllida reaches the closed French doors to the second parlor.

She opens one and slips noiselessly into the room.

There, Phyllida Remington Harper is jolted, in one stunning, fleeting, yet unmistakable glimpse, by the biggest shock of her life.

PART IV

THE FOURTH VICTIM

CHAPTER 14

Sunday morning, the sun rises brightly on a world scrubbed clean in yesterday's downpour. Charlotte is glad she decided to set the alarm for an early hour. It's a beautiful day to get up and moving.

If she could just seem to *get* moving, that is.

Rather than refreshing her and scrubbing the exhaustion from her soul, a shower seems to leave her only more tempted to crawl back into bed. Of course, if she had made it bracing and quick—rather than long, languid, and hot—she might be more capable of springing into action.

She yawns repeatedly as she dresses, putting on a conservative navy dress with white piping, a matching broad-brimmed hat, and spectator pumps with a coordinating handbag. Around her neck, she fastens a simple gold-cross necklace her Grandaddy gave her for her sixteenth birthday.

It's time she went back to the little white Baptist church overlooking the sea, across the highway from Tidewater Meadow. She used to go every Sunday with

Grandaddy—and sometimes Royce, and Lianna when she was forced—but Charlotte hasn't been there at all in the weeks since he passed away.

Reverend Snowdon visited the hospital in Savannah this week to pray with her and Royce, thanking God for sparing his life. When he left, she promised she'd see him at Sunday services.

"Stay for our coffee hour after," he invited. "You'll see lots of familiar faces, and they'll certainly want to see you. Everyone has been praying for y'all."

She promised to try, but she knows that she won't linger.

It would be pure torture to face all those people wanting to know how Royce is, and wondering how Gib could have done such a thing, and telling her that her poor dead Grandaddy would have been simply devastated by this turn of events and the shame brought to the family name.

No, she doesn't need that at all.

And anyway, she has other things to do on the south end before hurrying back up here to Royce. She wants to finally stop at the supermarket to get the ingredients for that seafood dish she's making. The prospect of all that work and the busy day ahead is daunting now, but of course she'll be fine once she's on a roll.

Oh, and she needs to take that radio to Mr. Goldberg to be fixed. She'd have gone yesterday, but she called ahead in the morning and learned that his little shop was closed for the Jewish Sabbath.

Which worked out better in the end, because she felt just as tired and lazy yesterday. Plus the rain persisted well into the afternoon, and it was a good day to stay in and cuddle with Royce on his first day home.

He's still grumbling about the hospital bed, which was delivered late Friday night and set up in the parlor.

But he refused to agree to let Charlotte sleep down there with him, on the couch. She hated to leave him alone, feeling the almost compulsive need to keep watch over him, lest something terrible happen again.

This anxiety is probably perfectly normal. All the bereavement counseling she endured told her that. But shouldn't it be lessening with time and distance from the trauma, rather than growing in intensity?

She can't quite convince herself that Royce isn't in danger, even now that he's home and Gib is in custody.

But she didn't tell her husband of her uneasiness— just that she knew he might not be able to get around unassisted if he needed something in the middle of the night.

"I won't need anything, believe me," he said, yawning profusely before turning in. "But if I do, I'll holler."

As she and Aimee made their way to the kitchen with the dishes and cups from the tea—sweet for her, hot for Royce and Aimee—and honey toast they shared earlier, Charlotte commented in a low voice, "The thing is, I'm so tired I'm afraid I wouldn't hear him if he did holler."

"Don't worry," Aimee said. "I'm not that tired. I'll definitely hear. Anyway, trust me—with those painkillers he's on, he's not going to budge. I just gave him a slightly bigger dose so he'll be out like a light all night."

"Is that a good idea?" Charlotte asked, concerned.

Aimee laughed. "Oh, don't worry. I didn't give him that much, although it was tempting, what with the way he was going on and on about you and me trying to baby him too much, and then he turns right around and calls me 'Baby Girl.' But that's Daddy. He's always liked to be the manly man. He thinks medicine is for wimps, you know?"

"Do I ever." Charlotte laughed, then fought another enormous yawn, overcome by the need for sleep. "I'm so wiped out I feel like I've been drugged myself. But I'll try and check on him a few times in the night."

"I'm sure he'll sleep through, with no pain. That's why I upped the dose a little. He probably wouldn't stir if a train went through there."

As far as Charlotte knows, he didn't stir—not Friday night, or last night, either. After the first good night's sleep, he wanted to try the stairs last night, but she and Aimee have convinced him to give it a few more days.

Whenever he's alone with Charlotte, he likes to take her in his arms to tell her—and show her—exactly why he's so anxious to get back up to their bedroom with her soon.

She feels the same way, and not just for romantic reasons.

Even with her night-light, she isn't comfortable being alone in that room all night.

Then again, it's not as though she's been lying awake worrying. Her own exhaustion is catching up with her: these last two nights, she's slept better than she has in weeks.

Which would be great if she didn't feel like she could have gone on sleeping for hours after the alarm went off.

"Good morning, Mrs. Maitland," Nydia says from the sink as Charlotte steps into the kitchen, now fragrant with fresh coffee and bacon grease.

"Good morning, Nydia." She pats a yawn from her lips. "You haven't seen my cousin Phyllida since yesterday, have you?"

The woman turns back to her sudsy water, but not before Charlotte glimpses a decidedly disagreeable expression on her face. "No."

Just *no?*

Irritated by the curt reply, Charlotte presses, "She

hasn't been down for breakfast at all? Not yesterday, not today?"

"When does she ever come down for breakfast? She's lucky if she's up in time for lunch."

All right. It's no surprise that Nydia is less than fond of the resident prima donna. Still, she might be a little more pleasant about it.

Charlotte takes a travel mug from the cabinet, deciding a dose of caffeine is in order if she's going to come fully awake for the drive down south.

As she pours it, Nydia comments, "Anyway . . . I thought she was leaving before the big storm."

"No, she wasn't supposed to until last night."

"Not yesterday's storm. There's a big one coming in a day or two, Tropical Storm Douglas. She wanted to get out before that. Did she go last night, then?"

"I don't know. I didn't see her all day. I was going to make sure she had arranged for a ride to the airport, but I . . . didn't want to bother her in her room."

The truth was, Charlotte was too busy lying around watching television with Royce to give her cousin much thought until they saw a story on the evening news about residual delays at the airport because of the weather.

"I just wondered if her flight was canceled in advance and she didn't bother to go," Charlotte says now, as she stirs more sugar than usual into her coffee. "I figured she might not have left the house if she knew about the delays, or that maybe she would have come back if she couldn't get out."

Nydia shrugs. "Haven't seen her," she reiterates, "but if she's gone, I'll go make up her room again before I leave."

"Leave?"

"It's Sunday, my day off."

Oh, that's right. Nydia always leaves Oakgate after breakfast and doesn't return until Monday morning. Where she goes, Charlotte has no idea—not that she's ever given the topic much thought. She supposes the housekeeper must have an apartment somewhere, or maybe a friend she stays with.

She has to have some kind of life beyond Oakgate. Charlotte certainly hopes she does.

That way, it'll be easier for her to move on after the place is sold.

"Well, then," she tells Nydia, as she opens the wooden file box where she keeps the seafood recipe, "you should just go ahead, and don't worry about the guest room now. There's no rush."

"No, really, let me get it ready. That way, your visitor can move right in there this morning."

"You mean Aimee?"

Nydia nods.

Charlotte shakes her head in response, rifling through her recipe cards with growing irritation.

Earlier this week, the woman also wanted to move Aimee into Gib's vacated, ransacked premises—and would have probably transferred her things single-handedly if the police hadn't cordoned off the room and asked them to leave it untouched for the time being.

Sensing she's about to get an argument now, Charlotte informs Nydia firmly, as she plucks the recipe card from the box and slams it closed, "I'd hate to make Aimee move now that she's settled in. And the room she's in"—*your grandaddy's room,* Nydia's disapproving look reminds her—"has its own private bathroom."

Yes. The bathroom where he died.

The unspoken words dangle between them as Nydia says only, "Your grandfather's things are still there. I never had the chance to clean them out before she showed up."

She says it with a deliberate emphasis on the pronoun, as though Aimee has no right to be here . . . and, come to think of it, as though it's up to Nydia, and not Charlotte, to go through Grandaddy's possessions.

She supposes the housekeeper does have a certain proprietary sense, having lived here since before Charlotte was even born. Still . . .

The woman is household help, not family.

"I'll go through Grandaddy's things after Aimee leaves," she tells Nydia, a bit coldly.

And Aimee, by the way, is family.

Before Nydia can comment, she adds, "Nobody's going to disturb anything in the meantime, so don't worry."

The housekeeper meets her gaze head on. "I would hope not," is all she says, before turning back to the sink.

Charlotte sets the recipe card on the counter, consults it, and opens the cupboard door to check for dried tarragon.

"Can I help you find something?" Nydia asks, startling her, having come up right behind her.

"Tarragon . . . Do you know if we have any?"

"No, I don't. Why don't you let me check?"

Sensing that the woman's offer stems more from reluctance to see her precious cupboards disturbed than from genuine helpfulness, Charlotte says, "Never mind."

Forget about checking for the herbs and spices she'll need. Unwilling to spend another moment in Nydia's company, Charlotte takes her coffee and her purse and leaves the room.

The housekeeper usually isn't this unpleasant—but then, Charlotte usually doesn't deal with her at this hour. Maybe she, like Lianna, just isn't a morning person.

No problem. Charlotte can buy everything she needs at the supermarket, including the herbs and spices. Fresh would be better anyway.

The longer she takes to shop and drop off the radio after church, the better the chances that Nydia will be gone for the day by the time she gets back.

She moves quietly through the house to the closed French doors to the parlor, where Royce is still asleep.

Darn it. She should have thought to get the radio from the mantel before she went to bed last night, so she wouldn't have to disturb him. Why didn't she do that?

Because you were too caught up in having Royce home to give anything else, including Phyllida, a second thought.

Again, she wonders whether her cousin made it home to California, and why she didn't at least say good-bye before she left. True, they aren't on the best of terms after all that's happened, but Phyllida must know Charlotte doesn't hold her responsible for her brother's actions.

Gib.

Even now, after all these days, she still can't quite grasp the enormity of what he did. Every morning, the shocking truth settles over her anew, like an ill-fitting uniform you can't wait to strip off when the day is done.

She supposes she'll get used to the idea that the enemy was lurking under this very roof—behind the mask of a loved one, no less.

Crossing the threshold into the parlor, she finds the heavy amber-silk draperies still pulled across the lace curtains, to block out the morning light.

When her eyes have grown accustomed to the dim interior, she glances toward the hospital bed on the far side of the room, in a nook beside the window. Royce is there, his mouth thrown open, obviously in a deep sleep.

After crossing the carpet on tiptoe, Charlotte realizes she'll need to tuck her car keys into her purse to free her hands for carrying the radio.

Unfortunately, she misses the zippered pocket, and the keys plummet to the floor. Of all the luck, en route, they strike one of the antique brass andirons with a deafening jangle.

Gasping in dismay, Charlotte swivels her head to look at Royce.

He doesn't even appear to have moved a muscle.

Panic overtakes her as she remembers the sight of Grandaddy's corpse, looking as though he had fallen sound asleep in the tub. In fact, she had almost convinced herself that Nydia was hysterical over nothing, jumping to conclusions . . .

Until she touched his skin and found it as cold as the bathwater and hard as the porcelain tub.

Heart pounding in dread, she walks over to Royce.

No, she thinks. *This can't be happening.*

I can't lose him now, after everything.

Slowly, she reaches for his hand, exposed on top of the sheet.

Thank God, she thinks as her fingers graze her husband's unmistakably warm flesh.

He doesn't even flinch as she gives him one last, firm stroke, just to be sure.

Aimee was right, she thinks, amused as she goes back to retrieve the keys. That painkiller he's on is good stuff. A freight train could roar through here, and it probably wouldn't even wake him.

On her key ring, the plastic frame that holds the Grand Canyon photo of herself and Royce has cracked.

Taken aback, Charlotte sees that a jagged line now appears to divide it in half, right between their smiling faces, almost as if it's a harbinger to . . .

No. Don't be ridiculous. Nothing is going to happen to Royce.

Anyway, the whole picture is an illusion in the first place: artificial backdrop, smiles, and all. They'd had a rare argument shortly before it was taken. Over what, she can no longer remember. It doesn't matter.

She gives her sleeping husband one last, grateful glance. He's going to be fine. Really.

"I won't be gone long," she whispers. "I love you."

Now she just needs to grab the radio, dash back to the kitchen for the recipe card, which she forgot on the counter, and be on her way.

There's just one problem.

The spot in the center of the mantel . . .

The spot where the radio sat for decades in its place of honor . . .

Is now conspicuously empty.

After a quick, fruitless search of the room—indeed, the entire first floor—Charlotte, dumbfounded, concludes that her Grandaddy's radio seems to have somehow vanished altogether.

With little to do each day but observe his own thoughts, Gib has grown to loathe Detective Williamson.

Dorado is tolerable—you get the feeling that he's at least human, that you might actually like him under regular circumstances. His partner, however, is thoroughly abrasive in every possible way.

Thus, when Gib is summoned to face him in a windowless room no different, really, than a jail cell, it's all he can do not to—

What? Spit in his face? Give him the finger?

Yeah, that'll go over big. Especially with Tyler here. Gib can't help but notice that the lawyer seems to be growing less benevolent with every passing day.

In fact, this morning, Tyler sits, arms folded, as though he's waiting impatiently for the detectives to begin . . . or end, so he can get on with his day.

He also refuses to meet Gib's eyes.

That isn't a good sign.

Gib assumes they're all here for another attempt at plea bargaining. If so, they're wasting their time.

"We have a few more questions for you, Remington," Dorado informs him, and something in his tone warns Gib the case has taken a turn. For better or worse, he isn't certain. But he senses that there's been a new development.

His brain is immediately fraught with possibilities—and fear. Still, he's careful to maintain an utterly blank façade, lest the circling predators sniff blood in the water. Gib knows now, from experience, that they will feed off the slightest hint of vulnerability.

What the hell is going on?

Did they do another search of his belongings?

Did they look more closely at the items in his Dopp bag?

Could they possibly have found the contents of the receptacles disguised as a shaving cream can and hair product?

No! Of course not. If they didn't find it the first time, they aren't going to keep going over and over the same evidence, Gib reminds himself.

Still, it takes every bit of his concentration to keep from betraying his foreboding as Williamson says, "We're not going to beat around the bush with you, Remington."

Gib shrugs, even as a shrill voice in his head shrieks, *They've found it. They know everything. You're fried.*

"I'm going to ask you a straightforward question, Remington." Williamson leans forward, his voice menacingly low, "And I want a straightforward answer. Got it?"

Gib nods, holding his breath, reminding himself that this whole nightmarish situation is getting blown out of proportion.

Seriously, it's not like I've been accused of murder.

But Williamson's next words make quick wreckage of that particular thought, hitting Gib like a cyclone.

"Where were you on the night your grandfather died?"

Royce sighs, watching Charlotte once again look at the empty spot on the mantel, almost as though she expects the missing radio to have miraculously materialized there.

"Charlotte, there has to be a logical explanation for this," he says gently, and not for the first time since he woke from a sound sleep to find her moving the couch to search behind it.

"I know there is."

He can't help but say, "I promise that the house being haunted by your grandfather's ghost isn't it."

"I know it sounds crazy . . ." She smiles sheepishly, turning away from the mantel to return to his bedside. "It's just that when it wasn't working, I thought maybe it was because Grandaddy's spirit did something to it."

"Which makes a whole lot of sense." He returns her smile to show that he's teasing.

"Royce, don't laugh at me."

"I'm not laughing, honey. I'm just trying to convince you that somebody—a human being in this house— must have moved the radio. Or taken it."

"Who would possibly do that?"

"Think about it, Charlotte. Who do you think?"

She shrugs. "I've already checked with Nydia and Aimee. I know Lianna couldn't have had anything to do with it . . ." She gives a purposeful nod, and he can tell she hasn't let go of his earlier insinuation about the pain medication.

This probably isn't a good time for him to mention that he's noticed the supply seems to be dwindling. He'll bring it up later, when she isn't as distracted.

"The only other person in this house is Aunt Jeanne," Charlotte points out, "and unless she told her nurse to come down and grab it, she's out of the question."

"Maybe she did just that."

There's a long pause.

"Why would she?"

Why? Because she's a nutcase, is what he wants to say.

But he opts for the more sensitive, "You know she's not exactly of sound mind. Why does she do or say anything?"

Charlotte shrugs again. "I'll ask her nurse tomorrow. She doesn't come on Sundays, and there's no use asking Aunt Jeanne directly."

"I don't think that matters," Royce says meaningfully.

His wife raises a brow. "Why?"

"Think about it, Charlotte. You forgot about one other person who's been in this house."

"Who? Phyllida?"

"Bingo."

"You think she took the radio? Why would she do that?"

Now he shrugs. "Out of spite? Because she knows that of everything in this house, it had the most sentimental value to you?"

The light dawns blatantly on Charlotte's face . . . along with unmistakable outrage. "You're right. I bet she did take it. I can't believe that. What should I do?"

"Write it off as a loss, and good riddance to your cousin?"

"No. I'm not going to just drop it." She looks at her watch. "It's still too early to call California. But believe me, as soon as it's a reasonable hour, I'm going to get ahold of her and ask her about it."

Having finally worked up her nerve to call the telephone number she had committed to memory in her misguided youth, Mimi is immediately discouraged when a recorded voice greets the call. *"We're sorry, you have reached a number that has been disconnected or is no longer in service. If you feel you have reached this reading in error, please check the area code and the number and try your call again."*

All right, so maybe her memory isn't fail-proof.

Still, she gives the memorized number another try, pressing the buttons more slowly. After all, it's not as though her hands weren't shaking like crazy when she dialed the first time, nor was she taking her time.

Once her mind was made up to take the plunge and make the call to Oakgate, she couldn't connect fast enough.

But she's going to have to wait a little longer.

Once again, the voice informs her that the number isn't in service.

She hesitates only briefly before calling directory assistance. They'll have to come up with the extra fifty cents, or whatever it costs, when the bill comes next month. This is important . . .

Life or death, she thinks, brooding as she waits to by-pass the automated response.

When the operator comes on the line, Mimi requests the number for the Remingtons, only to be informed that it's unlisted.

Plunking the phone back into its cradle, she paces across the kitchen to the doorway and peeks into the next room.

Jed is still sound asleep on the couch, courtesy of the prescription painkillers he finally agreed to take during the day, but only after she showed him that he still had plenty to spare.

Mimi's mother, God bless her, kept Cameron overnight again and promised to bring him home tomorrow morning, first thing. Today, she insisted on having him stay for church and a little picnic at the playground.

Maude Gaspar has been a godsend these past few days, keeping her grandson happily occupied so that Mimi can attend to Jed—and the newly complicated matter at hand.

I have to speak to Gib's cousin, she thinks resolutely, watching Jed's chest rise and fall in reassuring cadence. *The second Mom gets here tomorrow, I'm leaving her here with Jed and Cam and going straight over to Oakgate.*

She's never officially met Charlotte Remington Maitland, but she used to see her at the beach when she was a lifeguard. She remembers watching the beautiful and sophisticated Charlotte in admiration as she sat reading in the shade of her beach umbrella. She remembers wondering if it was hard for her to be on the beach at Achoco, after losing her son in that awful drowning accident there.

She remembers, too, daydreaming about what it would be like to be a Remington herself.

As if Gib ever would have married the likes of Mimi Gaspar.

Well, thank goodness he didn't want me, she thinks now, acknowledging what's become of her former boyfriend.

She shudders and pushes away the very thought of him, as she has all week, not even wanting to acknowledge Gib Remington's role in her past—let alone hers in his apparently dismal future.

But that hasn't stopped her from reading the papers. Not this time.

There's been no mention of the tip that led to Gib becoming a suspect in the first place, thank God.

The accounts are full of background about the illustrious family, with details about every player—from Royce Maitland's twenty-five-year-old daughter, Aimee, rushing to his bedside from New Orleans to Gib's sister, Phyllida, age respectfully omitted, and referred to as a Hollywood starlet, though there's never any mention of which films or TV programs, exactly, she has starred in.

There is, of course, plenty of media speculation about what could have driven the disgraced scion to such violence.

But Gib is no longer the family member who is most important to Mimi.

Nor, at the moment, is the secret that is far more likely to destroy what is left of her husband's life than to save it.

Charlotte is the only Remington Mimi is interested in contacting.

First thing tomorrow, she promises herself again, wishing she didn't have to wait that long. But she can't leave Jed here unattended, no matter how pressing her need to get over to Oakgate.

It's all right. Tomorrow will be here before you know it.

It has a way of doing that lately, she thinks grimly, wondering why time seems to stand still only when you long to savor precious moments. These last few weeks have flown by, each day seeming to alight fleetingly before being swept away, like the rapidly flipping calendar pages in a silent movie scene depicting the swift passage of time.

Yes, tomorrow will dawn all too soon, Mimi tells herself, brushing away the tears that spring to her eyes.

I just have to ask Charlotte what she knows about her mother . . . and just hope it's not too late.

Gib is lying.

Tyler is certain of it.

Alone with his client at last, he looks Gib in the eye. "Let me make one thing clear. Your grandfather is the only reason I'm even here in the first place. He was a close friend of mine throughout my life."

"I realize that." Gib's tone is sullen.

Standing over him, Tyler slaps his hands, hard, on the table and lowers his face to Gib's level. "If I'm going to even consider being remotely involved in your defense from here on in—and I'll say right now that it isn't looking likely that I am—you're going to tell me everything you know about your grandfather's death. Got it?"

"I'm not going to say anything to you that I didn't already say in front of them," is the wrathful response, as Gib jerks his head in the direction of the door through which the two detectives had just departed. "This whole thing is bullshit."

"Watch your tongue," Tyler says sharply.

To his credit, Gib apologizes.

"I hope you know that I'm this close to walking out of here." Tyler presses his thumb and index finger together and thrusts his hand into Gib's face.

"Please don't." Slumped in his seat, appearing more exhausted than dejected, he tells Tyler, "I just can't believe they're trying to pin this on me, now, too."

"Who?"

"The detectives, who else? Just like they planted those shoes, shirt, and cufflink in my room."

Tyler says nothing, having heard that ludicrous claim repeatedly ever since Gib's arrest.

He again hears an echo of his own voice, so long ago.

I don't know how the cigarettes got into my room, Headmaster Swift. I didn't put them there.

I don't know how the answer key got etched onto my desk, Mr. Anderson. Somebody in another section must have left it there.

"My grandfather had a heart attack," Gib goes on, gazing at the Persian carpet. "We all saw the autopsy report."

"And we all know that cardiac arrest can mask other things." At least, they know that now, thanks to Williamson's ever-informative spiel.

"We also know"—as Williamson also pointed out— "that bodies can be exhumed for a number of reasons, not the least of which is suspected murder."

Gib's head is still bent. He doesn't flinch. It's impossible to gauge his reaction to that news, but Tyler would stake a hefty bet that there was one.

What Gib doesn't grasp—but what Tyler has come to realize, having spoken with the detectives prior to the confrontation—is that Williamson and Dorado are operating purely on a hunch.

There's no evidence that Gilbert Remington's death

was anything but accidental. But in checking out all the avenues leading to Gib's possible motivation for Royce Maitland's shooting, the detectives aren't about to avoid this one.

As Dorado put it, it's awfully coincidental that the old man died just a few weeks before Royce Maitland was shot, and that the assault occurred shortly after Gib learned for the first time that he had been disinherited.

He was willing to do anything to get his hands on that money, Dorado told Tyler.

And Tyler couldn't bring himself to argue the point.

Having witnessed Gib's reaction to the will that day in his office, Tyler has no doubt that his surprise was as genuine as his dismay, which transformed right before the attorney's eyes to full-blown rage.

Tyler, of anyone, saw firsthand how much that money meant to Gib.

Tempted as he is to walk out of here and never look back, Tyler needs to take care of a few details first. There's no telling what might come to light if there's an ensuing investigation into Gilbert's death—and his life.

He owes it to his late friend—and to the memory of the Telfair Trio—to at least attempt to unearth the truth that lies beneath this latest Remington calamity, while making every effort to keep the near-miss of the past safely buried, where it belongs.

That doesn't mean he's going to represent Gilbert's grandson in court. But perhaps he can help him locate a criminal lawyer who has no potential conflict of interest—and nothing personal to lose.

No matter the eventual outcome . . . whichever way this turns out—whether Gib is exonerated or proven guilty—Tyler's loyalty to Gilbert will remain unsevered.

Yes, he thinks, *but if there really is the slightest bit of hard evidence that Gilbert's death was anything other than from natural causes . . .*

Then Gib Remington is entirely on his own.

Rounding the corner into the kitchen, Charlotte nearly slams into someone.

"Oh, I'm sorry!" Aunt Jeanne's nurse exclaims, taking a big step back, clutching a steaming mug. "I'm so glad I didn't burn you!"

Surprised to see her, Charlotte asks, "What are you doing here?"

"Just fixing your aunt some hot cocoa. Not the kind from the mix. I brought everything to make it from scratch. She likes a nice hot drink in the afternoon, and she was telling me that her mother used to make it for her that way when she was a little girl, so I—"

"No," Charlotte cuts in, not in the mood for idle chitchat, "I meant, what are you doing working today? I thought Sunday was your day off."

Melanie lowers her gaze to the mug. "It is. I just thought your aunt needed me here today. She's been so down, so it seemed like a good idea to come."

Charlotte digests this news with a twinge of guilt— she has neglected her elderly aunt these last few weeks, with all that's gone on—but also with a speck of suspicion.

It's not as though she can't afford to pay the nurse overtime. But that wasn't part of the original arrangement made by Grandaddy, and she can't help but wonder if Miss Sunshine, here, might not be a bit more shrewd than she comes across.

"Melanie," she says, after contemplating the best phrasing, "my grandfather had budgeted Aunt Jeanne's care and until I can look more closely into her daily needs to see if that warrants a change, I'm afraid—"

"Oh, you think I'm here today for the money? Don't worry, Mrs. Maitland. I wasn't expecting to get paid. I'm just visiting."

Really? Or are you an opportunist who cleverly shifts gears when put on a spot? Charlotte wonders as she looks into Melanie's big, seemingly earnest, blue eyes.

She decides to keep her suspicions to herself, at least for now. "Well, it certainly is nice of you to give up your day off," is all she says.

"Oh, I don't mind at all. Your aunt is such a wonderful woman. I love spending time with her." Melanie's tone isn't the least bit reproachful, but Charlotte gets the silent message loud and clear.

I love spending time with her . . . and so should you.

"Well, thanks," she murmurs to Melanie, resolving to pop upstairs later to see her aunt.

"You look really nice today, Mrs. Maitland. That color looks great on you."

"Thank you."

"And where did you get those shoes? They're darling!"

Charlotte repeats her gratitude, and tells Melanie she doesn't remember where she bought the shoes—which isn't the truth. They were purchased at a boutique where the least expensive item would cost several weeks' worth of Melanie's hourly wage.

"Are you going someplace special?" the nurse chatters on.

"Oh, I was going to head to church, and—" She slaps her head, remembering.

"What is it?"

"I meant to get some ingredients at the supermarket

for a seafood recipe I'm making for my husband, that's all."

"Would you like me to run out for you?"

"No, that's okay, you don't have to do that."

"I really wouldn't mind. I love being out and about! Especially when the sun is shining and the birds are singing, like today."

Sometimes, Charlotte thinks, Melanie's bubbly demeanor is a little hard to stomach.

"Really," Charlotte assures her, "that's okay. I'll go to the store later, or tomorrow. But thanks anyway."

"You're very welcome!"

The nurse is leaving the room when, as an afterthought, Charlotte calls, "Melanie?"

"Yes?" She looks expectantly over her shoulder with a jaunty swing of her long blond ponytail.

"Have you seen an old radio upstairs?"

"Oh!" Having turned around too quickly, Melanie accidentally sloshed cocoa over the rim of the cup onto her fingers. "I'm sorry, that that was really hot! What did you want to know?"

Charlotte repeats the question, watching the nurse set down the cup, cross to the sink, and rinse her hand under cold water.

"No, I haven't seen anything on the third floor, but I'll ask your Aunt Jeanne about it when I go back up."

Charlotte dismisses that notion with a wave of her hand. "Oh, that's all right. She probably won't even know which radio I'm talking about."

"You might be surprised." Melanie turns off the tap and dries her hands on a dish towel. "Your aunt remembers more than y'all think."

As the nurse retrieves the hot cocoa and leaves the room, her last words ring in Charlotte's ears.

Your aunt remembers more than y'all think.

She can't help but find the comment ominous, whether it was intended to be, or not.

"You heard what I told the detectives. I wasn't even in Savannah the night it happened. I was in Mexico, on vacation."

"I heard you, Gib," Tyler acknowledges, tapping his black wing tip impatiently on the Persian carpet, "and I was a little taken aback that you were able to recall in a split second your exact whereabouts on a specific date weeks ago without even glancing at a calendar."

"I didn't need to. It was a memorable trip, and I was in the company of a very memorable woman when Charlotte called about Grandaddy."

"Where were you?"

"In the airport. Charlotte can vouch for that if you talk to her. I remember the background noise was so bad I could barely hear her."

"What about your lady friend? Can I talk to her?"

Gib hesitates before answering. Just for a split second, but it's long enough to spark further suspicion in Tyler's mind.

"Sure," Gib says, "talk to her any time you want. Her name is Cassandra."

Pulling out a pen, Tyler asks for her last name and phone number, which Gib promptly claims not to know.

"You don't have her telephone number?" Tyler asks in disbelief. "Come on, Gib."

"I have it," Gib scowls, "but not here. Unfortunately I didn't have a chance to grab my little black book before I left the house."

Having had just about enough of Glib Gib, Tyler puts away his pen. With luck, she'll be in the Boston phone listings; if not, he'll commandeer Gib's cell phone—the modern-day equivalent of a little black book—which, come to think of it, must already be in police possession.

Dammit. Tyler simply wasn't cut out for criminal law, even at this stage of the investigation. Maybe he should cut his losses and refuse to have anything further to do with this.

The trouble is, he's not just here out of legal obligation, or even loyalty to Gilbert. He's here, too, because of what he did. He and Silas Neville, all those years ago. Not just out of friendship and loyalty. They weren't immune to the deadly sins they learned about in Bible School many years ago: greed was also a factor. Gilbert compensated them well for their risk.

So, yes, Tyler Hawthorne has something at stake, should the police start looking for skeletons in the Remington closets.

So he wants to know—no, *needs* to know—if Gib Remington's greed could have possibly pushed him as far as murder.

If he were a betting man, and inclined to listen to his own intuition, he'd say *no*.

But he's a pragmatic attorney, and the evidence seems to say *yes*.

"This Cassandra," he asks Gib, "does she live in Boston proper? Or in the suburbs?"

Again, the slight hesitation.

"You don't know," Tyler says flatly, "is that what you're going to tell me? You went to Mexico with this woman and you don't even know where she lives? And you expect me to believe that?"

Tyler would love to slap the insolent look off Gib's handsome face.

Then the younger man unexpectedly admits, "I didn't go to Mexico with her. I just met her in the airport."

"Who did you go to Mexico with, then?"

"I went alone."

"You expect me to believe that?"

"It's the truth."

No, it isn't, Tyler thinks, watching his client intently. *It isn't the whole truth, anyway.*

A female voice answers the phone with "Harper residence" on the first ring, but it doesn't belong to Phyllida.

Charlotte asks for her, going over again in her mind exactly how she's going to phrase her question about the radio. She decided not to make it a confrontation, as tempting as that is. No, it should be more of a . . . query, like a casual, *You wouldn't happen to know where Grandaddy's radio is, would you?*

She won't even jump right in with that; first, she'll ask about the flight last night and apologize for not having had a chance to say good-bye.

Yes, it's a good idea to remain civilized. As Charlotte's mother always used to say, *"You catch more flies with honey . . ."*

"Mrs. Harper isn't here," the voice says, effectively bursting her bubble—for now. "Mr. Harper isn't, either. Who's calling, please?"

"This is her cousin Charlotte. Who is this?"

"Lila—I'm Wills's nanny," the woman says edgily, before blurting, "Are you in Georgia? That cousin?"

"Yes . . ."

"Mr. Harper has been trying to call you all morning. He tried yesterday, too. He thought something must have happened to the phone because we saw on the Weather Channel there was a hurricane coming—"

"You mean the tropical storm? No, that hasn't hit yet. We've just had rain—"

"Well, we saw there were flight delays, and whenever he tried to get through to you, the recording kept saying the phone was out of service."

"Oh—the number's been changed." *And I would have told you if I had seen you, but you didn't even bother to say good-bye,* she mentally scolds Phyllida.

Then, realizing what Lila just said, she asks, puzzled, "Why has Brian been trying to call me all morning?"

"He wasn't trying to call you—he was trying to get Mrs. Harper on the phone. He's been leaving voice mails for her, too, but she isn't picking up her cell phone."

Charlotte frowns. "You mean she isn't there? In California?"

"No. Isn't she *there?*"

"No. At least, I don't think so. I haven't seen her."

"Mr. Harper is worried sick, and poor little Wills keeps asking where his mommy is . . . When he woke up Saturday morning I told him she was coming back that night. Mr. Harper even brought him to the airport, even though the flight was scheduled to get in so late . . . but no Mommy."

"Maybe it didn't come in," Charlotte suggests. "The weather was horrible. I bet she spent the night here at the airport and she's probably on a flight now."

"No, the flight came in, just an hour late. But she wasn't on it."

"Did you check with the airline?"

"They wouldn't release any passenger information. It's against the law. We don't know where she is. But we thought you would."

No," Charlotte murmurs, her thoughts reeling. "I'm sorry, I have no idea."

* * *

Deep in the marsh, unseen creatures scamper, slither, and fly away from approaching footsteps. The steel utility blade swings relentlessly at irksome Spanish moss, grayer and drier than an old lady's hair. The hilt glints silver in the sunlight as it hacks a cleaner path to the old slave cabins.

The mud in most places is knee-deep here, making each step a challenge, and high rubber boots a necessity.

This is hard work beneath the hot midday sun, but not nearly as arduous as it was to travel this same path the other night, in the dark and rain, dragging one hundred and twenty-five pounds of tarped dead weight. The hand truck did no good, having been left here at the cabin. But the flashlight, so thoughtfully provided by the victim herself, guided the way.

You could have thrown her into the trunk, weighted her with a concrete block, and tossed her off the Achoco Island causeway, like you said you were going to do.

Right. But this is better. Harder work yields prolonged enjoyment in the end.

Not that there's much time to linger for fun today . . .

And not that this plan is without significant risks.

Then again, it's like you mentioned to Lianna just the other day . . .

Nothing worthwhile in life comes without risk.

Yes, and she looked about as attentive as she would be listening to an English teacher droning on about literary devices . . .

Such as foreshadowing.

Tsk, tsk, Lianna. You really should listen when people talk.

Anyway, the risks of this overall plan became apparent way back in the beginning, when a trolley full of tourists happened around the corner onto Drayton Street unexpectedly just before Tyler Hawthorne's little rainy-day "accident" was to have occurred the first time.

It took another whole week to wait for a suitable deluge so that the hit-and-run could be restaged. That time, it worked like a charm.

Except that he lived.

But it did get him out of the picture long enough for the plan to proceed.

And he fits in rather nicely now, doesn't he?

So yes, there are risks at every turn. But really, who in their right mind is going to venture out here for any reason whatsoever in this day and age?

Chances are slim to none that anyone might have noticed that one cabin has been newly outfitted with a steel-reinforced door and a padlock, both conveniently purchased at the sprawling Home Depot over near the causeway.

It's just fortunate that the place was ready to accommodate yet another guest, this time ahead of schedule.

Well, in this family, one must always be prepared for the likelihood of unexpected company. That's just good old-fashioned Southern hospitality.

With an abrupt fluttering of wings, a great flock of nocturnal herons lifts from an overhead roost, their squawks mingling with the maniacal cackle of laughter that startled them.

"*There* you are!" Casey exclaims, hearing Lianna's voice. "Where have you been?"

"Where have *I* been?" Sprawled on the couch in the upstairs study, Lianna winds the curly phone cord around her index finger, watching the bulging tip turn white. "Y'all are the ones who've been away, like, forever. You said you'd call the second you got back on Friday."

"Well, I've been trying. God, I thought something awful had happened to *you* now!"

"Huh?"

"I mean, I know your freak cousin is in jail—Devin filled me in before she left."

"Where did she go?"

"To visit her dad for the weekend. And by the way, she couldn't get ahold of you, either. God, Lianna, I have been totally thinking the worst ever since I heard what happened to your stepdad. I swear, I've been trying to call you all weekend."

"On my cell?"

"Yes! Didn't you get my messages?"

"No, my cell is—the, um, battery died and I can't find the charger."

"Well, I tried you on your regular phone, too, and the recording kept saying your number was out of service."

"I guess that storm yesterday knocked it out," Lianna says, before remembering that she had used it several times, to call Kevin. The last time she talked to him, Friday afternoon, he asked her to try to sneak out Sunday afternoon to meet him. She told him she'd think about it.

Which is all she's done since . . . not that she's made any decision yet, even though Sunday is here.

"Maybe the storm did something to the line so it just can't get incoming calls," she muses aloud.

"Yeah, it says the number's not in service. You better tell your mother."

"I will. Right now, actually," Lianna says hurriedly, thinking her father or Kevin might be trying to get in touch with her today.

She tells her friend she'll call her right back, and

goes downstairs to hunt down her mom. She finds her, conveniently located right in the first-floor stair hall, standing on a tall stool in front of the open door to the coat closet beneath the stairs.

"Mom, there's something wrong with the phone. Casey's been trying to call for days and she keeps getting some recording."

"Oh." Mom's voice is muffled as she stretches to reach inside the closet, moving things around on the top shelf. "That's because I changed the number."

"You what?"

"Changed it. Because of all those nosy reporters who kept calling."

"Are you serious? And you didn't even tell me?"

Mom's head pops out of the closet and she flashes Lianna an apologetic look. "I'm sorry . . . I honestly forgot to. I've had a lot on my mind."

Okay, that's totally true. She has. But still . . .

"Have you seen Phyllida lately?" Mom asks.

_"No-oo,"_ Lianna says, "but I doubt you're going to find her up there."

Mom doesn't even crack a smile. "What about your Great-Grandaddy's radio? Have you seen that, by any chance?"

"What radio?"

"The one that was on the mantel in the parlor?"

"Which parlor?"

"Never mind," her mother says, climbing down to move the stool forward a few inches. "I didn't think so. Come on, help me look for it."

"In the closet?"

"In the house. I thought maybe Nydia moved it because it stopped working, and stashed it someplace."

"So why don't you ask Nydia?"

"She has Sunday afternoons off. Listen, go into the utility drawer in the kitchen and grab the flashlight, will you? I can't see in the back."

Grumbling under her breath that she thought the days of slavery ended in the Deep South almost a hundred and fifty years ago, Lianna follows her mother's instructions. Or rather, she tries to.

"There's no flashlight in here," she calls, slamming the drawer shut.

"There is. You're just not looking in the right place," comes the maddening reply.

She opens the drawer again and gives the contents a cursory glance. "Nope. Not here."

Hungry, she turns to the refrigerator and has about as much luck there as she did with the drawer. Nothing to eat. Nothing she wants, anyway.

She's about to pour herself a glass of sweet tea from the full cut glass pitcher when she hears a sound in the doorway and looks up to see her mother.

"What's up with Nydia, Mom? She's totally slacking off on the grocery shopping. Can you send her to the store?"

"She's off today. I meant to go myself this morning, but I got sidetracked." Her mother jerks open the utility drawer.

Lianna pours the tea, replaces the pitcher, and finds an apple. Not the reddish-orange Fuji ones she likes, but this green one will have to do.

She watches in smug satisfaction, polishing the Granny Smith on her T-shirt as her mother conducts her own fruitless search for the missing flashlight.

"See? I told you it wasn't in there."

"Well, it must be around here someplace," Mom snaps, opening the next drawer down and rifling through stacks of dish towels. Next, she rummages through the cooking utensils, clattering metal against metal in growing frustration before finally giving up.

She turns on Lianna. "Have you borrowed it lately?"

"No! Why do you always think I have something to do with whatever you can't find?"

"Because," Mom says, opening the silverware drawer, "things don't just vanish into thin air."

"Are you sure about that?" Lianna asks, biting into the crisp-tart apple.

"Actually"—her mother slams the drawer so hard that the glass rattles in the overhead cupboards—"I'm not sure about that at all today. Maybe things *do* vanish into thin air. For all I know, people do, too."

The cabin's sturdy new door is still closed and padlocked, just as it was left in the wee hours Saturday morning . . .

And then there were two.

"Yoo-hoo! Ladies!"

Oh, wait, it's not good manners to neglect to knock before dropping in, so . . .

The rubber-grip end of the heavy flashlight beats a satisfying rhythm on the new door of the small brick house.

"Little pigs, little pigs, let me in . . ."

The key turns easily; the padlock falls away with a clanking sound. The door doesn't even creak as it swings open . . .

Yes, thanks to my expert installation job. You just never know what you can accomplish if you put your mind—

A wall of stench rolls out through the open door, so putrid that it makes crossing the threshold out of the question.

"Yoo-hoo . . . I *said*, little pigs, little pigs, let me in—though I think I've changed my mind."

No response.

The flashlight's beam arcs across the exposed brick walls, the doll furniture, the maggot-filled, eyeless carcass that used to be Pammy Sue. Then it falls on what looks like a heap of rags on the dirt—or rather, *mud*—floor in the far corner.

"You're supposed to say 'not by the hair of my chinny-chin-chin.' What's the matter, did you forget your line? What kind of actress are you?"

Forget about staying outside. That isn't any fun.

It takes a moment, after crossing the threshold, to grow accustomed enough to the horrible odor to be able to speak without gagging.

"Pammy Sue? I hate to be the one to break it to you, hon, but you have terrible BO."

How satisfying that Pammy Sue, who was allowed to borrow Mama's fancy perfume any old time she wanted, now stinks worse than Pigeon Creek roadkill.

Yes, and how satisfying that I'm the one who has the fancy perfume now.

Real designer perfume from a department store cosmetics counter; not drugstore toilet water sold, along with bonus talc powder, in a cardboard gift box with a cellophane window.

But back then, Mama's drugstore perfume was the epitome of elegant femininity, and only Pammy Sue got to partake.

Aside from that one morning when you snuck into Mama's room before Sunday School and splashed some Eau de Something-or-Other behind each ear.

Bobby Lee Garrett, who was supposed to be impressed, didn't even notice. He was too busy gazing in blatant adoration at Pammy Sue as she handed out bible pamphlets.

But Mama noticed, afterward. Her pointy nose sniffed the air and her eyes, beneath a swoop of thick reddish bangs stranded with gray, narrowed in suspicion.

Naughty, naughty child . . . what have you done this time?

The punishment for perfume pilfering: being locked in the windowless woodshed overnight without food or water. Alone in the dark, listening to rustling vermin at your feet and overhead, feeling creepy-crawly creatures skittering over your skin without warning.

That was Mama's punishment for a lot of things.

And now, it's my punishment to dole out to those who deserve it.

Starting with Pammy Sue.

Too bad she can't stay here for much longer. Not in this heat.

Not if I have to come back here and catch another whiff of her.

"You're going to have to go soon, Pammy Sue. But first things first."

After a swift, hard kick, the pile of rags in the opposite corner squirms to life.

Phyllida Remington gazes up from the filth, blinking into the light.

Ah, Miss Beverly Hills is beautiful no more.

The artfully sculpted nose was shattered by the antique andiron she never saw coming at her.

Those surgically enhanced cheekbones are swollen purple and smeared with blackened streaks of dried blood.

And her blue eyes are round with fear, bewilderment and, most satisfying of all: horrified, shocked recognition.

CHAPTER 15

Monday morning, Royce is still sipping his steaming first cup of coffee, delivered with a plate of buttered toast and honey and a kiss from Aimee, when he hears the crunch of tires on the crushed-shell drive outside the parlor window.

From his propped-up position in the hospital bed, he can see an unfamiliar pickup truck with a dented fender pulling toward the house. Charlotte must have left the gate open again.

His first thought is that maybe she did it deliberately and that the truck might belong to the contractor. Royce had asked Charlotte to invite him out here to meet with them to go over the final steps for the Oglethorpe Avenue house renovation.

But he mentioned it less than an hour ago, when she was getting ready to leave to go to the supermarket. She didn't seem particularly enthusiastic about making the call and said she'll get to it later, when she has time.

Anyway, the contractor's pickup is red, and it sure as heck isn't this beat-up.

And, he sees now, there's a woman at the wheel—he just caught a glimpse of long blond hair and sunglasses before the truck disappeared from his sight range.

He hears it pull past the window toward the center of the portico before the driver cuts the engine. She must be a reporter. Damn.

He wonders whether Nydia has returned yet from her day off yesterday, so she can get rid of the reporter.

If not, I'm sure Aimee will welcome the pleasure, he thinks with a sly smile as he takes a bite of toast.

Through the screen, he can hear brisk footsteps crossing the drive, then tapping their way up the steps and across the flagstone.

The doorbell rings.

"Nydia?" Royce calls. "Are you here? There's a reporter out front."

Ever-efficient, the housekeeper must have already been on her way from the kitchen; he can already hear the faint, familiar creak of the front door opening.

Then comes the hum of female voices, followed by the unmistakable groan of the screen door.

"Nydia, no, don't!" he calls, wondering why on earth she'd let a reporter into the house.

Too late.

He can already hear footsteps clicking across the tile and hardwood floors, heading right for him.

Then a stranger appears in the doorway.

A stranger who looks familiar . . .

Why?

She must be on television, but she doesn't have that polished journalist appearance. Her hair falls loose past her shoulders without a hint of hair spray, and the blond streaks are from the sun, not a salon. That much is obvious in her tawny, freckled face and golden arms and legs.

Plus, she's wearing shorts, a T-shirt, and Dr. Scholl's—hardly camera-ready attire.

All right, so if she's not a reporter, who is she?

"Mr. Maitland, I'm so sorry to bother you—"

The moment she speaks that preamble, in precisely the words she spoke to him once before—*Mr. Maitland, I'm so sorry*—Royce recognizes her.

Not from the six o'clock news . . .

No, Royce realizes, as the toast and honey roil on a churning sea in his gut, she was a lifeguard at the beach on that fateful Labor Day weekend.

"So, we meet again," Williamson says, baring his teeth in what doesn't quite pass as a smile as Gib settles into the interrogation room for what promises to be yet another round of relentless questioning.

Tyler is here, which is a good sign. When he left yesterday, Gib wasn't entirely certain he'd see the lawyer again. Which might not be such a bad thing.

After Tyler had badgered him for every detail of his trip to Mexico—which, of course, Gib claimed not to recall—he left, saying he was going to verify that Gib really had been on the flights he'd claimed to have taken, and that he was going to locate Cassandra, provided she's listed in the Boston white pages.

Gib would venture to guess that she is, but who the hell knows?

If Tyler really wants her number that badly, Gib isn't about to keep it from him. It's in his cell phone's memory.

Along with a couple of other numbers he isn't particularly anxious to have come to light.

In response to Williamson's smarmy greeting, because it seems the detective is waiting for a response,

Gib says, "Yes, we're all in our places with bright, shiny faces."

All right, that probably wasn't the kind of response Williamson had had in mind.

Tyler glares at Gib, then asks the officers to explain the reason for this meeting.

"I'm glad you asked," Williamson says, "because I'm pretty anxious to tell you. In fact, I couldn't wait to get here."

He shoots a significant look in Gib's direction.

Terrific.

Are they going to: (a) have Grandaddy's body exumed, (b) try to pin a murder on him, to complement the assault charge, or (c) come up with some bogus witness who claims to be able to place him in the cemetery that night?

The answer, Gib discovers as he listens to Williamson's preamble with mounting anxiety, is (d) *none of the above*.

In the end, it's Dorado who delivers the sucker punch.

"We went through the evidence we took from your room again, Remington," the detective says, a gleam in his dark eyes, ". . . and we found something very interesting hidden in what looked like regular-old containers of shaving cream and hair gel."

"Hey, where have you been?" Kevin's voice asks, so loud in Lianna's ear that she instinctively shushes him, then feels ridiculous.

It's not as though anyone can hear his voice coming over the phone line in the study with the door closed.

Royce is safely stuck downstairs on the couch; her mother's car isn't in the driveway.

"I've been stuck at Oakgate, where else would I be?"

"You said you'd try to meet me yesterday afternoon. You never even called to set it up."

"I know." Her tone is hushed. "But I couldn't."

"How come? Was your mother up your butt now that she's hanging around at home again?"

"Actually, I fell asleep."

He snorts.

"It's the truth," Lianna tells him with a shrug. "I was really wiped out. I slept all afternoon." Which is probably why she managed to wake up so early this morning. It wasn't even nine o'clock when her eyes opened of their own accord.

"Anyway," she tells Kevin, "I found out my mother changed the number here last week and didn't tell me. Were you trying to call me at all?"

"Uh . . . Yeah. All weekend."

"That's why you couldn't get me. Sorry."

"It's okay. I'm glad you called. Let's hook up tonight."

"Tonight?" Lianna hesitates. "I don't know if I should sneak out, Kevin. If my mother catches me again . . ."

"Come on, she'll never know. And I miss you."

A smile curves her lips. "I miss you, too."

"So then let's go. I'll pick you up."

"What time?"

"Midnight?"

"Midnight? That's so late."

"Take another nap. You'll be fine."

"How about this afternoon instead?" she suggests.

"This afternoon? What are we going to do in the middle of the day?"

"You know . . . talk." *Kiss* . . .

Except not like we would if it was night and we were alone together.

It'll be safer.

Safe is good.

She'll just tell her mother she's going to take a nap for a few hours since it's such a crappy day out, and nobody will even realize she's gone.

Kevin hedges. "I don't know . . . I might have to work."

"I thought you said before you were off today."

"I'm supposed to be, but—"

"Look, do you want to meet me, or what?"

"I do. Just . . . tonight."

"Yeah, well, I don't want to wait that long," she says softly. "You know . . . I miss you. A lot."

"Okay, okay. What time?"

"Two?"

"I'll pick you up."

She hangs up, thinking that if her mother seems suspicious when she says she's taking a nap in the middle of the day, she'll just—

Lianna freezes.

A floorboard creaked just now, in the hallway outside the closed door.

Was somebody eavesdropping on her call?

With a whispered curse, Lianna contemplates the wisdom of opening the door to see who it is.

Nydia? Aimee?

It can't be Mom. She would have burst in here making accusations.

Unless she decided to catch me in the act.

Lianna frowns, pondering the situation.

There's no way to check from here whether her mother's car is back. The upstairs study faces the back of the house.

Okay, so she has two choices: She'll either have to disappoint Kevin by staying put this afternoon, or take the risk.

Nothing worthwhile in life comes without risk.

Right.

Who was it who said that to her recently?

Devin . . . ?

Dad . . . ?

Definitely not Mom. No, she's not about to go around telling Lianna to take chances.

Well, whoever it was, Lianna tells herself now, they were absolutely right.

How could you have been so stupid?

Why didn't Mimi ever consider, in her urgency to get to Charlotte, that she might find herself face-to-face again with Royce Maitland?

She saw the recognition in his eyes before she even had a chance to introduce herself.

Now, still taken aback both by his reaction and at finding him in a hospital bed, it feels lame to interrupt her apologetic introduction with a blurted, "I heard you say I'm a reporter, but I'm not. I'm Mimi Johnst—"

"I know who you are." His gaze is harder than the marble mantelpiece on the far end of the room.

She thinks quickly, determined to salvage the conversation. "Yes, I'm the one who went to the police with the tip that led them to Gib's arrest in your attack."

He raises a dark eyebrow at that.

He didn't know, she realizes. *Okay, so maybe that'll help me. I put his attacker behind bars.*

But his expression quickly reverts to stone as he responds, "No, you're the one who let my only son drown."

"Mr. Maitland—"

"Why are you here? And how did you even get in?"

"The gate was open, so—"

He curses. Then he demands, again, "Why are you here?"

She falters.

She could tell him she wanted to pay him a visit, to make sure he's recovering after the terrible shooting.

But she doesn't even have a bouquet of flowers or a box of muffins to enhance the ruse. The truth is, she never even thought twice about what happened to Charlotte's husband when she decided to come running over here.

She was thinking only of her own husband, consumed by the need to save his life, and desperate to ask Charlotte about what Dr. Von Cave revealed.

Now, she dismisses offering any false pretense for her visit.

"I'm here to see your wife," she says, plain and simple.

"My wife isn't here. She won't be back for a few days. So please leave."

He's lying.

Mimi can tell.

"Mr. Maitland, if you would just listen—"

"As I said, please leave."

"Mr. Maitland—"

"Good-bye!" He folds his arms and turns away as much as his position in the bed will allow.

Still, she wavers, knowing this might be her one chance, and Jed's last chance.

"If you don't leave now, I'll call the police. You're trespassing on private property. I swear, they'll come and take you to jail for days."

That can't happen. Jed needs her. Cam needs her. She doesn't *have* days to spend away from them, days to sit in jail.

Still, she doesn't move. If she could just—

"That's it." Royce Maitland reaches for the phone.
There's nothing for Mimi to do but go.

The parking lot, aisles, and checkout lines of Achoco
Island's only supermarket are jammed with locals and
summer residents alike, snapping up cases of bottled
water, plus batteries, canned meals, and all kinds of
other staples to make it through the approaching storm.

Next door, the hardware store is equally busy, doing
a brisk business on generators, flashlights, and blue-
plastic roofing tarp. There's already a generous supply
of that in the basement at Oakgate, thanks to leaks in
the attic during last year's harsh hurricane season.

Already weary, having woken up drowsy once again
today, it takes Charlotte nearly two exhausting hours to
plod through the store filling her cart, and another
twenty minutes to make it through the line. The job
would have been much easier had Lianna agreed to
come along, but she simply glowered when Charlotte
poked her head in this morning to ask her.

Oh, well. Between the solo drive over and the prolonged trip through the aisles she has plenty of time to
ponder her cousin's inexplicable disappearance. But it
doesn't appear that Phyllida met with foul play—at
least, not as far as Charlotte can tell.

The guestroom her cousin was using, when Charlotte
looked into it yesterday, bore no trace that she had ever
been there. Her clothing, toiletries, and luggage were
gone; the bed made up neatly with Nydia's unmistakable perfectly creased hospital corners.

So it doesn't seem as if Phyllida vanished from the
house under extraordinary circumstances. When she left,
it was apparently under her own steam, with her personal
belongings in tow. It really looks as though she must

have gone to the airport, but maybe she took another flight to California. Or maybe she went to Rhode Island, to visit her mother.

Charlotte decides to call Brian when she gets back home, even if it is still early on the West Coast. If Phyllida turned up last night, Charlotte will be relieved. If she didn't, Charlotte will ask if he has checked with Aunt Susan.

At last, she makes it through the long line and wheels her cart out to the parking lot. The sky over the water is ominously dark, and a warm, indisputably tropical wind is blowing in from the southeast.

After the pleasantly air-conditioned store, the air feels terribly oppressive. Charlotte's white sleeveless T-shirt and gray cotton-knit shorts stick uncomfortably to her skin as she works to hurriedly load the groceries into her SUV.

Her cell phone rings as she's loading the last bag, the one that holds the frozen items. Hoping the rapidly softening ice cream—mint chocolate chip, Lianna's favorite—won't melt entirely before she gets it home, she slams the hatch and checks her caller ID.

Private name, private number.

Okay, good, at least it isn't from Oakgate. Despite her growing uneasiness, undoubtedly augmented by the fact that her cousin seems to have vanished into thin air, nothing terrible has happened to Royce or Lianna . . .

Or has it?

What if the call is coming from the hospital ER, or—

"Hello?" she blurts into the phone.

"Charlotte Maitland?"

"Yes?" She holds her breath.

"This is Detective Dorado. I tried to reach you at home, but the number—"

"I'm sorry, I had to change it and I forgot to let you know." That's becoming her mantra. "Is something wrong?"

There's a pause.

Her heart quickens.

"Actually, there's been a new development in the case. Would it be possible for us to come right out to the house to speak to you?"

"How about if I come there?" she suggests, thinking quickly. The last thing she wants now is for poor Royce to have to deal with the police showing up again.

She's anxious to get back to him. But Aimee is there. She told Charlotte to take her time shopping and not worry about anything. He's in capable hands.

"That would be fine," Detective Dorado informs her, after conferring with somebody else in the room, probably Williamson. "Just as long as you can get right over here. We don't want to delay this."

"I'm headed straight to the causeway," she promises, sliding into the driver's seat, the ice cream in back forgotten.

"Looks like the storm really is coming, Jeanne," Melanie comments from the window, which she just lowered to a crack to keep the rain from blowing in. "Tropical Storm Douglas. The sky is getting dark out over the water."

Jeanne nods.

"I don't think it'll be upgraded to a full-blown hurricane, though. At least, I hope not."

"So do I," Jeanne lies.

A hurricane would be wonderful, really. A hurricane that would flatten the whole darned place. Then it would no longer be in her hands.

Hers . . .

And Melanie's.

I can't do it without her help.

But she'll be happy to oblige, as she always is.

You know I'd do anything for you, hon . . .

Anything?

There's only one way to find out.

"Melanie," she says heavily, "I hate to send you out in this, but I need you to do something for me before the storm gets any worse."

With another high-pitched, desperate grunt, Phyllida slams her bare feet against the door.

It refuses to budge.

She sinks back in exhaustion, her legs raw and bleeding where they're bound at the ankles and knees with unforgiving nylon rope. It's the same with her wrists, bound behind her. And her shoulders and upper back throb unbearably after hours—days . . . weeks?—in this excruciating position.

She has no idea how long it's been, or even where she's imprisoned. She only knows that she's in some kind of brick, windowless room, maybe a cellar or an underground bunker.

There's no food or water in the room, but it's far from empty.

The first thing she found was her Grandaddy's antique radio, of all things. At least, she thinks that's what it is. She accidentally struck the object when she was rolling around the mud floor, in a futile search for . . .

Something. Anything that might help her to get out of here.

It was only when her fumbling fingertips found the big, old-fashioned dials that she realized what the object was—and that it was useless in terms of a possible means of escape.

She's simply trapped here in the dark, with the radio—and other things.

At first, she thought she had found a child's body. It would explain the fetid odor that hovers in the stagnant air.

Then she realized it was a doll.

There are three of them. Doll furniture, too.

She stopped exploring when her hand grazed what felt like a coiled snake, and waited in terror for it to strike.

But it didn't.

She isn't going to explore anymore. Not in the dark.

There's not even a hint of daylight around the perimeter of the only door; no way of sensing the passing of time . . . when she's even conscious to think about it.

Most of the time, she's out cold, which is a blessing.

Then she won't have to think about what happened to her . . . or of what might happen next.

But somebody has to be looking for her out there.

Brian will try to find her.

Once he realizes I'm missing. God only knows how long it's been.

Or even Charlotte . . . Charlotte might realize . . .

Please, Charlotte. Please open your eyes. Please take a look at what's going on right under your nose, for God's sake! Please!

But her cousin won't see it. Nobody will.

Not unless they stumble across it, as Phyllida did. And even when she saw the shocking truth, she couldn't quite process it, couldn't bring herself to believe her eyes. She just stood there, slack-jawed—

Until something slammed into her, and everything went black.

If only I had fallen asleep that night . . .

If only I had gone out into the rain to call Brian . . .

If only I had decided to honor my marriage vows, and pick up the pieces instead of deciding to run away . . .

None of this would have happened.

She'd be safely at home in California, instead of waiting to be rescued from this living hell . . .

Or waiting to die at the sadistic hands of the last person she ever would have found menacing.

CHAPTER 16

"So what you're telling me," Charlotte looks from Dorado to Williamson and back again, "is that my cousin Gib is a drug addict?"

"For what it's worth, he says he's not an addict. He's a courier."

"Reliable as Federal Express," Williamson adds with a sardonic shake of his balding head. "Only they use trucks and envelopes, instead of commercial aircraft and fake hair spray containers."

Charlotte shakes her head, unable to believe Gib would actually smuggle drugs into the country from Mexico. "Why would he do something so stupid?"

"Cash," Dorado says. "That's usually the motive for anything, including attempted murder."

"So you don't think my cousin is the one who shot Royce?"

"We didn't say that . . . only that the alibi he gave us—his real alibi, not the original one he used—checked out. He was networking with some Colombian pals that night."

"Networking? What do you mean?"

"Savannah is a prime port city on the I-95 corridor between Miami and Boston," Williamson informs her, as if that explains everything.

At her blank look, Dorado jumps in. "I guess he decided that Savannah was convenient for business and decided to try and drum up some while he was here—once he realized he wasn't going to fly home to Boston an instant multimillionaire, anyway."

Charlotte shakes her head, trying to absorb what they're telling her. "I thought he was a lawyer up North."

Williamson is shaking his head.

"So he's . . . just a drug smuggler? Did he really even go to law school?"

"Yes. But he blew through most of his trust fund when he got it, and he's been in debt for years," Dorado tells her. "He wound up going to a loan shark at some points, figuring that if he could just get the money up front and keep himself afloat, he could eventually bail himself out the old-fashioned way."

"By getting a job?" Charlotte asks, still not following.

"By inheriting millions," Dorado counters. "We think he was banking on your Grandaddy to kick the bucket the whole time he was in law school, and when that didn't happen . . ."

"He helped him along," Williamson supplies.

Dorado throws him a cautious glance. "Maybe."

"Maybe," the other detective echoes grudgingly.

"And not by his own hand. He really was in Mexico the night your grandfather died. We checked it out."

"Was he dealing drugs?" Met with twin nods, Charlotte asks, "But why?"

"Why not? Fast, easy cash. Plus, he was a fine, upstanding citizen. Who would ever suspect him?"

"Not me," Charlotte murmurs, numb. "How did he do it?"

"It was a nice little gig," Williamson informs her, sounding like every detective on every cop show she's ever watched.

Except this is real. Chillingly, horrifyingly real.

"He'd jet down to Mexico—he even bought a nice timeshare down there—and come back with a pricey souvenir every time." Pausing to looking at her more closely, Dorado slides over the cup of water he poured her from the cooler when she first sat down. "Why don't you drink some of that?"

She shakes her head. "No, thanks, I'm—"

"Really. You should take a sip. You don't look like you're feeling that great."

"I'm just . . . I've been really tired the last few days."

"You've been through hell."

She nods. "I guess it's catching up with me."

"So listen to Florence Nightingale over here and drink some water," Williamson says gruffly, and ignores the dark look Dorado shoots in his direction.

As Charlotte sips, Williamson tells her, "We're going to look more closely into your grandfather's death, Mrs. Maitland. And your husband's shooting."

"And your cousin is still our prime suspect," Dorado inserts.

"I thought you said he was in Mexico when Grandaddy died, and when Royce was shot, I thought he—"

"His alibis don't mean crap," Williams says, and adds, "pardon my French."

"He could have had an accomplice," Dorado tells her.

"Or hired a hit man," Williamson adds.

Charlotte looks from one detective to the other, utterly overwhelmed. "So what now?"

"So now we check out the alibis of anybody else who could have had the slightest motive to hurt Maitland," Williamson says, as much to his partner as to Charlotte.

"We've been trying to reach your ex-husband," Dorado informs her. "Do you have any idea where we can find him?"

It's all she can do not to squeeze the water right out of the cup in her clenched hand. "He lives in Jacksonville. You should check his apartment, I would think."

"No shit, Sherlock." That, of course, comes from the ever-eloquent Williamson.

Dorado elaborates, "We haven't tracked him down there yet. We'll go over the contact information again with you. We also need to speak to your cousin Phyllida. Is she still staying with you?"

Charlotte hesitates only briefly before shaking her head. "No, she was supposed to fly back to California Saturday night."

"Supposed to?"

"I'm assuming she did. But when I talked to her nanny yesterday, she hadn't come home yet. They said she wasn't on the flight."

Again, the detectives exchange a glance. Dorado asks for the flight information.

"How was their marriage?" Williamson wants to know.

"Not great, I don't think."

"Would you be surprised if your cousin Phyllida lied to her husband, or you, about where she was going?"

Charlotte contemplates that and finds herself relieved at the possible explanation for Phyllida's whereabouts. Maybe she's having an affair or something. "I wouldn't be surprised at all."

"Would you be surprised if she was a conspirator with

her brother to harm you, your husband, or your grand-father?"

"Not really, no." Nothing would surprise her at this point.

Not even if she was to find out that Grandaddy had discovered what they were up to, and so wrote them out of the will because of it.

What doesn't make sense, if that was true, is his failure to confront Gib and Phyllida about it.

Unless he did.

But why wouldn't he go to the authorities?

Williamson is moving on brusquely, as if he's ticking off a mental checklist. "I understand your husband also has an ex-wife in New Orleans?"

She nods, her thoughts tumbling over each other like shells in an incoming tide. "But I don't know her address or her number off the top of my head."

"We'll get it. What about his daughter?" Dorado asks, hand poised on his notepad.

"She'd know it, but—"

"No, I realize that she'd know where to reach her mother. What I'm asking is whether she would have had any reason to hurt her father."

"None at all. And anyway, she was in New Orleans when he was shot."

"How do you know that?"

"Because I called her there several times after it happened to—"

"Land line or cell phone?"

She frowns. "Cell phone."

"She could have been anywhere, Mrs. Maitland."

"No, she flew in."

"After it happened?"

"Yes, the next morning."

"Did you pick her up from the airport?"

"No, she took a cab, but I saw her luggage," she adds, knowing they're about to tell her the cab doesn't prove Aimee even came from the airport.

She closes her eyes, then triumphantly tells them, "I remember, she had checked the suitcase. There was a white baggage claim tag folded around the handle. I remember because I asked her about checking it."

"Did you notice the date on it?"

"No, but it did say ATL-SAV. My husband's luggage always says the same thing when he gets back."

"It could have been an old tag of his, then."

She vacillates for a troubled moment, wondering if Aimee could have possibly—

"Wait!" she says, remembering. "I'm positive she was in the airport, in New Orleans. I heard the announcement for her flight boarding that morning while I was talking to her."

The detectives look at each other. "Do you remember which flight it was?"

She nods, pleased with herself. "Delta. Connecting through Atlanta. That's why I remember the announcement, because my husband has taken that same flight when he comes back from visiting her."

"So he visits her a lot?" Williamson asks, while Dorado jots down the flight information.

"He does now."

Too late, she realizes what she said.

"I mean, he *does*." She nods vehemently. "They get along very well."

"But there was trouble between them in the past?"

"Detective, my husband lost his son, Aimee's little brother, a few years ago. It just about ripped his family apart. He and his wife and daughter—well, they had to blame somebody. I know what that's like. Royce blamed himself. So did Aimee and Karen."

It's Williamson who breaks the uncomfortable silence.

"We'll need to check out your stepdaughter's alibi, Mrs. Maitland."

"It'll be our first priority," Dorado promises. "We'll make sure she really was on that flight. If she was, then you have nothing to worry about."

"She was," Charlotte tells him, lifting her chin resolutely.

But God knows she has everything to worry about.

Aimee . . . Karen . . . Vince . . .

They're going to put everyone who has anything to do with the Remington family under a microscope.

And God only knows what they're going to find.

An unbroken line of crawling traffic stretches from the Achoco Island Causeway all the way to the interstate. There's been no order to evacuate yet, not a mandatory one, anyway. But the storm system took another slight shift in the last few hours, according to the radio meteorologist. They're saying to expect flooding in low-lying areas, and you can't get much lower than the Johnstons's home on the canal.

I'll be back within the hour, she silently promises herself—and her family, who has no idea where she is.

She just couldn't go straight home after leaving Oakgate. Not without some answers. And she's going to try to find them in the local archives at the library's main branch on Bull Street in Savannah.

As she picks up speed, pulling onto the northbound ramp of I-95, the rain seems to come down harder. She increases the wipers' speed, leaning forward over the wheel to see through the windshield, careful to keep a safe distance from the taillights of the eighteen-wheeler that got on in front of her.

Okay, this isn't the best weather for a road trip.

But she has no choice.

If what Dr. Von Cave suggested is actually true, then she might be on to something.

It would be so much easier if she could just have spoken to Charlotte directly.

When she ran into the young, vaguely familiar blond woman in the hallway as she was about to let herself out, she almost spilled the whole sad story in response to a simple, "Can I help you with something?"

Mimi fleetingly confided that she lives on the island and needs to speak with Charlotte about an urgent personal matter.

"She isn't here. Is it something I can help you with, maybe?"

"I don't think so," Mimi said. "It's . . . a medical issue."

"I'm a nurse."

A nurse . . .

Is that why she looks familiar?

"Do you by any chance work at the Magnolia Clinic in Savannah?"

"No, I—"

"It doesn't matter, actually, where you work. I just need to get in touch with Charlotte as soon as possible. It's about my husband—he's been diagnosed with a rare stomach cancer, and I found out that Connie June Remington—"

"Mrs. Johnston!" The housekeeper scurried into the hall just then, far less welcoming than she was when she let Mimi in. "Mr. Maitland asked me to see that you had left. I'm sorry . . . You need to be on your way."

Mimi nodded and looked at the blond woman. "Can you tell Charlotte I was here, and to call me as soon as she can? My name is Mimi Johnston; I live down on the south canal."

She doubts Charlotte will get the message, let alone call her.

But then, she thought the same thing about Dr. Von Cave.

Of its own volition, her foot sinks slightly lower on the gas pedal.

And then, brazenly, lower still.

She's caught up to the truck, close enough to read the "How's My Driving?" sign on the back, despite the downpour and the spray.

Impatient to get to the library, heedless of the weather and the slick road, she decides to pass.

The moment she pulls out, a car horn blares, close behind her.

Too close.

It sends her swerving back into the right lane, out of control.

But only for a second.

A second is all it would have taken! her inner voice shrieks. *You could have been killed.*

Where would that leave Cam and Jed?

The steering wheel clenched in her white-knuckled hands, she has no choice but to slow to a relative crawl once again, staring bleakly through the windshield at the pouring rain.

This is becoming too precarious.

Much, much too precarious.

An exhilarating, healthy little risk is one thing; fool-hardiness is altogether something else.

And I'm no fool.

Complications are escalating like the wind speed off the ocean. There's only one thing to do: eliminate them, step by step.

First things first.

Time to do away with Miss Beverly Hills. It shouldn't take long—and she'll make some hungry gator a nice, filling lunch, just like Pammy Sue did. It didn't take long after she was dumped in a shallow pool for the snapping jaws to emerge and devour her fetid remains. Lingering in the marsh to witness that frenzied feast was almost as gratifying as it would be to watch Pammy Sue die all over again.

In the end, there was nothing left of Mama's golden girl. Nothing at all.

Too bad alligators don't eat radios.

It, too, will have to be hidden . . . again.

The first time, it was to prevent Charlotte from taking it to a repairman who would open it up, undoubtedly see that it had been immersed in water, and tell Charlotte that was why it had stopped working.

Who knows what conclusion she might draw from that? She's smarter than she looks—unlike her West Coast cousin.

Hmm . . . maybe the radio can be weighted with a rock and sunk in the marsh on the way to the house.

That will have to do. The important thing is to get back to Oakgate before the storm's full fury descends.

A dank sea breeze incessantly rustles the palm fronds and moss-clotted foliage overhead, and the rain is picking up along with the wind. The sky has turned an ominous yellow-black over the Atlantic to herald the arrival of Tropical Storm—or perhaps it's Hurricane, by now—Douglas.

Ah, yes . . . the professional chef's knife is even more

effective at clearing away troublesome vines than the utility knife was.

It will have to be thoroughly cleaned of blood—not to mention furtively sharpened—before it's been returned to the kitchen drawer back at Oakgate. Just in case.

In case, say, somebody would like to prepare a fancy French seafood recipe . . .

Or if a good, freshly whetted blade is needed for some altogether different purpose.

"So, like, he just called me to say that there's this really bad storm coming," Lianna tells Devin, practically whispering into the telephone receiver.

"Right. My mom is freaking out. Tropical Storm Douglas."

"Whatever . . . he has to work now because all these people are gassing up their cars to leave the island . . . so he said forget it and let's do it tonight instead."

"Where would you even go?"

"He said we could just, you know, hang out in his car, but . . ."

"What, you don't want to? That sounds romantic. Especially in a storm."

Lianna hesitates. "I don't know. I just don't know if I believe him."

"About what?"

"Having to work. Even though I could hear, like, all this noise in the background . . ."

"What did it sound like?"

"Like he was working at a gas station in the rain."

"Yeah, well, that doesn't mean anything," Devin says dismissively. "When my dad was having his affair before my parents split up, he used to make all these bogus staged calls to my mom to cover his butt. Like, he'd say he was calling from the car, stuck in traffic, or from the airport or something, and he wasn't. It just sounded like it because he was using this software-download service on his cell phone to make it sound like he was calling from somewhere else."

"You're kidding."

"Nope. I checked it out myself, actually, a while back. Before I figured out that now that my dad's gone and my mom's in charge, I can pretty much do what I want anyway. But if I wanted to come up with a good lie and cover my butt with fake background noise, I easily could, and Kevin could, too."

"So you think he's lying, too?" Lianna asks, incredulous that he would go to such lengths to make her think he's at work.

"I wouldn't be surprised."

"So what should I do?"

"Meet him tonight and call him on it. That's all you can do."

"Yeah, or not show up," Lianna says, glancing toward the window as the panes rattle in the wind. "Hey, the weather does look pretty bad. Did you say this is a hurricane?"

"Nah, just a tropical storm. At least, so far. My step-dad says it's no big deal. Trust me, it isn't."

"Yeah, well, you're up in Savannah. I'm stuck out here on this stupid island. I swear, I can't wait until we move back to the—"

There's a booming crack and then a deafening crash outside.

"Did you hear that?" she asks Devin. "God, it sounds like a gun just . . . Devin? Devin?"

The phone, Lianna realizes with a sickening feeling, has gone dead.

* * *

Waiting in the windowless interrogation room at the police station, where the detectives abandoned her ages ago with a promise to be back shortly, Charlotte is growing increasingly claustrophobic.

Her cell phone doesn't work in here, and she really should call home and let them know where she is. They must be getting worried, especially if that storm is still blowing in. It might even be starting to rain already; it could take her longer than usual to get back.

On top of that, most of the groceries she bought are going to be a total loss, sitting in the back of the SUV in the warm parking garage.

She supposes she could have stashed them in the fridge at the new house, conveniently located just down the block. But that would have meant setting foot in there again, and she isn't ready to do that. She couldn't even bring herself to drive down Oglethorpe Avenue to get here, instead going out of her way to avoid it.

She checks her watch again, wishing the detectives would at least stick their heads in, so that she could ask if she can leave the room to make a call.

Then again, she's almost afraid to call home, especially knowing that Aimee might pick up.

Of course Charlotte doesn't believe Royce's daughter, of all people, had anything to do with the shooting . . .

But the detectives don't seem as convinced.

And now, with all this time to sit and think, Charlotte is starting to get paranoid.

What if it *was* Aimee? What if she's so bitter over the loss of her brother that she wanted to hurt her father?

No. I can't be that poor a judge of character, can I?

No. I can't be that poor a judge of character . . . can I?

Still . . .

What if Aimee really did use an old baggage tag, like they said?

But I know she was calling me from the airport. I heard it in the background. I heard the flight announcement. Delta Flight 6—

"Mrs. Maitland?" Detective Dorado strides through the doorway, sans Williamson. "I'm sorry to have left you here for so long."

"It's okay, I just—I really need to call home and let them know where I am."

"You should—and you should probably stay here until the storm is over."

"What?" she asks in dismay.

"It's getting pretty nasty out there—especially down off the coast. Williamson was headed down to Jacksonville to look up your ex-husband but he just called and said he had to get off the road."

"The storm started already?" She pushes back her chair. "I can't stay in Savannah. I have to go back."

He holds up a hand. "Before you do, you should know one thing about your stepdaughter."

Once again, a corpse is dragged from the cabin to the nearest pool of water, considerably deeper already because of the tropical rain.

There, Phyllida Remington Harper's headless corpse is unceremoniously deposited with a splash.

Her head was inadvertently nearly severed when she tried to bolt in terror as her throat was cut.

Her fault, not mine. I only meant to slash her throat.

After she stopped flailing and gurgling, the sharp chef's knife finished the job with a neat, satisfying slice through the remaining tendons and spinal cord.

Satisfying, yes, but I should have left her head dangling if only to save an extra trip through this godawful storm.

No rest for the weary. Not today.

It's probable that the gators will have disposed of the torso and limbs by the time the head is retrieved from the cabin.

But surprisingly, the snapping jaws have yet to appear when the return trip has been made. The gators remain submerged and the body is still there, bobbing in the storm-tossed water.

Maybe the lurking creatures are waiting for the storm to end before they surface. Who can blame them? The weather is getting nastier by the second.

This time, there can be no loitering to watch the gators do their grisly work. Not with the storm raging and so much going on back at the house.

"Good-bye, Phyllida dear."

With that, the disembodied head of the would-be Remington heiress is tossed like a bowling ball into the churning, gator-infested water.

Charlotte holds her breath, fearing whatever Dorado is about to tell her about her stepdaughter, trying to prepare herself for the worst.

"Aimee was telling the truth about being on that flight from New Orleans."

"Thank God." Charlotte releases the breath audibly, through puffed cheeks. "Oh, thank God," she says again.

Then, with a pang of guilt and a silent apology to Aimee for even considering the worst, she adds, "But I never really had any doubt."

Not really.

"We confirmed everything with the airline. She went

through Atlanta, just like you said, Mrs. Maitland—and just barely made the connection to Savannah because the first flight was way behind schedule getting in and then back out of New Orleans. In any case, we tracked her all the way through, and her bag as well. She did check it. You were right about her being innocent all along."

Weak with relief, Charlotte manages to say only, "Thank you."

I knew it . . . I knew Aimee could never hurt Royce. Whatever she blamed him for in the past, she loves him . . . I couldn't be mistaken about that.

But Karen . . .

"Did you contact Royce's ex-wife?"

"No. We tried to find her in New Orleans, but there's no listing. We'll need to talk to your husband about her, and we'll need to get an address and phone number for her."

"I'll call you with it as soon as I get home."

"Actually . . ." Dorado gestures toward the door. "Let's call your husband right now."

"Do we have to do it this way? Over the phone? Please, Detective, he's recovering from a major trauma."

"And we're trying to investigate the source of that trauma." His voice is gentle, but firm. "Let's call."

"Aimee?" Royce calls from the parlor. "Aimee! What the heck was that crash?"

"I don't know," she calls from the far side of the house. "I'm trying to see."

It sounded as though one of the tremendous trees came down alongside the house. This storm is far worse than he had anticipated. And where on earth is Charlotte?

She should have been back from the grocery store hours ago.

This day has gone downhill fast, ever since he looked up and saw that lifeguard standing in the parlor.

He hears Aimee's hurried footsteps in the hall. "Did you find out what it was?"

She appears in the parlor doorway. "One of the live oaks right next to the driveway. It almost crushed Nydia's car and it took down some wires, too. I can't believe we didn't lose the electricity."

"I'm sure it'll go sooner or later. The lights keep flickering." He exhales nervously. "Where *is* Nydia?"

"Still upstairs somewhere, I guess. I haven't heard her."

That doesn't mean she's not around, Royce thinks, knowing how the housekeeper tends to creep around the house, popping up where you least expect her.

For all he knows, she could be eavesdropping on the other side of the parlor door. It wouldn't surprise him in the least.

"This storm is nasty," Aimee comments, as the wind lashes at the closed parlor window.

"And Charlotte is out in it somewhere."

"I know. Try to get her on her cell again. Maybe she'll pick up this time. Here, I'll dial; you talk."

Royce nods, taking the receiver Aimee hands him.

She begins pressing buttons, but he quickly shakes his head.

"Wait, there's no dial tone."

"Sorry." She jiggles the cradle button, then begins dialing again.

"Still no dial tone," he says sharply. "The phone is dead."

"What about your cell phone?"

"I have no idea where it even is. Probably in a pocket somewhere in my closet or the hamper."

"I'll go upstairs and look for it."

"I'll help you. It'll be faster."

"What about the stairs? And your leg?" Aimee asks.

"Don't worry. I'm fine . . . and everything else is going to be fine, too."

"I'm not worried."

"Yes, you are. About Charlotte. I can tell."

"So are you," she accuses.

"You're right. But I know her better than you do. There's no way she isn't doing everything in her power to get home. I'm sure she'll be here any minute now."

"I hope so."

"She will." He opens his arms wide. "Come over here, scared little Baby Girl . . ."

"Don't call me that," she protests, but her mouth quirks with a suppressed smile.

"You come over here and let your daddy give you a hug," he says, grinning too as he pulls her close and tenderly strokes her blond hair. "We're going to be just fine. I promise."

In the library, Mimi sits before the microfiche screen, disappointed.

Obituaries sometimes mention the precise cause of death—or at least indicate what it was, with a request for a donation to a charitable fund for Kepton-Manning Syndrome.

But according to every old newspaper she checked, Connie June Remington *"died at home after an extended illness. Donations can be made to the new Remington Ambulatory Wing at—"*

The lights flicker.

Disconcerted, Mimi glances up, then out the window at the gale. She has to get out of here. She really does.

But first, she'll check the Internet for any further information on Charlotte's mother.

"Excuse me, ma'am, the library is going to be closing early because of the storm."

Not looking up from the computer keyboard, Mimi nods. "I'll be finished in just a few minutes."

Googling Connie June Remington's name yields no new information.

Even as Mimi tells herself that she should give up and go home, her left index finger strays toward the T key, and her right immediately slips one space over, to the H.

No! Don't do it! That has nothing to do with this.

No, it doesn't, but seeing Royce Maitland today brought it all back.

It doesn't take much.

Her middle finger on the left hand presses the E key.

Why are you doing this? What do you think you're going to find?

At the time, she refused to read the papers, or watch the news, or listen to people discussing the tragedy. And never once, in the past three years since, has she allowed herself to look for it on the Internet.

But maybe it's time she did.

Maybe seeing it here, and facing head-on her own role in the tragedy, will help her to put it to rest. Maybe she'll stop having that awful nightmare that haunts her even now, when she's sleeping beside her dying husband, living a nightmare that's even worse.

After Theo, she quickly types Maitland, hits ENTER, and holds her breath.

Detective Dorado was right. The storm has definitely begun, and with a vengeance.

Charlotte keeps one eye on the rain-spattered window, and the swaying trees beyond, as she calls her home telephone number.

A recorded voice comes on the line. *"All circuits are busy. Please try your call again later."*

She looks at Dorado, who must have overheard.

He nods. "Try again."

"They said later."

"It's later. Try again."

She does. This time, there's a click, followed by a rapid busy signal.

"Oh, I must have dialed the old number," she realizes, and disconnects the call. "Sorry."

"Try again."

"I will," she snaps—and immediately wishes she hadn't. Not at him, anyway. He's just trying to do his job—trying to help her, and Royce—she should appreciate his kinder, gentler approach, as opposed to his partner's.

It's just that her nerves are rapidly fraying. Genuine premonition or irrational fear . . . all she wants is to get back home before something happens.

She calls the number again, more slowly this time, taking care to dial the right one.

Again, the unnerving up-tempo busy signal.

She looks anxiously at Dorado. "You don't think anything is wrong over there, do you?"

"The storm," he says with a discouraged shake of his head. "The phones must be out of commission."

"I'll try my husband's cell phone."

She does, but it goes right into voice mail. Listening to his reassuring voice on the outgoing message, she wonders how much to tell him. Now isn't the time to get into the detective's request, or the investigation. She opts to leave a brief message: "Royce, it's me. I'm on my way home right now, but it might take me a while because of the weather. I love you. See you soon."

She hangs up. "Can I please go now? If it's that bad I really have to get back there to my family."

"If it's that bad," Dorado returns, "I really wouldn't advise your going anywhere."

"I have to. My husband is injured and my daughter is only thirteen, and my poor aunt is old and feeble. They all need me at home."

"Are they alone?"

"No," she admits. "My stepdaughter is there, and the housekeeper—and my aunt does have a nurse, but . . . I need to be there."

"It sounds like they're in good hands, Mrs. Maitland. Don't you have a house right down the block? Why don't you stay there?"

"Because I'm going home." She meets his worried brown eyes with a defiant glare. "*Home* to Oakgate."

Huddled beneath a black umbrella that does nothing to shut out the rain blowing sideways, Tyler crosses the deserted expanse of Forsyth Park. He moves as quickly as his old legs can carry him. That isn't saying much, thanks to increasingly fragile bones and his recent injury, which happened a stone's throw from here, on a day almost as blustery as this.

Today, as then, he would much prefer to be snug at his home on Abercorn Street, perhaps enjoying a Cuban cigar and a single-malt scotch.

Ah, but Gilbert wouldn't approve, he finds himself thinking, then acknowledging, once and for all, the irony that a man who disapproved of such "immoral" vices as smoking and drinking would go to the immoral lengths he did to save his fortune, and his pride—at the expense of countless people's lives.

And you helped him to do it, Tyler reminds himself as he steps into the crosswalk where he was nearly killed last winter. *You and Silas.*

Silas's role in the cover-up was far more incriminating than his own. But in the end, were any of them any less, or more, guilty?

Tyler's injured leg is aching, but he forces himself to take the stairs, rather than the elevator. Punishment, he thinks wryly, but hardly harsh enough.

His mind flashes to Gib Remington, sitting behind bars, having confessed to the drugs but not to attempted murder. He won't be jetting off with a beautiful blonde any time soon.

Tyler wonders, again, about Gib's role in what happened here in Savannah—and at Oakgate.

Perhaps the truth about Gilbert's death will never be known.

But the truth about his life will.

In his office, Tyler goes to the tall wooden file cabinet and opens the locked bottom drawer using his key—the one whose duplicate nobody, including his grandnephew Jameson, has.

It takes him a long time to remove all the hanging files and stack them neatly on the floor beside the cabinet. Then, prying with a pocketknife on his key ring, he lifts the false bottom from the drawer and removes the manilla envelope beneath it.

Unlike the other two members of the Telfair Trio, Tyler Hawthorne won't carry blind loyalty—or toxic guilt—to his grave.

Nothing comes up in response to Mimi's Google request.

Nothing that pertains to a child's drowning death off Achoco Island, anyway. She scans the beginning of a long list of references to the names Theo and, separately, mentions of the last name Maitland. It would take her hours to wade through this.

She types in Theodore Maitland AND drowning, a trick she learned in a college computer class, to narrow down the search engine's hits.

The results pop up with plenty of entries that contain either Theodore or Maitland or drowning, or even two of the three words. But none of it is what she's looking for, at least, not right here at the top. She has hardly begun scanning the lengthy pages of entries when the librarian interrupts her.

"Ma'am? We really are closing."

"I'm sorry, I'm just about finished here."

She can't waste time wading through this list.

Biting her lower lip intently, she types in Theo Maitland AND Royce Maitland AND New Orleans AND drowning.

There!

The name Royce Maitland jumps out at her.

"Ma'am! Please!"

"I'm sorry. I'll shut down."

But before she does, she scrolls rapidly to click on the link for the first Royce Maitland entry.

Moments later, Mimi is running for the exit in a race that has nothing to do with the library's closing or the impending storm.

You are such a freaking baby, Lianna scoffs at herself as she cowers on her bed against the inner wall, as far from the rattling windows as she can possibly get. She closed and locked them when the rain started blowing in . . . as if that can really keep a storm this fierce at bay.

Yes, but this is a solid old house. It's been here for nearly a hundred and fifty years.

Uh-huh. So has the tree that came crashing down outside.

The thought of the wind gusting strong enough to destroy the formidable oak—and, possibly, implode the house's original windows—is enough to make her want to bolt from the room.

She forces herself to stay put.

First, you screw things up with your boyfriend because you're afraid he'll try to go too far.

Now it's all you can do not to go running downstairs to find your mommy because you're scared of a little storm.

A tremendous blast howls against the glass as if the storm begs to differ with her inner bully.

Okay, so it's a big storm.

But it isn't a hurricane.

If it were a hurricane, Lianna tells herself, *you could go running to your mommy.*

Her mother must be home by now, although she wasn't a little while ago, when Lianna had asked Nydia. That's when Lianna also found out it was a tree out front that had knocked out the phone lines when it came down.

Terrific.

The only thing worse than being stuck at Oakgate in bad weather is being stuck at Oakgate in bad weather without a phone.

Hey—maybe I should go find Mom and ask her if I can have my cell back, Lianna thinks suddenly.

After all, this is an emergency. It's not like she can use the regular phone. And it's probably going to be days before they fix the lines. She can't go for days without talking to her friends . . . or Kevin.

Right, Kevin.

Her mother isn't going to give her the phone back. No way.

All right, so I'll just have to go find it myself.

Yeah, and when she sees the bill, she'll know you used it when you weren't supposed to.

True, but that's probably a month away. Lianna will deal with the fallout when the time comes.

Her mind made up, she slips quietly out of her bedroom and down the hall.

The door to the room her mother shares with Royce is closed.

She opens it slowly, pleased when it doesn't creak like most of the other old doors in the house . . .

And what she finds on the other side is the most sickening shock of her young life.

Praying the tires won't lose traction and hydroplane, Charlotte steers the Lexus forward through yet another flooded low spot on the highway leading from the interstate to the Achoco Island Causeway. At least she's driving the SUV today, and not Royce's little Audi that she often takes.

Still, it isn't a good idea to be out in this storm in any kind of vehicle—unless it's a boat, she acknowledges, steering carefully around a wide, deep puddle.

She just has to get home.

They must be so worried about her—and God knows, she's worried about them. Chances are, everything is fine and the storm just knocked out the phone service . . .

But she would feel a whole lot better if she could just get home to Royce and Lianna.

At least Aimee is there, she reminds herself.

And it's not as though she won't know what to do in a storm like this. She's from New Orleans, for heaven's sake. She's survived worse. Much, much worse.

New Orleans.

Charlotte's thoughts instantly dart back to the conversation she just had with Dorado. There's something . . .

New Orleans . . . ?

Karen . . . ?

There's something she should be remembering. Something about . . .

Maybe not New Orleans . . .

Then what?

Vince . . . ?

No. There it is again! Some elusive thought that flits like a firefly into her consciousness, only to be instantly extinguished before she can catch it.

Think, think, think . . .

Maybe once she's safely back home, rather than making this treacherous drive from hell, it will come back to her.

For now, all she can do is drive—

Startled by a loud crack, she watches a tree crash to the earth in a flooded field off the road.

Yes, drive, and try not to get myself killed in the process.

Listening to the torrents of rain pouring onto the roof just overhead, Jeanne is surprised it hasn't started leaking yet in its usual spot on the far side of the room.

This is almost as bad as a hurricane, and she's weathered quite a few of those in all her years here at Oakgate. The roof leaks; the basement is bound to fill up with a foot of water—it always does.

Yet Jeanne supposes that she—or at least, the old house—might weather this storm as well.

But this time, she isn't planning on sticking around to witness the outcome.

Where on earth is Melanie?

Pushing aside the wheelchair parked beside the bed, Jeanne gets to her feet and goes, a bit unsteadily, to the window overlooking the front of the house.

Gazing down at the driveway, the first thing she sees is that an enormous tree has fallen alongside one of the cars. From here, she can't tell whether it's Melanie's.

Then a movement closer to the house catches her eye, and she strains to see what it is.

Oh. Somebody is down there.

She can't tell who it is; they're wearing a long black-vinyl rain cloak that whips wildly about in the wind.

As the figure comes fully into view, she realizes that he—or she—is oddly stooped over.

Oh! That's because whoever it is happens to be dragging something that must be heavy down the steps of the portico . . .

Something that looks for all the world like a dead body swathed in a sheet of blue plastic.

Heedless of her wet, windblown hair, Mimi paces the tiny room that she was ushered into while she waits to speak with one of the detectives on the Remington case.

Her heart rate—catapulted to a lofty height the moment she opened that Web link—has yet to return to normal. When she closes her eyes, all she can see is the shocking link to that Louisiana newspaper.

How can this be?

And why?

It doesn't make sense.

There has to be some mistake, or some coincidence.

Yet what are the odds of that? All the details match . . .

But the photos don't.

The door opens.

Aimee turns to see Detective Dorado—the nice one—standing in the doorway.

"What is it, Mrs. Johnston?" he asks, catching sight of her face. "What's going on?"

"I don't know," she says in a rush, "but you've got to get somebody out to Oakgate right away because I think Charlotte Remington and her daughter are in terrible danger."

Incredulous, Jeanne watches the hooded figure below come to a stop with its tarp-shrouded burden.

Why now? Why there?

Whoever it is went to tremendous effort to drag whatever, or whoever, is wrapped in the tarp quite a distance from the house. Jeanne assumed they were headed for the nearest car, but the car was bypassed in favor of the sprawling branches of the newly fallen tree.

Now what?

Her own plans forgotten, her view partially obscured by cascading moss and foliage, Jeanne sees the flapping tarp come away completely, released to blow into obscurity, carried by the gusting wind. By the time the storm is over, it might very well have been ripped to shreds, or swept out to sea, or tangled in tree limbs miles from Oakgate, mingling with other innocuous storm debris.

Nobody will ever know that this particular tarp shielded not a roof, but, indeed, a corpse.

A female corpse with light-colored hair that Jeanne, even at this distance, finds chillingly familiar.

PART V

THE FINAL VICTIM

CHAPTER 17

"There"—Aimee expertly secures the last strip of clean gauze over the wound—"how does that feel? Too tight?"

"Not at all. You're an expert." Royce begins to lower his leg, propped on the toilet seat, with a grimace.

"Don't hurt yourself."

"I won't." He sets it gingerly on the floor and tries to stand, testing his weight on it.

Watching him, Aimee says, "The stairs were too much for you."

"I'm fine."

"No, you aren't."

"Well, I will be . . . as soon as Charlotte gets back. And she said she's on her way, so—"

"She left that message a while ago. How long does it take to drive home from the supermarket, even in bad weather? And why isn't she picking up her cell phone?" Aimee shakes her head worriedly. "What about Lianna?"

"She's still in her room, right? We'd better go talk to her now."

"And tell her . . . ?"

"That this is getting much too dangerous and as soon as Charlotte gets here," Royce says resolutely, "we're going to have to evacuate. We can't waste another minute."

"That'll go over like a lead balloon."

"No, come on . . ." He hobbles to the door and out into the hall. "It'll be fine. Let's tell her now."

"You go ahead. She hates me."

"She doesn't hate you."

"Wanna bet?" Aimee folds her arms across her chest and watches him knock on the closed door at the end of the hall.

"Lianna?" He can hear the television blasting, as usual, on the other side of the door. She must be thrilled they have yet to lose power. But he has a feeling that will be short-lived. "Lianna!"

"Are you sure she's in there?" Aimee asks, coming toward him.

"The TV is on. Lianna!"

"Try the door," Aimee says hurriedly.

He does. "It's latched. She has to be inside. Lianna!"

The only sound from within is an eruption of canned laughter from a studio audience.

His heart sinking, Royce commands tersely, "Aimee, get me a chair from the guest room."

"I told you your leg was going to give out," she says, shaking her head as she scurries to oblige.

"No, the chair isn't to sit on. I need to use it to break down this door."

"I'm sorry, ma'am," the uniformed officer, dressed in bright orange rain gear, shouts when she rolls down the driver's side window. "I can't let you go over the causeway. It's closed."

"But I live out there!" Charlotte protests. "I have to get home to my family."

"Ma'am, that would be too dangerous. The storm surge is getting higher by the second. Already we've got waves washing over the road."

"But it's the only way to get back on the island!" she protests. "The other one washed away last fall."

"Exactly," he says with a meaningful nod. "That's why I can't let you drive out there."

"Where am I supposed to go?"

"There's a school back that way that's been set up as a temporary storm shelter. Go wait it out."

"But that could be days!"

"Nah. It blew in faster than they thought. I expect it'll blow out faster, too. See where my car is parked?" He indicates the narrow road ahead. There's a police car perpendicular to the causeway with red lights flashing, acting as a makeshift barricade. "There's a slight shoulder over there. It's wide enough for you to make your U-turn. Do you need directions to the high school?"

"The one on Topsail Road?"

"That's the one! Good luck!"

He waves her off.

Disheartened, she pulls slowly ahead, the windshield wipers now set at triple-time doing little to clear the view.

Her cell phone rings as she pulls onto the shoulder where the officer indicated.

Good. She hasn't been able to get a signal in a while now. Snatching it up, she's certain it will be Royce, wondering why she's not back yet.

"Hello?"

Her greeting is met at first with just a burst of static.

Then she hears a male voice and the name, "Dorado."

"Detective? Is that you?"

"Yes! Mrs. Maitland . . . Are you . . . ?"

"I'm sorry, your voice is breaking up." She shifts hurriedly into PARK and steps out of the car, hoping to get a better signal. It works.

"Mrs. Maitland, where are you?"

"I was trying to get home, but the causeway is closed."

"Don't go home. Whatever you do, don't go home! Do you hear me?"

"Not very well. It sounded like you said *don't go home.*"

"I did! Listen to me very carefully . . ."

More static.

Behind her, she hears a shout and sees that the cop who stopped her is waving his arm in a circle, signaling her to get back into the car and turn it around.

"In a second! I have a phone call!" she shouts to him. But her words are drowned by rain and borne away on the wind.

"Detective Dorado . . ." Frustrated, she steps farther from the car, buffeted by the gale. "What did you say?"

His next words are punctuated by another burst of crackling interference, but the few she does make out chill her to the bone.

"Royce . . . and . . . Aim . . . kill."

Clutching her cell phone against her ear, Charlotte is certain she misunderstood, because . . .

She can't have just heard what she thought she did.

Heart racing, she moves farther away from the car shouting over the wind, "What did you say, Detective? I sounded like—"

"I *said*, Royce Maitland and his daughter Aimee were killed in a car accident ten years ago in New Orleans."

* * *

The manilla envelope is tucked safely into the waistband of Tyler's trousers, beneath a protective layer of shirt and his soaked trenchcoat.

The wind repeatedly turns the umbrella inside out as he zigzags his way northeast, toward police headquarters on the corner of Oglethorpe and Habersham. Finally, the metal spokes begin to pop away from the center, and he shoves the umbrella into the nearest trash can. It was useless, anyway, in this storm.

He supposes that a man who wasn't hell-bent on self-punishment would have gone home with the envelope, figuring the contents will keep for another day or two.

But this has waited long enough.

Come hell or high water—and Tyler is enduring his share of both at the moment—he will get this information to the authorities today.

At last, he's arrived at the familiar station house where his business has brought him so often in the past.

The desk sergeant greets him by name.

"Mr. Hawthorne, what brings you out in this weather?"

He hesitates only briefly before answering.

Just long enough to send a silent apology to Silas and Gilbert, wherever they are.

"I have no idea what you're trying to say to me!" Charlotte protests into the phone, screaming to be heard above the roar of the storm, and the louder roar of panic beginning to mount inside her. "Royce and Aimee are at Oakgate. I'm trying to get home to them now."

Even as she speaks, his baffling words echo in her brain.

Killed . . .

Ten years ago?
Ten years ago!
What in the world is he talking about?

"No—please, Charlotte . . ." Gone is the masterful interrogator; gone is the Mrs. Maitland—or, for that matter, Ms. Remington.

Dorado's voice is strained as he says, "You have to listen to me; I just read the obituaries myself, I saw the pictures myself. Royce was forty at the time of the accident ten years ago, and bald. Aimee was fifteen, and a redhead . . ."

"No, no, no," she says, relief melding into the river of panic within. "That isn't them. They—"

"Charlotte—"

"You have their names mixed up with somebody else . . . Aimee is a blonde, and Royce certainly isn't fifty, or bald," she protests with a brief, brittle laugh, wondering how on earth he got so confused. "You met—"

"Charlotte! For God's sake, listen to me. Your life and your daughter's life might depend on it."

Your daughter's life . . .

"Royce and Aimee Maitland are dead. They were hit by a drunk driver near the French Quarter during Mardis Gras ten years ago." His tone leaves no room for argument.

"Then who—"

She tries again, struggling to stay sane in the face of her own hysteria.

"Who is at my house with my daughter?"

When Dorado speaks, the three words are drenched in the same frantic anguish that has broken like a tidal wave over Charlotte.

"I don't know."

* * *

Anxiety gnawing at her gut, Mimi sits on a bench in the station house outside the office where Dorado is presumably attempting to alert the authorities on Achoco Island.

Why would the imposter known as Royce Maitland have fooled his own wife, for God's sake? And it isn't just him—it's his daughter as well.

Mimi can't help but remember a movie she once saw, about the witness protection program—or so you were led to think. In the end, it turned out the hero and heroine really were running for their lives, and had taken on the identity of a dead couple to save themselves.

But even if that's the case with the Maitlands . . . Where . . . How does little Theo fit into the picture?

Another wave of nausea sweeps through her, along with yet another memory of the drowning on her watch.

All she wants is to go home, but she can't. Dorado convinced her that she's stuck here now, for the duration of the storm.

She did manage to reach her mother by telephone and learned that they've lost power out on the island, but that she found candles and flashlights. Cam is doing just fine playing shadow puppets on the wall.

"What about Jed?" Mimi asked, unable to forget her husband's ominous comment about hurtling himself into the Atlantic during a storm.

Her mother told her that he'd been sleeping all afternoon. Mimi made her go check him again, and held her breath until her mother came back on the line to say that he was there, in bed, snoring.

So here Mimi sits, mulling over the latest incredible turn of events involving Gib's family, and then noticing an agitated elderly man talking to the desk sergeant.

He's a distinguished-looking fellow, despite a shock of wet, windblown white hair and a soaked trench coat.

Intrigued when she overhears him say, "Remington," Mimi casually gets up and goes to get a drink of water at a fountain within earshot of the conversation.

"No, it isn't life or death *this very moment*," she hears him saying, "but it is life or death for anyone who—" He breaks off, glancing at her.

She realizes she's forgotten the water fountain and is staring directly at him.

Embarrassed, she stoops over the spout and presses the lever.

The man resumes his conversation with the sergeant in a stringent whisper, all but drowned out by the running water.

But Mimi releases the lever just in time to hear the one phrase that compels her to instantly give up all pretense of good manners: *Kepton-Manning Syndrome*.

"Stop! Hey!"

Charlotte ignores the angry shout of the police officer behind her; ignores the black-and-white car with the flashing light as she sprints past it, onto the causeway.

It's about a mile, she calculates as she hurtles herself forward, driven by sheer panic.

Thank God she had jammed her feet into sneakers, and not her usual sandals this morning.

Each footstep that lands in the streaming roadway sends up a spatter of spray; she's being soaked and battered from every direction by stinging rain and a wind so strong it's all she can do to stay centered on the causeway.

I've got to get to Oakgate.

Got to get to Lianna.

Got to get to—

No, not Royce!

He isn't—

Yes, he is. He has to be.

He's her husband. She loves him.

And Aimee—Aimee is his daughter. Her stepdaughter.

Aimee wasn't lying. Detective Dorado said it himself.

Aimee was telling the truth . . . You were right about her being innocent all along.

Yes, she was right.

Aimee is innocent.

I knew she wouldn't hurt Royce. I knew it.

So what in the world is Detective Dorado talking about?

Maybe that wasn't him on the phone right now. Maybe it was somebody who read something in the media and decided to play a cruel prank . . .

A sharp stitch pierces Charlotte's left side.

Panting, she slows her pace.

Just a little.

Just enough to relieve the pain in her side.

She can't stop altogether.

She's only a third of the way across the bridge. She can see the towering white foam hurled repeatedly against the man-made rock retaining wall on the distant shore.

Turning her head to look down for the first time, she realizes that angry green-black waves are breaking close to the road's surface, held back only by a low concrete barrier.

If that washes away, so will she.

And she'll be overcome quickly—no doubt about it.

The strongest swimmer couldn't survive more than a few minutes in that churning vortex.

She'll drown, just like her son.

Oh, Adam.

Oh, baby . . .

Maybe that's what is meant to happen.

Maybe she, too, is meant for a watery grave. Maybe—

No! Lianna. Lianna needs me. I can't die.

There's nothing to do but go on. Keep her feet moving, one splashing down right after the other. Get to the island. Get to Oakgate. Get to Lianna.

And Royce?

What about Royce?

Royce is as much a victim as she is.

Somebody tried to kill Royce . . . Or were they trying to kill her?

Well, it couldn't have been Aimee. She was in New Orleans.

And obviously it couldn't have been Royce. He was the one who got shot. He didn't do the shooting.

So who was the phantom figure that Charlotte saw lurking among the tombstones in the cemetery?

Who shot her husband?

"Excuse me? Hello?"

Jeanne stiffens, hearing the door open at the foot of the stairs leading up to the third floor.

"Is anybody up there? Jeanne?"

She doesn't answer.

She just sits in her wheelchair, and she waits, her hands clutching the mother-of-pearl handle beneath the woolen shawl on her lap.

Footsteps creak on the worn wooden treads.

Tentative footsteps, climbing toward Jeanne's private roost—the only part of this old house that is hers . . . if any part of it ever really was.

The top of a blond head grazes the bottom of her line of vision down the steps.

"Jeanne? Are you okay up here? I'm looking for Lianna. Is she up here with you?"

Jeanne doesn't reply.

The next stair tread creaks; more of the blond head appears.

The bangs, Jeanne notices, are still damp from where they peeked out from the hood of the black rain cloak.

This is insane, Charlotte tells herself, nearing exhaustion. She stoops into the wind, dragging each foot forward as the furious sea spits vehement waves over the concrete barrier on either side of her.

What is she doing here?

What is she trying to prove?

Dorado's voice reverberates through her mind.

Aimee was telling the truth . . .

Yes! She was!

So why is Charlotte risking her life out here?

Rising water is beginning to lap at her feet. She's almost across. Just a few more yards, and she'll be there.

She just has to keep on going.

We confirmed everything with the airline. She went through Atlanta, just like you said . . .

Why did Dorado call?

It had to be Dorado; it couldn't be a prank. He knew too much . . .

But then, why would he say what he did?

Royce Maitland and his daughter Aimee were killed . . .

Who's lying? Royce? Or Detective Dorado?

Not Aimee.

Aimee was telling the truth . . .

" . . . *just barely made the connection to Savannah because the first flight was way behind schedule . . .* "

Yes, she was on that same flight Royce takes.

Of course she wasn't lying.

I heard the airport in the background. I heard the flight announcement. Delta Flight 6—

What was it?

Six-something.

Royce takes it whenever he comes home from New Orleans.

Delta . . .

Delta Airlines Flight 640.

Yes, that's it. Flight 640. The one that's always on time.

"*Delta Airlines Flight 640 to Atlanta is now at the gate and will begin boarding momentarily.*"

Yes!

Yes . . .

There it is.

At last, the firefly-thought alights, barely within her grasp, flickering faintly like a birthday candle in a breeze.

No . . . Don't . . .

Charlotte desperately lunges for the memory before it can be extinguished.

"*Please have your tickets ready so we can board the plane for an on-time departure . . .*"

Yes, that's it.

The thought fully ignites, burning into her like a flame to scorch her world—her precious new life—to ashes.

An image flashes into her brain. Herself and Royce, seemingly standing at the edge of the Grand Canyon on a picture-perfect day.

The souvenir photo was a staged visual backdrop.

Is it possible that the airport announcement could have been a staged audio one?

Come on, Charlotte, think. Think about it.

She heard the airport announcement with her own ears, the plane was at the gate and they would be making an on-time departure. Aimee later mentioned it went smoothly.

But on that day, the first flight was late getting into New Orleans and back out again to Atlanta. Dorado said so himself.

Charlotte covers the last few yards toward the end of the causeway.

Somebody's lying.

But not Royce. Royce was shot. Royce has been her lone ally in this mess over the will. Royce doesn't care about money. He told her to go ahead and give it away.

But did he really think you would?

Was it all an act, her husband's utterly refreshing lack of greed?

No. It couldn't have been. Whatever the explanation for this chaos, Royce wouldn't lie to her. She believes in him. She *believes* him.

So who else are you going to believe?

Detective Dorado or Aimee?

Hearing a roar, she turns to see a towering wall of seawater coming at her.

It slams into her, sweeping her to blackness.

CHAPTER 18

Mimi watches as Detective Talibah Jones, a stunning African-American woman with a no-nonsense attitude, impatiently rifles through the sheaf of damp papers she just removed from the envelope the elderly gentleman tossed on the table.

"Start at the beginning, Mr. Hawthorne. I'm not following what you're trying to tell me."

"It's all there, like I said," responds the man who earlier, and hastily, introduced himself to Mimi as the Remingtons's attorney, Tyler Hawthorne.

"But what, exactly, is 'it'?" The detective looks questioningly from him to Mimi, who shrugs.

Hawthorne replies, "You're holding pertinent medical records and legal contracts—"

"Which would take me hours to go through. And believe me, Mr. Hawthorne, I don't have hours to spare."

"When you find out what I'm telling you, Detective Jones, I'm sure you'll agree that it's worth your while."

"I hope so. But tell me. Don't show me." She waves

the papers at him. "What's going on with this? And how is Mrs. Johnston here involved?"

"She isn't. She happened to be here dealing with another issue altogether and she overheard me. It turns out that her husband has been stricken by the same terminal illness—Kepton-Manning Syndrome, an incredibly rare condition for which there is no cure—that is referred to in these files."

No cure.

That isn't news to Mimi. Yet hearing her husband's inescapable doom affirmed again makes her want to stick her fingers into her ears and scream.

She refrains. That isn't going to help anybody. Certainly not Jed.

Nor is her being a part of this disclosure likely to help him, but she manages to maintain control of her emotions, just as she did when she revealed Gib Remington's incriminating comment the day of the shooting.

That was even more difficult. Gib might have committed far worse crimes than she, but that doesn't alleviate the guilt she's lived with for three years.

The night of Theo Maitland's drowning, Jed was working a double shift.

But Gib was there, on the beach, watching the search for the boy's body. He was the one who comforted Mimi when they gave up looking—comforted her with bourbon from his silver flask, then with kisses that quickly led to passion.

It was just that one night. And Jed never knew.

But Mimi will forever be haunted by the consequences of that day, for reasons that go well beyond the drowning on her watch.

"Kepton-Manning Syndrome?" Detective Jones frowns. "I've never heard of it."

Mimi informs her, "That's because it's so rare. Chances of coming down with this disease are one in a million—"

"They're much lower than that," Hawthorne interrupts. "Statistically speaking, there's a relative handful of documented Kepton-Manning cases *worldwide* each year."

"And . . . ?" Jones looks from Hawthorne to Mimi, and back again.

"And there have been more than half a dozen cases on Achoco Island."

Jones nods, steepling her hands as if in prayer. "What does this have to do with the Remingtons?"

Tyler Hawthorne clears his throat. "For one thing, Connie June Remington, Charlotte's mother, died of this disease, but nobody ever knew it. Not even Connie June herself."

"She didn't know she was ill?"

"Oh, she knew she was ill." Tyler's abrupt laugh is utterly devoid of mirth. "There was no doubt about that."

Fists clenching in her lap, Mimi pictures Jed, gaunt and helpless, wasting away before her eyes.

Tyler leans forward, resting his forearms on the table. "But her physician told her it was cancer."

Both Mimi and Jones gape at the attorney, who goes on to reveal, "The physician's name was Silas Neville."

Silas Neville . . .

Yes. Old Doc Neville. He treated Mimi's family for as long as she can remember; it was he who referred Daddy to a lung specialist in Atlanta.

Daddy—

"That's it!"

Mimi doesn't realize she'd spoken aloud until both Jones and Hawthorne look over at her, startled.

"I'm sorry," she murmurs, shaking her head, brows knit. "I just remembered something."

She knows where she's seen that nurse before—the one she encountered in the hall at Oakgate this morning: at the Baywater Hospice office on the mainland.

She was there on that awful, memorable day when Mimi went to set up her father's care, when he first became ill three years ago.

Only back then, the nurse was a good thirty pounds heavier, her hair was short and dark . . .

And her eyes were brown, not green.

Plunged into the raging tide at the causeway's island edge, Charlotte narrowly misses striking a concrete piling that juts from the frenzied water.

She attempts to paddle away from it, toward the island's rocky western shore that, hours ago in this spot, would have been dry land beneath her feet.

Dragged under by the relentless current, she struggles to surface.

I'm drowning, she realizes in disbelief.

Is this what Adam felt?

Oh, Adam . . . my baby.

Her resolve rapidly weakening, she flails helplessly where the surface should be, finding nothing but water.

Lianna . . .

Lianna needs me.

I have to get to her . . .

With a burst of adrenaline and a mighty upward thrust, she manages to get her head above water.

Immediately, a rogue wave hurtles her back toward the piling; this time, fighting her way to the surface inches from it, she instinctively grabs hold.

Her feet claw helplessly at the smooth cement surface and, miraculously, find a toehold. Propping her arches on what feels like a jutting metal prong, she hoists herself upward so that the incessant waves batter her knees and thighs instead of repeatedly sweeping over her head.

I'm still going to die, she thinks, looking helplessly at the shore just yards away.

I'm going to die and Lianna will be left alone.

No, not alone.

Charlotte closes her eyes against the spray.

Lianna will be left with her stepfather and step-sister—who inexplicably call themselves Royce and Aimee Maitland.

Charlotte's eyelids snap open abruptly.

Gazing, with a renewed vow to survive, at the cobble-stone boat ramp on the rocky shore, she never sees the monstrous wave bearing down on her from behind.

"Dr. Neville treated Connie June along with the other patients on Achoco who were ill with the same disease," Tyler informs his rapt audience. "Most of them were former employees of Remington Paper, and two were children who lived in houses at Tidewater Meadow."

"And where is that?" Detective Jones asks, now taking notes.

It is Mimi who, wide-eyed, replies before Hawthorne has a chance. "It's the low-income housing develop-ment that was built on the old Remington Paper factory site. Both my husband and I grew up there."

Tyler isn't surprised. He continues his tale, "There's a doctor in Europe—"

"Dr. Petra Von Cave," Mimi cuts in.

"Yes. She's been the world's foremost Kepton-Manning research scientist for decades. Gilbert managed to locate her and she did attempt to treat his daughter-in-law.

But that was before Gilbert realized just how many people had been affected—and that there was nothing Dr. Von Cave could do anyway."

"She does have some kind of experimental treatment she's working with now."

Tyler looks at Mimi, sees the consternation in her eyes. "Thanks to Gilbert," he says quietly, "by now, she may. He'd been quietly financing her research foundation ever since Connie June died."

"What a guy," Detective Jones says dryly, shaking her head as she makes a note. Clearly, she already suspects where this is going.

Tyler opens his mouth to defend his friend as noble, but his conscience won't let him.

It's too little, too late and you know it. Possibly saving lives in the future doesn't make up for the ones that could have been saved in the past, if he had just come clean with everything.

But all that ever mattered to Gilbert in the end was protecting himself and the Remington name—even posthumously. He didn't have the decency—or the guts—to make a bequest to the foundation in his will. Tyler suggested it many times, but Gilbert was afraid it might establish a link between himself and Kepton-Manning.

"When I called Dr. Von Cave," Mimi speaks up, "she recognized my area code and that I lived on or near Achoco Island. She made the connection between Jed and Connie June's case. That's why she called me back. But she didn't tell me there were so many."

Tyler averts his gaze. "That's because she didn't know."

"Do you mean," the detective says, "that this Dr. Von Cave wasn't part of the cover-up?"

"No. She was just Gilbert's attempt to save his daughter-in-law's life." *And ease his own guilty conscience.* "Dr. Von

Cave long ago isolated the cause of this disease to a few possible environmental factors. One of them is the exposure to a toxic chemical that happens to have been a by-product of Remington Paper. It was dumped on-site for years."

"Was that legal?"

Tyler lowers his head but only briefly. "No. But I wasn't aware of that when it was happening. Nobody was. Gilbert only involved me later—when things got complicated."

"Complicated how?"

Tyler draws a deep breath. "Like I said, nobody, not even Dr. Von Cave, ever realized there was a cluster of cases on Achoco Island—not even the patients themselves. Their local physician diagnosed them with various terminal diseases, and sent them home to die. They did, and quickly."

"Are you telling me that they all used the same doctor? And that he was a part of a conspiracy to conceal the health risks?"

"Yes, and so was I." Tyler's voice is level. "But it was Gilbert who engineered the whole thing. He was desperate to cover it up. He would have been ruined if it had ever gotten out."

Mimi looks as though her head is spinning. So, apparently, is Detective Jones's, because she shakes her cornrows, clattering the wooden beads. "Back up. How on earth did Gilbert ensure that every one of those patients saw the same physician?"

A brisk knock on the door startles all three of them.

A sergeant pokes his head in. "Mrs. Johnston? Detective Dorado needs to see you right away."

Mimi leaps to her feet, murmurs an apology to Tyler and Jones, and is quickly escorted from the room.

Tyler looks at Detective Jones, who is still waiting for a reply to her question about Silas Neville.

"Just how many doctors do you think there were back then on Achoco Island, Detective? One. And how many employers?" Again Tyler answers his own question. "Aside from the fishing industry and a couple of restaurants and stores, Remington Paper was it. Gilbert provided an employee health plan. Mandatory free physicals twice a year eventually became a part of it."

"I think I understand how the doctor fits into Gilbert's cover-up," Detective Jones tells him, "but where do you come in?"

Tyler swallows hard. "Gilbert discreetly arranged to pay for everything for those patients right-up front: medical care, funeral expenses, ongoing benefits for their families. He did it under the guise of philanthropy."

Tyler shakes his head, remembering the gratitude of those poor people. They were profoundly touched that their benefactor didn't even want his generosity publicly acknowledged. Indeed, so humble, so honorable was Gilbert Remington that he forbade them to reveal his financial support.

"Mr. Hawthorne . . ."

"Yes, I'm sorry, I'll continue." He clears his throat. "Each patient and their family or guardian had to sign a legal contract stipulating certain conditions."

"You drew up and executed those contracts."

"That's right." Tyler heaves a sigh, relieved that after all these years, the whole shameful business is out in the open.

"Why, Mr. Hawthorne? Why would an otherwise respectable lawyer and doctor stoop to this level?"

He looks Jones in the eye, wondering if she can possibly understand about the Telfair Trio, or being raised with so much that you always want more.

No, she can't.

Because I don't understand, myself.

In the end, all there is, all I can do, is accept the blame.

"Because Gilbert was our friend," he says simply, with a shrug.

This is it, Charlotte comprehends as she is ruthlessly wrenched from the concrete refuge, a helpless pawn in a raging battle at sea. *It's over.*

Her flailing limbs are powerless; her furious, terrified scream snuffed by the tempest's mighty roar.

She is engulfed . . .

And then, miraculously, she is not.

It is an excruciating landing, her body catapulted onto a rocky bed of shoreline.

She can feel jagged edges slicing into her tender skin, leaving her raw and bleeding, drenched in saltwater that mercilessly stings her fresh wounds.

For a moment, she's certain she's going to die, so brutal is the agony.

But the moment passes, and she's alive.

Alive, and heaving herself onto the battered, wobbly legs that will carry her straight to Oakgate, and her daughter.

"Did you get in touch with the police on the island?" Mimi asks Dorado, finding him waiting for her in the office where she left him earlier.

He answers without looking up from his computer screen, still rapidly tapping the keyboard. "I did, but I had a hell of a time getting them to agree to go check things out at Oakgate. They've got their hands full with this storm and it won't be easy for them to get up there.

They said a tree fell across the road just north of the causeway. It cut off the only route that leads up there."

"Can't they go on foot or by boat or something?"

"They'll get there just as soon as they can, however they can."

He looks up at her at last. "I need you to look at something, Mrs. Johnston. I don't think you noticed it the first time. Neither did I."

"What is it?"

He gestures for her to come around behind his desk.

She leans over his shoulder to see the computer screen and finds the New Orleans newspaper write-up she'd read earlier.

Once again, the unfamiliar faces of the doomed father and daughter smile at her, and she suppresses a shudder.

"They look so happy," she tells Dorado, shaking her head. "What am I supposed to be seeing in the picture?"

"You're supposed to be reading the article. Here."

He jabs an index finger at a paragraph of text.

She reads it aloud.

"Arriving at the scene of the accident, where a steady stream of Aimee Maitland's friends have been leaving flowers, notes, and candles, her mother, Karen, broke down in tears. 'She was my baby—my only child. She and Royce were everything to me.' The anguished mother—"

Mimi breaks off and looks up at the detective as it dawns on her.

He nods. "Her only child." He grabs the mouse and scrolls down the page. "Here, look at the obituaries. See here? It says Royce Maitland is survived by his wife, his mother, two aunts, and several cousins. Period."

"But . . ." Shaking her head, Mimi asks, "What about his son? Theo? Ten years ago, Theo was still alive."

"Not according to this."

"I don't . . ." She trails off, trying to wrap her brain around the impossible until Dorado states it for her.

"Mrs. Johnston, Theo Maitland never existed at all."

The fist-sized cobblestones of the boat ramp leading away from the water make it impossible for Charlotte to run. Even in sneakers, she has to pick her way slowly over the rough surface, lest she twist an ankle.

Can you imagine having to run for your life on this surface?

Was it only weeks ago that she asked that seemingly absurd question of her husband, on their way out to dinner in Savannah?

His answer, so reassuring then, now fills her veins with an icy current.

Why would you be running for your life?

Why, Royce? Why am I running for my life—and running from you?

Dragging his throbbing leg behind him, Royce limps over to the closet door.

He jerks Lianna's clothing back and forth, hangers clattering and rasping along the metal pole, half-expecting to find her concealed among the garments.

But the closet is as empty as the space beneath the bed, and behind the bathroom door, and alongside the dresser and armoire. He even wedged himself painfully into the fireplace and looked up, thinking she might somehow have stuffed herself into the chimney.

No Lianna.

All right, so where can she be?

She was in this room, and she didn't leave through the door. He pushed it in; it was latched from the inside.

She couldn't have gone through the windows, either. All of them are closed and latched from the inside.

That leaves only two explanations: either Lianna is a little witch, and she used her magical powers to vanish into thin air, or there's another way in and out of this room.

She can be a little witch, Royce thinks, his jaw set as he surveys the layout of the room, *but I sure as hell don't believe in magic.*

He smirks, remembering that he said just the opposite to his wife, back when they first met. She just about swooned over the corny line, and he made sure to kiss her good and hard after he said it.

Yes, if ever a woman was ripe to fall in love, it was Charlotte Remington . . .

And that was precisely what he was banking on the day he first met her, as if by chance, at the one place where she was willing to open up and show her vulnerability: the bereaved parents group.

Of course, before he could join, he had to *become* a bereaved parent . . .

A simple enough task, if you really put your mind to it.

As he likes to tell Odette, *No children or animals were harmed in creating this scam.*

But he doesn't expect that to hold true for much longer.

"Lianna!" he bellows, running his hands over the molding around the closet door. "Lianna!"

An eternity seems to have passed from the time

Charlotte dragged herself to her feet and the moment she arrives at the stone entrance to Oakgate.

The gates are closed; she can't open them without her electronic remote.

She runs alongside the old stone wall until she reaches a spot low enough to easily scramble over. On the other side, she darts across the stretch of well-tended lawn dotted with old trees and blooming shrubs.

The summer lush and verdant landscape is littered with downed tree limbs and clumps of wind-tossed Spanish moss, the ground spongy and flooded beneath her feet. Several times Charlotte skids in the muddy grass, but manages to keep her balance somehow; manages to propel herself toward the house.

At last it looms ahead, framed by swaying oak branches against a turbulent black sky; its windows darkened and tightly closed against the gale.

Charlotte stops short as she reaches the top of the drive, where a massive oak has fallen beside a car: Nydia's car.

Her heart takes a death plunge as she spots a pair of feet protruding from the mountain of boughs.

Dear God in heaven . . .

The tree took a human casualty on its way down.

For a moment, Charlotte can only stare. Then she rushes forward, propelled by sheer dread; knowing she is bound to discover that the feet belong to one of a handful of Oakgate residents. Charlotte prays fervently that the victim is still alive—and that it isn't the child she loves more than anything on this earth.

No.

It isn't Lianna.

Numb with shock and revulsion, Charlotte moves

closer, whimpering, her feet becoming entangled in the vinelike branches that snake at her ankles.

Charlotte gazes into the eyes of Grandaddy's housekeeper, frozen within a grotesque mask of terror as Nydia stares at the last thing she ever saw on this earth.

She must have seen the tree coming at her.

Her skull is split, a gaping wound bisecting her forehead from the bridge of her nose straight up through her blood and brain and rain matted hair.

"Drop the gun, Jeanne." Aimee's voice is no longer as deadly calm as it was the first time she said it. Frozen on the stairway, her hand still clutching the rail, she doesn't dare to take a step forward, or back.

She's afraid.

She thinks I'm going to kill her.

I think I'm going to as well.

"Jeanne, this is ridiculous. Drop the gun."

Jeanne shakes her head, clutching her mother's pearl-handled revolver in both hands, aiming directly at the woman on the stairs. The woman who murdered poor Nydia and dragged her body out into the storm.

"Where is Melanie?" Jeanne demands again.

"I told you a hundred times. I have no idea. She isn't here."

"What did you do to her?"

"I haven't seen her, Jeanne. She left hours ago. I have no idea where she went."

Jeanne knows where she went: to the liquor store on the island's southern end, to buy Jeanne a bottle of bourbon.

"Please, Melanie, my nerves are just shot with this storm and all that's happened with my grandnephew,"

Jeanne had told the nurse, handing her a couple of
twenty-dollar bills.

"Where did you get this?"

"I saved it. Keep the change."

"Oh, Jeanne, you don't need liquor to calm your
nerves. How about if I sing to you?"

In that moment, Jeanne knew she was doing the
right thing.

Nobody in this house, not even Melanie, can possibly
understand the depth of Jeanne's misery.

Nobody understands that it will take more than a little song to lift her spirits; that it will take more, too,
than bourbon.

The only two souls who would have understood—
Mother and Eleanore—departed this earth years ago:
one in a suspicious freak accident, the other by her own
hand.

Sleeping pills and liquor.

A lethal combination.

Just as effectively lethal as firing a bullet through
one's brain. But Eleanore lacked the courage, or perhaps merely the means, to do that.

Jeanne has the means. In the end, what she inherited from her mother is far more valuable than china
and crystal.

But she doesn't have the courage. If she did, she'd
have done it weeks ago, when she learned that Gilbert
had left her nothing.

All these years, she had foolishly held out hope that
he would defy their father.

All these years, she had been a fool.

All these years, she had feigned dementia, thinking
that if he saw that she was incapable of taking care of

herself, he would feel sorry enough for her to take care of her.

And had it worked . . . to an extent. He didn't put her in a nursing home—she knew he wouldn't. It wouldn't do to have all of Savannah buzzing about Gilbert's batty sister. The family honor had to be protected, at any cost.

So, ever since she "lost her mind," Jeanne has had a familiar dormered roof over her head, a sturdy tabby foundation beneath her.

Oakgate is her home.

Just as it always should have been.

Just as it always should be.

Surely he should have seen that.

But her brother didn't leave her the house.

He didn't leave her anything at all.

It doesn't matter now.

Tucked beneath Jeanne's mattress is the orange plastic bottle of Gilbert's sleeping pills, pilfered from his medicine cabinet weeks ago.

She was dismayed to find that the prescription must have been almost due for a refill.

In and of themselves, there weren't enough capsules in the bottle to do the job.

But Eleanore's lethal recipe called for one other ingredient, and unwittingly Melanie agreed to provide it.

"Your hands are shaking pretty badly, Jeanne," Aimee observes. "How are you going to shoot me? It takes steady hands to shoot a gun. Believe me, I'm aware of that. Do you know why?"

Jeanne doesn't reply, just struggles to keep the gun trained on her target.

"I'll tell you why. Because I spent the last two years— two *years*, Jeanne—in marksmanship training. I can hit a terrorist on a predesignated freckle on his arm from a

block away." She emits a short laugh. "Or I can hit a regular Joe in the leg from just across the street, and,
thanks to my medical background, be sure to take him
down . . . without permanent damage."

Jeanne's jaw drops. "Are you talking about Royce?"

"Royce?" she echoes. "Sure, we'll call him Royce for a
little while longer if you like. But we don't have much
time."

"For what?"

"It's almost over, Jeanne. You've lived a long life. Is
there anything you want to tell me?"

"What . . . What do you mean?"

"You know . . . anything you'd like to share, before
you die. People like to do that, Jeanne. And I like to listen. It was part of my job, and I kind of miss it, you
know?"

Aimee moves to take a step forward, believing that
Jeanne might be so engrossed in her story that she
won't notice.

"Stay there!"

Aimee obeys Jeanne's sharp command. But she
keeps talking.

"I'm a nurse. Did you know that? Just like your friend
Melanie. So I know all about people like you."

"And I know all about people like you." Jeanne glares
at her.

Ignoring that, Aimee goes on, "I used to take care of
lonely old people. Some of them didn't have anybody
else in the whole world who would take care of them, or
anybody to leave their money to. A few of them actually
left it to me, not that they had much. Still, it was nice of
them, don't you think? And you'd be surprised how
many of them had lots of cash hidden right there in
their houses."

Jeanne thinks of the wad of twenty-dollar bills, now

sealed in an envelope with Melanie's name on it. Just yesterday, Melanie finally revealed that her benefactor was a married congressman. He died a few years ago, leaving her with only the condo he bought for her.

So Melanie can use Jeanne's birthday money—meager a sum as it is. Along with the cash, she's leaving Melanie a note: a suicide note, as it were, to thank Melanie for all she did, and apologize for what Jeanne has to do.

"A lot of old people don't believe in banks. Do you, Jeanne? Oh, wait, I guess it doesn't matter. I guess you don't have any money to start with."

Jeanne's finger tightens over the trigger.

"But my favorite part of the job was just listening. Some of those deathbed confessions can be really interesting. Take Silas Neville's, for instance."

Silas Neville?

The vaguely familiar name seems to hover before Jeanne in a fog.

Then Jeanne plucks the recollection from the chasm of lost memory. He was a friend of Gilbert's, she now recalls. Ever since he was a boy.

"Remember him, Jeanne?" Aimee smiles. "His was the most interesting confession of all. And I was the only one who heard it. Just like I'll be the only one to hear yours. So, Jeanne, do you have any final requests? Any profound last words?"

Jeanne swallows hard, staring into green eyes—unnaturally green—that are ablaze with madness.

"No?" Aimee asks, after a short pause. "Then I'd say it's time to call it quits."

In one abrupt movement, she reaches for her pocket.

She's going for a gun, Jeanne realizes.

Then a deafening blast swoops her to a place where there can be no more pain.

"Lianna!"

Her stepfather's voice is faint, drifting to her ears from someplace above her, up in the house.

Cowering on the stairway in the damp, dark tunnel concealed behind the wall of her room, she wonders if she should go down and try to escape through the basement after all.

She decided against it earlier, afraid that somebody would see her through one of the windows as she tries to flee the house—or, even more frightening, that *she* might be lying in wait in the cellar.

Royce's daughter.

Aimee.

Thinking again of what she saw upstairs in the master bedroom, Lianna closes her eyes to shut out the disgusting vision of father and daughter—in each other's arms.

So engrossed were they that they never even realized they had been seen.

Not that Lianna lingered in the doorway for more than a nauseating split second.

That was all it took for her to realize that her stepfather isn't the man she and her mother believed him to be . . .

And that her stepsister is precisely what Lianna instinctively perceived her to be: a lying, conniving fraud.

Hearing an explosion overhead, Lianna believes for a moment that another tree has fallen—this time on the house.

Then she realizes that it wasn't a tree.

That time, it really was a gunshot.

Charlotte hears a loud bang, and this time, she instantly realizes what it is: a crack of gunfire.

And that it came from inside the house.

She never even considers running down the driveway toward the gate and the old stone wall; running for help.

That isn't an option.

Her only thought is that she has to get to her daughter.

Please, God, let her be all right.

Her oozing sneakers pound up the steps and across the wet flagstone of the portico.

Please let her be alive.

Too late, she realizes that the door is locked, and that she doesn't have a key.

Lianna's instinct is to hurl herself down the stairway in the dark, anything to get away from whoever has the gun.

But she's outnumbered already; there are two of them.

Royce is somewhere above, but there's no telling where Aimee is.

Well, Lianna will have to take her chances.

She has to try to get away.

This is her own fault. She should have been braver. She should have gone shopping with her mother this morning, instead of sulking, and then cowering, in her room.

Now she has nobody to blame but herself.

Nobody is going to come and save her, just like nobody could save Adam.

But that wasn't his fault.

It was mine.

And now I'm being punished for what I did . . . just like I always knew I would be.

* * *

Royce has just encountered what feels like a loose panel beside the fireplace when he hears a gun go off upstairs.

"Aimee?" With a curse, he rushes to the hallway, dragging his bad leg. "Are you all right?"

Odette appears, holding her pistol. "She was armed up there, Joe."

"Shhh!" He gestures wildly to alert her that she's slipped up and called him by the wrong name: his real name. Not that anyone else gets away with the shortened version of it.

Aside from his mother back home in Chicago, who calls him Joey, he's been Joseph his entire life, Joseph Borger . . . well, that is when he's not busy being Royce Maitland or whatever dearly departed soul he's had the pleasure of impersonating for the purpose of a well-planned con.

"Oh, give it up already, Joe. Who's going to hear?" Gone is the honey-sweetened N'Awlins drawl, replaced by the twang of the Tennessee mountains, where Odette Krupp—AKA Aimee Maitland—was born and bred.

"The old lady's dead, and so is the housekeeper," Odette informs him. "All we have to do is grab the kid and Charlotte, and we're home free."

Incredulous at her laid-back attitude, he snaps, "All we have to do? It's not that simple."

"Sure it is. Remember, *Daddy*? You came up with the plan yourself. We just use this"—she waves the gun— "to convince your lovely wife and stepdaughter to get into the car and drive. Then I grab the wheel and make sure that they overshoot the foot of the causeway—so easy to do in this nasty weather—and land in the water. Oh, but first I have to remember to jump out."

She flashes the dazzling row of white teeth Joseph paid a fortune to have capped. That was almost as expensive as the liposuction, but not as much as what he spent on the colored contacts, the frequent hair salon visits, the gym, and the personal trainer.

But it was worth all the money and well worth the wait. Odette Krupp was transformed into a tawny Southern beauty. She looked at least ten—or twelve, to be exact—years younger. She could easily pass for a nubile twenty-five, virtually unrecognizable as the mousy nurse who had once worked for the hospice clinic—and stumbled across a multimillion-dollar secret.

At first, when she told Joseph, he thought they might just blackmail the old man with what they knew.

Then Joseph looked a little more closely at the illustrious family tree, and realized that there might just be an old-fashioned, legitimate way to inherit the entire Remington fortune: by marrying into it.

Maybe he should have left it at that. As Charlotte's husband, even with Charlotte inheriting just one-third of the fortune, he would be set for life. Nobody would ever have to know who and what he really was.

But his own greed, and Odette, got to him.

He wanted it all.

So he took a gamble—and he won.

He'd guessed that Gilbert actually had a conscience—and could be convinced that leaving Charlotte all his money was the best way to appease it. What better way to compensate his unwitting granddaughter for Gilbert's own role in her mother's premature death?

What Joseph didn't count on was that Charlotte would work her way under his skin—or that it would be so damned hard to see this thing through to the end.

Odette is much more cavalier about it than he is. As she likes to tell him, *"You've just got to do what you've got to do. You can't let emotions get in the way."*

He's come to realize that she's absolutely right.

And that when the time comes, he will push aside his emotions to do exactly what he's got to do.

Heedless of the howling wind and driving rain, Charlotte races around the perimeter of the house, trying first the side door, and then the back.

Locked, both of them. Just as she expected.

But that's okay. She knows where Grandaddy keeps the key.

Heart pounding, she scurries across the garden to the old stone sundial. With trembling fingers, she reaches into the overgrown plantings around the base.

Where is it?

She begins to claw frantically at the rain-drenched weeds and perennials.

The key has to be here . . .

It has to, because now it's her only means of getting to Lianna.

Finally, she gives up the fruitless search.

Think! There just *must* be another way.

Joseph Borger watched Charlotte for months, while making an honest living for a change, thanks to the technological skills he learned after a youthful stint in prison. Fortunately, he hasn't been incarcerated since he became proficient at his illegal career and computer-savvy at his legal one.

Not that the computer training hasn't been beneficial in other ways. The document forgery was a snap; so was implementing the software to fake that airport phone call from Odette's cell phone.

It wasn't hard for Joseph to initially keep a low profile in Savannah, or even on the island. Not many people paid much attention to a quiet "computer nerd," as Odette liked to call him back then.

But she wasn't the only one who was undergoing a physical transformation.

Eventually, Joseph had his teeth done, too. He hired a trainer, too, and bought gym equipment that he used religiously. He also bought a new wardrobe, with the help of a personal shopper.

All the while he was preparing to become the dashing Royce Maitland and sweep Charlotte off her feet, he was noting that the grieving mother kept to herself, didn't date, didn't have friends or a social life. That the only people who seemed able to permeate the walls she had built around herself were her daughter, her grandfather, and the members of her support group.

Creating a fictional son was as easy for Joseph as it was for him to come up with a fake identity for himself and Odette. Nobody ever questioned that his name was Royce Maitland, or that his son had been lost in the water that day.

The beach was jammed with people. Nobody paid him any attention at all until he ran screaming for the child who didn't exist.

But "Royce" had the documentation to prove that Theo had, should anyone think to question it: birth certificate, social security card, death certificate . . . Anyone who knew their way around the Internet as well as he did could come up with that stuff.

He'd done it plenty of times, for simple insurance cons.

But none of those could compare to this.

No other scam demanded the patience, the complex planning; none promised to deliver the staggering pay-off.

Not yet, though. We're not there yet.

"Why'd you go and shoot the old lady?" he asks Odette in disgust. "There wasn't supposed to be another body left behind. It was hard enough to cover up what we had to do with our little eavesdropper."

Nydia.

Yes, if she had just minded her own business, she'd still be alive. But she always did have a way of popping up when you least expected it. Chances are, she didn't overhear anything, but Odette wasn't taking any chances. And when Nydia popped up one time too many, she happened to be conveniently within reach of the same brass andiron that silenced Phyllida Harper when she walked in on them in bed in the wee hours of Saturday morning.

"I told you we should have drugged her, too," Odette hissed to him back then, as she prepared to drag Phyllida out of the parlor.

"How? I doubt she's any more likely than you are to touch that disgusting sweet tea. Too many carbs," he added, echoing Odette's response to just about every food she must avoid to maintain her new figure.

But it's worth it. He enjoys being with a woman who looks like her—as much as he's secretly enjoyed being with Charlotte.

That was the part that just about did Odette in, more than once. It killed her to know that he was making love to his new wife, though he repeatedly claimed that he didn't enjoy it. He swore that he thought only of Odette when he took Charlotte in his arms.

What a shame that he didn't get to do just that to celebrate his return from the hospital.

Ah, but a jealous Odette saw to it that it wouldn't happen. He found it almost amusing that she ingeniously rendered the elevator inoperable, just so that he wouldn't be able to share a bed with Charlotte these last few nights. Amusing, too, that she made sure Charlotte would sleep soundly through the night so there was no risk of "father and daughter" being caught sharing the hospital bed behind closed parlor doors.

Phyllida Remington Harper did catch them—which rendered her yet another casualty of the best-laid plans going slightly awry.

But nothing will go wrong from here on in.

Just as long as he doesn't get sloppy and leave a trail.

"We have to do something about the old lady," he says, his thoughts racing.

"Oh, don't worry about dear Aunt Jeanne, Joe. She took care of herself. I didn't have to."

"What are you talking about?"

Odette laughs. "Poor thing put a gun into her mouth and blew her brains out before I could do it for her."

Her palpitating heart constricted in her rib cage, Lianna doesn't linger on the unstable third step, feeling the old wood begin to buckle beneath her weight.

She swiftly lowers her foot to feel for the next, more solid, tread below. Safely there, she proceeds to the next, and then the next . . .

Step-by-step, she descends into the black void, remembering that day; that awful, awful day eight years ago.

Her brother wasn't supposed to have his autographed

baseball at the beach, or anywhere outside the house, for that matter. Dad had bought it for him, and told him he had to keep it on a shelf in his room.

But Adam couldn't part with it. He snuck it into the beach bag so that he could show his friends. Lianna saw him do it; he made her swear not to tell.

She didn't.

No, she did something far, far worse.

When Mom was opening the cooler to set out the sandwiches she'd brought for their lunch, Lianna grabbed Adam's precious ball and threw it with all her might, into the surf.

It was a joke.

She laughed at Adam's dismayed expression, then snickered behind her hand as he snuck back down to the water, away from Mom.

But Lianna's amusement transformed quickly into fear as she watched the current sweep the ball farther and farther from Adam's grasp.

The lifeguard was blowing his whistle, but Adam paid no heed.

Then, suddenly, he was gone, swept away in a riptide, leaving Lianna to stare in shock as her mother looked for him on the sand—her puzzled, then frantic voice calling Adam's name.

That was the first time, the first of many, that Lianna wished she had been the one . . .

Wished *she* was the one who had died, not Adam.

Now, as she continues the long, slow descent to the cellar, step after painstaking step, she can't help but wonder if the first part of that wish might be about to come true.

"Jeanne killed herself?" Joe asks Odette in disbelief.

"Yup. I've never seen anything like it. What a mess."

He shakes his head, not sure whether to believe her. She isn't the most honest gal in the world . . .

Which is why we're a perfect match.

He didn't always think so. He was originally smitten by her older sister, Pammy Sue: the slender, green-eyed blonde who, ironically, the formerly frumpy Odette now resembles so closely.

But Pammy Sue lacked her younger sister's clever ingenuity. Fortunately for Odette and Joseph, she also lacked the natural curiosity that might have made anyone else at least wonder why they were being asked to take an early-morning flight from New Orleans to Savannah.

Dull-witted Pammy Sue did it, no questions asked, carrying her sister's ID and baggage, for a couple hundred bucks. Odette had assured him that after she picked up her sister—with the luggage and ID—at the airport that morning, she drove Pammy Sue straight to the bus station and put her on the Greyhound back to Tennessee. Still no questions asked.

Joseph sometimes forgets that he had ever chosen Pammy Sue over Odette. And he isn't the only one who did. Their mother, the volatile redheaded Mrs. Krupp, blatantly favored her eldest daughter. No wonder poor Odette always resented her big sister. No wonder she worked her butt off to get out of Pigeon Creek and make something of her life. Nursing school was her ticket . . .

Nursing school, and later, Charlotte Remington.

So look who's on top now, Babe, Joseph likes to point out to her. *Forget Pammy Sue. You're the one who's got it all: looks, brains, me . . . and, pretty soon, millions of dollars.*

"I'm serious, Joe," Odette is saying now, ever industrious. "All we have to do is leave Jeanne just the way she is. The gun is still in her hand; her prints are the only ones on it. All the forensics experts in the world will come to the same conclusion: that she killed herself. It's the truth."

"Why do you think she did it?"

"Because she's a nutcase? Because she was watching out the window when the tree fell on poor old Nydia, and she just lost it? Who cares? We can use this, Joe. You'll say that the tree fell, the old bat shot herself, and Charlotte and Lianna took off in their car to get help. They were driving too fast, all shaken up, and . . . *Bam!*" She slips the palm of one hand across the other, simulating a car going over a precipice.

"It could work."

"It *will* work. This is a terrible storm. People get killed in this kind of weather. It happens all the time. Nobody's going to question it."

"No, I know. That's why we took advantage of the storm. But we weren't counting on the old lady, and the housekeeper, and—"

"Joe, relax. You were already shot once. Nobody's going to suspect anyone but Gib of anything. And even if they do, they'll assume Gib hired someone to pull it off. He's connected. The cops didn't miss that, trust me. They didn't miss much, when it comes to Gib."

Joe's lips curve into a smile as he recalls how he slipped the cufflinks out of Gilbert's jewelry box, leaving them on the ledge outside the back door, with the dress shoes, for Odette to take.

Joseph teased Odette relentlessly when she informed him that with the addition of a few cotton balls to stuff the toes, Gib's shoes fit her oversized, clodhopper feet perfectly.

Then she had the nerve to complain that they were hard to run in, that she nearly twisted an ankle that night as she fled across Colonial Park Cemetery.

Twisted an ankle? he echoed. *At least you didn't have to get shot in the leg.*

But it was worth it in the end, just as he'd known it would be. The worst part was taking that bullet—made slightly more bearable thanks to a local anesthetic, courtesy of Odette, that he had injected into his thigh while pretending to remeasure the bathroom.

If Gib Remington hadn't been so easily framed, thanks to the unexpected bequest of the cufflinks that enhanced things so nicely, the whole plot might have become transparent at any given stage.

But it had all fallen into place.

Now, nobody in Savannah, or on Achoco Island, will see Royce Maitland as anything but a fine, upstanding citizen, and a victim himself.

Gib Remington can rot in jail, protesting his innocence until the day he dies. Nobody's going to believe him.

As for Gilbert Xavier Remington II—the old man got what he deserved that day in the bathtub.

It's just too bad he didn't suffer as much as the many people whose lives he destroyed.

So Joseph doesn't feel bad about him. Nor will he feel bad about Charlotte's pain-in-the-ass kid.

Not as bad as he's going to feel about—*No. Don't even think about that until you have to.*

Instead, he remembers what it was like to hold a classy, beautiful woman like Charlotte in his arms.

What lies ahead is going to be hard on him. He has a heart, after all.

But what has to be done will be done. She just won't deserve it.

Not like Gilbert did.

When Royce approached him to say his shady cover-up had been detected, Gilbert didn't even ask how. With resignation, as though he had been waiting for the day somebody would discover his duplicity, he simply asked his grandson-in-law how much he wanted to keep quiet.

When Royce told him it would take more than a little hush money—that indeed, he would have to change his will to make Charlotte his only heir—Gilbert balked. But only until Royce showed him the letter detailing the cover-up, and promised him there was a duplicate in a safe place that would come to light if he didn't acquiesce.

So Gilbert changed the will, undoubtedly spurred as much by his own guilt as by his need to protect his secret.

There's no doubt that he adored Charlotte. No doubt that he knew how destroyed she would be if she found out what he had done.

Gilbert must have believed, as Royce had anticipated, that leaving his entire estate to her would somehow justify it in the end. He didn't care about Gib and Phyllida anyway. Charlotte was the only one who had ever loved him, or respected him.

If Gilbert had known what Royce was really up to . . .

But he never suspected. He must have believed that his granddaughter's husband had stumbled across the secret and was perhaps at worst an opportunist looking out for her best interests in addition to his own.

"Come on, I think I just found some kind of false wall in the bedroom," he tells Odette now, heading in that direction.

"Why didn't you say so?" She brushes past him. "I told you the other day, these old houses are full of them. Come on, let's get her, so we'll be ready when Charlotte comes."

* * *

At last, Lianna is nearing the bottom of the second flight—and salvation.

No longer worried about what might await her in the cellar, she clings to the railings and cautiously lowers her foot, remembering that this is another spot where the treads have rotted away.

Then, as she feels around for a rung to stand on, she hears the groan of an old wooden door from somewhere above.

It can mean only one thing: they've found her.

She can hear voices, Royce's and Aimee's, tumbling down the shaft from two stories overhead.

Maybe they won't realize I'm still here. Maybe they'll think I'm long gone.

She goes absolutely still, hands clenching the rails, one foot precariously balanced on the wobbly step, the other dangling down behind her.

"It feels like some kind of a stairway," she can hear Aimee saying. "It must go down to the basement."

"Get a flashlight," Royce responds tersely. "She has to be down there."

"Not if she got away."

Lianna holds her breath, statue-still. If they just leave long enough to get the flashlight, she can steal away in silence, and they'll never—

Something—some creature seeking higher ground—crawls over her hand.

An involuntary scream escapes her.

She lets go of the rail and plummets to the storm-flooded earthen floor a good five feet below.

"She's there!" Royce bellows overhead. "I'll go down this way; you go around to the outside entrance and block the basement door."

As Lianna scrambles to her feet in half a foot of muddy water, she can hear the pounding of Aimee's retreating footsteps.

Above, Royce is testing the stairway. As she feels her way back from the foot of the stairs toward the secret entrance to the basement, she hears him limp down the first two steps.

Then he reaches the precarious third.

The old wood groans in instant protest beneath his weight.

Then, with a splintering sound, the step gives way altogether.

Royce Maitland's petrified scream echoes in the tunnel as he falls.

He lands with a deadly splash in the very spot Lianna has just vacated.

Without even a whimper, she flees, knowing she has to make it out of the basement before Aimee gets there.

She wades through the muck and water that have flooded the earthen floor, adrenaline pumping, feeling her way in the darkness. She crosses the cellar, foot by painstaking foot, guided by memory of where she thinks the door is located.

But when she reaches the spot, there is only clammy tabby wall.

Sobbing now in fright, Lianna feels her way along the wall, hoping she's going in the right direction.

Then, all at once, the door opens . . . and she sees that she was wrong.

Thank God, she was wrong.

She's several yards away from the opening, well beyond the block of gray daylight that spills through.

Silhouetted in the doorway is the unmistakable figure of Aimee Maitland . . . And she's holding a gun in her right hand.

Lianna flattens her back against the wall, vowing not to move a muscle, not to make a sound, not even if a snake wraps itself around her ankles.

"Lianna . . . Where are you, little sis?" Deranged laughter echoes eerily off the tabby walls. "Are you afraid of the dark, like your mommy? Here, this will help."

It's only then that Lianna sees the object in her left hand.

A flashlight.

She doesn't stand a chance.

She holds her breath and waits for the beam to flood her hiding spot; waits for the blast of gunfire.

Maybe Adam will be waiting for me, is her last thought before she's blinded by the light.

She squeezes her eyes shut, knowing that any second now . . .

"No!" With a mighty shove, Charlotte catches Aimee off guard from behind.

Aimee drops to her knees in the waterlogged doorway, the gun flying out of her hand to land with a splash somewhere in the darkened basement beyond.

"Mom!"

"Lianna, stay back!" Charlotte shrieks, spotting her daughter just inside the cellar door as Aimee crawls after the gun.

Charlotte tackles Aimee, clawing at her clothes, her face, her hair.

"Lianna!" she screams. "Run!"

"Mom—"

"Get help! Hurry!"

"But the phone—"

"Not here! Run out to the highway! Keep going until you find someone!" Charlotte screeches before Aimee gets hold of her and flips her onto her back with a guttural curse.

Hearing her distraught daughter sloshing frantically away, Charlotte prays she'll follow through, escape . . .

Whatever happens to Charlotte now, Lianna's life must be saved.

Yet she'll fight ferociously for her own.

As Aimee reaches for her throat, Charlotte bites her wrist as hard as she can.

A yelp of pain, a window of opportunity.

Fueled by rage, Charlotte seizes the moment, grabbing hold and heaving her attacker with all her might.

Aimee lands beside her.

Go for the eyes, Charlotte thinks frantically.

Coated in thick slime, Charlotte struggles to get on top.

But Aimee is quicker.

Stronger.

As Charlotte goes for Aimee's eyes, Aimee's hands close around Charlotte's throat, constricting her windpipe.

It is Charlotte who is flipped to the flooded floor this time, landing on her stomach in the sludge.

Aimee is on top of her, riding the small of her back, fingers splayed on Charlotte's head. Charlotte's arms are clamped between viselike thighs as Aimee presses her face underwater.

Try as she might to turn her head or buck her attacker, the effort is futile. Charlotte is hopelessly, help-lessly pinned.

Oh, God, please help me . . .

She holds her breath as long as she can.

Then, overcome by the reflexive urge to inhale, her aching lungs are swamped.

No, oh, no . . .

This time, she really is drowning.

She's going to die.

There's no one to save her . . .

Lianna has escaped, but help will be too late for Charlotte now.

But Lianna is safe.

Charlotte's chest is burning.

Her useless arms have given up the struggle.

She's delirious, dying . . .

In the distance, a brilliant light . . .

Adam . . . Adam is waiting for me.

Then comes the violent explosion in the distance—and everything goes black.

Lianna is halfway across the great lawn when she hears the gunshot.

"Mommy! No!"

She takes off running, toward the basement and the gun, not away from it. Toward her mother. She can't leave her there to die alone.

Aimee's got a gun.

I don't care.

Aimee's going to shoot me, too. *I'm running right into a death trap.*

I have no choice.

It's all I can do.

She slips wildly through a grass-slick puddle, falls, picks herself up.

Runs a few more steps, falls again.

Keep going. Get to Mommy . . .

At last, Lianna skids around the back of the house.

Her mother's body, limp, lies face up just outside the basement door in the pouring rain.

Royce is on top of her, trying to choke her.

"Stop!" Lianna screams.

Just before she spots the gun lying at the edge of a puddle in the grass, a few feet from Royce and her mother.

She lunges for it.

"I swear to God, I'll shoot you, Royce!"

"Help me, for God's sake, Lianna!" he commands hoarsely without even flinching, and she realizes that he isn't trying to choke her mother after all.

He's doing compressions.

Royce, bleeding from a gash in his own forehead, is trying to save her mother's life.

"Oh, my God!" Lianna wails, dropping the gun and sinking to her knees beside her mother. "Mom . . . !"

It is then that Lianna spots Aimee, face down in the muddy water beyond the basement doorway.

A pool of scarlet is seeping into her blond hair where the back of her head has been blown away.

Royce pumps furiously.

Lianna prays.

Her mother gasps.

"Yes," Royce whispers. "There, babe. Yes."

Charlotte sputters and chokes, water spouting from her lips.

"Thank God." Royce's voice is ragged as he cradles her in his arms.

Lianna clings to her mother's hand, sobbing in relief—and shame. "Royce, I'm so sorry, I thought you—"

Were trying to kill me.

She can't say it.

How could she even have thought it?

Because she walked in on him and Aimee upstairs.
His own daughter. He was in bed with his own daughter,
kissing her . . .

At least, that was what it looked like in the fleeting
glimpse Lianna caught before she fled, sickened.

Now she replays the scene again, and again, trying to
make sense of what she saw. Or thought she saw.

Because it couldn't have happened. Royce shot
Aimee to save his wife's life, so . . .

*So maybe I was wrong about what they were doing. He and
Aimee . . .*

*Or maybe I imagined the whole thing. God knows I was in
a crazy state of mind up there . . .*

Right now, the only thing that seems obvious is that
Royce loves her mother. He isn't trying to harm
Charlotte—or Lianna, for that matter.

"It's okay, Lianna," her stepfather says simply, as if
he's read her mind—and forgiven her.

"When I heard you coming down those stairs, trying
to get to me—"

"I thought you were in some kind of trouble down
there."

"You fell. I was sure you were—"

"My arms broke my fall. But I hurt my leg. The same
leg," he adds ruefully.

"Lianna . . ." Mom thrashes her head; her voice is
weak.

"Shhh, Charlotte, it's okay." Royce gently strokes her
soaked hair. "Lianna is here, too. She's all right. You
don't have to worry."

Mom's eyelids flutter. She's trying hard to come out of it.

Lianna swallows a lump of regret, hating herself for thinking that her stepfather was trying to hurt her—and her mother.

"I thought Mom was dead when I heard the gun go off," Lianna says, trembling as she attempts to grasp all that happened. "I thought Aimee shot—"

"No," Royce interrupts, "I managed to get to the gun in time. I shot Aimee. I had no choice."

"She's your daughter." Lianna shudders.

Tears glisten in Royce's eyes. "I had to, Lianna. She's insane. I had no idea she was caught up in what Gib was doing . . ." His voice breaks; he buries his face in his hands, sobbing. "My God, if I hadn't gotten there when I did . . . I can't even think about what might have happened."

"Lianna . . ." Mom's eyes, her voice, are ravaged.

"Lianna is fine." Royce presses a kiss on Mom's forehead as, dazed, she looks from her daughter to her husband. "Can you see her, Charlotte? She's fine. Show her, Lianna. Tell her."

"Yes, I'm okay, Mom." Crying, Lianna bends forward to lean her cheek against her mother's shoulder.

Royce says softly, "Everything is going to be okay, now, Charlotte. We're going to be fine: you, me, and Lianna."

At last, Charlotte manages to speak coherently. "The police—call the police. Please . . . Royce . . ."

"I will. The phones are down, but I'll use my cell phone. Lianna, stay here with your mother."

"I will." Lianna watches Royce limp away in obvious agony, thinking she won't leave her mother's side again for a long, long time.

Neither, she's certain, will her stepfather.

His body torn and bruised, his leg shattered, it takes Joseph a long time to drag himself into the house.

Clasping the cell phone against his ear, he presses 9-1-1 and begs for help.

"What's going on there, sir?"

"Please . . . We've been attacked. Please send some-one—"

"Calm down, sir. Tell me where you are and what happened."

He does. But not, of course, everything.

Nobody will ever have to know everything.

He learns that a tree has fallen across the highway, cutting off Oakgate from the rest of the island.

It's going to be a while before the police can get up here.

"But we're working on moving it out of there now," the voice on the telephone assures him. "We'll be there as soon as we can, Mr. Maitland. I know you've been through a lot. Just hang on."

"We'll try."

Joseph hangs up his cell phone, tucks it into the pocket of his soaked slacks.

Hang on.

Yes.

Later, you'll clean your wounds, change your clothes.

Later, you'll take care of yourself.

Right now, he must begin the long, painful, final journey back to Charlotte.

Odette never saw it coming.

Joseph's one comfort is that she never turned her head, never sensed his betrayal.

It was over quickly. One courageous squeeze of the trigger, and Odette was gone.

She was gone, and Charlotte was saved.

What if you had been too late?

He nearly was.

If he was too late to save Charlotte, he could have gone back to the original plan: Odette's plan. The one she assumed he was following all along.

He was careful not to let her suspect anything.

Odette had no idea that in his effort to make Charlotte love him, Joseph had fallen in love with Charlotte as well.

Odette couldn't know that he had no intention of murdering Charlotte.

No, not his beautiful, beloved Charlotte. Just Lianna—along with her beautiful blond stepsister, Aimee, in a tragic accident as they tried to flee the island for help.

Cringing in anguish as he uses his arms on the rail to pull himself down the back steps, Joseph is satisfied with the way things have turned out.

Big sister has been taken care of.

In time, when all the fuss has subsided, little sister will be, too.

Or maybe not.

Maybe Joseph should try to learn to live with Lianna after all. For a while, at least.

Maybe he should spare his wife the loss of another child.

Because he does love Charlotte. He really does.

And now he has it all. Everything he ever wanted . . .

With the exception of Lianna.

Oh, well, there's always boarding school—or Vince. Let Daddy's little girl go live with him for a while.

I can talk Charlotte into it. I can talk her into anything.

Outside, it's still raining steadily, but the savage gusts have subsided.

The worst of the storm is over.

Isn't that the truth, Joseph thinks wryly.

He limps painstakingly around the clump of shrubs that lead to where he left Charlotte—

Only to find that she's vanished.

A wave of panic sweeps through him.

Then a voice commands, "Stop right there and put up your hands."

Charlotte's voice.

She's on her feet—and she's pointing a gun . . .

At him.

As Charlotte watches the taillights of the police car disappear through a curtain of rain down the winding drive, she sinks onto the top slate step of the portico.

Handcuffed in the backseat is the man she knew as Royce Maitland.

In time, she might find out exactly who he really is, or was.

Maybe she never will.

It doesn't really matter now.

It's over.

Their universe shattered, she and Lianna are nevertheless alive.

That's something.

No.

It's everything.

"Mom?"

She looks up to see Lianna behind her, still pale, still quivering, still covered in mud.

"Is he gone?" she asks in a little-girl voice that wrings the last bit of emotion from Charlotte's heart.

"Yes, Lianna," she manages to say, "he's gone."

"Mom . . . You saved my life."

Charlotte shakes her head, remembering what happened back there in the treacherous sea.

If it wasn't for her daughter, she would have readily joined her son.

"You saved *my* life, Lianna. Twice."

Her voice gives way then, and she raises her arms in mute invitation.

Not so long ago, Charlotte had told herself that when it comes to her daughter, all she can do is hold her breath and let go.

I was wrong, she thinks now, as she gathers Lianna into her arms at last. *Dead wrong.*

All I can do is breathe a tremendous sigh of relief . . . and hold on tight.

EPILOGUE

The beach is postcard-perfection on this, the first official weekend of summer.

Down beyond the dunes, where sea oats sway in the warm salt breeze, bright-colored blankets and umbrellas dot powdery sand. Crisp white sails skim the horizon. The ocean air is rife with the sounds of gleeful children splashing in the surf, the incessant roar of the waves, the squawking of circling gulls, the hum of banner-toting planes cruising the coast.

Charlotte sits in her blue and white canvas chair, protected from the midday sun by her cotton cover-up and the umbrella's shade. Romance novel in hand, woven sweetgrass hat on her head, she smiles, watching a little boy splash, shirtless, in the surf.

On his shoulder is a telltale birthmark.

Charlotte told him it's an angel's kiss, just as she told little Adam years ago.

Adam would have graduated from college last month, had he lived—another unreached milestone to join the others in Charlotte's mental scrapbook. If she closes her eyes, she can see her lost son: proud teenager in cap and gown, dashing groom in a wedding bouton-niere, tender new father cradling an infant.

Milestones . . .

Next month, Charlotte will kiss her daughter good-bye and send her off to her freshman year at Princeton.

Initially, Lianna didn't want to go that far from Oakgate. She likes to stay close to home. And Charlotte would secretly love to keep her there, safely tucked under her wing.

Yes, it's tempting to just hang on tight, forever.

But I can't.

It's time to let go at last.

Milestones . . .

The little boy in the water will be starting first grade in September at Telfair Academy, just as his mother did almost three decades ago.

He, too, will be on a scholarship—of sorts.

Charlotte has arranged to pay little Cameron John-ston's private school tuition. She'll send him to college, too, when the time comes.

For his mother, Mimi, one more semester at Georgia Southern will yield that elusive degree in international studies at last. But she's already been to Europe. Many, many times. Not on business, or pleasure, but a mission.

Mission accomplished.

"How can I ever repay you for all you've done for us, Charlotte?" Mimi asks, often.

Charlotte simply tells her that payback isn't necessary.

She never mentions what she figured out on a July day three years ago, the first time she joined the John-stons at the beach . . .

That little Cameron is family.

Nor does she ever remove her swimsuit cover-up when Jed is around. If he ever noticed the identical angel's kiss on her shoulder, he would realize that his son has Remington blood in his veins.

Devoted, loving Jed is Cameron's father in every way that counts.

Gib Remington, sentenced to a long prison term on drug-smuggling charges, will never have to know that his long-ago one-night stand with Mimi Gaspar resulted in a pregnancy. She and Jed were married soon after she found out she was expecting, and she had opted never to tell him the truth.

"It's better this way," Mimi had said when Charlotte confronted her and she admitted that Gib had indeed fathered her son. *"Jed's suffered enough pain. He'll never have to know."*

Charlotte may not necessarily agree with Mimi's decision, but who is she to judge?

She herself has made mistakes.

Everyone does. It took three years of therapy for Charlotte and Lianna to come to terms with their own, to forgive themselves—and each other.

To learn to communicate, to trust, to take chances again.

So Lianna will go off to college next month.

As for Charlotte . . .

If she hadn't gotten to know Mimi and Jed, hadn't seen the strength of their love in the face of death-defying odds, she might never have dared to take the biggest chance of all.

A young child's sudden squeal reaches Charlotte's ears, and her heart skips a beat.

She darts an anxious glance at the shoreline to see Cameron, gleeful as his robust father swings him into a wave, holding tight to those capable hands.

Don't let go, she thinks, watching as the wave washes over father and son. *Not yet.*

"Don't worry, Charlotte. Jed's got him."

In the next chair, Mimi is smiling reassuringly.

"I know he does . . . I just . . ." She trails off.

There are some wounds that never fully heal.

Some you carry with you forever, with only time—and love—as balm.

Mimi touches Charlotte's arm gently. Mimi knows. She came harrowingly close to losing someone she loves desperately.

But that didn't happen. Charlotte paid for the trips to Europe, for the experimental treatment that saved Jed's life and has since saved countless others.

The only thing that makes Grandaddy's crime bearable is the final irony that his secret, sizable contributions funded Dr. Petra Von Cave's research for all those years—and ultimately provided the cure for Kepton-Manning disease.

Grandaddy's estate covered the vast, ongoing cost of cleaning up the former chemical waste dump on Achoco Island. Tidewater Meadow was torn down; it will be years before the site is safe for habitation. Its residents have scattered, most to other islands.

Maude Gaspar is one of the few who stayed. She lives with her daughter and son-in-law now, in the little canalside cottage that's bursting at the seams. She's content to care for Cameron and his baby sister, Jeannie, while their parents work, and study—and labor on the new four-bedroom home they're building near the beach.

But it's slow going. Jed is busy with another job, one with good pay and benefits: overseeing the ongoing renovation of Oakgate.

The brick slave cabins have been torn down, that patch of marsh filled in. A memorial garden marks the spot where Phyllida Remington Harper's remains were found, along with those of Odette's sister, Pammy Sue

Krupp. Brian came from California with his son for the garden's dedication. Charlotte was glad they came, and glad Phyllida's life insurance policy paid off the Harpers's debts.

Charlotte created a trust fund for little Wills, who has no memory of his mother or Oakgate, no comprehension of the Remington legacy. Perhaps in the end, he's better off.

Inside the mansion, beyond the enduring brick façade, countless walls have come down.

There are more windows, to banish the shadows and let in the sunlight.

Central air-conditioning was added, the duct-work filling what was once a secret passageway from the second floor to the basement.

The entire third floor has been reclaimed as attic space for countless antiques: Remington relics Charlotte can't bring herself to part with.

Maybe someday she'll go through them.

But this isn't a time to revisit the past; it's a time to look ahead.

On the second floor of the old plantation house is a brand-new master suite: the honeymoon suite, Phil insists on calling it, though the newlywed period officially ended with their first wedding anniversary last month.

A year already.

It took longer than that for Charlotte to agree to their first date. Gradually, she learned to trust the handsome detective, to recognize that his concern for her and Lianna had shifted from professional to personal.

Their wedding last June was in the fragrant rose garden behind Oakgate, with Lianna crying happy tears as maid of honor and Williamson at his partner's side, as always, grinning proudly as best man.

Who would have imagined that behind the crusty façade was a human teddy bear?

It just proves what Charlotte learned in the most tragic way possible: that no book should ever be judged by its cover.

In her life, the chapter involving Joseph Borger is closed. He'll be in prison long after her cousin Gib is released—most likely for the rest of his life.

For Charlotte and Lianna and the Johnstons, a new chapter has begun.

Survivors need a fresh start, just as houses sometimes do.

Adjoining the master suite at Oakgate, the cozy room that was once Gilbert Remington's study has been done over in shades of pastel blue.

Baby blue.

With luck, the white nursery furniture will be delivered by the Fourth of July, as promised . . .

A long shadow falls over the sand.

Charlotte looks up to see her husband standing over her, his brown skin glistening with droplets of seawater, mocha-colored eyes twinkling down at her. "Hey, how's the beach ball?"

"Just fine." She smiles as he gently pats her enormous stomach and is met with a reassuring kick from their son's tiny foot.

"It's a boy, Mr. and Mrs. Dorado," the obstetrician said the day she gave them the amniocentesis results.

It's a boy.

A son.

A son who will one day soon be rocked in his mother's embrace, and swung high above the surf in his father's hands, and who will ask his big sister a million curious questions when she comes home to visit.

But for now, for one last summer, Lianna is home—and soon, the baby will be, too.

Home at Oakgate.

Pressing her thumb to her eyebrows, Charlotte shields her eyes to cast a reassuring gaze out over the ocean.

Yes, Lianna is there, just beyond the breakers, floating serenely in the sparkling blue sea beneath the golden summer sun.

And above her, a lone white gull soars to the heavens.

Romantic Suspense From
Lisa Jackson